CU00825632

I Spy Bletchley Park

George Stratford

To Zubie,
with very best wishes,

George Stratford

Copyright © George Stratford 2018

The author asserts the moral right under the Copyright, Designs and Patents Act 1988 to be identified as the author of this work. All rights reserved. No part of this publication may be reproduced, stored in a retrieval system or transmitted, in any form or by any means without the prior consent of the author, nor be otherwise circulated in any form of binding or cover other than that which it is published and without a similar condition being imposed on the subsequent publisher.

ISBN: 9798508818890

DEDICATION

This novel is dedicated to my dear late mother, who served as a WAAF for two years (1940-42) at Bletchley Park. Just like all the others who worked at this most vital World War II code breaking centre, she never once breathed a word to anyone of her time there until long after the secret was made public over thirty years later.

What was achieved at Bletchley Park was truly incredible. And for me, even in a non-Facebook and Twitter world, the fact that the thousands of people who worked there during those war years were able to 'Keep Mum' about what they knew for so long afterwards is also pretty bloody amazing.

I raise my hat to each and every one of you.

ALSO, A BIG THANK YOU TO....

A special thanks to Robin Upshon for his excellent work in creating this book's cover. Also, to John Bladen, one of the dedicated volunteers at Bletchley Park, for his invaluable advice on numerous matters of detail.

A WOMAN'S PLACE

Of the ten thousand or so people who worked at Bletchley Park during WWII, nearly eight thousand of them were women. As both service personnel and civilians they played an indispensable role in every level of activity, right up to making vitally important cryptological breakthroughs of their own that were certainly on a par with those achieved by their more fabled male counterparts.

But little is ever written about all those young women who fulfilled slightly less glamorous but still essential roles at the Park: women such as the Wren helping to operate huge cryptographic machinery, and the WAAF wireless or teleprinter operator working around the clock to send and receive encoded vital intelligence. There were also the translators and traffic analysts, usually working under intense pressure in dimly lit and poorly heated huts. These tasks, and many more besides, were all undertaken by women.

Far from being just a small clique of intellects, Bletchley Park was a team of thousands. And eighty-percent of them were female. Just for a change, I thought it would be rather nice if one of these less spoken about heroines were to take centre stage in a novel based around BP's secretive existence in the dark days of WWII. I hope you agree.

George Stratford

PART ONE

Pride before a fall

ONE

S he had been warned time after time not to attempt it. Reminded all too frequently of the terrible injuries that had befallen so many of those who had gone before. It made not a scrap of difference. She had made a promise to herself, and the only thing those cautionary words had achieved was to make her more determined than ever.

Now – today - the moment was finally here.

The pounding of her horse's hooves on the turf was music to Lady Margaret Pugh's ears, even though it felt as if her heart was racing along equally quickly and might burst at any moment. Now twenty-three years old, even as a small child with wayward pigtails stuffed uncomfortably beneath her riding hat while trotting around on a small pony, it had been her heartfelt ambition to one day clear this huge obstacle that was now rushing toward her. And with good reason. Not for nothing had it been known for nearly one hundred and fifty years as Stanley's Folly.

Her great-great-grandfather, Sir Stanley Pugh, the ninth Earl of Dewksbury, had been the first to see this jump as a personal challenge. However, although renowned as a most determined man, after numerous painful falls and twice breaking his right leg, he perhaps wisely chose to abandon any further attempts.

In wry testimony to his own failure, he named this short section of boundary hedging on their Buckinghamshire estate eponymously and decreed that it should henceforth be kept regularly trimmed at its present dimensions of exactly seven feet high, and two foot six inches wide. A splendid silver trophy was purchased and placed for safe keeping with the firm of family solicitors. Should any future member of the Pugh family become the first to clear the Folly, then they could claim the cup as rightfully theirs. Oh yes, and if possible he would personally come back from the grave to offer his congratulations.

To this day, June 9th 1933, the cup remained unclaimed and Sir Stanley was yet to reappear.

Margaret had been secretly building up to this moment for several months. Despite countless failed attempts by her ancestors, her optimism was high. Her mount, a five-year-old smoky black stallion called Soldier, was fearless and would not let her down. Many other Pugh family riders in the past had found themselves being thrown violently out of the saddle when, at the very last second, their horse suddenly realised the enormity of what it was being asked to do. But Soldier was an altogether different breed.

This was Margaret's final thought as the stallion launched itself upwards. Just like all the many other times when rehearsing this jump at slightly lower heights, the sheer power generated by the animal's muscles seemed to race all the way through her, as if for that fleeting moment they had become a single entity. It was the most joyous feeling imaginable.

"Bless you," she breathed as Soldier's leading legs cleared the uppermost foliage with inches to spare. An instant later they were beginning to straighten out in preparation for the landing.

Then, at the last second - at the *very* last second - the stallion's trailing hoofs somehow just clipped the hedge's final few inches. It was little more than a tickle, but it was a touch, nonetheless. And sufficient to deny them a clear jump.

Soldier landed cleanly, allowing Margaret to quickly bring him to a standstill. "Good boy," she leaned forward to whisper in his ear. "Now I know for sure we can do it."

The horse gave a small neigh, bobbing his head as if nodding in agreement.

In truth, this attempt had been far more of a success than a failure. Even if they had gone clear, they would still have needed to do it again in front of two independent witnesses in order to qualify for the cup. Margaret was already analysing today's jump and making minor adjustments to ensure that, next time, they *would* go clear. She would also make certain that there were the required eyes in attendance to officially certify their triumph.

The ride back home was spent debating whether to tell her father about their near miss, and of her absolute conviction that very soon she would actually win the famous cup. He would be thrilled and appalled in equal measures. Thrilled for her in that she had come so close to success, but also appalled that she should be taking such an enormous personal risk.

The bond between them had become stronger than ever since the death of her mother three years ago from tuberculosis. Quite soon after that, Margaret had even been allowed to play a far larger part in the management of their estate, despite the fact that she could never actually inherit it. Women over the age of twenty-one may have won the right to vote five years ago, but some ancient customs were still carved in granite. As the earl's only child to date, unless he remarried and produced a male heir, both his title and their estate were certain to pass over to a distant branch of the family that neither of them had much liking for.

Not that this was of immediate concern. Her father was only fifty-one; there was time enough yet for a young brother to appear. In truth, Margaret had never felt equally as close to her somewhat unloving mother who had clearly wanted a son, and three years seemed to be a perfectly sufficient mourning period.

She thought some more. It would be wonderful to see him happily married once again. Several times lately she had caught glimpses of his need when saying goodnight and heading for his lonely bedroom. Yes, she would do it! The very next time she popped down to London she would start enquiring amongst her extensive social network about suitable candidates. Who could say what might result?

Hadley Hall, a little over fifty miles north-west of London, came into view, prompting an affectionate little smile. No matter how many times Margaret gazed upon her ancestral home, that first glimpse of the old place as she returned from her daily ride always had the same effect. It was impossible for her to imagine a time when it might not be a part of her life.

On turning into the stable courtyard, she could see the head groom waiting for her. Tom Harris had been with the estate all of her life. His equine knowledge was exceptional, and she had gone out of her way to learn as much as possible from him. Because of this, their relationship was rather less formal than might be expected.

"A good ride this morning, My Lady?" he asked, taking the reins after she had dismounted.

"Excellent, Tom. Absolutely excellent," she replied.

He was well aware of her ambitions regarding the Folly. She wanted to tell him more, but her mind was now made up. She *would* tell Father. He must be the first to hear the news of her near accomplishment. She couldn't wait to see his face.

Her anticipation was rapidly rising as she entered the house.

"Ah, Davis!" she exclaimed on spotting her father's valet descending the grand staircase. "Do you know where the earl is?"

He paused briefly in his stride. "I believe he is in the library, My Lady."

She hurried on. The library door was closed, which Margaret felt to be a little unusual but not terribly significant. Thrusting the door open, she burst into the room.

"Father! You'll never guess what—"

Her words came to a juddering halt at the sight before her. Henry Pugh, the twelfth Earl of Dewksbury, was slumped in an armchair with his face buried deep in his hands. Margaret thought she even heard a sob escape. But that couldn't be so. Never in her life had she seen him remotely close to tears. Not even after the death of her mother. Like so many generations of Pughs before him, he was renowned for his staunchness of character.

She rushed to his side. "Father, what's wrong? Please tell me."

His hands remained stubbornly in place and he made no attempt to sit up. A second sob slipped out. "Leave me alone, Margaret," his muffled voice instructed her. "Close the door behind you and issue strict orders that I am not to be disturbed. Not for any reason whatsoever."

Normally, she would have done as he wished without hesitation. But this was not normal circumstances. He was in terrible distress over something. The fact that it was entirely against his nature to openly display such emotion only made the situation even more disconcerting.

She drew a deep breath. "I can't leave you like this. You must tell me what is troubling you."

After waiting a few seconds and not receiving any answer, she attempted to gently prise his hands away from his face. The reaction was almost instantaneous. Before she knew it, the earl was on his feet and glaring at her.

"Didn't you hear me?" he roared. "I said leave me alone."

Never at any stage of her life had he ever spoken to her in such a way. Even when chastising her over something, he always remained in full control of himself. Now, seeing his face at last exposed sent a thudding sensation racing straight to Margaret's heart. His eyes were red raw from tears: his features heavily lined and haggard. He seemed to have aged at least ten years since she had seen him only a short time ago at breakfast. For a moment, the sheer shock of it all rendered her speechless.

And then, as quickly as it came, his anger was gone. "I'm sorry, Margaret," he told her, at the same time raising a hand to his temple. "I had no reason to shout at you. Whatever must you think of me?"

Barely had he spoken when he seemed to lose his balance slightly. Margaret took hold of an arm to steady him. "Sit down again," she urged. "I think you must have made yourself dizzy by jumping up quickly like that."

With her assistance, he did as she suggested. After settling, he then said something further to her. This time though, his speech was badly slurred and she did not understand a word.

"I beg your pardon," she said. "You'll have to speak more clearly, father."

He tried to reach out to her, but the arm dropped back into his lap after raising only a few inches. Margaret then saw one side of his face beginning to droop.

Realisation came with a rush. Her father...her dear lovely father...was ....

"No!" she screamed.

Literally seconds later, the valet Davis came rushing into the room.

"The earl is having a stroke," she shouted at him. "Call Doctor Grant immediately."

NEARLY SIXTY MILES away, in the back room of a modest semi-detached house in south London, twelve-year-old Betty Hall was preparing to play Beethoven's Für Elise on an upright piano that, although it bore several minor scuffs and dents, was perfectly tuned.

Shifting slightly on her stool, she glanced across at the other side of the room where her mum and dad, together with her tutor Agatha Wright, were sitting waiting for her to begin. The looks of anticipation on her parents' faces only served to increase Betty's nervousness. Despite Agatha's assurances that she was now more than ready to play her first little proper recital for them, the butterflies in her tummy simply refused to settle. What if her performance did not live up to mum and dad's expectations? Of course, neither of them would ever say as much directly, even if they did feel that way. They were far too kind to do that. But she would be able to tell if they were disappointed anyway, no matter how much they might try to hide it.

Agatha gave her a quick nod of encouragement, to which Betty flashed a grateful smile in return. The unspoken message was clear. *I believe in you. Just believe in yourself.*

Doing her best to brush away all negative thoughts from her mind, not to mention the troublesome butterflies from her tummy, she placed both hands precisely on the keyboard and began to play.

EXACTLY AS BEETHOVEN had intended, the opening part of Für Elise was a relatively simple melody that even a modest performer could play well enough. But that was before the great composer underwent a dramatic change of heart well before its completion.

As the piece began moving into the far more technically challenging phase of its latter stages, Agatha could not prevent a smile of pride developing. Her pupil's fingers, including the often difficult to manage fourth and fifth digits of each hand, continued to move with nimble assurance over the keyboard: the beneficial result of numerous hours spent practising scales. It was hard to believe that young Betty had begun lessons with her only six months ago as a complete beginner. She was now without doubt one of the most promising students that Agatha had ever taken under her wing.

She had a great deal of respect for Betty's parents as well. With Dan a carpenter in precarious times when there was certainly no guarantee of regular employment, and Mabel a part-time secretary, they were a far from wealthy couple. Yet despite this, they had done everything they possibly could to support their daughter's musical ambitions. The second-hand piano would have cost them far more than they could normally afford, and Agatha was well aware that they frequently struggled to pay her fees. She also knew they were far too proud to accept the occasional free lesson. She compensated for this as much as she could by charging them considerably less per hour than she did her wealthier, mainly middle-class clients.

With a final flourish of the fingers, Betty concluded her recital and immediately twisted around on her stool to look at her audience. Her look of apprehension was quickly replaced with a grin of delight as all three gave her an enthusiastic round of applause.

"I really don't know where she gets it from," a proud looking Dan remarked. "Neither me nor Mabel have got a musical bone in our bodies."

"It's the same with both of our mums and dads," an equally proud Mabel added. "None of them can play a note on anything, though I do remember how old Uncle Charlie used to bash out a bit of a tune on the spoons sometimes at Christmas." She laughed at the memory.

"We need to take some pictures," Dan declared, stepping over to the sideboard. From this, he produced a Kodak box camera. "Come on everyone, over by the piano with Betty."

Agatha smiled again while following him, but this time it was mostly to herself. The pair of them would remember this occasion with joy for years to come: the day when their daughter showed them the first real glimpse of her undoubted talent. It was a fitting reward for all the many sacrifices they must surely have made on her behalf.

As for Betty herself, exactly how good would she become? The girl practised diligently and possessed a true passion for the music, so she clearly had the potential to go a long way indeed. Perhaps even all the way to the very pinnacle of the profession.

But who could say with certainty? At sixty-nine years old, Agatha had seen much in her life.

Sometimes events had an unfortunate way of interfering with a person's true destiny.

THE QUALITY OF FURNISHINGS inside the private waiting room told Margaret that it was a place reserved exclusively for those of considerable wealth or status. She had also been treated by all of the hospital staff with every bit of the deference that someone of her social position might expect. Not that she had ever paid anywhere near as much attention to formal etiquette as most others from the aristocracy. One had to keep up certain appearances, of course. But being an earl hadn't protected her father from suffering a stroke, and it damn sure wouldn't make a blind bit of difference to his chances of survival whether she was addressed by those working here as 'My Lady', or a plain and simple 'Miss'.

The waiting was agony. She was well aware that, even in this modern age of the 1930s, there was still virtually no effective treatment for a stroke. The first two or three days would be critical. If a patient survived these, then the best that could normally be done was to limit the damage with intense bouts of therapy. Basic skills such as walking, eating, and dressing would all usually have to be relearned. She could not help but wonder if her fiercely independent father would rather have died.

The door opened, leaving little time to dwell on this depressing notion. Doctor Grant, the family GP, entered. She had known him since she was a toddler. Quite a small man – at five feet, four inches he was a good inch shorter than Margaret herself – he sat down facing her and gave a comforting smile.

"I've been fully briefed by Mister Carter, the head neurologist," he began. "Given my long association with your family, he thought that you might prefer to have me bring you up to date on your father's condition."

Margaret gave a slightly impatient wave of the hand. "Yes, of course. Just tell me everything you know please."

"Well, My Lady, the good news is that his condition seems to have stabilised quite early."

"And the bad news?"

The doctor shifted in his seat for a moment. "He is extremely restricted in movement all the way down his right-hand side. His speech is also affected. You may struggle to understand much of what he says until you get used to this."

"But it will improve? With the right rehabilitation therapy, I mean."

"That's possible. It depends on many things, including the strength of the earl's own desire to improve." He paused briefly. "On the bright side, all the tests so far indicate that his cognitive functions are working normally. He knows exactly what people are saying to him and responds in the best way he can."

Margaret considered his words, wondering fearfully once again if her father would find life trapped inside a body that would no longer perform to his needs even vaguely tolerable.

"I would like to see him as soon as possible," she said.

The doctor stood up. "Of course. I will take you to him straight away."

AT THE BEGINNING, MARGARET'S fears appeared to be unfounded. Throughout the earl's period in the hospital, and when at first arriving back home, he applied himself fully to all of the exercises prescribed. Every day, hour after hour was spent shuffling about the house with a walking stick until totally exhausted, all of the time muttering demands to his incapacitated right leg that it become more active.

Even when sitting down, the fightback continued. With teeth gritted and growling from the effort, more hours were spent attempting to raise his equally immobile right arm. Any improved elevation, no matter how slight, invariably produced a loud grunt of satisfaction. Having been a naturally right-handed person, being forced to now struggle with his left to perform relatively simple tasks was a major source of both embarrassment and annoyance to him. He was absolutely determined to overcome this.

As the initial tests had suggested, his mind appeared to be as sharp as ever. What's more, considering the short space of time that had passed, his speech was showing a truly remarkable improvement. Margaret was now able to understand him perfectly well, in spite of a small lingering slur.

Yet even though communication was not a problem, there was one matter that the earl refused outright to discuss. Any questions regarding the reason for his distress immediately prior to the stroke were invariably brushed aside. Nothing Margaret could say would shift him on this. It became an ever-increasing weight on her mind.

Aside from this concern, life at Hadley Hall was settling into a new routine. With Margaret already well-versed in estate management and her father remaining capable of making any major decisions if it became necessary, the short-term future appeared to be secure.

Then, on the fifth week of her father's return home, the family solicitor John Bridle came to visit. He and the earl immediately went into the study together, where they remained for almost two hours. When a tight-lipped Bridle eventually emerged alone, on encountering Margaret he departed with what she felt was undue haste. Seeing as how they normally enjoyed at least a short friendly chat whenever their paths crossed – like Doctor Grant, they had known each other ever since her early childhood - this was more than a little mysterious.

With concern rising, Margaret headed straight for the study.

The earl was sitting motionless behind his desk, staring blankly at the facing wall. He did not display even a flicker of acknowledgement when she entered the quite small room.

She touched him on the shoulder. "Father."

He gave no response. An awful feeling of *déjà vu* came over Margaret. The only difference this time was a lack of tears. In fact, there was no emotion or sense of awareness at all.

And then his head moved slightly so that he was looking directly at her. He started to whisper something that she could not quite make out. "I can't hear you," she said, leaning down to place an ear close to his mouth. "Tell me again."

Now she could understand him better. Not that he was making any proper sense. It was just a string of self-recriminatory words spoken in a distant, emotionless tone.

"Shame...gullible...guilt...fool...."

"Shame. Shame of what, father?"

"...humiliation...ridicule...remorse...finished."

"I don't understand. Why are you talking like this?"

"All gone...everything."

At that point, her father's flow of words came to an end and his gaze returned to the wall.

Nothing Margaret could think of to say was able to shift his attention away from this.

TWO

Despite being a family business with just one office that was located in the rural town of Bletchley, Bridle & Bridle solicitors enjoyed a far-reaching reputation. The firm had been handling affairs for much of the landed gentry in Buckinghamshire and surrounding counties for more years than people could recall. And in just the same way that these country estates changed hands with each new generation, so too did the running of Bridle & Bridle pass from father to son. It was an arrangement that suited everyone involved.

John Bridle had been expecting a visit from Lady Margaret with some trepidation ever since his last trip to Hadley Hall. It had not taken long to materialise. Torn between a sense of loyalty to the earl and an even greater sense of responsibility to 'do the right thing' by his daughter, he'd spent hours debating over how much of recent developments it would be correct to reveal. Even now, when she was sitting just a few feet away on the other side of his desk, his mind was still not made up.

In spite of the determined set to the young woman's face, this did little to disguise the fact that she was extremely attractive. With her well-proportioned figure, shoulder-length auburn hair, quite large eyes and full lips, she often reminded him in some ways of his own dear wife when they had first met some thirty years ago. There could also be no doubt that Lady Margaret had always been one of the most charming and friendliest of people he had ever encountered in the course of his professional life.

But now, suddenly and brutally, her entire world had been turned upside down. No wonder she currently had such a resolute air about her. And the awful thing was, she did not yet know even a fraction of the hard truths being kept from her.

He produced his professional smile. "So how may I help you, My Lady?"

She looked him directly in the eye. "Perhaps we can begin with what you said to my father when you came to our house the day before yesterday."

Bridle leaned back in his chair. She was certainly not beating about the bush. "It was in connection with a particular investment the earl made a few months ago," he began cautiously. "One that ..."

He cleared his throat. "One that unfortunately did not transpire quite as he hoped for."

"Please, do not spare me the facts, Mister Bridle. "I know full well that my father has lost a disastrously large amount of money. He as good as told me that himself. What I want to hear from you now are the details."

"The thing is, My Lady, the earl has specifically requested that you should be protected from such concerns. He does not wish for you to—"

She raised a hand to stop him. "I'm afraid that whatever he has wished for in recent days is no longer relevant." She sighed. "Let me be perfectly open with you. Since your last visit to Hadley Hall, my father has not spoken a single coherent sentence to anyone. Until he does, and his current condition strongly suggests that this may not be at any time in the foreseeable future, I am the one solely responsible for the administration of our estate. In order to fulfil this duty to the best of my ability, I need to know precisely where our financial position stands."

She paused to let this sink in before concluding: "I do not wish to be rude, Mister Bridle, but please consider this to be an instruction, *not* a request."

With a rush, the solicitor knew that he had little choice but to comply. The earl may have wished to shield his daughter from the harsh realities of the situation, but right now it was clear that only hard facts would be sufficient to satisfy her. Even though she would never be able to inherit the estate, that was of little consequence. The present circumstances were about to affect her enormously. The sooner she was made aware of these, the better it would be.

He sighed. "Very well, Lady Margaret. But I must warn that you should prepare yourself for bad news."

She waved a hand. "I am already prepared for that. Please, just tell me the worst quickly."

Bridle decided to take her at her word. Like pulling away a sticking plaster from sensitive skin, it would probably best be done in one rapid go.

"Your father is virtually penniless," he stated bluntly. "The entire estate, including the house, is to be sold in order to settle an overdue tax bill."

He braced himself for her reaction.

A lengthy silence followed, during which Lady Margaret's expression remained impassive. The solicitor could only marvel at her self-control. He knew that, inside, she must be in absolute turmoil. The Pugh family's ownership of Hadley Hall and the estate dated back hundreds of years. Discovering that everything was lost had all but broken the earl completely.

Bridle had been fearing that a similar reaction might now be about to take place right here in his office. That this had so far not occurred produced a feeling of enormous relief, together with a surge of utmost respect for the young lady sitting in front of him. Right now, the fact that she was an earl's daughter meant nothing to him. The only thing he could see was a young woman scarcely out of childhood handling a piece of truly devastating, life-changing news with all the fortitude and maturity of a fully-grown man.

When she finally spoke, her voice was quiet yet firm. "I take it there is no possibility of this bill being settled in any other way?"

"I am afraid not. Not unless the earl has considerable assets that I am unaware of."

"If that were so, then I doubt that he would have been so severely affected by events."

Bridle acknowledged the truth of this with a nod, but said nothing.

Placing both elbows on the arms of her chair, Margaret leaned forward. "Speaking of how all this has affected my father, did you happen to first make him aware as to the dire result of his investment on the same day that he suffered his stroke?"

The solicitor swallowed hard. "I called on him that very morning with the news of his financial loss. I believe you were out riding at the time."

She gave a comprehending nod. Bridle did not need to be told what she was thinking.

After a short reflective silence, she said: "Now I want to know everything about this calamitous investment. Most importantly of all, I want to know who sold it to my father, and who it was that advised him as to the merits of it."

The implication was clear. "Let me say at once, My Lady, that I strongly advised the earl against such a risky adventure. However, in the light of what had gone before, he was determined to press ahead with it regardless."

"In the light of *what* that had gone before?"

"The stock market crash of four years ago. Like many other members of the aristocracy, he lost a substantial amount of money in that catastrophe."

A long stream of air escaped from Margaret's mouth. "I knew nothing of this. He never spoke a word of it to me."

"With all due respect, My Lady, why would he? You were still not of age at the time. And I know for a fact that he did not even choose to discuss this loss with your mother. To be honest, I don't know of any man of his social standing who would have shared such a private matter with the female members of his family. It is simply not the done thing."

Whatever she was making of this rather forthright assessment, Margaret kept it to herself. "Please continue, Mister Bridle," was her only response.

He sighed, as much with relief as anything. For a moment he'd feared that he might have overstepped the mark with his frankness. But having set the benchmark, he may as well now continue in the same open manner.

"The stock market crash, of course, was quite closely followed by your mother's sad death. In my opinion, these events combined to make your father rather more vulnerable than he might normally have been. He was desperate to restore the family fortune to its former level, so when this apparently gilt-edged latest investment opportunity was offered to him, he was unusually eager to take advantage of it."

"And what exactly was this investment opportunity?" Margaret asked.

"A gold mine in South Africa. A gold mine that—"

"Are you saying that father still owns shares in this mine?" she cut in. "Even if the investment is not currently paying off, surely there must be a good chance that it will do so in the future."

Bridle gave a sad shake of the head. "As I was about to tell you, it was a gold mine that does not actually exist."

For the first time in their conversation, one of his revelations did succeed in inducing a significant reaction. But it was not one of shock or distress. It was one of pure rage.

Margaret's grip on the chair arms tightened so much while forcing herself into a half upright position, Bridle could clearly see the whitening of her knuckles. By contrast, her face had become a dark shade of red.

"Doesn't exist!" she exploded. "That's not an investment, that is fraud. An outright crime. Why didn't you stop this?"

"I tried to, My Lady. Please believe me, I did. But the truth is, most of the arrangements were made with undue haste without my knowledge at a location somewhere in London that the earl was strangely reluctant to share with me. The funds had already been transferred into an alleged holding account before I was even presented with what ultimately turned out to be a worthless contract. I wanted to make enquiries as to the authenticity of the mine, but what with it being located so far away in South Africa, that would naturally have taken a little time. Time that your father was convinced he did not have."

Margaret dropped back down into her seat. Bridle could see how much effort it was taking for her to control her temper. "If it helps, My Lady, I will swear right now on a holy bible that I played no part whatsoever in this deception," he told her.

Her features gradually returned to a more natural colour. A faint smile even briefly formed, giving the solicitor a fleeting glimpse of the polite and lively young lady he had come to know so well in the years before the earl's misfortunes had struck.

"That will not be necessary, Mister Bridle, she told him. "I know you to be a thoroughly honest man in all respects. I will of course have many more questions for you in the coming days, but for now, there are just two more things I need to ask. Firstly, how long will it be before the estate is sold?"

The solicitor sucked in a long breath before answering. "I'm afraid that an auction has already been arranged for two weeks from today. Unfortunately, despite my best efforts, the tax authorities are not willing to wait even a day longer."

He paused. "And your second question?"

Her face became grim. "Do you have any information as to who was responsible for deceiving my father in this most foul and callous manner? Also, is there any hope at all that they can be brought to justice?"

"I will tell you what little I know on that score," he said. "But I fear it will not bring you very much satisfaction."

ONLY WHEN WELL AWAY from John Bridle's office did Margaret cease walking and sit down on a public bench opposite the Shoulder of Mutton public house. There was so much to take in. Though she had arrived for her meeting with the solicitor already steeled for bad news, what she had actually heard far exceeded even her worst expectations.

She tried to place herself in her father's situation. No wonder he was so devastated when she'd found him in the library moments before his stroke. To discover out of the blue that he had been swindled out of almost every penny he owned was enough to reduce anyone in his position of responsibility to despair. The fact that he had very quickly found the fortitude to fight back against this massive loss, and the debilitating effects of his stroke, only served to increase her admiration for him.

She could see it all now. Even at this low point, his relentless efforts at regaining at least some degree of personal mobility had been directed toward just one purpose: to be strong enough to somehow find the means to hold the estate together. He had still honestly believed that, given the time, he could achieve a reversal of fortune. And with such unyielding determination, not to mention a whole raft of influential contacts to call on, who was there to say that he couldn't?

The damnable taxman! That was who.

To have picked himself up from such a low ebb, only to have it all snatched away again with news of the enforced sale was cruel almost beyond belief. What difference would a few more months have made to the tax authorities? They could have given him at least a chance to get back on his feet. Especially after all the large sums of money the Pugh family had contributed to their coffers over the years. But no. Even though the estate must be worth vastly more than any debt due, they had to demand their pound of flesh immediately. And in the process deliberately ruin a decent and honest man.

Yet much as she despised the heartless bureaucrats responsible for enforcing this decision, it was nothing compared to the virulent hatred that was boiling up inside for the swine of a confidence trickster who had set this whole series of disastrous events in motion. He was the one truly to blame for this terrible situation. She would happily see him locked away for the rest of his life for all the suffering that he had brought upon her dear father.

The last few minutes of conversation with John Bridle had given her little hope that the man would ever be brought to justice. According to the scant information Bridle had established from the earl, the fraudster had presented himself as an affiliate of the Johannesburg Stock Exchange. Carrying impeccable looking references in support of this identity, together with glowing geology reports and estimated production values for the mine, he'd assured the earl that a select few investors could be confident of truly remarkable returns in a very short space of time. But speed and discretion were vital. New exchange controls due to be enforced at any moment would make international trading many times more difficult and expensive. This factor alone would be sufficient to instantly double the value of any stock purchased beforehand.

"It goes without saying that, almost as soon as the funds were transferred, both the man and money disappeared without a trace," Bridle had told her in conclusion. "As you would expect, the matter is now in the hands of the police, although with nothing more than a bogus identity to work with, it is hard to be optimistic of their achieving any success. This appears to have been a meticulously planned fraud, so the perpetrator was sure to have made adequate arrangements to cover his trail. I would suspect that he is already many miles away from these shores by now."

With a heavy heart, Margaret was forced to concede that the solicitor was almost certainly correct.

NO MATTER HOW HARD Margaret tried to discuss the situation with her father in the days leading up to the auction, he remained unresponsive.

Although soon recovering from his state of shock and being fully aware of everything she said, it was as if he'd been broken to such an extent that he was prepared to passively accept whatever further blows fate cared to throw at him. Any suggestions that he might like to resume his rehabilitation exercises were totally ignored.

Doctor Grant offered a theory that, given the strength of his pride beforehand, it was most likely a deeply ingrained sense of guilt and shame that was now making her father so isolated. How long this condition might continue was impossible to say. It could be days, months, or years. Possibly even permanent. Sometimes it needed just a small trigger for the sufferer to snap out of the condition. If the earl were to suddenly discover a powerful enough motivation to re-involve himself with daily life, that might be all that was required. Beyond this, any kind of accurate prognosis was impossible to state.

Then, just when Margaret imagined that matters could not get any worse, they did.

Although not personally affected very much until now by the economic depression that had been hanging over the country in recent years, she was still sufficiently aware of it to understand that money was not so freely available as before. Even so, what happened on the day of the auction still came as an enormous shock.

Neither the house, nor the estate grounds, attained even their reserve prices. Margaret had been fully expecting them to bid up to at least double these figures before the hammer finally came down. As it was, everything was automatically withdrawn from sale without a penny being raised.

Her one sustaining hope throughout all of this trauma had been that, after the tax debt was settled and some goodwill payments made to any long-serving staff who faced unemployment, there would still be sufficient funds remaining for her father to purchase a decent replacement home. It would obviously be in much reduced surroundings, but a home nonetheless where he would be comfortable and well cared for. Now, given this failure to sell up for even sufficient to cover their tax obligations, what would be the Inland Revenue's next move?

The answer arrived with indecent haste.

John Bridle, together with a rather tall man with hawk-like features, arrived at the house just two days later. To her astonishment, her father agreed to their request for a private consultation in his study. To her even greater astonishment, while she was pacing about the front lawn speculating on what was being decided in this meeting, Bridle emerged from the house just half an hour later to say that she had been invited to join them.

"The earl refuses to conclude matters without you being present," he told her.

"You mean my father is actually discussing matters with you in detail," she responded, a surge of hope rising. Could this be the trigger that Doctor Grant had spoken of?

Bridle frowned. "Not exactly *discussing*, My Lady. Other than stating his wish for your presence, he has made only one other stipulation. However, seeing as he had previously made his requirements in this matter known to me via a telephone call last week, a lot of talk from him during today's meeting has not been necessary."

"He called you last week? I didn't know that."

"Yes, he had clearly foreseen the situation that has arisen today and wished to mitigate your ongoing circumstances as much as possible. That is what I have been attempting to do for him."

Margaret's relief that her father had after all acted with some measure of awareness – albeit without her knowledge – was overcome by the apprehensive expression on the solicitor's face.

"What precisely is the situation that has arisen today?" she asked.

He ran his tongue over the top lip. "The gentleman accompanying me is representing the government. They will be making a purchase of the house and entire estate for the sum total of four thousand pounds."

So great was the shock, it took a second for Margaret to fully grasp this.

"Four thousand pounds!" she repeated. "That's not even a third of the reserve price. Just the house and the three hundred acres that go with it must be worth at least ten thousand, and there are another six thousand acres of prime farmland on the estate as well."

Bridle shifted his feet uncomfortably. "That's all perfectly true, My Lady."

"Then I will go in there and make sure your companion from London knows this as well."

"I'm quite certain that he already does. Unfortunately, there is little room for negotiation. In essence, this is a compulsory purchase so that the tax liability may be paid off."

"But that's tantamount to robbery! Surely they can't do that?"

"I very much regret to say that they can."

She steadied herself. "So what were these terms that my father stipulated? Were they met?"

"Only to a degree, My Lady."

Moving over to a nearby bench seat, Margaret plopped herself down. "You had better explain, Mister Bridle."

He nodded. "In return for signing the agreement without creating an enormous fuss and embarrassment for the government – which, given his status, he would possibly be quite capable of achieving - your father initially demanded a fitting home for you and himself to be provided once the sale was completed. That was to be the case, even if there was insufficient money left over to fully pay for one. Sadly, this condition was refused."

Now that she had had time to digest things a little more, although still incensed, Margaret was not totally surprised by the government's vindictive attitude. Her father's outspoken criticism of the Prime Minister, Ramsay MacDonald, had been going on for very nearly a decade: ever since MacDonald during his first stint as PM in 1924 had suspended all charges against the communist newspaper editor J R Campbell for publishing an article inciting mutiny within the British armed forces.

In the earl's opinion, MacDonald's decision was nothing less than an act of treason, making him entirely unfit to hold any public office. And while it was true that the affair had soon brought down his government after only nine months in power, MacDonald quickly bounced back and was now at the head of the current coalition running the country. Infuriated by this, her father had been repeating his views loud and clear right up to the very day of his stroke.

"So what *has* been agreed?" Margaret asked, surprised by how much she was managing to keep her anger from showing.

The solicitor sat down a few feet to one side of her. "I have done my very best in these negotiations, My Lady. Please believe that."

"I am sure you have, Mister Bridle. But the final outcome, please."

"As a gesture of goodwill and acknowledgement of the earl's place in society, the government have agreed that you both may be allowed to take up residence in the head gardener's cottage. Although the state will now own the property, your father will have a guaranteed right of residency for the rest of his life."

"And when he dies?"

Bridle spread his hands in a gesture of helplessness. He did not need to say a word.

"I see," Margaret murmured. "And has father agreed to this?"

"Only with your assent. That is why he wishes to see you in the study now. However, before you go in there, you should be aware of one final, last-minute stipulation he has made today. He has insisted – absolutely insisted, and got his way – that for as long as he remains living in the cottage, you must retain full control of the stables and all of the horses. It is quite clear that he knows how much they mean to you."

Margaret felt a renewed rush of love for her parent. Even in his darkest hour of humiliation, he was still thinking of what he could do for her. And his humiliation was most certainly what certain people within this government was seeking. To hell with their magnanimous gesture of goodwill. They damn well wanted to keep her father living as a dependent in clear sight of what he had once owned; it would be a blow to his dignity and pride every single day he lived on. This was to be their revenge for him daring to speak the truth so openly about the closet communists in their midst.

Nevertheless, Margaret told herself, if he could bring himself to tolerate such a humiliating situation, then so must she. Besides, it wasn't as if they had any realistic alternatives at present. Her father's pride would never allow him to go cap in hand to any of their relatives, or be reduced to seeking charity from his wide range of friends and acquaintances. For him, that really would be the final nail in his coffin.

Another thought then dropped into Margaret's mind. With the stables remaining in her control for the foreseeable future, this could also be seen as a business opportunity – a chance for her to earn what might be a very reasonable living. At the very least it would give her a purpose in life and hope for the future. Perhaps that was the intention in the back of father's mind all along? The Pugh family had a long history of fighting back against adversity. He knew full well that she wasn't some pampered little princess who would be unable to adapt to their vastly reduced circumstances. Now she would prove it to him by supporting them both.

Margaret rose from the bench. "Very well, Mister Bridle. Let us go and finalise matters," she told the solicitor.

PART TWO
The turning point

THREE

The middle-aged gentleman walking with Margaret gave her a quick smile. "We really are most grateful for your assistance, My Lady. Some of the terrain here on your estate is an excellent match for what the chaps are expecting to face in the cross-country section of competition."

They were heading for the stables, and the speaker was Colonel Timothy Albriton, the chairman of a small committee appointed to oversee the British equestrian team's preparation for the soon to take place 1936 Olympic Games in Berlin.

Margaret was already well aware of what he'd just told her, having heard exactly the same thing from all three members of the eventing team who had been making regular use of her facilities. However, she could not resist an inner smile at the colonel's tactful phrasing of *'your estate'*. He knew as well as she did that her father was no longer owner of the land, nor was he ever likely to be so again.

Owners or not, in the close to three years that had passed since taking up residence in the former head gardener's cottage, little else appeared to have changed. Aside from a couple of visits by government inspection teams, Hadley Hall had apparently been forgotten. In one way, Margaret found this rather comforting. At least the old place was not being maltreated by occupants who did not appreciate its history. On the other hand, to see such splendid accommodation going to waste could at times be infuriating.

In the early days after its sale, she had often taken to wandering alone through the magnificent old mansion, almost every one of the countless rooms and corridors evoking a special memory of some kind. But these visits had ceased more than a year ago. As time progressed, they became simply too painful. The hard truth had prevailed. Even in some impossible dream world in which the house was miraculously bequeathed back to her father, without the income from all the farms on the estate, he could never afford to run it in anything remotely like its former manner. His swine of a swindler had put paid to any possibility of that.

Not that they were entirely without income. Margaret had blessed her parent's foresight a thousand or more times in negotiating what was virtually ownership – albeit temporary – of the stable block and horses, including her beloved Soldier. It was with a much-relieved heart she was able to tell head groom Tom Harris that, should he wish to, he could continue living in his small apartment above the stables. He eagerly agreed to this, and just as quickly to her following business suggestion. Since then, they had built up what was now the most highly regarded riding school for miles around. Such was the demand, a telephone had even been installed in the cottage hallway to deal with the steady flow of enquiries.

Margaret's good relations with their former tenant farmers was also a factor in this success. Each one approached freely gave his consent for her and her pupils to ride across agreed sections of their land. The Pugh family had always been fair and considerate landlords to them, so they were now quite happy to do what they could for her. In any case, whatever her and the earl's present circumstances, they were still leading members of the local aristocracy, and as such, respect was deeply ingrained.

This same level of accessibility had now been extended to the British three-day eventing team, together with the Hadley Hall stables and Tom Harris' vast expertise whenever it was needed.

"I'm happy to have been able to help in some small way," she told Albriton in response to his words of gratitude.

They paused outside the stable entrance. "Please, My Lady, do not underestimate the value of your assistance. I believe it has even been noted at government level." He gave a small laugh. "That's not altogether surprising, of course. If truth be known, they are rather more keen than usual for us to put up a good show this time around. You know, what with this Hitler chappie getting a bit too big for his boots."

Margaret raised an eyebrow. "Is that what they think? Some of the people I talk to whenever I go down to London seem to take a rather different view. They say Mister Hitler is just a strong leader who has performed wonders for the German economy. Also, that he is the best man available to prevent the spread of communism throughout Europe."

Albriton cleared his throat. "Yes, I have heard that opinion expressed as well, My Lady."

After a slightly uncomfortable pause, he brightened. "But we digress, and I have news to bring. In appreciation of your hospitality, it has been unanimously agreed by our committee that you and the earl should be offered the opportunity of joining our team in Berlin as our guests of honour. Naturally, your provided accommodation during the final week of the games will be at the Hotel Adlon, the city's finest."

For a moment, Margaret was completely taken aback. She quickly recovered. The Hotel Adlon, she told herself. It would be wonderful to experience that kind of luxury once again, even if only for a short time. And she would love to be there for the equestrian events, all of which were scheduled for that final week. But there were other matters to consider.

"I can't speak for my father," she began. "The truth is, he does not venture far from home these days. As for myself ...."

Her hesitation was quickly noted. "Please, My Lady, I was not expecting you to provide an answer immediately. There is plenty of time for you to think on matters, and to make whatever arrangements might be necessary to cover your absence if you do decide to go."

"I will certainly let you have an answer as soon as possible," she told him.

"Then I will look forward to receiving it."

Opening the stable door, he extended an arm. "For now, shall we continue?"

"Yes indeed," Margaret replied, leading the way through to the horses.

SOMETHING ELSE THAT had changed little during the last three years was the earl's state of mind.

Physically, he was better than could be expected, especially seeing as how he continued to shun all of his former rehabilitation exercises. However, sheer necessity had forced him into becoming quite adept with his left hand, making him capable of doing most things for himself if he felt like it. And that was where the problem lay. Other than occupying an armchair by the sitting room window and gazing out of it for hour after hour, he showed scant interest in doing anything beyond merely existing from day to day.

Just occasionally he would initiate a conversation, but it was always one full of regrets and memories. Never once did he raise a topic that was forward looking or optimistic. Even when Margaret told him of the successful business that she and Tom were building it generated little more than a brief nod. It was as if, having focused his mind long enough to gain the cottage and stables for their use, there was now nothing else left to hold his attention. Margaret had spent many hours wondering about the trigger that Doctor Grant had spoken of. If such a thing existed, she had no clue as to what it might be.

Colonel Albriton had mentioned that her assistance to the Olympic team had been noted at government level. She took this with a pinch of salt. If that was really true, then they had a damn funny way of showing their gratitude.

With Ramsay MacDonald now gone from Downing Street, she had recently written a letter to the present prime minister, Stanley Baldwin, in the hope that a conservative government might be more sympathetic to her father's plight. She had spelled out in detail his disturbed and apathetic mental condition, stating that she was certain the humiliation of living in a property that was now owned by someone else was at least partly to blame for his current state of mind.

She also spoke of how the success of her riding school would now allow them to place a reasonable size deposit on the cottage and stables. If the Prime Minister would only sanction a sale back to them of these two properties, they would undoubtedly be able to pay off the balance in a respectable period. As a result, the knowledge that he was once again living in a Pugh family owned property would undoubtedly go a long way toward restoring at least some of the earl's former pride. In fact, she added with weighted significance, it might even significantly extend the number of years that he had left to live.

She could not say for sure that the letter had been read by the PM himself, but the manner in which her plea had been regarded by whoever in Downing Street did deal with it was all too clear. The curt reply that arrived just a few days ago amounted to little more than a single line, stating: *It has been decided that the sale of the properties in question is currently not in the best interests of HM Government.* Not a single word was written regarding the state of her father's health. It was signed by someone from the Treasury.

If the passing of time had succeeded in slightly diminishing Margaret's resentment of the way her father had been treated, this snub succeeded in fully rekindling it. These people actually wanted him to die as soon as possible, she told herself. They were refusing to sell the two properties because they wanted full control over them with a minimum of delay. Hadley Hall and its grounds could then be sold in its entirety without the inconvenience of a sitting tenant vastly reducing the price.

The sheer cynicism of this appalled Margaret. Though she still loved her country, she loved her wonderful father far more. Not a single day passed when she did not spend time searching her mind for a way to bring him out of his apathy and restore some of his former pride. The sale of the cottage and stables, she had been certain, would have gone a long way toward achieving that. But now someone in Westminster had seen fit to kill any hope of even that small concession.

They truly were testing her patriotism to the limit.

SOME TIME WAS SPENT considering Colonel Albriton's offer, and it was an hour or so after dinner that same evening before Margaret decided to raise the matter. Her father was in his usual armchair by the window.

She took a seat nearby. "Father, there's something I'd like to discuss with you."

His head turned to face her, but he said nothing.

"I had a conversation with Colonel Albriton today," she began, "and you'll never guess what. He's invited us to—"

"Berlin! He's invited you to Berlin."

So sudden was the interruption, she blinked quite hard. "Yes, that's right. But how on earth did you know?"

"Stands to reason. After all the help you've given them, it's the very least they can do."

Despite his rather gruff tone, Margaret found herself smiling. There was certainly nothing wrong with his deductive powers. They were as sharp as ever. He might spend the vast majority of each day gazing out of the window in an apparently vacant manner, but he obviously saw quite a lot. This though, was the very first time he'd ever passed any kind of meaningful comment on what he observed.

Who could tell what else was passing through his mind during those endless hours? If only he would talk to her about his innermost feelings. She had tried so hard to coax them out of him on numerous occasions.

Margaret leaned a little closer. "All the equestrian events are taking place during the last week of the games, so that's when our invitation is for. And guess what? They are even paying for us to stay at the Hotel Adlon."

The earl grunted. "Someone must have plenty of money to spare then. It's a splendid place. Make the most of it, Margaret my dear."

"The invitation is for both of us, father. Please say you'll come too."

"No, that's out of the question."

"But I know you love the riding events almost as much as I do."

"I said no, Margaret."

The earl's voice then softened. "But you go, my dear. I absolutely insist on that. It's only for a week. Just find someone to fix me my meals while you are away and I'll be fine. Tom will be close by if I ever need help with anything."

She frowned. "I'm not sure about this."

"It's decided, and that's the end of the matter," he told her, turning his face back to the window.

His expression stated plainly that there would be no further debate.

TOM COULD NOT HAVE been more supportive about the proposed trip, agreeing at once to everything she asked of him. Not only that, he also offered to bring a camp bed over and sleep in the cottage so that the earl would not be alone at night should some emergency arise. With a dependable woman from Bletchley agreeing to come in daily to cook and clean up, Margaret at last felt comfortable enough to accept the colonel's invitation.

On hearing that the earl would not be going, Albriton had asked if there was anyone else she would like to nominate as a travelling companion. She said no. There was a good reason for this: her rapidly rising curiosity.

Although now living in vastly reduced circumstances, Margaret was still the daughter of an earl. Without any sense of conceit, she also knew that most men considered her to be extremely attractive. These two factors were sufficient to ensure that invitations to some of the best parties in London continued to arrive in the post. Every so often she would accept one of these.

A few months previously she had attended one such occasion at the Cafe Royal. Although there primarily to seek out new business opportunities with the equestrian set, she soon found herself drawn to a group centred around Diana Mitford, who Margaret was informed had recently returned from attending a major Nazi rally in Nuremberg. Already quite infamous for her close association with Sir Oswald Mosley, leader of the newly formed British Union of Fascists, Diana was enthusing about the many wonders that Adolph Hitler had achieved in Germany. With hugely ambitious building plans underway and unemployment plunging to just 1.7 million, there was money aplenty for the German people to spend, she told all of those listening.

After chatting with others at the party, Margaret found that quite a few of them shared the Mitford girl's opinions, particularly when she had spoken of Hitler's determination to stamp out the communist threat that seemed to be spreading so freely throughout Europe. This had struck a powerful chord with Margaret too, bringing to mind her father's past vigorously expressed opinions on the matter.

At the end of the day she had been left with a surprisingly intense curiosity to see some of this German economic miracle for herself. And now, out of the blue, she had been presented with the perfect opportunity to do so.

But if she *was* going to do this, she would need to do it properly. Without the company of her father or any other companion to take into consideration, she should have adequate time to attend all of the riding events, and explore well beyond the confines of the games as well.

Anticipation was growing fast. Who could tell what she might see? Or who she might meet there?

She could hardly wait to be on her way.

FOUR

Margaret was so glad that she had come to Berlin. With the three successive days of eventing competition all being held at different venues across the city, time had rushed by in a flurry of activity. This culminated in their final test, the show jumping, taking place inside the vast Olympic Stadium on the very last day of the games before a crowd estimated to be well over one hundred thousand.

The equestrian events had been a resounding success for the hosts, their riders winning all six team and individual gold medals in dressage, eventing, and show jumping. From a British point of view it was rather less of a triumph, with just one bronze medal between them from all competitions. But at least this had been won by the eventing team, so Margaret could feel a touch of satisfaction. However, in spite of all their preparations, there had been one aspect of the cross-country course that no one apart from the German team could possibly have anticipated.

The numerous large barriers and ditches were all well accounted for, but obstacle number four on the 22-mile course turned out to be the world's very first official water jump in eventing competition. Most riders approached this at full speed, easily clearing the low fence only to discover that the depth of water on the other side was at least two feet deeper than might be reasonably expected. Not only that, the footing was treacherous.

Of the forty-six competitors that jumped into the pond, only eighteen made it out again without either the horse or rider falling. Sadly for the British team, this included one of their own riders. Compounding the issue many times over, his horse then bolted off into the far distance, all the time clocking up a huge number of penalty points until it was eventually caught and the rider back in the saddle.

Germany completed the eventing team competition with 676 penalty points; Poland were second with 991; and Britain came a distant third with a staggering 9,195 points.

There were now two more days in Berlin before Margaret's journey home: days that she was determined to use well. It was time to get away from all the carefully scripted Olympic agenda and discover if everything she had heard about the new Germany was true. She needed to mingle with the ordinary citizens, hear what they were saying to each other, and if possible, engage some of them in conversation. Her German was certainly good enough to do this.

Conveniently, one of the best places of all to start on this adventure was right here on her hotel doorstep.

FROM AN ARMCHAIR IN a discreet corner of Hotel Adlon's spacious lobby, a man aged in his late twenties carefully observed all the comings and goings of the guests. His well-cut suit, together with an understated air of entitlement, allowed him to blend in easily with the opulence of his surroundings.

He spotted Margaret the instant she appeared at the top of the stairs. The thought of how attractive she looked in her floral summer dress and lightweight cardigan briefly formed. Quickly though, he raised the newspaper on his lap to cover his face. Only after what felt like a suitable pause did he lower it slightly, just in time to see her heading for the exit.

He immediately prepared to follow her.

AFTER STEPPING OUT from the front of the hotel, Margaret strolled a short distance along Pariser Platz and then on through the Brandenburg Gate. As with all the places she had visited during the last few days, the red flags with a black swastika at its centre were impossible to miss. Whether fluttering from flagpoles, strung out on a line across streets like bunting, or suspended from the sides of large buildings, they were literally everywhere.

Olympic or various national flags were also much on display, but it was the swastikas that left an indelible impression.

Directly ahead was Berlin's green breathing heart: the Tiergarten Park. Once inside, she wandered along a path leading north. Lots of people were moving in both directions, with some of the gentlemen even making a point of raising their hats to her while passing. Other visitors to the park, mostly small family groups, were sat on the grass enjoying the mid-morning sunshine. The smiles on their faces together with the buzz of their animated conversations, predominantly in German though she caught snatches of English and French as well, only served to further enhance the sense that this was a city at peace with the world.

After about two hundred yards her eyes wandered over to the right where she caught sight of the badly fire damaged Reichstag. She paused, then sat down on a nearby public bench.

Margaret continued to stare at the country's historic former parliament building, unused and ignored ever since being set ablaze more than three years ago. She wondered why it had not been restored. Especially with the world coming to Berlin for the games.

A voice speaking in impeccable English broke into her thoughts. "My word, what an amazing coincidence. How wonderful to see you, Margaret."

She looked up into the face of the young man standing there. "Richard...Richard Forest? Is that really you?"

He gave a broad smile. "It most certainly is. Though since I am now living in Germany, I have reverted to my original family name of Forst. A mere single letter of difference, but it somehow feels right." He pointed to the vacant space beside her. "Do you mind?"

"No, of course not. Please do."

As he settled down, Margaret recalled their first meeting. Their fathers had both been members of the same gentleman's club in London, and because of this friendly acquaintance, Lord Forest and his wife had often been invited as guests to Hadley Hall. On the second occasion they had brought Richard, their only child, along with them. Whether this was a rather obvious attempt at matchmaking by the two sets of parents was uncertain. Margaret was only eighteen at the time, and Richard just two years older.

Whatever the case, the pair of them soon became good friends without ever displaying any sign of becoming romantically involved. It was strange really. Although she'd had plenty of admirers and several brief flings during the years that followed, the need for that kind of relationship with a man had never been a particularly important aspect of her life. She was well aware that some of those in their social circle whispered of how she was too much of a daddy's girl, and that most of her emotions were invested in him and the estate: that this was why none of her affairs had ever lasted for long. Nevertheless, she and Richard remained close and had continued seeing each other on a platonic basis throughout, even for a time after her father's stroke.

He was a huge motorcycle fan, she remembered, often turning up to meet her on one of his powerful machines, the like of which she had never encountered before. At first she had been apprehensive about becoming a pillion passenger with him, but he soon proved to be an expert rider and gained her confidence. After that, she began to find their high-speed jaunts quite exhilarating. Not quite as exhilarating as being on a horse at full gallop, but very close.

Then tragedy struck. Both of Richard's parents were killed in a car accident. After that, she had seen him just once. They had dinner together in a little Mayfair restaurant, during which his distressed state of mind made conversation incredibly difficult. Two years had passed since then without any kind of contact. He just seemed to disappear completely. Now she could understand why.

"Is your move here permanent?" she asked.

"Most definitely," he told her. "Please forgive me for saying this, but even though I was born in England, it is my grandfather's heritage that I now associate most strongly with. These days I see myself as being completely German. And why not? Believe me, very soon Germany will become the most powerful nation in the world."

Before Margaret could respond to this claim, he pointed across the park. "I saw you gazing at the Reichstag as I approached."

She nodded. "Yes, I was wondering why it had been left in that terrible condition. It's such an important building."

"You are right," he said. "It is important - important in the sense that it remains that way. At least for a time longer. In its present condition the

Reichstag is a constant reminder to all those who pass by of the need to continue our fight against the evils of communism. The Bolsheviks who started the fire may have been caught and dealt with, but there are countless more of them still infiltrating our society with their poison. They seek to destroy our democratic society and are constantly looking for ways to start an uprising against the legitimately elected state."

Not once during this little speech did he raise his voice in the slightest. Margaret had to admit that everything he said came out as sounding perfectly reasonable. And it was true that her father had often made similar statements before suffering his stroke.

Richard must have sensed what was passing through her mind. "I know that if the earl was with us right now he would agree wholeheartedly," he added. "How is he these days?"

She sighed. "Much the same as ever. He could have come here with me for the games, but he still appears to have little motivation to do anything other than just sit around the cottage."

She went on to explain about her involvement with the British eventing team, their subsequent offer of accommodation at the Hotel Adlon, and of her father's refusal to even consider travelling with her.

"That is so sad to hear," Richard remarked. "He was such a vigorous man before ...."

He hesitated, as if reluctant to rake up bad memories.

"Before the government of the time ruined him," she completed.

He nodded. "Yes, it's true they treated him appallingly. Far worse than a man of his standing should ever have been. But of course, the one really to blame for all of his problems was the swine who sold him shares in that non-existent gold mine. It makes my blood boil when I think of how he fooled so many people and yet still got away with it."

Margaret stiffened. "So many people?" she repeated. "Are you telling me that father was not the only one who was cheated?"

"Oh, perhaps I was speaking out of turn." Richard held up a hand. "Please forget that I said anything, Margaret. It's all water under the bridge now, anyway. They'll never catch him."

"No...no, you must tell me everything you can about this. I insist. I need to know."

A reluctant sigh slipped out. "Very well. Seeing as how it's obviously so important to you." He drew a deep breath. "The truth is, my father invested in this fake mine as well. So did many others at the London club they frequented. That's where all the relevant discussions took place."

"I heard nothing about this," Margaret said. "Not a single word."

"That's hardly surprising. It was a huge embarrassment to all of those involved and got hushed up as much as humanly possible. Most of the members, including my father, invested with a degree of caution. So when the whole thing was exposed as a sham, they were at least able to absorb the financial shock. The general attitude was: Better to keep mum about it rather than let the world see what fools they'd been made of by a cheap confidence trickster."

He paused. "The earl, unfortunately, chose to go the whole hog so to speak. Which meant he was hit far harder than the others."

Margaret shook her head. "Why? Why would he be so rash? Especially when no one else was doing the same."

"Because he loves you so much."

"I don't understand. What's that got to do with it?"

Several seconds passed before Richard replied. "I really shouldn't be talking about any of this. Our two fathers were much closer friends than you might have realised, and they shared a great deal of their private thoughts. Mine told me a few details of their discussions in the utmost confidence. That's why I've never said anything to you before."

"Well you certainly can't stop now. Not after having told me this much."

When he did not respond quickly enough, she prompted: "You said it was because my father loves me so much."

"Yes, and I do not want you to start feeling guilty in any way."

"Why on earth would I feel that?"

Another sigh, the longest one yet, slipped out. "It weighed very heavily on the earl's mind that you could never inherit Hadley Hall or the estate. He also knew full well that you would receive precious little acknowledgement from any of the male heirs in line. That being so, he wanted to provide as much as he possibly could for you after his death. His shares in the gold mine were to be your inheritance and provide a good income for many years to come."

Margaret felt a lump forming in her throat. She tried to swallow it away, but it remained stubbornly in place. There was so much her father had kept to himself. It must be tormenting him every hour of every day. And Richard was right. There was an irrational feeling of guilt creeping up on her. The guilt of not having been born a son.

"Thank you for being honest, Richard," she told him. "So many things make more sense to me now." She passed a hand over her brow. "I take it that you never met this confidence trickster yourself?"

"Unfortunately not. All I know is that he was a temporary guest of the club and his references appeared to be immaculate. Oh, and father positively believed him to be Jewish. He said that the man's features, particularly the nose, were unmistakable. Also, that he could not help but notice in the club washroom one day that the fellow had been ...."

He gave a slight cough. "Circumcised."

"Really." Margaret was briefly too taken aback by his candour to say anything more.

"At the time, this was not considered to be an obstacle," Richard continued. "Indeed, two extremely wealthy members of the club who invested modestly were also Jewish. You might even say it was their example that played a big part in prompting others to follow."

A flicker of suspicion rose in Margaret. "Do you think they were involved in the crime as well? Perhaps as part of a deliberate ploy to lure others in?"

Richard shrugged. "Who can say for certain? But if they were, it didn't do them very much good. Both of them were fairly old and died quite shortly afterwards." A short laugh slipped out. "One of them actually expired while eating dinner in the club. Apparently he was tucking into a particularly large second helping of roly-poly pudding at the time."

Margaret took a moment to digest all of this. She had also heard a few vague stories back in England of how the Nazis had been conducting some sort of purge against Jewish citizens, though nothing of this nature had so far been apparent during her visit. She tentatively put this thought to Richard.

"A small part of what you say is true," he agreed. "As I have since discovered for myself, a number of the Jews living in Germany, just like the fellow in your father's case, are nothing but criminals feeding off the law-abiding members of society. But rest assured, Margaret, whatever measures are being taken against them, it is merely a case of removing a few rotten eggs for the sake of the greater good."

She gave a slightly uncertain frown. "Yes. There are bad people in every society, I suppose."

Even though it went against every one of her natural instincts to discriminate purely on the grounds of nationality, she could feel these new disclosures trying to make her do precisely that. She fought to repel the instinct. The hatred she had long felt for the foul beast who'd deceived her father so cruelly was undeniable. But it was the man's despicable actions that made her feel that way. Nothing else. She had not even been aware of his national background or religion until a few moments ago.

Nevertheless, Richard obviously knew what he was talking about. And he would certainly never lie to her. The truth was, it didn't really matter where the criminals and violent political activists currently causing problems in Germany originated from, they still needed to be dealt with if there was to be good public order. What's more, everything she had so far seen in a peaceful and thriving Berlin indicated how well the Nazi policies were working.

And that, she reminded herself, was to be the purpose of today's expedition. To explore wider afield so as to confirm this impression.

"I'm so glad we bumped into each other, Richard," she said, rising to her feet. "Your enthusiasm for the new Germany is infectious, and you've given me such a lot to think about. But I really must move on now. There are only two days remaining before I return home, and there is still so much of Berlin I want to see. Perhaps we can ...?"

The hanging question was seized upon, as she half-hoped it would be.

He rose to stand alongside her. "Then you will be needing a guide to ensure that your limited time is put to the best possible use. And who could be better qualified for the job than an old friend who just so happens to know the city very well indeed?"

She smiled. "Well...if you are sure you can spare the time. And it would be lovely to talk some more. You've never written, so I'd be most interested in hearing how things have been for you since moving here."

"Then your wishes shall be granted, My Lady," he told her with a grin.

MARGARET MADE A POINT of explaining that it was not historic buildings and monuments that she wanted to see, but the places where ordinary German people went to relax and enjoy themselves. She was not disappointed by Richard's choices.

After continuing to explore the open spaces of the Tiergarten for a short while longer, he then took her to the nearby Bellvue railway station. From here, they caught a train to Strandbad Wannsee.

"It is the largest inland lido in the whole of Europe," he informed her proudly during the fifty-five-minute journey. "People come from many miles around to enjoy the facilities."

Even forearmed with this information, Margaret still found herself gasping with delight on first seeing the vast stretch of sandy beach running along the lake's shore. By now the sun was high in the sky, and what seemed like hundreds – possibly even thousands – of joyful looking people were packed onto the golden sands. Virtually all the men were wearing nothing but shorts or bathing trunks, while some of the women's beach attire, to Margaret's eyes, appeared more than a little bit daring. Spaced at regular intervals in the sand between all these sun worshippers, small Nazi flags on short poles fluttered happily in the breeze.

Her earlier impressions gained in the Tiergarten were confirmed. Few tourists were present here. This was the German people enjoying their leisure. Mister Hitler's economic miracle was clearly working well enough for them.

After strolling for a time and then enjoying lunch in the beach front restaurant, Richard suggested that they head back toward the city centre.

"I know just the place for us to go next," he told her.

This time they got off the train near Charlottenburg and took a tram down into the heart of Wilmersdorf. Here, Margaret was ushered to a table at an open-air bar/restaurant with live music and a dance floor that was full of couples spinning enthusiastically about. The band was playing the song Goody Goody, which she knew had been a huge hit for American orchestra leader Benny Goodman earlier that year. The bouncy rhythm had her tapping her toes almost immediately. When the waitress came to their table, Richard ordered a gin and tonic for her and a beer for himself.

"Just to prove I haven't forgotten your favourite libation," he smiled.

They danced once or twice and chatted freely, just like the old days. So relaxed did Margaret become, before she knew it the time was approaching six o'clock.

"Goodness!" she exclaimed after glancing at her watch. "I didn't realise it was so late."

"Is the time important?" Richard asked. "Do you have special plans for later?"

"No, not really."

"That's good, because I was about to ask you if you would care to accompany me to a small party this evening. There will be someone there who, given your obvious curiosity about the new Germany, I know you will be most pleased to meet. A very important man indeed."

Margaret leaned closer. "Very important, you say. Are you going to tell me the name of this mysterious person?"

"Absolutely not," he told her, his smile returning. "You will just have to trust me. All I will add is this: You may find it very much to your personal advantage to speak with him."

She tapped the table sharply. "You rotter, Richard. Are you teasing me?"

"Would I do that?" he grinned.

AFTER ESCORTING MARGARET back to the hotel, Richard arranged to return there for her with a car at nine o'clock. He then set off at a brisk walk in an easterly direction along Unter den Linden before turning right into Wilhelmstrasse.

Everything had gone exactly to plan. Sometimes he thought he knew Margaret better than she knew herself. On discovering that she was booked into the Hotel Adlon for the last week of the games, it had simply been a matter of following a carefully planned script.

The first few days of her visit were not important; she was most unlikely to see anything untoward. On the Führer's direct orders, Berlin in general, and especially any area that Olympic visitors were liable to encounter, had been thoroughly sanitized for the duration. No trace of anti-Jewish notices or graffiti could be seen anywhere, and hundreds of potential troublemakers in the form of communists, gypsies and Jews had been arrested and interned in a camp well to the east where they could not be an embarrassment.

It was the day after the closing ceremony that Richard chose to move in.

Even before leaving England he'd been well aware of Margaret's disgust for the establishment figures she held responsible for ruining her father. She'd spoken to him about it on almost every occasion they'd seen each other, and he'd taken full opportunity to subtly encourage her animosity. By then, he had already become deeply fascinated with the rise of Nazi fascism and could well envisage a future when Britain and Germany might end up on a collision course. Now, having lived in Berlin for two years, he was convinced of it.

His grandfather's aristocratic connections and military background had served him well when first arriving in the country, opening doors that would otherwise have remained firmly closed. Once passing through these, he set about ingratiating himself with the right people to such an extent that within a year he'd become a member of Hermann Goering's personal staff, with special responsibility for the recruitment of informants. Granted powers and access equal to that of a senior Gestapo officer, he had so far been commendably successful in this role.

His boss, he quickly learned, was constantly seeking ways of advancing his own cause and digging up dirt on real or imagined rivals. Richard's suggestion to him regarding Lady Margaret Pugh, describing her as a disillusioned member of the British aristocracy, was enthusiastically endorsed. Goering understood very well what a feather in his cap with the Führer it would be if he could have direct access to someone in England with Margaret's important social connections. More than that, after being told of her father's recent fall from grace, he fully agreed that there appeared to be a good possibility of gaining her cooperation.

"Keep me informed of your progress," he had instructed Richard.

He was now about to do exactly that.

FIVE

E ven amongst all the other luxury vehicles gracing Hotel Adlon's car park, the gleaming black Mercedes-Benz cabriolet was still by far the biggest eye-catcher of all.

"Your transport for the evening, My Lady," Richard said, sweeping an arm ceremoniously toward the passenger door and then opening it for her.

"What a magnificent car," Margaret told him, nodding appreciatively. "Is it really yours?" Whatever she had been expecting, it certainly wasn't anything as grand as this. She had almost forgotten what it was like to travel in such style.

"It actually belongs to my employer," he admitted. "Just one of three delivered to him only a few days ago direct from the factory. But he has provided me with use of this one so that I may convey you to his little gathering in style. He is most keen to ensure your comfort."

His eyes ran over the elegant black evening dress and pale green silk shawl covering her otherwise bare shoulders. "And may I say how lovely you look, Margaret."

She smiled in response to the compliment, at the same time noting that he was now wearing formal evening dress. He had told her earlier of the dress code expected and could not help but wonder yet again who their host this evening would turn out to be. Clearly it was someone who enjoyed the whole 'dressing up' thing. Richard had described him as his employer, which was another surprise. Up until now she had imagined her old friend to be living off his father's inheritance. Not that this would last him forever. Certainly not in a city as expensive as Berlin.

"How far are we going?" she asked after they were both inside the car.

"Ah, a good question," he responded. "I would say something close to..." He paused for a moment to stroke his chin, as if pondering the matter. "Six hundred metres perhaps."

"Six hundred metres!" Margaret could not help but laugh. "You mean to say that this beautiful car has been provided for a journey that we could actually walk in just a few minutes."

Richard sighed. "I fear that your recent life has made you forget how a lady of your rank deserves to be treated, Margaret. To expect you to walk any distance at all when responding to a formal invitation, especially when you are so splendidly attired, would be an unforgivable insult."

She laughed again. "I didn't mean that literally. But a taxi would surely have been sufficient?"

He shook his head. "Most definitely not. Our host would not hear of it."

They drove south for a short distance before turning into Leipziger Strasse. To their left, a high wall and thickly foliaged trees completely screened off what lay behind from public view. The car paused at a pair of large metal gates, but these were quickly opened by one of the two armed soldiers on duty there, allowing them to follow a tree-lined driveway all the way to a large, four-storey house. A short flight of steps led up to the main entrance. Two more soldiers standing rigidly to attention were positioned left and right of the door. Between these two, holding himself in a slightly more relaxed manner, was a quite senior looking officer.

He came down the steps to greet them as they got out of the car and gave a brisk bow. "Good evening, Lady Margaret. I am Colonel Karl-Heinrich Bodenschatz, and it is my honour to escort you through to this evening's proceedings."

With a brief nod of acknowledgement to Richard, he led the way back up the steps and into the house.

Almost at once they were confronted by an elaborately decorated white alabaster staircase that, to Margaret's mind, had been designed purely to instil a sense of awe in visitors. What's more, it probably succeeded in a lot of cases, she felt. However, having lived for most of her life daily ascending the infinitely grander and beautifully carved main oak staircase at Hadley Hall, this white creation made little impression. In fact, by comparing it to what she was familiar with, all this did was acutely remind her of how much she missed living in the grand old house.

On reaching the next level, they were led along a hallway where the improbably deep pile of the carpet muffled all sound of their advance. Bodenschatz then paused outside a set of double doors. As he opened these, the hum of several simultaneous conversations drifted out.

They moved forward into a large reception room with paintings and tapestries adorning every wall, together with the ubiquitous swastikas and one exceptionally large portrait of Adolph Hitler. Approximately fifty guests were stood about, mainly in small groups. Most of the men were wearing evening dress similar to Richard's, although a few, like Bodenschatz, were in full military dress uniform. As for the women, all were elegantly attired and dripping in expensive looking jewellery. Margaret's hand briefly touched her throat, where just a simple necklace was hanging.

Even amongst all these people, she was able to identify their mystery host almost at once. Though a little portlier than the photos she had seen suggested, in his white, medal-bedecked uniform he was still unmistakable. Richard had not been exaggerating; Hermann Goering *was* one of the most important and influential men in Germany. Probably second only to Hitler himself. In spite of this, on spotting their arrival, he came striding over immediately.

"My dear Lady Margaret, how good of you to join us," he said in excellent English after Bodenschatz had formally introduced him. "I have been so looking forward to making your acquaintance ever since Richard told me of his chance encounter with you earlier today."

She accepted his outstretched hand and allowed him to kiss her lightly on the fingers. "I thank you for your hospitality, Herr Goering. And for the use of your magnificent car."

By now, Bodenschatz had already summoned a circulating waiter with a raised arm and a sharp click of the fingers. Margaret and Richard were both handed flutes of champagne.

Goering waved a hand across the room. "As you can see, I have a number of civilian guests here this evening. They are mostly leading members of the business community, and as plenipotentiary of the four-year plan to restore Germany's economy, I must work closely with these people to implement measures that will ensure the plan's success. Gatherings such as this can play an important part in the process."

"From what I have seen and heard, you are already enjoying a more than reasonable measure of success," Margaret told him. "And to have been able to host the Games in such a triumphant way is quite an amazing turnaround given the circumstances."

Goering did his best to look modest without coming even close to achieving it. "An excellent beginning, that's true. But still a long way to go."

"I would be very interested to know more about this four-year plan of yours if you have the time," she continued. "Perhaps England could learn something from your methods."

"For you, Lady Margaret, I will definitely make the time," he responded. "We can talk as much as you wish a little later on: just the four of us in a private room where there will be no distractions. Until then, unfortunately, I am compelled to attend to some of my other guests."

He beckoned Bodenschatz in a little closer. "Karl is my adjutant and trusted friend. He will be able to introduce you and Richard to some of the more interesting people here while I am otherwise occupied. Please feel free to mingle as freely as you wish."

With that, he moved off to speak with a middle-aged couple in the centre of the room.

After watching him go, Margaret took a sip of champagne. Something was telling her that this could turn out to be an even more interesting evening than expected.

IT WAS JUST AFTER ELEVEN o'clock when Bodenschatz showed Margaret and Richard into a small study adjacent to the reception room. Goering followed them in a couple of minutes later. With all of them settled comfortably in leather armchairs, the talking began.

For more than half an hour Goering spoke of nothing but his ambitions to make Germany the most powerful economy in Europe. He seemed to be highly confident of success and took the trouble to answer all of Margaret's questions in a fair amount of detail. He even complimented her on her understanding of the subject.

Gradually though, the roles were reversed and Margaret found herself becoming the one who was answering questions. First of all it was just her general impressions of the new Germany that she was asked about. Then things became rather more specific. How did she think Germany's efforts to recover its economy compared with the way in which the British government was handling things? Could those in Westminster be doing more to help their own people through the current hard times?

It was this final question that prompted a flicker of derision to register on her face.

Goering spotted it at once. "I understand exactly how you feel," he told her.

"No you couldn't," she snapped back, for a moment completely forgetting social niceties.

He merely smiled. "Please allow me to be honest with you. I know all about your father's outspoken views on communism, and of how the Ramsay MacDonald government sought to ruin him because of this."

A flash of anger ran through Margaret. She glared across at Richard, suddenly aware that neither he nor Bodenschatz had uttered a word since entering the room. "You spoke of my father's private business," she accused.

He shook his head, a hurt expression forming. "No, Margaret. I wouldn't do that."

"Then how would Herr Goering know of it?"

"Your good friend is entirely innocent, Lady Margaret," Goering cut in. "All he did was confirm what I already knew. Under pressure, I might add."

"So who did tell you?" she pressed. "It was hardly a topic that would feature in any of your German newspapers."

"That's true. But as you will be aware, a considerable number of the British aristocracy possess German origins, plus there are many more who simply share your father's distaste for communism and have a strong liking for the way we are managing our recovery. People such as two of the Mitford sisters, both of whom are still here in Berlin after attending the Games as guests of the Fuhrer. The possibilities for casual talk are numerous."

"Even so, why would anyone consider my father's misfortunes worth passing on to you?"

"Perhaps because I am renowned as a man who abhors injustice. A righter of wrongs is how I like to see myself."

Margaret could not prevent an ironic laugh from slipping out. "Are you suggesting that you could somehow bend the British establishment to your will and correct the situation in my father's favour? Knowing them the way I do, I doubt that very much."

He merely smiled. "There are things currently happening at a very high level that you are entirely unaware of, Lady Margaret. Things which I'm sure you will understand I am not at liberty to discuss in detail at present. All I will say is this: You may be most surprised at what can become possible for both you and your father in the not too distant future."

For a moment, she could feel only confusion. The implied promise was clearly there, and no matter how hard she looked, she could not see a trace of deviousness in his expression. Nor hear anything but calm conviction in his voice. Yet in spite of this, it was an almost unbelievable claim. What situation could this admittedly extremely powerful and influential man possibly engineer that might restore Hadley Hall and the estate to their keeping? And even if by some miracle he was capable of doing so, what would he want from her in return?

Richard's words of earlier that day then returned to her. *You may find it very much to your personal advantage to speak with him.* Was this what he had been referring to?

She turned to face her friend. In return, she received an almost imperceptible nod. Imperceptible....but loaded with significance.

Her mind was now swirling with questions, but before she could give voice to any of them, Goering spoke again.

"I can see that my words have surprised you, Lady Margaret. And as you no doubt will have already suspected, I do have a proposition to put to you. But first, a question. How much do you love your country?"

"I love it very much indeed," she responded quickly, astonished that he should even be asking her such a thing.

She paused for a moment to choose her next words more carefully. "It is simply the inflexible attitudes of those who govern us that gives me cause to harbour a certain resentment. Considering all that they have done to ruin my father, it would be entirely unnatural if I did not feel this way. But that does not affect my sense of loyalty. Not in the slightest. I only want what is best for my country."

He nodded. "Just as I thought. A true patriot. Like myself, of course."

"Please do not patronise me, Herr Goering." She could not keep a sharp edge from her tone.

"My dear Lady Margaret, that was not my intention at all. Please accept my apologies. I merely wished to establish exactly where your allegiances lie before saying anything further."

"Well now you have. I am English and proud of it, despite the considerable failings of our leaders." He was beginning to annoy her, but the carrot had been dangled and she was compelled to hear him out.

Goering fiddled with the swastika hanging from the left breast of his tunic for a couple of seconds before continuing. "The Fuhrer not only wishes to improve life for the people of Germany," he began cautiously. "He also has plans to do the same for a significant number of other European countries. However, a strong hand is needed if Europe is to be cleansed of its many ills. A lot of people - myself included - feel that, although the ultimate aim is to bring nations together in harmony, the vigorous but necessary methods we must use to achieve this will eventually cause considerable conflict between our two governments."

He looked her directly in the eye before adding: "All the indications suggest that those in Westminster are determined to remain the dominant force in Europe. That being so, they are certain to be highly resistant to any change for the better if they feel it reduces their influence."

"I can agree with your assessment of their reaction," Margaret told him. "But when you speak of conflict, are you suggesting that our countries might actually go to war with each other once again?"

"Sadly, that is a very real possibility. Our Leader will not abandon his plans to restore Europe's fortunes just because your parliament objects to meaningful progress for the many."

At last Margaret began to see where this conversation was leading. "So if such a conflict were indeed to happen, I take it that you fully expect to win this time?"

"Without a doubt. Very quickly indeed and with a minimal loss of life on both sides. Soon now, Germany will possess the largest and finest armed forces in the world." He gave a short laugh. "What could Britain do to stop us? Your Royal Air Force is still using bi-planes from the last war, whilst the Luftwaffe..."

He checked himself, as if suddenly realising that he was saying too much.

Margaret continued with her train of thought. "And of course, any victory you secure would be followed by a significant change in the ongoing government of Britain."

Goering nodded. "The necessary adjustments would be made."

"Adjustments that would allow certain properties to be returned to their former owners?"

"You understand the position perfectly, Lady Margaret. Rest assured that Earl Pugh's property would be one of the very first to be dealt with."

Despite having anticipated a response along these lines, to hear it actually confirmed in words still drew an involuntary blink of surprise. Almost as a matter of course, the first thought that came racing into her head was Doctor Grant's trigger theory and how her father might react. Owning the estate once again would be certain to give him a whole new lease of life. Even if the effects of the stroke continued to limit him physically, in his mind he would surely be restored to his spirited old self. After the recent years of depression, what a blessing that would be. It might even extend his life expectancy by many years.

Goering spoke again. "There is also the matter of succession. Something could most definitely be done to ensure that you, and not some distant male cousin, will inherit the earl's estate when he finally passes on. That would be a most pleasing outcome for both of you, I should imagine."

Just when Margaret thought she was absorbing his first suggestion, this entirely unexpected second proposal hit her with even greater force. She closed her eyes for a moment to fully take it in. Something that she had longed for nearly all of her life but never considered remotely attainable was now tantalisingly being held out as a very real possibility.

She could never bring herself to wish for another war. That would be a terrible thing to do. But if a second conflict and a German victory was going to be inevitable anyway, why shouldn't her father stand to benefit from the situation? Especially after all that he had suffered. In fact, after what she had seen here in Berlin, the whole of Britain would probably be significantly better off under Nazi rule.

She drew a deep breath. Stop it, she told herself. You're racing ahead way too fast. Even if Goering was absolutely right about everything, such a situation would likely be several years away. Nothing much was going to change for her next week. Nor in a few months. And there was still one burning question yet to be answered.

What was expected from her in return for all these favours?

The question was met with a dismissive wave of Goering's hand. "Almost nothing, especially at first," he told her. "I would request only that you keep your eyes and ears open for any little scraps of information that you think might be of use in shortening whatever period of hostility eventually arises. Obviously, the briefer this turns out to be, the fewer the number of lives that will be put at risk."

Margaret frowned. "You mean spy?"

"No, not really. Perhaps see it more as an intermediary role in helping to bring matters to a swift and peaceful conclusion."

"I'm not a fool, Herr Goering. Please don't mistake me for one. I know exactly what you are asking of me. What's more, I will certainly sleep on the matter and provide you with an answer in the morning."

A look of surprise briefly showed. A smile then formed. "Splendid, Lady Margaret. I shall look forward to hearing from you. However, let me add just one thing before I return to my other guests. Believe me when I say that both the Fuhrer and I have a great affection for Britain and its people. In many ways we regard you as kindred spirits and long to share our prosperous future with you. It is only your self-serving politicians who will ultimately cause friction between our two countries."

He gave a small laugh. "So you see, in many ways you might say that we are on the same side with a common enemy to defeat."

Margaret's expression gave nothing away. "A point I have not overlooked," she remarked.

Her gaze then shifted to Richard. "I would like to return to my hotel now," she told him.

AS EXPECTED, NEITHER the comfort of her bed nor the lateness of the hour was going to lull Margaret into sleep easily. Not with her mind crammed so full of questions and possibilities.

Richard had said little during the short drive back to the hotel. If anything, she could sense a kind of nervousness about him, almost as if his own future might be affected by her final decision. Already she was beginning to question whether their meeting had been the chance encounter it appeared to be. Subsequent developments seemed to have fallen into place with surprising speed and convenience. Nonetheless, much as she tried to refute it, a great deal of Goering's logic was sound. And what he was offering in exchange for her help was tempting beyond belief.

A loving smile formed as Margaret pictured her father's estate being restored to him. The vision quickly expanded. He'd be a new man again in no time at all: she was sure of it. To see him once more back where he rightfully belonged inside Hadley Hall would be beyond wonderful. It would be just like it was before...no, even better. She knew how deeply it troubled him that their ancestral home could never be hers. Now, if she accepted Goering's proposition, even that dark cloud in her father's world could be removed. For a moment or two, while imagining him in this revitalised way, a great wave of happiness engulfed Margaret completely.

The feeling soon passed as the reality of things began biting deep. She had told Goering that she loved her country and wanted the best for it, and that remained unquestionably true. Now though, the question was: What *would* actually be the best thing for it in the long run. The status quo, or a new broom to sweep clean?

She may have been sheltered from such things before, but her father's downfall had opened her eyes wide to the harsh realities of Britain's economy. The Great Depression was still fresh in most people's memory: a time when unemployment had reached seventy percent in some parts of the country. Even four years later there were still over three million unemployed nationally. Having now seen Germany's economic miracle for herself – they had double the population and little more than half the unemployment - the contrast was astonishing. Would it really be so bad for Britain's people if the architects of that success were to do the same for them too? Those currently in Westminster were clearly failing.

But one question was key. Was another war between Britain and Germany really inevitable? She had heard little talk of such a possibility back home. This, despite the fact that Germany had marched troops into the Rhineland earlier that year in an act that went directly against the Treaty of Versailles. Many people were saying quite openly that they did not see why the Germans should not be allowed to re-occupy what was after all, a part of their own country. They seemed confident that this was as far as the situation would stretch. However, Goering was widely regarded as being privy to all of Hitler's intentions, so there had to be a significant element of fact in what he'd revealed to her.

It was only after several hours of soul-searching that Margaret made a tentative decision. No matter how far into an uncertain future they might be looking, it was impossible for her to turn her back completely on Goering's proposal. Not if there was even the smallest chance of seeing her dear father restored to anything like the spirited and happy man he used to be. After all the countless wonderful things that he had done for her throughout her life, the very least she must now do in return is explore the possibilities. She would never be able to live with herself if she failed to make even that small gesture on his behalf.

She would go along with Goering's proposal and play a waiting game. The man himself had said that very little would be required of her at first, so this should give her a breathing space to see how his prophesies developed. If and when a war did arrive, only then would she be compelled to appraise things more fully. Until such time, if pressured into making a few token gestures, she would stick to contributing only the very lowest grade information. The kind of stuff that could do little or no harm to anyone.

Several other questions remained, perhaps most importantly of all, how would she be able to pass and receive messages without placing herself at risk? Also, in the event of a German victory, what guarantee could Goering offer that his promises would be honoured? If issues such as these could be satisfactorily resolved then she would agree to his proposition, albeit with a great number of carefully concealed reservations.

She just prayed the day would never come when she regretted this decision.

AFTER THE INITIAL EUPHORIA of striking the bargain, it had not taken long following Margaret's return home for a sense of unease to set in.

Her father had never expressed an opinion on Hitler's rise to power, and any attempt by her to raise the subject with him was invariably brushed aside. She had already spent many hours wondering what he would make of Richard's deep involvement with the Nazis. Would he shrug it off and say that the boy was simply being true to his family heritage, or be outraged and insist that he should have remained loyal to the country he was born and raised in? If she could not be sure of the earl's response to such a straightforward question, how could she possibly anticipate his reaction to the deal his own daughter had made with Goering?

It was possible that her father's anti-communist sentiments would give him at least a measure of sympathy for current German policies. His fate at the hands of a Jewish swindler might add weight too. But would that really be enough for him to condone her actions in Berlin? In every other way he was a fiercely patriotic man who had served with distinction in the last war.

The agony of uncertainty lingered on for day after day. In the end, Margaret decided to say nothing for the time being. If and when the estate was eventually restored to him, perhaps another reason for this piece of good fortune could be conveniently manufactured. Until then, although it broke her heart to see him continue with his melancholy and meaningless existence, he must be allowed to remain this way.

PART THREE
The conflict begins

SIX

Three years had now passed since her visit to Berlin, and Margaret had been watching developments in Europe with equal measures of fascination and horror.

Following Germany's absorption of Austria into the Reich, matters had seemed to come to a head when Hitler insisted that the same thing should happen to a border region of Czechoslovakia known as Sudetenland populated almost entirely by Germans. After several months of mounting international tension, at a Munich conference in September 1938, an agreement was signed by Germany, Britain, France and Italy granting the Fuhrer his wish. With Czechoslovakia excluded from negotiations but forced to accept the outcome, British Prime Minister Neville Chamberlain returned home waving a non-aggression pact signed by Hitler and declared to the masses of waiting media: *'Peace for our time.'*

Knowing what she did, Margaret did not share his opinion.

Confirming this, just six months later, Nazi troops invaded the rest of Czechoslovakia. Appeasement had clearly not worked, prompting Chamberlain to publicly guarantee British aid to Poland if they were the next to be invaded. On the first of September 1939, the German battleship *Schleswig-Holstein* opened fire on the Polish garrison at Westerplatte to signal the start of exactly that.

The die was cast. Two days later, both Britain and France declared war on Germany.

AT FIRST, MARGARET had corresponded with Richard via normal mail to an address he had provided her with in Switzerland. By using a simple yet secure code based on the content of two specially selected books and always posting her letters from a different box in London, she felt as secure as could be expected. Little risk was involved in gathering the kind of next to worthless information that could be seen or heard by just about anyone if they kept their wits about them. In truth, without making herself rather obvious by putting leading questions to some important people that she knew quite well, there was little more she could report anyway.

But as the storm clouds of war gathered strength, things abruptly changed. Mass censorship of private mail was becoming a near certainty, and Margaret was very quickly given new directions for communicating. For the very first time, she was given a personal contact on home territory. And a more flamboyant character was difficult to imagine.

For several years now, a tipster going by the name of Joe Bull had been a highly popular character on English racecourses. Cheekily claiming to be a descendant of the iconic but fictitious John Bull, he could be seen sporting a vivid red and gold waistcoat with the English three lions and crown emblazoned across the front, a tail-coat made up entirely from a union jack flag, and a flat cap decorated with half a dozen Tudor roses. With his catchphrase of *'Give it a go with Joe'* lustily delivered in broad cockney tones, he was regarded by most punters as a pretty average tipster but well worth a few shillings for the entertainment value. Rumours also persisted that Joe was in fact a very rich man who did this purely for fun, and all of the money he collected was regularly donated anonymously to charity.

Margaret's instructions were to keep using the same code books as before, and to pass her messages over to Joe while apparently buying a tip from him. These tips were always handed out in a sealed envelope with Joe leaning in close to whisper: *'Don't let on the 'orse's name to no one else. That'll jinx it good 'n proper and it'll likely still be running this time next week.'*

Everyone knew he said pretty much the same thing to all of his customers; it was an expected part of the show. Except in Margaret's case, the envelope she received contained the latest message from Richard, and the whisper in her ear was usually to inform her of the next few race meetings that Joe could be found at. If he had a message for her, he would be wearing a green silk cravat. If not, it would be a red one. Also, in case of unexpected events, a warning black neck-tie would mean 'do not approach me for any reason'.

Although at first uneasy about this arrangement, Margaret was left with no other choice if she wanted to continue with things. On the plus side, with little of consequence to report anyway, her actual meetings with Joe were quite few. After nearly a year, during which she experienced just five trouble-free exchanges, she began to relax more. Even in the first few months after war was declared, nothing much seemed to be happening. People even began speaking of this time as the 'phoney war'. Margaret could thoroughly relate to that.

Then, to her absolute horror in March of 1940, after remaining uninhabited for close to seven years, work suddenly began at Hadley House to convert it into some kind of government department building. The process was brutal. Most of the house's beautiful furniture was either thrown down into the cellar or taken away completely in huge removal vans. Replacing these former Pugh family heirlooms, in came an almost endless stream of cheaply made desks, chairs, and filing cabinets. Despite Margaret's many heated protests, heavy-booted builders with no apparent regard for their surroundings tramped up and down the magnificent main staircase, leaving behind a thousand and one different scars as testament to their passing.

Much of the work consisted of dividing up the larger rooms with rough partitioning in order to create countless small offices. Margaret could hardly contain her tears as carpets and floorboards were torn up for no apparent reason, while intricately patterned plaster decorations on the walls and ceilings that were considered even vaguely obstructive to the job in hand were simply hacked away with crowbars and hammers.

Outside fared only a little better. Aside from the churning up of the forecourt and adjacent lawn caused by the passing of so many heavy vehicles, half a dozen ugly looking Nissen huts had also been erected. Exactly what the intended purpose of these was remained a mystery.

Then, as if to deliver a final kick in the teeth, three of the six horses in her stables were requisitioned by the army. And just like in the case of the house, there was no advance warning. A trio of soldiers carrying a government signed order simply turned up with a horse box one morning and informed her they would be taking whatever mounts they saw fit. The one saving grace was that, in an ironic way given his name, her beloved Soldier was regarded as

69

being too old for their requirements. She certainly wasn't going to tell them that he was still by far the strongest horse of them all, and neither would Tom. Now nearing his sixtieth birthday, the groom looked as healthy and vigorous as ever. The fact that his daily workload had been reduced by half did nothing to diminish his ire over their loss.

With their cottage being just two hundred yards away from the house and the activity on the forecourt clearly visible from their living room window, there was no possibility of Margaret concealing events from her father. As usual he said little, though the distress on his face was obvious. In spite of this, he gave no sign of sharing the same sense of outrage that was burning inside of her over seeing their ancestral home being so cruelly vandalised. If this could not stir him out of his apathy, she felt with a sinking heart, then surely nothing ever could.

But she had anger enough for the two of them. If there had been any stirrings of guilt over her agreement with Goering, these two latest assaults on their lives firmed her resolve once again. If anything, it was now stronger than ever. Instead of the virtually useless information she had so far relayed, she would now try to discover some genuinely useful intelligence. For a start, it might be useful to know what branch of government administration was going to be housed in Hadley House once all the work was completed. Who could tell? Perhaps there might be some benefit to be gained from this situation after all?

She would be watching developments very closely indeed.

DESPITE HIS HIGHLY convincing act, Joe Bull – real name, Joseph Flynn - was no more a natural born Londoner that Adolph Hitler.

He knew nothing of his parents, having been discovered as an abandoned baby in the pews of a Dublin church. His date of birth and given name had been scribbled on a label tied to his wrist, along with a plea to: 'Please care for my child'.

Raised in one of the city's harsh disciplined industrial schools where 'trade training' consisted mostly of back-breaking labour in the school's farm fields, he eventually escaped this environment at the age of fourteen. By now almost a man anyway, even if not in terms of age, he spent the next six years scratching a living in any way he could, mostly at the various racecourses and point-to-point meetings held in the area. Horse racing was popular virtually all the year round, and there were plenty of trainers and owners at these meetings willing to part with a small amount of loose change in return for a willing young helper with a strong arm. While earning his crust, young Joe made a point of listening and learning all that he could.

The next turning point came when, just after his twentieth birthday in December 1915, he decided to volunteer for military service and joined up with the Royal Dublin Fusiliers. Any aversion to siding with the British was far outweighed by a conviction that, if people like him did not go to the aid of brave little Catholic Belgium, his home country might well be the next to suffer a German invasion. There was also the lure of a proper pay packet every week and regular meals. These alone had to be worth getting shot at occasionally, he reasoned.

Fortune favoured him during the remaining three years of hostilities on the Western Front. Never ducking his responsibilities, he still managed to survive a series of encounters that included a major gas attack in April of 1916 that left over five hundred of his comrades dead, the horror of twice going over the top in the Battle of the Somme five months later, and then over the top yet again the next year in the stinking quagmire of mud known as Passchendaele.

It was during this final assault that the much-loathed mud ended his days of conflict, and most likely saved his life given the terrible casualties that his unit was still destined to suffer before Armistice Day. A misplaced boot slid erratically in the slime, sending him tumbling down into a particularly deep shell hole, snapping his left leg completely in half and leaving its lower section jutting out at a grotesquely unnatural angle.

Soaked by the pool of bitterly cold rainwater at the bottom, the battle raged on overhead in all its fury. Unable to crawl more than a few inches, he lay there in agonised solitude for hour after hour with rifle held constantly at the ready, never knowing which type of uniform might be the first to appear at the top. A heartfelt prayer of thanks slipped out when, long after dusk had fallen, two stretcher bearers from his own brigade slid down into the hole beside him.

Not that his ordeal was over. Amongst the horrifically wounded and dying in the nearest medical tent, a broken leg was nothing more than a minor wound. Several more hours elapsed before an overwhelmed and heavily bloodstained medic eventually spared him a few seconds. After a cursory examination, Joe was given a shot of morphine for the pain and then taken to the nearest casualty clearing station. Squeezed in between stacks of ration boxes in the back of a lorry and driven five miles over deeply potholed tracks, every jolt of the vehicle along the way sent fresh surges of pain racing through his shattered limb. Throughout the journey, all he could think of was how bad it might have been without the morphine.

By the time someone did actually get around to setting his leg it brought good news and bad. He would walk again, but not without a permanent limp. This meant a significant medical downgrading that would prevent him from returning to the front line. Instead, he would be temporarily assigned to light duties with the Labour Corps.

It was during this spell that he discovered a new talent. Now billeted with men from all over Britain rather than just fellow Irishmen, he took to mimicking many of their various accents as a form of entertainment for everyone during their off-duty hours. Scots, Geordies, Liverpudlians and Londoners were those that seemed to come most naturally of all. Once convinced he wasn't taking the mickey out of them, his targets quickly became amused and encouraged him to do more, saying that even to their ears his copying of their accents sounded completely authentic.

"Yee soond just leik yee come frem doon wor street," a particularly large lad from Newcastle told him. Joe smiled to himself. He'd never even heard a Geordie accent until a few weeks ago.

This period came to an end when, with the minimum of explanation, he was abruptly discharged and returned to Ireland with instructions to attend a Travelling Pensions Board in Dublin. Here, to his outrage, he was told that he would not be awarded any gratuity or disability pension due to doubt over the way he had sustained his injury. The presiding officer went on to say that, according to an unnamed officer's eye-witness account, it was deeply suspected that he had deliberately thrown himself into the shell hole to avoid taking any further part in the advance. That would make the resulting broken leg a self-inflicted injury. He should think himself lucky indeed not to be facing serious court martial charges and a long prison term.

"People have been shot for far less," the overweight and florid-faced officer concluded in a tone that suggested he would very much have liked to carry out the sentence himself.

Joe had always believed that Ireland should be freed from British rule. After this experience, that same belief became a burning passion.

Local support for independence had been growing ever since the executions and mass internment that followed the Easter Rising of 1916. Although initially targeted as a traitor by the newly formed IRA for having served with the Brits, Joe soon convinced their high command of his current loyalties by proving his worth as an intelligence gatherer. With his variety of utterly authentic sounding English accents he was more than capable of blending unobtrusively into unionist bars and clubs almost anywhere in the country, in the process picking up many snippets of priceless information, especially in the protestant areas of Belfast.

His lone wolf operations for the republican cause continued throughout the Irish War of Independence. Even after the Anglo-Irish Treaty was signed, he fully supported Michael Collins' view that the treaty was a mere stepping-stone and not a final settlement. Six north-eastern counties still remained within the United Kingdom. If his country was to be truly free, these must be included as well. It was all or nothing.

It wasn't until the summer of 1922 that this conviction began to waver. For a man who had already seen far too much of war and death, the civil war that flared up between pro and anti-treaty forces was a big turning point. Seeing fellow Irishmen now slaughtering each other was just too high a price to pay. When Michael Collins, who by now was effectively Prime Minister of the Irish Free State, was shot dead in August of that year, it was the final straw for Joe.

After cautiously raising his wish to leave with the people who mattered, it was emphatically made clear to him that: *'Once in, you're in for life'*. However, given the value of his service to date, there *was* one option that could be put on the table. If he was prepared to go live in England as part of a new sleeper cell being set up, he'd be provided with a fresh identity and enough cash to see him through the first few months. This was a one-time offer that he had just one week to consider.

Joe did not even need one day to think it over. A new start somewhere away from all the violence was what he now craved. If he could not find that in Ireland, then England would have to do. With a suitably worn birth certificate stating that he had become Joe Mason from Whitechapel in east London, he was on his way in less than a fortnight.

To his surprise, he settled into life as a Brit quite easily. In fact, he quickly became so much at ease with his new persona, speaking day after day with a cockney accent soon came as naturally as his former Irish brogue used to. Equally naturally, he found himself falling back on the racetrack experiences of his youth to carve a niche for himself. Thanks to a brilliant eye for detail and judicious betting, he began making a passable living and a fair number of friends among the regular punters with whom he'd occasionally share a winning tip.

With no incentive to change things, the years just seemed to slip by. Even after suddenly realising that he was now fast approaching middle-age, things might still have continued the same way had it not been for a flippant comment from the recipient of his latest tip.

"You should take this tipping lark up professionally," the man suggested while happily counting his winnings. "You know, like that Prince Monolulu bloke. He does pretty good for himself from what I can see."

Though meant as nothing more than a joke, the remark still registered with Joe. There had always been a bit of a showman in his personality, and the idea steadily took root. By now he'd been in England for ten years without hearing a single word from those back in Dublin. It looked as if they'd decided to release him from further obligations after all. How he prayed for that to be so. The troubles back in Ireland now seemed a long way off, and, contrary to expectations, he actually quite liked most of the English people he'd met. He rented a comfortable room in a large house in Brixton, and there was even a promising relationship developing with a barmaid who worked at his local pub. After close to three decades of knowing little but severe hardship and war as Joseph Flynn, in his current identity of Joe Mason he was actually enjoying life.

Another year passed without contact, taking Joe into the spring of 1933. Now confident that his prayers had indeed been answered, ambitions of becoming a rival *'character driven'* tipster to Prince Monolulu returned. If a pretend African prince could do so well for himself, surely he could come up with a personality equally as successful. And so, with a bit of thought and a definite hint of irony given his past republican involvement, Joe Bull was created.

With much of his patter picked up from the market traders of London and adapted for use on the racecourse, he was soon putting on a show that summer that had the crowds flocking around wherever he went. No one really cared much about the tips they received; they were paying for the entertainment more than anything else. Which was just as well. By naming all the runners that day at least once in the envelopes he handed out, someone was sure to have a winner in every race. That was more than enough to keep the punters happy. As for himself, he was loving every minute of it. He had never been so popular, and he was making far more money than ever before.

Once again, the years seemed to just slip by.

It was after a particularly successful afternoon at Sandown Park racecourse that reality at last forced its way back into Joe's life. Once outside his house, he had just parked up the Royal Enfield motorcycle that he used to travel to all of the meetings within an easy ride of London when he found himself suddenly facing three of his fellow countrymen. They did not appear to be especially friendly.

The reason for this quickly became apparent. "Your orders was to keep a low profile, not to go making a bloody showman of yourself," one of the men growled in his ear.

Joe felt a shiver. Was he in for a punishment beating? He was in his forties now, and every one of the trio was bigger and younger than himself. There was no hope of making a dash for the safety of the house either. Even though his limp was not a very heavy one these days, it was still enough of a handicap to squash any thoughts of making good his escape that way. He steeled himself, determined to land a few telling blows if the punches or worse started flying.

Relief came when he saw the trace of a smile form on the newcomer's face. "All the same, Joseph, the boys back home have come around to thinking that maybe this comedy act of yours is just about the best cover possible. So now you've started, be sure to keep it up. Especially seeing as how there's going to be some work coming your way soon."

Joe didn't know whether to feel relief at not receiving a beating, or despair that he was now being dragged back into a world he thought he had escaped.

"What kind of work?" he asked, only realising after the words were out that he was still speaking with his London accent. In a flash of insight he understood just how deeply he had become immersed into his new life. This was his natural way of talking these days. It would take a conscious effort to start sounding like a natural born Dubliner once again.

"You'll find out when the time is right," he was told. "But before you go, there is one thing you can do for me right now."

"What's that?" he asked warily.

"Give me a decent tip for tomorrow's races. And I mean a winner. None of that Joe Bull shite."

For a moment or two, Joe had a crazy impulse to burst out laughing.

A NEW CAMPAIGN OF IRA bomb attacks in England at the start of 1939 had Joe fearing the worst. Would he soon be ordered to take an active part in this? Though he could never agree with indiscriminate attacks on innocent citizens, he knew full well what would happen to him if he refused. There had already been over a dozen attacks during January, followed by two more in early February at London underground stations: one at Tottenham Court Road, the other at Leicester Square. Although these latter explosions had not caused any fatalities, there was much public alarm and outrage. As a regular user of the Northern Line himself, they were also uncomfortably close to home.

When the call to duty did arrive shortly after these February attacks, it was nowhere near as bad as he'd first feared. At least he wasn't being ordered to do anything violent, merely to exchange messages with an obviously aristocratic English lady. Why a woman like her would choose to be involved with the IRA was a mystery. Not that it mattered very much. It wasn't his place to know such things, and that suited him fine.

This attitude changed considerably when a second war with Germany became a reality that September. Joe suddenly found himself thinking quite a lot about the anonymous woman he had been dealing with for the last seven months. When put together with other snippets of information he'd gathered, a disturbing possibility began to take shape.

It was an open secret that the IRA had been fostering links with Abwehr, and that it had helped the German military intelligence service to embed several of their agents within southern Ireland. Joe was also well aware that some of those amongst the British aristocracy actually supported the Nazis: Sir Oswald Mosely and Diane Mitford, who was the daughter of a Baron, were proof of that. The couple had even chosen to get married in Nazi propaganda chief Joseph Goebbels' home with Adolf Hitler as the guest of honour.

So what if, instead of republican business, he was helping a British spy to pass her messages on to Germany through an Irish based Abwehr agent? That would be a much different matter for his conscience to deal with. As someone who had experienced far too many of the horrors that war could inflict, his heart went out to all of those who would be sent to the front lines. Just like the last time of calling, there would be many Irishmen volunteering as well. To feel that he may in some way be responsible for causing even one more death than was necessary amongst those brave souls would be a very heavy cross to bear.

Too heavy, perhaps?

Joe sighed. Even if all this was true, what could he do? Much as he wanted to know more, any move by him to investigate could have a very bad ending indeed. He'd stand a better chance of surviving if he played Russian roulette with only one empty chamber.

All the same, if a no-risk chance did happen to come along....

THE PHONEY WAR CAME to a sudden end on the tenth of May 1940.

In a move that seemed to come out of nowhere, German forces blitzed their way through the Netherlands and Belgium, then simply bypassed the supposedly impregnable Maginout Line at its northern end and carved their way into France. So great was the surprise of this blitzkrieg attack, just eleven days later they had the entire British Expeditionary Force together with a large chunk of the French army and the remains of the Belgian forces virtually surrounded and retreating to the coastal town of Dunkirk. In total, these numbered close to half a million men. And while over 330,000 of them were later successfully evacuated by sea in an exercise that newly installed Prime Minister Winston Churchill described as a 'miracle', they were forced to abandon vast numbers of badly needed artillery pieces, vehicles and tanks, plus thousands of tons of ammunition.

Paris fell on the fourteenth of June to complete France's defeat.

Britain was now truly on its own against an enemy that appeared to be unstoppable.

FOLLOWING THESE EVENTS, Margaret recalled how Goering had been utterly confident of a swift victory over Britain when the time finally came. His confidence was now looking to have been well placed. In spite of Winston Churchill's belligerent speeches, she was praying that he would bow to the inevitable and make some sort of agreement to hand the country over peacefully in order to prevent any further loss of life.

She thought of the letter she kept in the safest of places: the one hand-written by Goering that promised the return of Hadley House and the family estate following a German occupation. Could the invasion really now be close at hand? If so, was there any information she might be able to gather that would help to ensure its rapid success?

Given Oswald Mosley's many public demands for a settlement with Germany, his sudden internment following the Dunkirk evacuation had not come as a great shock to Margaret. His wife's incarceration at the end of June, however, did shake her rather more. She and the Mitford girl had spoken together in public - albeit as part of a group - on two separate occasions recently. Might this have been noted by the authorities? Hundreds of

Mosley's supporters had already been rounded up and were now also experiencing prison life without being charged. Whether she was under suspicion or not, Margaret knew she would certainly need to tread with special care for a time if she did not wish to join them.

As it turned out just a few days later, even treading with care became impossible. The vast majority of professional sport had already been suspended for the duration long ago. Now, despite furious protests from the Jockey Club, the government had finally decided that all horse racing meetings should follow suit. Margaret was abruptly left with no means of communicating, not even if she had something of vital importance to impart.

Perhaps nothing more would be required of her anyway, she considered. Many people were whispering that an invasion was sure to come in only a matter of days. With luck, it wouldn't be too long before the fighting was over and the Nazis were running the country.

Then life would surely become a whole lot better.

SEVEN

The Battle of Britain in the late summer of 1940 shattered any hopes Margaret might have had of a quick and relatively painless end to the war. With the RAF's dogged resistance preventing any possibility of a seaborne invasion until the following spring, the frustrated Luftwaffe switched its attention from Britain's Fighter Command bases to the country's major cities. Over a ten-month period of concentrated bombing that quickly became known to everyone as 'The Blitz', virtually every major city and port suffered heavy damage. At one point, London endured unrelenting raids for fifty-six out of fifty-seven consecutive days and nights.

Then, although the raids did not cease entirely, they suddenly became far less frequent. It soon became apparent why. In a move that appeared to make no military sense, in late June 1941, Adolph Hitler launched a huge offensive against the formidable forces of Russia, in the process diverting vast amounts of his Luftwaffe resources.

Britain gave a collective sigh of relief. A desperately needed breathing space and opportunity to regroup had been granted.

DAN HALL LOOKED AT his daughter sat at the other end of their kitchen table with a mixture of surprise and bewilderment. "The WAAFs!" he exclaimed. "Surely you can't be serious, Betty. Please think of your future before rushing into this."

"And you'll be safe in America away from this horrible war," her mother added. "I really don't know why you've insisted on waiting so long. Who knows what might happen here soon?"

In truth, Betty had been thinking long and hard over her future ever since war had first been declared. There had been so many things to consider, but she had finally made her decision and would not be talked out of it, even though she knew that her parents were speaking out of love and only wanted to protect her. She was now twenty years old, and with skills that she'd been assured would be most useful to them, volunteering for the Women's Auxiliary Air Force was definitely the right thing to do.

The last eight years seemed to have flown by. After leaving school she had first of all taken a job as an office junior. More recently, she had also begun evening classes to learn shorthand and typing. The piano lessons with Agatha continued as well whenever there was money enough to pay for one, although before long it had started to look as if her tutor's health was not what it used to be. And so it turned out. Sometime soon after Betty's nineteenth birthday, Agatha Wright died quite peacefully in her sleep.

Incredibly, it turned out that she had left £4,000 in her will for Betty to continue her musical education with a friend of hers: a former international concert performer who was now running a small but highly selective academy in New York. Successful graduation from here was regarded as a virtual guarantee of future acclaim. No one had ever suspected that Agatha possessed so much money, or that she had such high-placed contacts.

'You have a God given talent, my dear,' her tutor had written. *'Please allow another former pupil of mine who has long since surpassed me in ability to complete what we started together.'*

Betty's parents were thrilled for her, as was she herself for having been given such a wonderful opportunity. Even so, with her secretarial course only a matter of weeks away from finishing, she resolved to make sure of that qualification before embarking on this new adventure. The dexterity of her fingers over the piano keyboard had applied itself equally well to her typing skills, giving her a speed that was far in excess of any other girl on her course. This was a source of quiet pride.

With the qualification duly gained and a bright musical future beckoning, without knowing quite why, something prompted Betty to remember the newsreel pictures she had seen just over a year ago of the men returning home from Dunkirk. Their battle-weary faces spoke clearly of how much they had given, and the hell they had been through. Almost overnight, her priorities changed. Though the temptation to follow her dream was still strong, any thoughts of running away to New York at such a time were forced from her mind. If she could help in any way with the war effort, she knew that it was her duty to do so.

Conscription for men had begun at the very beginning of hostilities, and it was quite obvious that woman would become liable to call-up for some form of duty very soon as well. It would be much better to volunteer immediately and get a choice of what she did rather than wait for too long and find herself pressed into something unsuitable later on.

After talking to recruitment officers from all three services, she had eventually decided that the women's branch of the Royal Air Force was where she would fit in the best. Now all she had to do was break the news to her parents. As expected, it wasn't going well. She fell back on the only argument that she felt might sway them.

"I understand how you feel," she began. "But I won't change my mind. And remember, you both volunteered to do your bit in the last war. You can't blame me for doing the same thing."

It was a valid point. Her father had served on the front-line with the Army Cyclist Corps, and had even been presented with a Mentioned in Dispatches certificate for gallant and distinguished services in the field. Signed by Winston Churchill himself in his 1919 capacity of Secretary of State for War, Betty knew the certificate was one of his proudest possessions, even though it was always kept hidden away in a drawer and almost never spoken of.

As for her mother, she had joined a Voluntary Aid Detachment of the Red Cross and served in a variety of capacities, often putting herself a great personal risk while administering first aid during the Zeppelin air raids on London. Like husband Dan, she rarely spoke about any of this, but several neighbours had made a point of telling Betty how courageous they remembered her mother being during those dangerous days.

A short silence developed. The parents then looked directly at each other.

"I don't think we are going to win this argument," Dan said.

Mabel gave a sad nod. "You're probably right."

They both turned to face their daughter. "What about Agatha's money?" Mabel asked. "What will you do with that?"

"I'll just leave it in a savings account until the war is over," Betty told her. "I'll go to New York then if the woman there will still take me."

"I see. But what if...you know...if things don't turn out the way we hope they will?"

"There's no chance of that," Dan cut in quickly. "Not now our Betty is joining the fight. With her in the ranks, the Germans haven't got a hope."

His bullish comment, obviously an attempt to lighten the mood, drew a slightly strained chorus of laughter.

"Don't be silly, Dad," Betty told him. "I'm not going to be a hero or anything, just a teleprinter operator."

"Heroes come in lots of different disguises, my girl."

Mabel frowned. "We don't want her winning any medals, Dan. We just want her to be safe."

Having stated that, she stood up. "I think it's time for a cup of tea."

AFTER LISTENING TO the news on the BBC Home Service, Margaret switched off the wireless.

"About bloody time too," the earl remarked. "Hitler should have gone after those blasted communists right from the beginning instead of dropping his damned bombs on us. They're the real enemy. Haven't I always said so?"

Margaret glanced at him with something close to astonishment. Throughout the lunchtime broadcast he'd been sitting in his usual position by the window, apparently showing no interest at all in what the newsreader was saying. He had hardly ever spoken about the war before, let alone gone so far as to express an opinion on what he wanted to see happen. By his standards, this was an almost garrulously long speech.

She reacted quickly in an attempt to draw him into a conversation. If she could just get him to talk to her a bit more, that could tell her so much of what she needed to know.

"So you want Germany to beat Russia?" she asked. "Is that what you're hoping for?"

He gave a non-committal grunt.

"Do you think they can beat the Red Army?" she pressed on. "And what if they do and then come back here to have another go at invading us? Say they were to succeed this time. At least there would be no more communists to worry about. How would you feel then?"

He stared at her for what felt like a particularly long moment, his expression unreadable. "What a damn fool question, Margaret," he then snapped, turning his head away to once more gaze out of the window.

"I'm sorry. I only meant to—"

"You've said enough. No more!"

That was it, she realised. Past experience told her that she would be wasting her breath trying to persuade him to say anything further when in this mood. Why had she jumped in so quickly? If only she had been a little subtler in her approach, he might possibly have opened up quite a lot. Now, because of her over-eagerness, she was back to square one.

She followed her father's gaze out of the window. The Nissen huts were still as big an eyesore as ever, and although Tom and herself had successfully repaired most of the upheaval to the forecourt and driveway, the lawn was taking a long time to recover.

She felt her teeth grinding hard together as she stared at the scene. All that destruction both inside the house, and to the surrounding grounds. For what? The workmen had departed many months ago, and since then, absolutely nothing further had happened. The house was still empty and unused, a mocking tribute to the blundering inefficiency and callous disregard for national heritage displayed by the bureaucrats in Westminster.

Whatever their plan for Hadley House originally was, it appeared to have been abandoned. But it would now cost an absolute fortune to restore the place even remotely close to its former condition. Much of the fabulous interior décor had been utterly destroyed and could never be replaced. The government had succeeded in doing far more damage to the old house than any of the Luftwaffe bombers were ever likely to. And all for nothing, apparently. Whenever she dwelt on the matter for any length of time, it was only her rage that prevented her from weeping.

Aside from a couple of minor incidents, the area around Bletchley had so far escaped unscathed from the bombs, even when the blitz was at its height. Other than a railway station with fairly wide-ranging links, there was unlikely to be anything else of interest to the Germans in their small country town. The only industry was a brick-making plant. Not a target that would be exactly high on Goering's list of priorities.

That said, as the months passed, Margaret had found herself wondering a lot more about the unusual developments taking place at Bletchley Park.

The mansion there was only slightly smaller than Hadley House, and like so many of the big country houses, it appeared to have been requisitioned by the government for some use or another at the start of the war. Whenever out exercising Soldier in the vicinity, the sight of armed guards at the entrance pretty much confirmed this. As did the motorcycle despatch riders that could be seen coming and going on a regular basis.

But it was the non-military people who passed in and out of the entirely fenced-off mansion grounds that puzzled her the most.

Considering the eccentric appearance and behaviour that many of these newcomers displayed when seen in town, some of the locals were convinced that the manor must have been converted into a type of lunatic asylum. The 'inmates', as they were often flippantly referred to, could frequently be heard in pubs and cafes talking to each other in what sounded to any normal ear like utter gibberish. Coupled with some outlandish dress sense – one young woman was always seen wearing trousers, a bow tie and smoking a pipe, while one of her male friends made a regular habit of wearing a black shoe on one foot and a brown one on the other – they were generally regarded as being weird but pretty harmless.

Margaret was quite happy at first to accept the idea that the manor was some kind of hospital for people with mental disorders: perhaps as a result of the Blitz. Living in the cities during that relentless bombardment would have been quite sufficient to put a few rather deep cracks in some people's minds. Perhaps it was a bit like the shellshock she'd heard old soldiers from the trenches of the last war talk about. These patients had to go somewhere to recuperate, and a large mansion in the relatively safe countryside was as good a place as any. What's more, even a hospital was likely to need security at the entrance during wartime. Nonetheless, her attention had been drawn to the manor, and after making a note of gradual changes taking place there, her opinion as to its possible function began to shift.

In the beginning there had been only a handful of military personnel apparent, but as the months passed, so that presence grew. Mostly it was young women from either the Wrens or the WAAFs that she saw passing through the gates at what seemed like regular shift intervals. None of these were wearing the uniform of a nurse, so the mystery of their presence deepened. Could it be linked to whatever the despatch riders were delivering?

An ever-increasing number of questions were forming, none of which she yet had an answer to. Speculation alone was useless. She needed to know a whole lot more about what was going on inside those securely guarded gates before even considering passing on her suspicions to Goering.

The ban on horse racing had provoked a huge outcry, and lobbying by a large number of influential people had seen the sport reinstated shortly after the Battle of Britain. But then new restrictions severely limiting the number of courses permitted to operate had been introduced early that year. Of those that were, it came as some consolation that the quite nearby venue of Newmarket had been appointed as the temporary home to most of the remaining flat racing calendar, even staging classics like the Oaks and Derby that would normally be run at Epsom. A few National Hunt courses had also survived, ensuring at least limited communication opportunities with Joe Bull through the winter months as well.

Margaret had been following news of the German advance into Soviet territory closely. As in Europe, their forces appeared unstoppable. In less than a month they swept four hundred miles into Russia, and by mid-October of 1941 were closing in on the capital city of Moscow. Once that fell, the invasion of Britain was sure to become Hitler's priority once again.

This assessment led rapidly on to another consideration. She was becoming acutely aware that she had so far done little to earn Goering's gratitude. If German occupation did become a reality before she'd provided him with at least one piece of valuable information, he might well choose not to honour their agreement. The most recent message from Richard had even hinted at this possibility. That would be the worst outcome imaginable. It wasn't as if she'd be able to claim that the Reichsmarschall's letter was a legally binding document. Certainly not in a Nazi court of law.

Her reluctance to take unnecessary risks was slowly overtaken by the pressing need to prove her worth. And luck was on her side. A suspicion that something very important indeed was happening right here on her doorstep at Bletchley Park was becoming stronger than ever. Something that could be vital for the Germans to know of.

But how to change suspicion into certainty? That was the problem.

After pondering on this, she decided to take a chance. There was one person she knew of who might well be able to shed a little light on the matter.

But she would have to tread very carefully indeed.

THE TEST WAS OVER. With a sigh of relief, Betty removed the headphones and shifted her eyes to the RAF officer standing beside her table. Without saying a word, he leaned over to pull out the sheet of paper from her typewriter, pursing his lips as he carefully studied the row after row of five-letter blocks she had transcribed from a high-speed Morse code recording.

After what felt like an eternity, he finally placed the sheet down. "Remarkable," he said quietly, almost as if talking to himself. "Forty-five words a minute and one hundred percent typing accuracy. I've never seen anything quite like it before."

His voice then rose and he looked Betty directly in the eye. "Congratulations, Aircraftwoman Hall. You've passed with flying colours."

A surge of satisfaction ran through her. It had been an intense six months at RAF Compton Bassett learning the trade of Wireless Operator, and the standards set were particularly high. But not only had she made it and was already proudly wearing her trade flash on the right arm of her uniform jacket, apparently she had now passed some sort of special test that just herself and two other girls from their class had been selected to sit. Quite what the purpose of this extra test was had not so far been revealed. It was all a little bit mysterious.

After joining the WAAFs, following four weeks of 'square bashing' drill instruction together with endless kit and room inspections at a Spartan camp just outside of Harrogate, she had been given an aptitude test for sending and receiving Morse code. In many aspects, she took to this in the same way that she had taken to reading music: it was simply a different language that needed to be learned. With her typing skill already noted, she was told that, rather than setting off for the teleprinter training she had been anticipating at RAF Cranwell, she was being sent to RAF Compton Bassett instead.

And now she had arrived at this latest point. Was the mystery at last about to be explained?

"Do you know where I will be posted to next, Sir?" she asked.

"Oh yes," he replied. "You'll be going to a little place called Bletchley."

Betty frowned. "I don't think I've heard of that camp, Sir. Are you able to tell me something about what they do there?"

He gave a short laugh, as if she had suggested something quite ridiculous. "I'm afraid not, Hall. You'll find out all you need to know once you arrive there. Oh, and just so you know in advance, you will be given a copy of the Official Secrets Act to sign before you leave. Also, you'll have to remove that trade flash you are wearing. I know that you've only just sewed it on and are justifiably proud of having earned it, but no wireless operators are permitted to wear them while serving at Bletchley Park. Is that perfectly clear."

Betty blinked in astonishment. "Yes, Sir."

Her mind was racing. The Official Secrets Act? Wasn't that for spies and suchlike? And why the need to remove her trade flash? What on earth was she getting involved with?

A second, much deeper frown formed. Instead of being explained, the mystery had just become even more puzzling than ever.

BACK IN HER BILLET and sat on the edge of her bed, Betty was still speculating over her new posting. Every base she had been sent to so far had naturally required quite strict security, but what she was experiencing now, even before arriving at Bletchley, was taking things to a completely new level.

She was finding the need to remove her hard-earned trade flash strangely disheartening. Only a week ago, the hut she was based in had been full of newly qualified girls from her class all chattering excitedly while proudly sewing the 'fist and lightning' emblem of a wireless operator onto the sleeves of their tunics. Now, at least until tomorrow when a new intake of trainees arrived, she was the hut's only occupant. She was also the only one amongst her class who had been required to remove her flash again before setting off to her new posting.

Sadly, she picked away at the last few threads of cotton holding it in place. After gazing at the little rectangle of fabric for a few seconds, she placed it into the top right-hand pocket of her tunic and carefully secured the single brass button.

She wondered how long it would be before she was able to display it once again.

LIEUTENANT-COMMANDER Simon Straw was one of a group of young people that Margaret had socialized with in the years immediately prior to her father's downfall, although back in those carefree days he'd been a mere Sub-Lieutenant out to prove himself to his own father, a former Rear Admiral. Although they had never been the very closest of companions, unlike a few of the other so-called friends from that era, at least he had never allowed her vastly reduced circumstances to change anything. Whenever they encountered each other in London he was unfailingly polite and always willing to chat about the latest development in their lives. He was, as far as she was concerned, very definitely the solid and dependable type.

He was also someone who, for the last couple of years, was generally thought to be involved in something rather 'hush-hush' at the Admiralty.

Simon had sounded genuinely pleased to hear from her when she telephoned, and after exchanging the usual pleasantries, they agreed to meet up for lunch at the Savoy Grill. On entering the restaurant, she spotted him immediately sat at a corner table. Fair haired and of above average height, he looked quite handsome in his naval uniform as he rose to greet her.

"Margaret, how splendid to see you again," he smiled.

After he'd made sure she was seated comfortably, she felt a small stab of guilt. Simon was a genuinely nice chap and didn't deserve to be taken advantage of. But if there really was something top-secret happening at Bletchley Park, he was one of the few people who might know a bit about it.

"You must tell me what's been going on with you lately," he said once they'd settled and ordered drinks. "But first of all, take a look at the menu and see what you fancy. I hear that the salmon is very good. It's fresh in from Lord Trinkle's estate."

Margaret did as he suggested, running her eye down the list of starters and main courses available that day. As was the case in all of the large London hotels, there was little food rationing imposed here. A plentiful selection of meat and poultry dishes together with a variety of omelettes and soufflés were all there to enjoy if you could afford to pay for them. By contrast, the current official egg ration for each city dweller not wealthy enough to dine in such places was a miserable one per week.

Once again Margaret felt a twinge of guilt. She rarely went short of decent food. At home, the farmers on their former estate, although under strict government demands on what to produce for the war effort, still managed to look after her pretty well. Between them they provided sufficient vegetables, dairy produce and even meat to keep her, her father, and also Tom in good shape. As a major menace to vital crops, some of the rabbits that were regularly culled also featured quite frequently on their dining table.

She placed the menu back down. "Very well, I'll have the ham and egg on toast to start with, then the salmon with a side salad."

Their drinks arrived just as she spoke: a gin and tonic for her, a scotch and water for him. He lit a cigarette, prompting Margaret to groan inwardly. Neither she nor her father had ever smoked, and they both hated the smell of it. But so many people had fallen into the habit during these stressful days and it was hard to escape from. Another thing to blame on the war perhaps.

"So how is that riding school of yours doing?" Simon asked. "It must be jolly tough for you at the moment."

"It's not easy," she admitted. "But we get by, and it will get better again once the war is over. I'm sure of that."

"That's the spirit," he told her. "V for victory and all that."

She hesitated before speaking again. "Actually, Simon, I was wondering if you might be able to help me with something."

He drew deeply on his cigarette. "If I can, then of course I will. I'll be happy to."

"It's about Hadley House. The inside of it has been absolutely destroyed, and I have no idea at all what purpose it was meant to serve."

"Yes, I did hear that some work had taken place there."

"Work! Vandalism more like."

Although genuinely still mortified over the damage, Margaret was playing up her outrage for all it was worth. This was only a lead-in to the real purpose of their conversation.

"I know that we don't own the house any longer," she continued in a much more controlled tone, "but father and I both still love the old place dearly. It breaks our hearts to see what has happened to it. In fact, just between the two of us, the earl still dreams of restoring the family fortune after the war is over and buying it back again. As a privately owned property, he believes that this will allow him to leave the estate to me rather than see one of our distant cousins inherit it."

Leaning closer, she lowered her voice to a confidential level. "Of course, you and I both know that this is extremely unlikely ever to happen. Father is approaching sixty years old now. I think the stroke, together with the trauma of recent years, must have combined to seriously affect his reasoning. He is far from the man he used to be. All the same, if I could only give him some good reason as to why the house has been so horrifically transformed and then abandoned....perhaps tell him of some patriotic purpose it will be put to quite soon that will be of assistance to the war effort? If I could only do that, at least it might serve to make the current situation just a little more bearable for him."

Simon stubbed his cigarette out in the ash tray. "I'm afraid I can't help you much there, Margaret. I do believe that the place was originally going to be used by the Ministry of Food. It was something to do with rationing, I think. Then the plans were dropped."

He spread his hands. "That's all I know."

"Dropped! They damn near destroy the interior of our old home and then simply abandon it. Why can't it be put to good purpose? Most other big houses are. Houses like...like ...."

She waved a hand, as if seeking to find an example. "I don't know. Like Bletchley Park for instance. There seems to be plenty going on there every time I ride past the place."

Just for a moment – for a mere split second – Margaret thought she saw something close to alarm register on his face. Had she not been watching so closely, she might easily have missed it altogether.

He let out a long sigh. "I honestly haven't got the slightest idea what purpose Bletchley Park has been put to," he told her, both his voice and expression oozing sincerity. "And even if I did, you must know that I couldn't possibly talk about it."

But you were quite willing to tell me about the plans the Ministry of Food had for Hadley House, Margaret thought. So there was a definite line drawn somewhere in his mind between what could be spoken of, and what was strictly off-limits. She did not believe his claim of ignorance for one second: not with all those Wrens being brought into Bletchley every day on a fleet of buses. Everyone at the Admiralty of his rank would surely be aware of a naval presence like that, if not its precise purpose in being there.

All this confirmed her suspicions that something hugely important was indeed taking place right under her nose, and probably had been for some time. But it was an absolute certainty that Simon would not be drawn into saying anything more on the subject. And to press the matter even a little bit further was sure to bring way too much attention upon herself. She had already gathered as much as she could realistically have hoped for.

With a shake of the head, she slapped herself smartly across the back of the hand as if in self-chastisement. "Whatever am I thinking of? Please forgive me, Simon. I've put you on the spot, and that's the very last thing I intended to do. It's just that I've been so worried about father's mental health lately. I suppose I was hoping to hear some sort of positive news about the house that might help to buck him up a touch. It was silly of me really. I know how hush-hush most things are."

She even allowed a little moisture to creep into her eyes.

Simon reached across the table to touch her gently on the forearm. "There, there, old girl. Don't let it get you down. Give the earl my best regards, and if I do hear of anything that I think might make him feel better I'll be sure to pass it on."

Margaret rewarded him with a grateful smile. "Thank you, Simon. You've always been a good friend to me."

At this point, their hors d'oeuvres arrived and they began eating.

No more was said on the subject.

93

WHILE WALKING BACK along the Strand toward the Admiralty, Simon was in thoughtful mood.

It had been delightful to see Margaret again. At just one year older than her, back in the day he had often longed that their friendship could be on a more intimate basis. She was an extremely attractive woman though, and there had been quite a few other chaps around with similar intentions to contend with. Somehow or another, what with this abundance of rivals and the demands of his naval career becoming ever more pressing, they had sadly never got anywhere near as close as he would have liked.

He smiled to himself. Rather surprisingly, even after all this time, she was still single. Just like himself, in fact. In his case it had been the continuing pressure of his work that had prevented any serious relationships from developing. He wondered what Margaret's reason might be.

The smile faded. There had been one rather unsettling aspect to their lunch. One that he was not entirely sure how he should react to.

He had been working in Naval Intelligence for some time now, and was well aware of the vital role that the people at Bletchley Park were playing in helping to curtail the losses of Atlantic convoys bringing in desperately needed supplies from North America. It was no exaggeration to say that without these convoys, the war would almost certainly be lost.

Thanks to a collection of brilliant if often eccentric minds at Bletchley, the supposedly unbreakable Enigma codes used by the German U-boats *had* been broken. The Admiralty was being regularly updated on where many of their marauding wolf packs would be patrolling and were so able to guide the convoys safely away from the danger areas. Yet even with this information, the number of merchant ships being sunk was still critically high. It was an unending battle. The Germans were constantly devising new ways to increase the complexity of their messaging systems, and the codebreakers with their small army of support teams up in Bletchley Park were working around the clock to deal with these changes. What they were achieving was one of the most closely guarded secrets of the entire war.

And that was where Simon's problem lay.

Such was the strength of the security blanket wrapped around Bletchley Park, even the vast majority of the people working there had no proper idea as to the ultimate purpose of the place. The relatively tiny number of those such as himself who *were* fully 'in the know' were under the strictest of instructions. Even the smallest mention of Bletchley Park by unauthorised personnel, anywhere and at any time, especially if it came in the form of an enquiry, was meant to be reported to the security services immediately.

But this was Margaret, he kept telling himself. And what she'd said hadn't really been a question. Not in the proper sense. It was more of a simple observation than anything else: an attempt to make a comparison between the obvious high level of activity at Bletchley Park and the complete abandonment of her own former home. It was the sort of remark that anyone in her rather awful kind of situation might have been tempted to make. She hadn't pressed the point with him either. Not in the slightest.

If he did pass on details of their conversation as instructed, he knew that the 'funny people' at MI5 could well end up making the poor girl's life a misery. All for the sake of a perfectly innocent remark. Hadn't she and her father suffered enough in recent years? Despite their present situation, by birthright alone they were still the absolute pillars of British society.

And this was Margaret.

With his usually decisive mind still seeking the best course of action, Simon crossed Trafalgar Square and headed toward Admiralty Arch.

EIGHT

With a sigh, Betty glanced though the window of the slowly moving train. She could see nothing but countryside and heavily overcast skies. All alone in the eight-seater compartment, she wondered what had happened to the two other girls who had sat the Morse typing test with her. Clearly they were not also on their way to Bletchley. The mystery attached to her new posting was growing deeper than ever.

For three weeks she had been held in a kind of limbo at RAF Compton Bassett while she was security vetted prior to leaving. Other than being informed that Bletchley was situated in the county of Buckinghamshire, she was told nothing about the place, or what went on at the enigmatically named Station X that she would be joining. At first she had thought this was simply a case of people being deliberately uncommunicative, but later on began to feel it was more likely because they simply did not know themselves. As someone of a naturally inquisitive nature who normally liked to have a clear picture of what was going on in her life, she was finding this to be more than a touch frustrating.

At long last the train chugged its way into what she hoped was her getting off point, though she could not yet be certain of this. As instructed, she had counted eight stops since leaving Euston station in London, but the anti-invasion preparations designed to confuse the enemy had necessitated the removal of all road signposts and station names. The voice of the stationmaster making his announcement while walking up and down the platform then carried clearly into her compartment.

"Bletchley! This is Bletchley."

Betty put on her cap, grabbed her kitbag, and stepped off the train.

The only person on the platform apart from the stationmaster was another man. Like Betty, he was wearing an RAF uniform, though this one bore the two stripes of a corporal.

His eyes ran over her briefly. "Aircraftwoman Hall?"

"Yes, corporal."

He held out a hand. "Movement order and ID." After inspecting these to his satisfaction, he pointed ahead. "Follow me."

They set off at a brisk pace. Once outside the station they crossed the road and headed down a fairly narrow footpath that was almost totally enclosed by trees and bushes. Betty had a whole stack of questions that she was bursting to ask her escort, but one look at his stern features suggested that she would get short shrift if she attempted to do so.

After what could have been no more than three hundred yards they emerged onto a road and came face to face with what was obviously the camp's main entrance. Iron gates set between two stout brick piers blocked entry to a tree lined driveway. A guardhouse also of brick was directly to the left of these. Two soldiers with rifles were manning the gates, one on each side, while a third sentry was visible inside the guardhouse behind an open hatch. After exchanging a few words with the latter, Betty's escort waved her through the quite narrow gap available and along the driveway.

In the gloomy daylight ahead, an imposing manor house very quickly became visible; so too did a small lake with several geese wandering around the edge of it. A little further on, her eye was caught by a trio of rather scruffily dressed men along with a lone woman who looked as if she had stepped straight from the pages of a high society magazine. They were all sitting on a bench and laughing loudly at some humorous remark that one of their group had just made. In fact, there appeared to be more civilians than military personnel about. Betty frowned. Where on earth had she been posted to? This was unlike any RAF camp that she had ever seen before.

There were also quite a large number of brick and wooden huts scattered about the grounds, and she fully expected to be directed into one of these. But that was not the case. To her surprise, they continued on the path all the way up to the mansion itself and then inside. They eventually stopped outside an office door on the ground floor.

"Enter," called a man's voice in response to the corporal's knock.

With a firm prod, Betty was propelled inside. "Aircraftwoman Hall, Sir," the corporal announced before briskly withdrawing and closing the door.

Sitting behind an oak desk, Betty saw a middle-aged man with slightly thinning hair and a powerful jawline. He was obviously a person of importance, but seeing as how he was dressed in a smart suit rather than a military uniform, she was unsure whether or not a salute was required. She settled for dropping her kitbag and coming smartly to attention.

"Stand easy, Hall," he told her with just the trace of a welcoming smile. "We don't overdo the formalities here." That said, he made no attempt to introduce himself.

Though relaxing her stance a little, other than a snappily delivered, "Thank you, Sir," Betty remained silent. An explanation for all the secrecy surrounding this place was now likely to be forthcoming. She could not wait to hear it.

The man leaned back in his chair, for a moment regarding her with fingers steepled beneath his chin. "For several months now, I've been searching for an extra someone with truly exceptional ability in the receiving and typing of high-speed Morse code. From all the reports I've received, it appears that you fit the bill splendidly, Hall. Do you agree with that?"

"Well, Sir...I don't know what to say. It's true that I passed some kind of special test at Compton Basset. And you can rely on me to do my very best for you. I just hope I can live up to your expectations."

He smiled fully for the first time. "Well, we'll soon find out, won't we? You'll have the rest of today to sort out your billeting arrangements and other stuff, then you are to report for your first shift at 0.800 hours tomorrow in Hut Fourteen."

"Can you tell me a little about the nature of my duties here, Sir," Betty asked. "I haven't been able to find out anything up until now."

Any lingering trace of his smile instantly vanished. He leaned forward to place both hands flat down on the desk. "Apart from the basic necessities, nor will you ever," he stated bluntly.

Seeing the confusion on her face, he continued: "I can see that you are of an inquisitive nature, Aircraftwoman Hall, so I will remind you of something. You have signed the Official Secrets Act, and the penalty for breaching it is severe in the extreme. It is a penalty that, I can assure you, no one in their right mind would ever wish to experience. Is that perfectly clear?"

A chill ran down Betty's spine. What on earth was he threatening her with? She was well aware that there was a war on and secrecy over many things had to be maintained. But all she had done was ask about the purpose of her job. Surely she needed to know at least something of that in order to perform it properly.

"Absolutely clear, Sir," she replied, trying for all her worth to keep her voice from shaking.

The man's eyes bored uncomfortably into her for a second or two longer. He then nodded, and his voice became just a little less sharp.

"As I said to you just now, we tend not to overdo the formalities here. But understand this: the work we do at Bletchley Park is of the most vital nature imaginable to the war effort, and the one thing we absolutely insist on at all times is tightly closed lips. Whatever aspect of this work you do happen to learn of whilst stationed here, it must never be shared. I don't just mean with civilians outside of these gates, I mean with every single person you come into contact with aside from the small team that you will be working directly with. No one else...not even your closest family members, nor any friends that you might make from other huts during your time here...none of them must ever hear a solitary word about your personal duties. No matter how much you trust them. Once again, I have to ask you, Hall, is that fully understood?"

Although there were now more questions than ever racing around in her mind, Betty came sharply to attention once again. Given the moment, it just seemed like the right thing to do.

"Yes, Sir," she replied. "I can't wait to get started."

NINE

Two events taking place many thousands of miles apart in early December 1941 cast a dark shadow over Margaret's hopes for the future.

Despite having moved on to within a mere ten miles of Moscow, the German advance had ground to a halt. Hindered by deep snow and a lack of supplies, the up until now all-conquering force was preparing to regather itself before making a final push for victory. But then, on the fifth day of December, the Soviet defenders launched a surprise counterattack. Such was the ferocity of their assault, the invaders soon found themselves pushed back more than a hundred and fifty miles from a capital city that only a short time ago they had looked certain to take with the minimum of resistance. In a perhaps ominous sign of what was to come, it was their first major retreat of the war. And the freezing Russian winter was steadily getting worse.

Just two days later, in weather conditions about as far removed as possible to those in Russia, Japan attacked the American's Pacific naval base at Pearl Harbour in Hawaii. Up until this point, although providing a great deal of logistical support to Britain, the US had remained officially neutral in the war. That neutrality was now swept aside. From this moment on they would be throwing the full might of their military power into the conflict.

For Margaret, this was devastating news. Once the Americans began fighting alongside Britain, the Germans would be facing serious battles on two major fronts. She did not need to be an expert on military strategy to see how that could end in disaster. The need was no longer to simply prove her worth to Goering; it was now vital that she do all she could to ensure a German occupation of Britain before the Americans became too deeply involved. With Japan to contend with as well, they were unlikely to step into the European war if Britain were to fall first. Apart from anything else, they would have no other suitably large land base within the region from which to operate.

Following her revealing lunch with Simon Straw, she felt she already had more than enough information of value to make it worth passing on to Goering immediately. But there was a frustrating delay involved. The still reasonably busy flat racing season of the spring and summer months was gone, and wintertime national hunt meetings where she could link up with Joe Bull had been few and far between recently. In the end, she had to wait until a meeting only a few days prior to Christmas before an opportunity arose. In her message she stressed emphatically the importance of Bletchley Park. Although she could not yet say exactly what was taking place there, it was assuredly something of the utmost secrecy and importance. Its destruction would be certain to aid Germany's war enormously. In her opinion, the mansion and grounds immediately around it should be bombed without delay.

Feeling that she had done everything she could for the present, Margaret resigned herself to waiting for a reply. But it would not come quickly. There would be no opportunity of seeing Joe Bull again until a race meeting scheduled for the second week of February.

That suddenly felt like a long time away.

THE YEAR OF 1942 HAD not started well for Reichsmarschall Hermann Goering. Even though his Luftwaffe had performed well in Russia given the appalling conditions, recent setbacks on the ground meant that the anticipated rapid victory had failed to materialize. That was bad enough on its own, but when combined with the United States of America suddenly joining the war, the situation could now prove to be very troublesome indeed if Russia was not dealt with quickly. The Fuhrer had stated emphatically that he wished to avoid a war on two fronts, and such was his rage over the current situation, there had been times recently when he'd been almost impossible to talk to.

Yet today, whilst sat in his sumptuously furnished private apartment at the Reich Air Ministry headquarters in Berlin, Goering was in an excellent mood. One that might even be described as ebullient. The man sitting opposite him, his former adjutant and now promoted to a General, Karl-Heinrich Bodenschatz, remarked on his disposition, adding with a smile: "Is there anything else from this meeting that I should report back to the Fuhrer? Something more that you wish to mention before I leave?"

An expansive wave of Goering's arm waved the enquiry aside. "No, Karl. We've covered everything. I don't need to detain you any longer."

Despite them having been good friends for many years, Goering had no intention of sharing the reason for his current good humour. Not on this occasion. Bodenschatz was now the liaison officer forming a direct link between himself and Adolph Hitler, and everyone was well aware of the Leader's revulsion for anything that could be deemed as 'modern art'. *Degenerate* was one of his most widely quoted descriptions, along with the firm belief that any artist who chose to paint a blue meadow or a green sky belonged in an asylum or prison. And should most certainly be sterilized.

Thanks mainly to the plunders of war, both Goering and Hitler already owned large private collections. But where the Fuhrer failed to see merit in anything but the strictly traditional, Goering's tastes spread far wider.

Amongst the artists officially listed as degenerate and whose works were banned from even entering Nazi Germany, Vincent Van Gogh was a particular favourite of his. He could well recall seeing the artist's work *Trees with Ivy* for the first time at the Jeu de Paume Gallery in Paris at the end of 1940. He had been utterly spellbound, spending several minutes simply running his fingers over the painted surface while allowing his mind to luxuriate in dreams of ownership. Never had he desired a work more. It had become an all-consuming passion: a demand that could not be denied.

And now the dream was so close to becoming a reality. The delivery to his country home just outside of Berlin was due that very afternoon.

He was, of course, risking the Fuhrer's wrath if his plan the smuggle the Van Gogh into the country amongst a large consignment of other looted works deemed acceptable for Aryan eyes were to be discovered. But he had covered his tracks well, and what little risk remained simply had to be taken. The lust for ownership was irresistible. It was something only a handful of truly great connoisseurs such as himself would ever be able to understand.

Just as Bodenschatz was rising from his elegantly upholstered chair, a loud knock sounded on the study door. This then swung open to reveal Lieutenant Colonel Werner Teske, Goering's current senior adjutant. Goering sighed inwardly when spotting the sheet of paper in Teske's hand. No doubt this was going to be the cause of another irritating delay. And just when he was thinking he would soon be free to leave for home.

Following a sharp click of his heels, the adjutant moved closer and held out the paper. "This is the latest message Richard Forst has received from his agent in England, Reichsmarschall."

Bodenschatz raised an eyebrow. "Ah, the charming Lady Margaret, I presume. Do you want me to stay here while you assess that?" He placed both hands on the chair arms, looking as if he might well be preparing to sit back down again.

This was the very last thing Goering wanted. There were several security measures he needed to check at his home before the much-anticipated delivery arrived, and to be late back there might cause all kinds of difficulties. For now, this message would be receiving only his most cursory attention.

"No...no, Karl," he said quickly. "I know how busy you are. You go ahead and carry on with your next meeting." He gave an exaggerated sigh. "Believe me, her reports so far have contained nothing of significance. If by some miracle this one offers anything even remotely important enough to trouble the Fuhrer with, then of course I'll contact you immediately."

"Very well. If you are sure."

"Absolutely."

With a huge sense of relief he watched Bodenschatz depart. He then turned to his adjutant.

"So, Werner. I take it you have already looked at this message. Is there anything I really need to bother with? Up until now the quality of Lady Margaret's intelligence has been a severe disappointment to me."

Teske sank into the chair vacated by Bodenschatz, all air of formality gone now that the pair of them were alone. "You might want to look at this one a little more closely than usual," he suggested. "Even Forst said he was surprised when he decoded it."

Goering flicked an impatient hand. "Very well then. Give it to me."

A silence developed while his eyes ran over the typewritten page. When he finished reading, his expression was incredulous.

"A country house!" he exclaimed. "She wants me to bomb a single house in the middle of nowhere. Is she completely mad?"

"I fully understand how you feel," Teske began slowly. "But what if this Bletchley Park really is as important as she suggests?"

"What if....what if?" Goering sneered, tossing the sheet of paper down on the coffee table beside him. "Where is the actual proof for anything? All we have here is the speculation of a woman who for the last seven years has not provided us with one single piece of genuinely useful intelligence. Why should it suddenly be different now? For all we know, she might well have been captured by the British and turned into a double agent. Have you thought to consider that possibility?"

"That is possible," Teske agreed. "Though if this really is false intelligence deliberately fed to us, I fail to see a plausible reason for it. Perhaps...?"

He paused, clearly inviting the Reichsmarschall to suggest a motive of his own thinking.

The invitation was not taken up. Instead, Goering glanced at the magnificently crafted Vacheron & Constantin aviator's watch on his wrist. "Enough of this. It's time I was leaving. You take care of things for now, Werner."

Picking up a telephone on the small table, he jabbed down on a single button and barked out an order. "Have my car ready to take me home in two minutes."

"What do you wish me to tell Forst?" Teske asked as soon as the receiver was back in place.

Goering's face tightened. "For a start, you can tell him to stop wasting my time. Unless this so-called agent of his provides me with some solid proof – and I do mean proof, not more of her guesswork – not a single Luftwaffe aircraft will act on her information. Is that clear?"

Seeing the rising impatience in Goering's expression as they both stood up, Teske knew better than to detain him for a second longer. There must be something very important on his mind, he considered. When his boss was in this kind of mood, the best thing to do was simply agree with him as quickly as possible. As long as he did that, their normally relaxed relationship would be resumed soon enough.

"Yes, Reichsmarschall," he responded, jerking to attention and clicking his heels in the same manner as earlier.

Goering barely noticed. He was already striding rapidly toward the door, his mind occupied solely with thoughts of the treasured new addition to his art collection. If everything went to plan, he would most certainly be in the mood for a small private celebration later that evening.

AFTER STARING FOR SEVERAL seconds at the decoded message she had just written down, Margaret slammed her copy of Black Beauty shut in disgust.

Anna Sewell's novel had been her very favourite book as a child, and having read it from cover to cover countless times, she knew the story virtually word for word: an especially useful asset seeing as how it was now one of the two books that she and Richard were using to encode their messages. The other one, that was fallen back on only when the word or phrase needed could not be found in Black Beauty, was a 1930s printing of the concise Oxford English Dictionary. Black Beauty was coded as book A, and the dictionary as book B.

For a moment or two, the exasperation building up inside Margaret reached boiling point. What more did Goering expect her to do? It was easy for him to demand solid proof of Bletchley Park's importance, but he had no idea of how difficult and terribly risky that would be for her to obtain. If Simon's ultra-defensive reaction had been anything to go by, it might even prove to be completely impossible. She knew in her own mind that something vitally important was taking place there; why couldn't Goering just take her word for it? It wasn't as if the Luftwaffe raids had ceased altogether since the Blitz. What difference to him would one more make?

Gradually, her mood calmed to merely simmering. Much as she remained resentful of Goering's stubbornness, she was forced to concede that she had done very little so far to win his confidence. On top of that, she must never forget that he was still her only hope of ever regaining Hadley House and the estate.

With the demands of war taking an ever-tighter grip on the country, her riding school business had dried up almost completely. Recently she had been forced to start digging into the savings originally intended as a deposit on the cottage and stables. They could survive for a while yet on this reserve, but once it was gone there would be virtually nothing else of value to fall back on apart from the few bits of furniture and other items that they had been allowed to remove from the mansion when first moving out. And no one was buying stuff like that these days anyway. Not unless you were practically giving it away.

For a family with such a long and rich heritage, to lose their one remaining source of income and be reduced to an even lower status would be the ultimate humiliation. Such a situation would be impossible to hide from her father for very long. He said nothing much, but he missed little. After all the tribulations that had gone before, a further fall from grace might easily be enough to induce a second stroke. This time a fatal one.

Margaret's mouth firmed. That could not be allowed to happen. She would do anything...anything at all...to prevent it.

If Goering wanted proof, she would have to somehow find it. Whatever the risk to herself.

TEN

By late March, Betty was at last able to take up lodgings in a rather nice house on the outskirts of Bletchley town: one that boasted the quite rare and wonderful luxury of an indoor toilet. Better still, unlike some other girls' experiences she had heard of, the family here had gone out of their way to make her feel welcome. All in all, it was a vast improvement on the freezing cold hut situated just outside the perimeter fence that she had previously been sharing with the seven other WAAFs who were performing similar duties as herself.

From her new home she was able to ride a bicycle into Station X for her eight-hour shifts, though she had long since stopped thinking of it by that name. Most people working there who she had encountered commonly referred to the place as simply BP, which was short for Bletchley Park. She soon found herself doing the same thing.

The memory of how forcefully she had been warned about the need for secrecy when first arriving remained fresh in her mind, and she would of course follow that instruction to the letter. But that did not intimidate her sufficiently to smother her natural curiosity or prevent her from speculating.

The Morse code that she was receiving through her headphones was not coming directly from a radio. That much was plain to see from the connection. Also, there was no sign of any large external aerials anywhere within BP's grounds, so that meant the signals were most likely coming to her via a land line. All would be quiet for a time, then there would be a sudden burst of high-speed transmissions, nearly always in the same meaningless five letter blocks of code that she had been tested with at Compton Bassett. Exactly where the pages from her typewriter were taken after leaving her hut remained unknown, but she could make a darn good guess. If, as she strongly suspected, they were enemy signals, then it was likely to be somewhere reasonably close by to be decoded. Perhaps even the hut next door? Which of course, explained the need for such intense secrecy.

Work continued around the clock at BP in three, eight-hour shifts; at present she had just finished the first of six days on the 8am to 4pm duty. It was a welcome change from the almost universally disliked midnight to 8am shift that she had previously been stuck on.

Stepping out of the gloomy hut with its blacked-out windows, she blinked for a moment in the lingering hazy sunshine. It was pleasantly warm for the time of year. She would enjoy the ride home today.

While walking over to where her bicycle was parked, she found herself thinking of her parents. There would be a week's leave due soon, and she was eagerly looking forward to travelling home and seeing them again, even if she couldn't talk about the work she was doing. She'd have to cook up some kind of story. Most probably she'd tell them that, because of her college training, she had been forced into doing 'ordinary secretarial work'.

"Are you Betty Hall?" a rather posh sounding voice suddenly asked, dragging her mind abruptly away from south London.

She looked behind to see a blonde-haired woman just a little older than herself wearing civilian clothes. Clothes, that from the look of them, Betty imagined must have cost a fortune. This was one of the debutante types she had seen from time to time sitting by the lake. They had clearly not been conscripted into any of the services, so quite what these posh girls were doing here was a bit of a mystery.

"Yes, I am," she replied cautiously, remembering the instruction not to share too much personal information with anyone outside of her own hut.

A smile of relief formed on the newcomer's face. "Well I'm jolly glad to have caught you before you disappear off home." She extended an arm. "I'm Cynthia Bagsure."

Betty exchanged a handshake. The girl's grip was surprisingly strong for such a slender and fine-boned person.

"What can I do for you?" she asked.

"I've been told that you tinkle the old ivories a little bit. Is that right?"

For an instant, Betty found herself wondering how dear old Agatha might have reacted to this description of her pupil's piano-forte skills. She almost laughed out loud. Seriousness then quickly took over. "Where did you hear that?" she demanded.

"It's written down on your file under personal interests and hobbies." Cynthia held up a hand in mock defence. "Before you say anything, don't worry, I've not been snooping around in an underhand way or anything. I got that info quite legitimately from the admin officer."

Betty started to speak, but Cynthia pressed on. "I had to ask him if he could suggest anyone because, the truth is, we...that's our little revue group...are in rather an awful hole at present. Our usual pianist Gloria has gone down with bronchitis and can't stop coughing for more than a few seconds at a time. That's beastly inconvenient because we've got a show to do in aid of the Red Cross at Bletchley Road School and desperately need someone to replace her."

At last Betty was allowed a few seconds to speak. "I'm not sure if..." she began slowly.

"It really doesn't matter if you're not all that good. We just need someone who can bash out a bit of a tune. You can manage that, can't you?"

Betty nodded. "I think I probably can."

A huge smile lit up Cynthia's face. "That's super! You're in then. Welcome to the team."

"Wait a minute," Betty protested. "What is this show, and when are you performing it?"

"Oh, didn't I say? It's a sort of Victorian music hall extravaganza we've called *'Down at the Old Bull and Bush'.* You know the sort of thing: some lively songs that everyone can sing along to and a few good laughs from a cheeky-chappie comedian thrown in for good measure."

"And when are you rehearsing this?"

Cynthia wafted a careless hand. "Oh, rehearsals are all finished with."

"So when are you performing?" Betty could feel a frown developing.

"Why this evening, of course. Hence the panic. We start at eight o'clock, but if you get there by seven I'll run through a few things beforehand with you. By the way, can you read music?"

"Yes. A little bit."

"Wonderful! Gloria can't read a note." Cynthia gave her an exaggerated wink. "She'd better watch out or you'll be taking her place permanently."

FOR THE LAST MONTH, Margaret had been keeping as close a watch as was possible on the comings and goings at Bletchley Park without attracting undue attention to herself. The guards at the main entrance gave the impression that they were focused mainly on those people passing through the barrier, and not so very much on any activity that might be going on in the wider area outside. Even so, given the importance of the place, she remained sharply aware that there may well be more covert eyes watching out for this from other points. As it was, providing she did not linger in the immediate vicinity for too long, she felt that her horse-riding excursions in the nearby fields allowed her at least a small amount of credibility for being where she was.

No one, whether in uniform or not, was allowed inside without first showing a pass. Amongst the civilian girls regularly coming and going, even from a distance, Margaret sensed that she could recognise several faces. One of them, she was certain, was Cynthia Bagsure, Viscount Holding's youngest daughter and the sister of a former quite close friend. Cynthia had been by far the brightest of her siblings, and the last Margaret had heard of the girl she'd been studying mathematics at Girton College in Cambridge. What exactly she was now doing here in Bletchley was more than a little puzzling, but given her regular passage in and out, she must surely know a fair bit about what was going on behind that intimidating fence. Maybe, with a bit of careful handling, she could be induced into letting a few little facts slip?

Margaret's first thoughts centred on how to manufacture a natural looking meeting. She was still trying to discover something of Cynthia's social life outside of the Park so that they may 'accidentally' bump into each other when, out of the blue, a perfect opportunity presented itself.

Notices advertising an upcoming show by a section of the Bletchley Park Musical Society began appearing in church halls, shops and schools all around the area. Rather than the more usual serious classical recitals, this one was being promoted as: *A jolly good music hall singalong that everyone can join in with.* It was being staged to help raise funds for the Red Cross, and Cynthia's name was listed as being the producer and contact name for enquiries.

This could turn out to be a most interesting evening, Margaret decided.

JUDGING FROM THE FULL house attendance, it appeared that Bletchley's citizens were very much in the mood for a *Jolly good music hall singalong.*

Margaret had already made herself known to Cynthia, although so far it had been no more than a fleeting talk. She had though, promised to catch up more at the end. As producer, Cynthia still seemed to have a thousand and one last-minute matters to attend to. At present she was engaged in conversation with another young girl who was sitting on a stool behind an upright piano at the left-hand side of the stage. With no other instruments in sight, it appeared that this would be providing most, if not all, of the evening's musical accompaniment.

Margaret looked again at the quite pretty, dark-haired girl behind the keyboard. During their earlier brief chat, Cynthia had explained almost apologetically that she was a late stand-in for their regular pianist and *'a bit of an unknown quantity'*. Now, for some reason or another, Margaret herself began wondering about the extent of the girl's ability.

She did not appear to be nervous, even though the entire show might well stand or fall on how well she performed. Margaret knew from her own miserably poor attempts at piano lessons as a child what a devilishly tricky instrument it could be to perform well on. That failure had been just about the only time her father had ever expressed a feeling of disappointment in her. As pretty much a soloist, all eyes would inevitably turn to this girl if she happened to go off-key even briefly, especially if it were to happen during the quieter parts of any song.

There was little time left to ponder on this. With a final, 'good luck' pat on the shoulder for the girl – one which Margaret found herself mentally supplementing - Cynthia disappeared into the stage wings. A second or two later, several of the lights in the hall were switched off.

The show was about to begin.

AS THE LIGHTS DIMMED, Betty flexed her fingers. She had discussed each of the songs briefly with Cynthia and had the sheet music for them all balanced on the rather shaky wooden stand in front of her. There was just one problem. She had never played anything like this before.

Though she was perfectly familiar with such bawdy, singalong music from hearing it on the wireless, Agatha would quite possibly have fainted from utter shock if she had tried to play anything like tonight's opening song, 'A Little Bit of What You Fancy Does You Good', during one of their lessons. For her venerable tutor, with just one notable exception, it had always been a strictly classical world. All else was mere trivia. As for Betty herself, while she also dearly loved the work of the classical composers, she did find herself quite often tapping her feet to some of the more popular tunes of the day as well. The American composers Cole Porter and Irving Berlin were two of her favourites. In her opinion, there were many different styles of music out there to be enjoyed. She'd just never had the opportunity to play very many of them.

Until now.

THERE WERE THREE ENCORES for the closing song of 'My Old Man Said Follow the Van', with everyone in the hall, Margaret included, on their feet singing along and clapping throughout. Cynthia was positively beaming from ear to ear, especially when it was announced that the grand sum of fifty-five pounds and ten shillings had been raised that evening for the Red Cross.

Now, with the audience leaving, Margaret was at last able to get around to the main purpose of her being there. She sat down on a wooden chair alongside Cynthia in a corner of the hall.

For a few minutes she chose to tread on safe ground, keeping the conversation centred almost entirely on what they had in common: in this case, Judith, Cynthia's sister. She listened patiently to updates of the girl's situation. Like Margaret herself, Judith was now thirty-one years old and had escaped the conscription age for women introduced the previous December by one year. Mention of this gave a convenient link to switch the focus of their talk slightly.

"But you're still young enough to be liable for call-up," Margaret pointed out. She gave a short laugh. "Of course, you were always the brainy one, Cynthia. I heard you were studying maths up at Girton College, so I expect that's why you've escaped it so far."

"Actually, I finished there last August," the girl told her. She pulled a sour face. "It's so annoying. Do you know that those rotters at Cambridge still won't give us girls a proper degree, even though practically everyone is perfectly aware that Girton's course is just as tough as the BA they do at the chaps' college?"

"Your father will be proud of you, just the same." Margaret assured her. She paused before adding: "So why haven't you been called up since? What are you doing these days? At Bletchley Park, I mean."

This was a key moment. Margaret held her breath, hoping that she had made her question sound like a natural enquiry.

No look of alarm registered on Cynthia's face. She waved a casual arm. "Oh, nothing much. I'm just helping out a friend in the office with some accounting work for a while, that's all. Very boring stuff really. I'm sure my call-up papers will be arriving any day now. Who knows what I might be heading for after that?"

She may have spoken in an utterly convincing tone, but Margaret did not believe a word of it. Cynthia was renowned for her active mind and low threshold of boredom. Mentally stimulating challenges were her lifeblood. She could dash off the Times crossword in almost the blink of an eye. For her to happily settle for such a mundane existence was inconceivable, as was the idea of her just drifting into something. She had always been a girl with a plan. If she was called up into one of the services, with her brains, it would most likely be as an officer doing something of significant importance.

A thought then suddenly popped into Margaret's head. Almost at the same instant, Cynthia rose sharply out of her chair.

"Oh look!" she exclaimed. "There's the school headmaster. I simply must go and have a word with him before he disappears. It's been lovely to see you again, Margaret. Do give my best wishes to your father."

With that said, she hurried away across the now quite sparsely populated hall. The suddenness of her departure was not lost on Margaret. It certainly seemed as if she had touched a sensitive nerve. It would be wise not to push things any further for a time. Besides, the sudden thought that had occurred only a moment ago was already developing into something that now seemed to be making quite a bit of sense.

Just then she spotted the young piano player heading toward the exit, prompting her mind to switch directions. For some unaccountable reason the girl had been capturing Margaret's attention on and off all evening. It wasn't simply her playing, even though this had been very good indeed for an amateur production. No, it was something more than that. A strange feeling...a magnetic force almost...had slowly sneaked its way into her mind, telling her that this young girl and herself were destined to meet.

Exactly why this should be wasn't made clear, but Margaret could think of only one plausible explanation. As part of the evening's show, even as a last-minute stand-in, it was more than likely that the girl also worked inside Bletchley Park. Maybe it was her, and not Cynthia, who was the insider she needed to shed more light on what was taking place behind all that security? Margaret rose to her feet. If this was the case, she would have to act quickly.

She moved across to intercept her target before she reached the door.

BETTY SENSED THAT THE oncoming woman was intent on speaking to her, even when she was still several yards away. The feeling turned out to be correct.

"What a thoroughly enjoyable show," the newcomer said, placing herself squarely in Betty's path and pretty much compelling her to stop. "And as for your performance, my dear, I thought it was simply outstanding."

Betty frowned. "I don't know about that. All I did was provide accompaniment for the singers. They were the real stars."

"No...no, you are doing yourself an injustice. Without any rehearsal, it must have been difficult for you. But you managed splendidly."

"How did you know about—" Betty began.

The woman laughed. "Oh, I'm so sorry. Please allow me to introduce myself. I am Lady Margaret Pugh, an old friend of Cynthia's family. She was telling me just before the show started how you boldly stepped in at the very last second to save her from the disaster of having to postpone. She's enormously grateful, you know."

Betty regarded the woman a little more closely. Yes, now it was mentioned, she did recall seeing the pair of them exchanging a few words at the start of the evening. Their posh accents were quite a close match too.

"I'm Betty Hall," she responded. "I'm pleased to meet you, My Lady."

"Please don't bother with formalities," she was told. "Just plain Margaret will do."

Betty smiled, but did not speak further. She suspected that their conversation was leading to something specific. This was soon confirmed.

"Actually," Margaret began slowly, "I was wondering if you might be interested in providing me with a few piano lessons at my home. Nothing too advanced, of course. To be perfectly honest, I'm little better than an absolute beginner. I haven't really played at all since I was around fourteen years old, so we'd probably have to start off with the basic scales and suchlike all over again. But I would so like to improve. And I'd be happy to pay you whatever the current going rate is, naturally."

For a second or two, Betty had no idea how to react. This was the last thing she might have expected. Rapidly though, her thoughts pulled together.

Tonight's performance might not have been what Agatha had intended for her. Nor was it where her ambitions ultimately lay. Nonetheless, she had thoroughly enjoyed herself, even if she had felt a tiny bit rusty at the beginning. This had been the first time she had sat at a keyboard since joining the WAAFs nearly ten months ago, and it had showed. She still needed to practice regularly, otherwise who could tell how much she might backslide by the time this war was over? Then what might become of her dream trip to America?

Teaching someone else might be a useful way of keeping herself up to scratch, and earning a little bit of extra money at the same time. Things were certainly rather tight at the moment with just her meagre WAAF pay to rely on. Maybe she could send some of this extra cash back home to her parents as well? That would be nice.

"Where do you live, Margaret?" she found herself asking.

ELEVEN

The clock in the living room was showing 4.30pm when Margaret moved over to the window that gave her a good view of the long driveway leading up to Hadley House. Her eyes searched for a glimpse of young Betty approaching on her bicycle. The girl had promised to come directly to the cottage for their first piano lesson straight after her shift finished at 4.00pm. With Bletchley Park being just five miles away, she was due to be appearing any time now.

After a slightly uncertain start to their talk in the school hall, they had soon begun to get on rather well, Margaret felt. She had managed to confirm that Betty did indeed work at Bletchley Park, and that she was serving as a WAAF. These upcoming lessons would be an excellent opportunity to further gain the girl's trust and hopefully gather a few scraps of information about whatever it was that she actually did there.

The lessons themselves might prove to be rather useful in a way as well, although she doubted that Betty possessed anything like enough ability to pass on much in a strict musical sense. Certainly not of the sort that would impress her father. Before his financially straitened circumstances, the twelfth Earl of Dewksbury had been a particularly generous patron to the arts, most notably of all in the field of classical music. His love of this was almost certainly why he had employed one of the best piano tutors available for her when she was a child.

Not that a belated attempt at winning her father's approval was the objective of this musical adventure, she reminded herself. Betty was clearly from a very modest background, and although social structures were not quite what they used to be, there was still a degree of inbred respect and trust amongst most working-class people for members of the aristocracy. For Betty to sit down to tea with an earl and his daughter was sure to be a whole new experience for her. It was unlikely she would ever suspect there being an ulterior motive behind this hospitality.

Another look at the clock showed that a further ten minutes had passed. Margaret moved to the window again, and this time Betty was in sight. She stepped out of the cottage to greet her.

The girl looked somehow different in her WAAF uniform: perhaps a little more mature. Whatever the case, it was a warmish sort of day and Margaret could see that she was perspiring quite freely from her ride. In fact, straight after propping her bicycle up against the cottage wall, she removed her jacket and loosened her tie.

"That's better," she said, folding the jacket over her arm.

"Let me take that for you," Margaret offered. "We can hang it up in the hallway."

After handing the garment over, Betty cast her eyes around: first of all taking in the mansion and the Nissen huts nearby. Margaret could imagine what was going on in her mind. She probably believed that the big house had been requisitioned for the war effort, and this was the only reason why Margaret and her father were currently living in the cottage. There was no reason to set her straight on the matter.

Betty's eyes then shifted further across. "Is that your stables?" she asked.

"Yes, I run a riding school here," Margaret told her. "But what with the war going on, business is very slack these days. Practically nothing at all."

"I've often wondered what it would be like to ride a horse." Betty grinned. "The truth is, there aren't too many places for that kind of thing in my part of south London. And even if there were, what with one thing and another, I wouldn't have had much time for it."

Margaret was quick to spot the opportunity. "Maybe so. But you're in the countryside now, so why not think again about giving it a try? I can help you."

"You mean like a trade-off?" Betty laughed. "I teach you the piano, and you teach me how to ride?"

"Yes, if you like."

For a moment there was a definite sign of interest on Betty's face. But a look of doubt then formed. Margaret could guess the reason for this. "I'll still pay you for the piano lessons," she added. "All three of my horses need a lot of regular exercise, so if you were to take one of them out occasionally, that would actually be doing me a favour. As I said just now, there are hardly any customers these days."

The doubt on Betty's face remained, but it was lessening. "Let me think about it," she said.

Placing the girl's jacket over the bicycle's handlebars, Margaret beckoned. "Come on. Let's go and meet the horses. It will only take a few minutes, and maybe that will help you to decide."

There was a genuine flicker of interest in Betty's eyes now. "All right then," she agreed. "Why not?"

Margaret smiled to herself as they made their way over to the stable block.

FOR BETTY, STROKING a horse and seeing it react to her touch had been a captivating experience. She had never been anywhere near this close to one before, and it was an experience that she most certainly wanted to repeat.

While walking back to the cottage alongside Margaret, she thought yet again how fortunate she had been to meet this woman. But it would not be fair to take advantage of her new friend's generosity, even though she was probably very rich indeed. Betty had been intending to charge five shillings an hour for her lessons, which was still well below the normal rate. Now, having already decided that the offer of riding lessons was too good to miss out on, she mentally adjusted this price down to half a crown.

As they paused beside the bicycle to collect her jacket, Margaret touched her lightly on the arm. "I should warn you before we go inside," she began in a slightly quieter than normal voice. "Father had a stroke several years ago and doesn't really go out anywhere these days. He's not used to meeting new people, so when you see him, please don't be offended if he doesn't say very much at first. I know he can be a bit grumpy at times, but he'll get used to you after a couple of visits."

"I see." This put a sudden damper on things for Betty. She really hoped there was not going to be an awkward atmosphere. "Maybe I should come back another day?" she suggested.

"No, that's not necessary. I've already told him that you're coming. He's expecting you now."

"If you are sure?"

"Absolutely! I'm not going to miss out on our lesson now. I've been jolly well looking forward to it all day."

Still a little against her better judgement, Betty allowed herself to be ushered inside.

On entering the sitting room she immediately noticed two things. Firstly, to her relief, there was no sign of the earl. He was probably upstairs, she imagined. Possibly even making a deliberate effort to avoid her if he was as averse to meeting people as Margaret said.

The second thing that caught her eye was the object of utter beauty standing in the corner of the room: a black, Steinway Model R upright grand piano. This, she knew, was the same model as the two Steinway uprights that had been selected to entertain first-class passengers on the world's most luxurious ocean liner, the ill-fated Titanic. And now here was another one that she was about to give lessons on. Up until this moment, to have the opportunity of playing a Model R had been nothing more than a wonderful dream. To actually be paid for doing so was beyond her wildest fantasy.

She glanced across to see Margaret smiling at her. "You like it?" her new friend asked.

Betty moved across the room to lift the lid and run her fingers lovingly over the keyboard. "It's magnificent." She played a few notes. "It sounds to be perfectly in tune as well."

Margaret smiled again. "So now, all you have to do is teach me how to play the darn thing."

IT WAS FUNNY HOW THINGS sometimes turned out, Margaret reflected.

The piano lessons had been intended for no other purpose than to help her win over Betty's confidence. And earlier, when the girl's interest in riding lessons had come to light, it had been an unexpected bonus. Their rides around the estate would give her even more time to probe for information.

Yet in spite of her motives, after their first hour together sat at the keyboard, Margaret was feeling a genuine enthusiasm. This was the last thing she'd expected. The hugely expensive Steinway had been purchased by her father so that she could be given those long-lost childhood lessons, and because it had been privately purchased rather than inherited, it was amongst the few items of value they had been allowed to retain when vacating the mansion.

Not that the Steinway evoked any fond memories. The lessons she'd had on it had been demanding, and never something she looked forward to. As a result, her progress had been slow and extremely limited. Maybe it was simply a case of her tutor failing to inspire her? The woman had certainly been a bit sharp-tempered, frequently making her displeasure obvious if her young pupil were to make even the smallest of mistakes.

With Betty it was so different. Margaret no longer felt as if she was being pressured into aiming for excellence in the fiendishly complex world of classical works. Now, she was simply being given a helping hand in learning how to play along with some of the popular tunes of the day. They might not be to her father's taste, but she thoroughly enjoyed many of them. For the first time ever whilst sat at the Steinway, she was actually having fun.

Father had obviously chosen to remain upstairs in order to save his ears from as much torment as possible. As for herself, it wasn't that she had no appreciation of classical music. Some works by Tchaikovsky and Mozart gave her enormous enjoyment, and it would have been lovely to be able to play them well. But she was perfectly well aware of her limitations.

They paused for a break. Leaving Betty still sat at the piano, Margaret went into the kitchen to make them both a cup of tea. She was just about to return with a loaded tray when the sound of the piano starting to play reached her.

Almost at once she felt her jaw sag in astonishment. The tune was one that her childhood tutor had frequently tried - with a spectacular lack of success - to drum the basics of into her. The title was on the tip of her tongue, but it refused to come. What she did know, beyond any doubt, was that she was hearing an absolutely masterful rendition of the classic piece. Even her old tutor had not sounded so clear or confident when playing it. She stepped back into the room and placed the tray quietly on a table. She had no idea...no idea at all that ....

How on earth was it possible for a girl so young and from a working-class area of London to be so accomplished?

With her back to the room, Betty was totally engrossed in her playing and unaware of Margaret's return. Spellbound, she settled down in an armchair to continue listening. A distant memory told her that this was a quite short composition that would likely last for only a few minutes longer.

The memory was correct. Almost too soon for Margaret, the piece came to an end. As if only now suddenly sensing that she was being watched, Betty swung around on her stool. A look of embarrassment instantly came over her. She even turned a little red in the cheeks.

"I'm so sorry," she apologised. "I just couldn't stop myself. This is such an amazing piano and I really wanted to hear how Für Elise would sound on it. That was one of the very first pieces I ever learned to play properly, so it has special memories for me."

Für Elise. Yes, Margaret remembered now. A bagatelle, her tutor had called it.

She came across to sit on the stool beside Betty. "How old were you then?" she asked.

"I was twelve. Twelve and a half to be exact. I remember because mum and dad bought me an old piano as a birthday present and I'd been having lessons for six months."

Twelve years old! And only six months of lessons.

From Margaret's perspective, such precocious talent was amazing. For several seconds she found herself speechless with admiration. But there was somebody else nearby who had not temporarily lost their voice.

"That was remarkably well played, young lady," she heard her father say.

She looked across to see him standing in the open doorway. What's more, there was a smile on his face. How long had it been since he'd displayed one of those?

He moved fully into the room, stopping just a few feet short of the piano. All of his attention was centred on Betty. "We haven't been introduced yet," he said. "I am Lord Dewksbury, Margaret's father."

Rising from her stool, Betty hesitated, clearly uncertain as to whether or not a curtsy was required. In the end she settled for the compromise of just a slight dip of the knees. "I'm Betty, My Lord...Betty Hall."

His smile reappeared. "I am most pleased to meet you, Betty."

Introductions completed, he moved over to his usual armchair and settled into this before adding: "You must tell me who taught you to play so well?"

Up until now, Margaret had felt that nothing else today could surprise her. But to see her father willingly engaging in conversation with a total stranger was absolutely astonishing. Astonishing, but at the same time, simply wonderful.

"It was a lady called Agatha Wright, My Lord," Betty told him. "Sadly, she died a little over a year ago."

"I'm sorry to hear that. But I'm sure that she was very proud of you."

After a brief pause, the earl beckoned Betty closer. "I wonder, could I ask a favour of you? Would you be kind enough to play a little more for me? It's been such a long time since I've had the opportunity to hear someone perform in the flesh, so to speak. I do miss that pleasure very much indeed."

Betty glanced at Margaret, who gave her a quick nod of encouragement. "Father loves anything classical," she said.

Betty turned back to the earl. "Is there anything special you'd like me to play?" she asked.

He waved a hand. "I'll leave the choice up to you, my dear. Why don't you surprise me? What did your tutor Agatha particularly like?"

Margaret watched as Betty walked thoughtfully back to the piano. What would she choose to play? The effect she'd had on her father so far had been little short of miraculous. Margaret had not seen him this animated for many years.

Could this much longed-for improvement possibly continue?

AFTER SETTLING BACK on the piano stool, Betty continued thinking for several more seconds before turning to face the earl. He was already leaning back in his chair with fingers resting beneath his chin and a look of eager anticipation on his face.

She'd at first been intending to play something 'safe' such as Beethoven's 'Moonlight Sonata' or Edvard Grieg's 'Morning Mood'. Both were fully committed to memory and would be perfectly straightforward to perform. But where was the challenge in that? Or the surprise, for that matter? Pieces such as these were exactly what the earl was expecting to hear.

What Betty now intended to play would be the very opposite of all that.

She had always believed Agatha to be a strict traditionalist, so when her tutor first introduced her to the then quite recently written work, she was more than a little astonished. But that quickly changed. *You will find it challenging your skills in many new and exciting ways,"* Agatha had told her. She had been right, too. In its own highly unconventional way, the work was an absolute masterpiece, not to mention one of the most difficult Betty had ever so far tried to learn. Even after countless hours of practice, some of its more complex parts still felt elusive. Increasing the difficulty even further, it had been well over a year since she'd last attempted to perform them.

So why was she choosing to place herself under such pressure now? Also, equally pertinently, why was she risking the earl's displeasure?

She could think of only one reason. He had called her former tutor to mind. Now, because of that poignant reminder, Betty could feel a powerful desire to pass on Agatha's appreciation of a much-maligned composition that they had both come to feel passionately about. This was the one work that strayed away from the strictly conventional that Agatha had fully embraced. Although normally performed by a full orchestra, the composer had also written a special arrangement for a solo piano that lasted for just over thirteen minutes. That was what she would play now.

Hoping fervently that this particular thirteen would not turn out to be an unlucky number, she looked the earl squarely in the eye.

"You asked for me to surprise you, My Lord," she said. "I think this should do the trick."

MARGARET RECOGNISED what Betty was playing almost before the first bar was completed. It didn't matter that when under full orchestration, this part would be performed on a solo clarinet as a continuously rising *glissando*. The opening to George Gershwin's Rhapsody in Blue was unmistakable on virtually any instrument.

A rush of despair came over her. Of all the things that Betty could have chosen, what on earth had made the girl think that this would please her traditionalist father? The word 'controversial' barely began to describe the feelings that this work aroused. Ever since its first public performance less than twenty years ago, Rhapsody in Blue had been sneered at and dismissed as 'trite and formless' by the vast majority of serious music critics. Gershwin himself was branded by them as being nothing more than 'a tunesmith with pretensions'.

In contrast, most of the popular press had heaped enormous praise on the work, calling it: *'A ground-breaking fusion of classical music and jazz'.* It was a huge success commercially as well, with millions of people in both America and Europe purchasing copies of its various recordings in pre-war days. Margaret wholeheartedly agreed with them. She had adored the work ever since seeing it featured in the Hollywood movie The King of Jazz back in 1930. She had even been tempted into buying a recording herself, though she would never have dared to play it within a mile of her father's hearing.

Yet here it was now being performed directly in front of him. She glanced at the earl. He was still leaning back in his chair, but now had both eyes closed. His face was expressionless.

As the music gathered pace and volume, Betty's upper body swayed from side to side on her stool, her fingers continuously flashing across the keyboard and both feet dabbing up and down on the instrument's pedals in order to enhance and sustain the notes. The Steinway's rich tones swelled out with increasing vigour, seeming to fill every small portion of the room with the sheer quality of its vibrancy. It was quite literally music to Margaret's ears, eventually captivating her to the point that, for a brief space of time, she found herself forgetting all about her father's presence.

She held her breath while waiting for the transition that she knew would take place at about the eight-minute mark. This was probably her favourite part of all. The particularly loud and rapid section currently playing came to an almost abrupt end. A brief moment of total silence hovered teasingly in the air. Betty then raised her left hand high for a second before beginning to pick out the gently rippling opening notes of the haunting main melody. As it nearly always did at this point, Margaret felt her skin starting to tingle in anticipation. The subdued moment gradually built in pace and volume, jumping into a few unusual avenues along the way but ultimately leading to, what was for her, quite possibly the most wonderful of musical climatic finishes ever written.

And then, with a glorious melodic rush, it was all over. Utterly spellbound, for a breathless moment Margaret felt a compulsion to burst into applause. Only the sudden movement of Betty twisting around on her stool to seek the earl's reaction prevented her from actually doing so. With no small sense of trepidation, Margaret turned her gaze in the same direction.

Her father had not moved in the slightest since the last time she had looked at him. To all appearances, he might well have been asleep.

"I'm sorry if—" Betty began after a few seconds of rather tense silence.

The earl's eyes snapped open, stopping her in mid-sentence. "There is no need to apologise for your choice, Betty," he began. "You played what you imagined to be suitable. What's more, you certainly did succeed in surprising me. It was …."

He paused for a long moment before suddenly smiling. "A most pleasant surprise. Also, I have to say, an illuminating one. I have never heard Mister Gershwin's much talked about composition performed as a solo piano arrangement before, and now that I have, I can honestly say that it has opened my mind considerably as to its merits. Its complexity is considerable, and you Betty, played it close to perfection. You are an extraordinarily talented young lady."

Margaret could only stare in delighted astonishment at her parent. He had enjoyed it. He had actually enjoyed it. And he was smiling once again.

A sudden thought fell into her head. Could this be the trigger that Doctor Grant had spoken of all those years ago? Had something so straightforward as providing music - music performed right here in their own home - been the key all along? She had tried many times with only limited success to coax him into listening to concerts on the wireless. Now, the penny finally dropped. It was the 'being there' aspect that was so important to him.

Hadn't he said so himself only a short time ago how much he missed: *'hearing someone perform in the flesh'*. Why had she not realised this before?

"I was concerned about the two mistakes I made in the cadenza section," Betty was saying.

"Actually, I only picked up one of them," the earl responded, now leaning forward and obviously prepared to engage in earnest debate. "But then again, the occasional blemish is very much a part of the joy connected to an impromptu performance, don't you think?"

Betty frowned. "I'm not really sure. Don't you feel that it's a performer's duty to be constantly seeking perfection?"

"To a point perhaps. However, for me, the interpretation is everything. What a boring world it would be if every piece of music were to be played in exactly the same way on every occasion."

Margaret sensed that this conversation was very soon going to be passing completely over her head. She had not been able to detect even the hint of a mistake anywhere in Betty's playing. Carefully, so not to disturb their exchange, she skirted around the pair and picked up the tray of now cold cups of tea.

Thrilled at their ongoing engagement, she was perfectly happy to leave them to it: two people from vastly different backgrounds and generations brought together by a mutual passion for music. Such was the connection developing between them, Betty had even stopped addressing her father as 'My Lord', Margaret noticed. Not that it bothered her in the slightest. Just so long as this remarkable restoration of his *joie de vivre* continued, she would not even care if Betty were to start calling him by his first name of Henry. At this moment, all she could feel was an enormous debt of gratitude to the girl.

After entering the kitchen, she placed the tray beside the sink. Her father's voice drifted in, his tone full of enthusiasm while debating some technical detail about octaves. Margaret smiled to herself. On impulse, she opened the back door and decided to stroll around outside for a time.

Within just a few seconds, as if the fresh air had cleared her mind of cloying emotions over what was taking place inside, she realised that here was an opportunity she should not allow to pass by. Maybe she would learn nothing. On the other hand, she might well discover something very useful indeed. As long as she did not delay, there would be little risk involved.

Moving around to the front of the cottage, she eased the door open. There, hanging on a hook in the hallway, was Betty's jacket. From the sound of it, the pair in the living room were still absorbed in their discussion. As long as it stayed that way, everything would be fine. Even if one of them did happen to glance in the direction of the wide-open lounge door, the coat hooks were much further down the hall and well away from their line of vision.

With nimble fingers, Margaret checked each of the jacket pockets. Only the top right hand one produced anything of interest.

A wireless operator's flash was easy to recognise. The fist and lightning design was quite distinctive, and since the war had started she'd seen many RAF people walking around in London wearing one just like this on their right arm. Was this Betty's trade as well? And if so, why would she hide her flash away like this? Most service people she had ever met were inordinately proud of whatever qualifications they had managed to earn for themselves.

Betty must have been ordered to remove it.

For security reasons?

Given all the other secrecy about the place, this seemed to be the only logical answer, especially after a close inspection of the jacket's upper right arm revealed a faint trace of stitching marks in the appropriate rectangular shape. Which gave rise to other interesting thoughts. If Betty was a wireless operator, that sort of fitted in rather well with her theory of what function Cynthia might be serving at Bletchley Park.

Satisfied with what she had discovered, she returned the flash to the same pocket she had found it in and crept back outside.

IT WAS AFTER NINE O'CLOCK when Betty eventually left the cottage. With the blackout regulations insisting that the beam from the lamp of her bicycle be restricted to no more than a narrow slit, this may have posed a problem in navigating her way over unfamiliar territory. Fortunately, the sky was clear and there was a good three-quarter moon to illuminate the way until she got back onto more frequently ridden roads.

Throughout the ride, her mind remained full of developments at the cottage. The earl had insisted that she come back again as often as possible, even giving her a hand a squeeze of appreciation when they said goodbye. She explained about her constantly changing work shifts, but promised to return whenever she could. She meant it, too. Quite aside from Margaret's piano lessons, she was still looking forward very much to her first experience of riding a horse. Perhaps her next day off due this coming Sunday would be a good time for that?

After leaving the cottage, Margaret had accompanied her outside to where her bicycle was waiting. Now just the two of them, she explained what a huge difference Betty's playing and conversation had made to her father's well-being, and how much she appreciated it. They had even exchanged a brief hug before parting.

By now, Betty was very nearly back at her lodgings. Yes, she told herself, meeting Margaret had been a most fortunate encounter for all kinds of reasons. Maybe she was being a little naïve, but despite the vast difference in their social status, she could feel a genuine friendship developing between the pair of them.

She really hoped it would continue this way.

WHILE WATCHING BETTY pedal off into the darkness, Margaret experienced yet another rush of gratitude for what the girl had achieved with her father. This was a perfectly normal reaction of course, and one she could fully understand. Less expected was the growing feeling that she was actually becoming rather fond of her supposed new friend.

She shook her head in an attempt to remove such a silly thought. Her relationship with Betty was based on the need to gather information: nothing more. She must never forget that. Her father's apparent recovery, although a wonderful development, had come about mostly by accident. There were probably hundreds of pianists around who could have achieved the very same thing with him given the opportunity. It was her own fault for not having spotted this potential route to his rehabilitation much sooner.

She began to consider the information she'd so far gathered. Betty was a wireless operator, and Cynthia a mathematician. What common purpose could these two very different people be working toward? Margaret now knew thanks to Betty's mention of shifts that her section was on duty around the clock. That in itself said that their work was of a vital nature.

The fresh evening air was helping her to think, allowing her to speculate further. The role of a wireless operator was to both send and receive messages: there was no secret attached to that. Also, in a time of war, it was a certainty that nothing of any importance would be transmitted in simple plain language. Both sides would be using special codes. She was doing the same thing herself. Not that the military would be using a simple book code. No, they were bound to be employing something far more complex than that. Devilishly complicated codes designed to prevent even the finest brains on the enemy side from unscrambling their messages.

The finest brains!

The phrase sparked a memory that came back to her like a shot. It was one of those elusively familiar faces she had noted going in and out of Bletchley Park a few times recently. She could now remember exactly where she had seen the man before. They had never met personally, but she had read an article featuring him in Tatler Magazine several years ago. There had been a number of good photographs too. What was his name? Professor Frank Tweeny? It was something like that. He had been an Honorary Fellow at Trinity College, Cambridge and was reputed to speak nine languages fluently, including Japanese, Russian, and most significantly of all in this instance, German. For this, plus various other reasons she could not quite recall, he had been referred to as: *One of the finest brains in the country.*

And now, he too had turned up at Bletchley Park.

The picture was becoming all too clear. Linguists and mathematicians would be exactly the sort of minds ideally suited to codebreaking. That would explain some of the weird characters seen wandering around the town as well. Many academics and freethinkers were notoriously eccentric. Margaret also recalled again the ease with which Cynthia used to dash off the Times crossword. An expertise in wordplay was surely another great qualification for the task they were undertaking.

It all added up so well. Everything at Bletchley Park was there to support and protect an elite collection of brains. She was certain of it. Betty, talented pianist as she may be, was merely one of those receiving coded German messages and passing them on. Nonetheless, she might still have useful knowledge to let slip. And even if she did not, their friendship must continue for a time yet. If only to ensure her father's continuing recovery.

On stepping back inside the cottage, she saw him standing at the foot of the stairs. He was obviously waiting for her.

"I'm going up to bed now, Margaret," he said. "But before I do, I want you to know how deeply I appreciate you bringing young Betty here to play for me. I cannot remember the last time I enjoyed myself so much. In fact, I rather suspect that it was far more for my benefit than any renewed interest in piano lessons for yourself that really lay behind your engaging her."

He held out his left arm. Even the afflicted right one managed to raise almost half the way up. "No man could ever wish for a better daughter."

Astonishment swept over Margaret. The last time he had displayed anything like such open affection for her was before his stroke nearly a decade ago. They shared a warm hug, and for the second time that day she felt tears creeping into her eyes. She had no intention of correcting her father in his belief of her motives. It was simply too wonderful to bathe in the glow of his love and appreciation. Why risk spoiling such a special moment?

She watched him climb the stairs. In the first few years of his disability she had needed to assist him in this just about every step of the way. Even yesterday it had still seemed like a bit of a struggle for him. Now, by comparison, he appeared to be almost flying up there.

She could not help but wonder how great the improvement might be if she did ever succeed in restoring his estate to him. She had to continue believing that the country would be better off under German rule, and that they still had the military strength to prevail. Worryingly, American troops had been arriving in England ever since the end of January and were growing in numbers all the time. Any attempt at an invasion from now on would be certain to face far tougher battles than it would have done back in 1940.

It appeared that time was not on Germany's side, especially with vast numbers of their troops apparently still locked in a deadly kind of stalemate with resurgent Russian forces. Ever since the assault on Moscow had been repulsed, it was incredible how the Red Army seemed to be one step ahead of the invaders for much of the time.

Her thoughts quickly switched back to Bletchley Park. Could it be that the collection of brains working there were successfully decoding messages sent by the Germans serving in Russia and passing this intelligence on to Stalin? That would certainly go quite some way toward explaining the sudden success of the Soviet fightback.

More than ever she was convinced that the Park's destruction would be of major benefit to Germany's cause. It might even be sufficient to provide them with a war-winning advantage if achieved quickly enough. In her own mind, she now had plenty enough proof for Goering to sanction an air raid. If it wasn't, then she would damn well invent some more to force his hand. It was that important. He would thank her in the end.

The Two Thousand Guineas was due to be run at Newmarket in a little over four weeks, and Joe Bull was certain to be there. This time she would be far more forceful in her message.

Bletchley Park *must* be destroyed.

TWELVE

Lieutenant-Commander Simon Straw stepped out through the main doors of Bletchley Park mansion and immediately lit a cigarette. Thank God for a break in the meeting, he told himself. Tempers with a few people were becoming more than a little frayed.

Discussions had centred on the still relatively new Naval Cipher 3, which a few of the most highly regarded brains working at the Park seemed to think was vulnerable to being broken by the Germans. His role here today was to listen to all of these concerns and then report them back to the Head of Naval Intelligence at the Admiralty. The problem was, there were several conflicting opinions as to the best way of rectifying the problem, and everyone seemed to think that their solution was obviously the most effective one. Complicating matters still further, Naval Cipher 3 had been set aside for Anglo-United States use, so quite understandably the Americans were being pretty darn vociferous in their opinions as well.

He wandered over in the general direction of the lake, eventually settling down on a bench seat close to the edge. Several ducks drifted by as he stubbed the cigarette out and continued to dwell on the meeting. The lunch break would hopefully provide the means for a calmer atmosphere to take over.

"Simon Straw! I thought it was you. How jolly nice to see you again."

The young woman's voice jerked him away from his deliberations. She was standing just a couple of feet away. Though her face looked to be familiar, he could not quite place it.

"It's Cynthia...Cynthia Bagsure," she continued. "You were part of the gang my older sister Judith used to run around with in pre-war days."

He laughed. "Oh yes, I remember you now. I came to your house quite a few times, didn't I? But you must have still been very young the last time I saw you there."

"Fifteen, I think," she told him.

"And what have you been doing with yourself since then?"

She sat down beside him. "After finishing school I went up to Girton College and bagged myself one of those beastly degrees without a name in mathematics. You know, the ones they reserve especially for us girls."

Simon nodded sympathetically. He had heard this same lament several times before, and in his experience the girls who'd qualified at Girton were usually more than equal to their male counterparts in ability. All the same, Cynthia must have done exceptionally well to have been recruited here at the Park. The memories were returning. Yes, she had been an extremely bright child, he recalled.

A grin suddenly appeared on her face. She leaned in a little closer. "I'll tell you a secret if you like. I used to have this enormous schoolgirl crush on you. I always thought you looked so dashing, especially when you were wearing your uniform."

He blinked in surprise. "Really? I had no idea." He did not know what else to say. He had certainly never seen himself in that sort of light. Not in the slightest.

"I mentioned about it to Judith once and she told me not to be so silly. She said that you would never be interested in me."

"Well, you were still rather young," he pointed out tactfully.

"Oh, it wasn't just for that reason. Judith reckoned you were secretly in love with Margaret Pugh and didn't have eyes for anyone but her."

Her words struck a sensitive spot. Simon realised that his face had coloured a little. Had he really been in love with Margaret back then? Actually *in love*? And even if that was true, had his innermost feelings – feelings that he had clearly not admitted even to himself - been so blatantly obvious to all the others in their little circle of friends? Despite the passing of years, it was still embarrassing to think that he might have been so transparent.

"I certainly did like Margaret a lot," he began, feeling somewhat on the defensive. "But I'm not so sure about the whole *being in love* bit. We never actually got it together you know. Not even for a short time."

Cynthia brushed this detail aside with a small flick of the hand. "She still lives pretty close to here, even after her father's misfortune. But I'm sure you're well aware of that fact already. Why don't you pop over to see her while you're in the area?"

"I'd rather like to, but I'm afraid there won't be time. My driver has orders to take me straight back to London as soon as my meeting here is over." He gave a short laugh. "Anyhow, seeing as you are so interested in my private life, you might like to know that I had lunch with Margaret at the Savoy Grill not long ago. We got on rather well, as it happens."

"Actually, I saw her recently too," Cynthia told him. "She came along to a show our little revue group put on at a local school the other evening. We chatted for a short time at the end, but then I had to beat a rather hasty retreat when she started asking me about my work here." She waved a hand. "All perfectly innocent of course, but you know how it is."

A small jolt ran through Simon. "What exactly did she say to you?" he demanded, aware that his voice had suddenly become sharp. He tried to offset this by adding in a more casual tone: "I'm sure it was innocent as well, but it's still best if we know about these things."

She frowned anyway. "I'm not a fool, you know. I didn't let on a thing. She asked why I hadn't been conscripted yet and wanted to know what I was up to these days. I told her I was just doing some boring old accounting work to help out a friend until my call-up came along."

Simon nodded, but made no reply.

"They were perfectly natural things to ask someone if you haven't seen them for a long time," Cynthia continued. "And this *is* Margaret we are talking about. She was one of my sister's crowd, not some bally stranger."

Yes, thought Simon. That's exactly what I told myself about her as well.

Although hating himself for thinking this way, he began analysing their conversation at the Savoy Grill once again. All of Margaret's enquiries about what was happening to Hadley House had eventually led on very conveniently to her observations about Bletchley Park. These had been framed as a question, but not a direct one. Which of course, if a person really was seeking to subtly extract information, was exactly how they might set about things.

Still finding it almost impossible to think of Margaret in this way, he nonetheless knew that, coming on top of his own experience, her subsequent questioning of Cynthia was simply too great a coincidence to ignore.

"You've gone awfully quiet," she remarked. "Are you worried about something?"

He ignored the question. "Have you seen Margaret again since then?"

"No, not a glimpse. But I'm rather annoyed with her, all the same."

"Really? Why is that?"

"It's a bit of a story, actually. There was a young WAAF called Betty who helped us out that evening. She stood in at the very last minute for our usual pianist who was sick. As it turned out she was spiffingly good, even without any rehearsals. I just gave her the music sheets she needed and off she went, note perfect all the way through."

"But why are you annoyed with Margaret?" Simon pressed. He glanced at his watch. Their meeting was due to reconvene soon.

"I was mad keen to get Betty involved with this super new production I'm planning," she continued. "I sounded her out about it...practically begged her if the truth be told...but she turned me down flat. She said she no longer had any spare time because she was too busy with giving Lady Margaret piano lessons. I spotted them talking together that same evening after the show had finished, so I imagine that's when they fixed it all up. It was just after I'd scuttled away to avoid any more awkward questions."

She slapped herself lightly on the wrist and gave a lopsided grin. "Bad move, Cynthia. How to lose a cracking pianist in one easy lesson."

Her attempt at wry humour was lost on Simon. "What is this Betty's full name, and where does she work?" he asked.

"It's Betty Hall, and she's in Hut Fourteen."

"And you are in...?"

"Hut Eight."

Simon nodded. Alan Turing's section: a man who was playing such a major part in the very meeting on naval security that he now needed to get back to. It was as he suspected; Cynthia had a key role in things here.

She might give the impression of being a bit light-headed at times, but underneath all that there was a very sharp brain indeed.

He rose to his feet. "I must go now," he said. "Remember, Cynthia, do not mention a word of what we have just discussed to anyone. Especially to Betty herself."

She looked him directly in the eye. "I know the house rules as well as anyone. Mum's the word at all times. As I told you just now, I'm not a fool."

In spite of the deep concern eating away at him, he managed to produce a genuinely warm smile. "Believe me," he said. "I never thought you were. Not for a single second."

SIMON ARRIVED BACK in London that same evening. After having made his report to the Head of Naval Intelligence, it was with a tangle of conflicting emotions that he went on to share his concerns over the recent conduct of Lady Margaret Pugh.

Once finished, he went on to stress quite strongly that the motive behind her asking to meet for lunch might well have been what it appeared to be: nothing more than a sincere concern over her father's health. As for Margaret's approach to Cynthia Bagsure, he repeated Cynthia's assertion that the two questions she had posed were: *perfectly natural things to ask someone if you haven't seen them for a long time.* All the same, given the extremely sensitive nature of BP's work, it was clearly his duty to report these developments.

The Vice-Admiral had considered what he'd heard for a few seconds, then told Simon to come back to his office first thing in the morning. That moment had now arrived. While standing in front of his superior officer's desk, he felt a quickening of his pulse as the man began to speak.

"I've spoken directly to the PM about this, and he is definitely concerned. Even though, as you have quite rightly pointed out, there is no solid evidence whatsoever to suggest that Lady Margaret is up to something she shouldn't be, Winston still wants the matter to be thoroughly investigated. He demands that it's checked out from every conceivable angle."

This was precisely what Simon had been expecting to hear. All those in the know were well aware of Winston Churchill's absolute determination to preserve the utmost secrecy over the work of those at the Park who he had frequently referred to as his 'Golden Geese'.

What he most certainly was not expecting to hear was what the Vice-Admiral said next. "He wants it to be done by you, Simon. You are the one who will be doing the investigating."

It was impossible for him to conceal his surprise. "Me, Sir? But surely this is a job for MI5 or Special Branch."

"Under normal circumstances, yes, it would be. However, if there is any grain of truth in your suspicions, we don't want to spook Lady Margaret. As you will know, she is an exceedingly clever and observant woman who would likely spot a Special Branch man taking a close interest in her activities a mile off."

Simon had little choice but to agree with this assessment. He gave a nod, but said nothing.

"On top of that, in spite of her and her father's much reduced circumstances, she is still a highly regarded member of the local aristocracy. She does a great deal of good work for charities in her area of Buckinghamshire, and it would cause numerous problems if she were to be arrested and subsequently proven to be innocent."

"That is another valid point, Sir. Even so, I don't see how—"

"She and you are long standing friends, Simon. You know her well. Well enough, Winston feels, for you to be capable of quickly spotting any little abnormalities in her behaviour. You know what I mean, the kind of personal stuff that a stranger might miss out on completely."

"That's possibly true, Sir. On the other hand, we only see each other occasionally these days. And even when we do, it's mostly here in town. She is hardly likely to react well to me suddenly appearing in Bletchley and attempting to become far closer pals than usual. If she is guilty of something, that would surely put her on her guard more than anything."

"Of course it would. And that won't be your role. But we do want you to go up to Bletchley again and stay there until this thing is sorted out one way or another. An office has already been reserved for you inside the manor, so you'll be able to direct operations from there."

"Are you saying that I'll have a team working for me?"

The Vice-Admiral smiled. "I don't know about a team exactly. Even within the Park, the less people who know what's going on the better. But you can certainly make use of Cynthia Bagsure if the need arises. And as it happens, you do appear to have one important agent already in place."

"Really, Sir. Who might that be?"

"Why this WAAF girl of course. The one who Lady Margaret appeared rather keen to obtain piano lessons from."

He checked a sheet of paper in front of him. "Yes, Betty Hall, that's her name. A particularly talented young lady from all accounts. Handled correctly, she might well turn out to be your trump card."

THIRTEEN

During the last three weeks, Betty had cycled over to see Margaret and the earl as frequently as her work would allow her to. Even while on her current night shift, she had still so far been able to pop in twice during the early part of the evening.

It was a rewarding experience for her in so many ways. First of all there was the opportunity to continue practising her own skills with a piano that was infinitely superior to anything she had ever played on before. At the same time, she was also benefiting from a most appreciative yet knowledgeable audience.

Her talks with the earl after each performance were never less than stimulating. What's more, he appeared to have an increasing vitality about him every time she came. It was now almost impossible to imagine him as the withdrawn and depressed man that Margaret had described to her prior to their first meeting. So relaxed had they become in each other's company, by now she almost ceased to regard him as an earl at all. His title was hardly ever used by her, nor was it ever referred to by him.

As for her relationship with Margaret, Betty was convinced more than ever that she had found a genuine and generous friend. With Margaret always keen to maximize the time that was set aside for her father's benefit, their piano lessons had become ever shorter. Not that this affected the payments she made. Despite Betty's protests, she always insisted on paying at least five shillings an hour, regardless of how that time was spent.

"Both father and I are so grateful," she would say whenever passing over the money.

For Betty, this was the only uncomfortable part of the arrangement. Especially as she had already received several of the promised riding lessons from Margaret. In fact, had she not been convinced of her friend's considerable wealth, she would have refused to accept any further payment at all. As it was, she knew how much her parents were struggling to get by and fully intended to give them most of what she'd collected when her first week's leave from Bletchley became due the following week.

A chance remark she'd made about the mansion the previous week had given her the opportunity of seeing for herself exactly how wealthy the Pugh family must be. Obviously deeply attached to the place, Margaret immediately offered to give her a brief tour.

Betty was shocked by the state of the house interior. After she remarked on this, Margaret's face tightened. All of the damage would quickly be put right as soon as the war was over, her friend assured her. Betty could not even begin to imagine the cost of such an extensive restoration, but the determined set on Margaret's face showed that she fully intended for the work to be done, regardless of the expense involved.

It became increasingly obvious from the way Margaret spoke how terribly upset she was over the virtual wrecking of their sumptuous home. But then, as they arrived on the top floor, a change came over her. Her voice lightened. So too did her footsteps.

"This is what I really wanted you to see," she began, "the one part of the house that has thankfully so far escaped any damage." She threw open a pair of heavy oak doors. "I pray things will remain that way, and that it can be put to its proper use once again very soon."

For Betty, after seeing all the scarring on the walls and office type functionality of the cheap partitioning, it was like stepping into a completely different world.

"This was our ballroom," Margaret sighed. "I can remember so many wonderful occasions being held in here." She moved over to one of the many casement windows overlooking the countryside. "And the view from this high up on a clear day is simply spectacular."

Betty gazed around, for a few seconds awed by the sheer size and splendour of the immense room. It was by far the biggest in the house, measuring probably ten - possibly even twenty times - the entire floorspace of her own little home. But from amongst all of the surrounding decor, one feature drew her eye far more than any other.

High above, spanning very nearly half of the entire room's ceiling, she could see a vast domed skylight with a multitude of thin gold veins running through it. But this was only a part of the attraction. Suspended on a chain from the centre of the glass dome hung an unbelievably large chandelier with so many individual lights that they were impossible to count. Supplementing this magnificent centrepiece, dozens of elegantly crafted wall lights adorned the walls all the way around the room's perimeter.

The mid-afternoon sun was catching the dome's edge, creating a brilliance that Betty was unable look at directly for more than a few moments. To compensate for this, she had found herself trying to imagine the room as it might have been in bygone evenings, with the chandelier lights blazing and a grand ball in full flow. Picturing all those elegant ladies in their stylish gowns and hearing the strains of a Strauss waltz as they whirled around and around, she had been well able to understand Margaret's wistfulness. It was the kind of occasion that most girls from her part of south London only ever experienced in books or trips to the pictures.

The memory faded. Right at this very moment there were other things for her to concentrate on. With a cloudy sky overhead, it was virtually pitch dark as she picked her way carefully along the path to Hut Fourteen to start the latest of her night shifts. Just two more of these to get through, she told herself. After that she could start preparing for her visit home. She would be so happy to see mum and dad once again.

She was still thinking of this happy reunion as she entered the hut. To her surprise, a naval officer was standing directly beside her usual work station. He was only about ten years older than herself, but judging from the amount of gold bands on his sleeve he was reasonably senior.

He smiled as she approached. "Aircraftwoman Hall?"

"Yes, Sir."

"I am Lieutenant-Commander Straw. Would you come with me please?"

The order was issued in a pleasant enough voice. Even so, Betty could not help but wonder if she had done something wrong. Also anxious over leaving her post just as she was due to start work, she glanced toward her supervisor sitting nearby. The woman merely nodded.

Her head spinning with possible reasons for this mysterious change to her routine, Betty followed the officer back out of the hut.

SIMON LEANED BACK IN his chair to regard the young woman standing a little nervously on the other side of the desk. He had already gathered quite a lot of information about her from her file, especially details of her quite obvious high level of intelligence. Seeing Betty Hall in the flesh now convinced him even further that she would be eminently suitable for the task he was about to put to her. Although pretty in a decidedly feminine way, there was also a discernible air about the girl that spoke of a natural determination and strength of character.

The only possible drawback was, would she willingly go along with what he was about to propose? He could not force her to do so. She was a WAAF wireless operator who was doing a vitally important job exceptionally well. Beyond that, there was no duty requirement compelling her to undertake a completely different role for which she was totally untrained. A role that, if things did turn out the wrong way, might place her in serious danger. This job had to be accepted voluntarily.

He sighed inwardly. If only he had the same choice. Even putting aside any previously unadmitted deeper feelings that he might or might not have held for Margaret, she was still a friend of long standing. To be spying on her in this way felt like the worst kind of betrayal, especially as he was still very much inclined to believe in her innocence. But unlike Betty, he *was* a trained intelligence officer. And no one in their right mind queried an order from Winston…whatever the grounds. All he could do was get on with it.

He gave Betty a friendly smile in an attempt to put her more at ease, then indicated a nearby chair. "Why don't you pull that up and sit down?" he suggested. "From now on we will try to keep this on a completely informal basis. I will call you Betty if that is all right with you?"

After sitting down, she looked him squarely in the eye. "Perfectly all right, Sir."

"Let's drop the 'Sir' bit as well shall we, Betty? At least when no one else is around. I want you to be fully relaxed before we move on."

The first glimmer of a reciprocal smile showed on her face. "Can I take it that I am not in any sort of trouble then?"

"Absolutely not," he assured her.

Barely had he spoken when a thought flashed through his mind.

No trouble. Not yet, anyway.

But if Margaret really was up to her neck in something bad, could he honestly guarantee that trouble would not somehow find Betty if she agreed to do as he asked?

BETTY SHIFTED SLIGHTLY in her chair. Although relieved at this confirmation that she had not unwittingly done something wrong, it also served to further increase the mystery. Why had she been brought to this small office on the top floor of the mansion? Not once since her day of arrival had she so much as set foot inside the place. She had always felt that the grand house was reserved for only the most important people at the Park.

She remained silent. The reason was sure to be made clear soon enough.

"I understand that you have recently been giving piano lessons to Lady Margaret Pugh," he eventually said. "Are you still doing so?"

Of all the questions he might have asked her, this was the last thing Betty was expecting. This was her personal life, and had absolutely nothing to do with her work here.

"Yes, I am," she replied. "As a matter of fact we have become rather good friends. We've been out riding together a few times as well."

For some reason, he appeared pleased to hear this. "Do tell me more, Betty? In fact, I would like to hear everything there is to know about your friendship." He waved a hand. "You know the sort of thing. How often you see each other? Where you go to on your rides? What you might chat about together other than all that piano stuff?"

It was the final one of these suggestions that prompted a rush of indignation within Betty. So that was where all this was leading. They suspected that she might be leaking information.

"I have never discussed my work with Margaret," she said in a voice rather louder than normal. "Nor would I do so in the future. I *have* signed the Official Secrets Act, you know."

He raised a calming hand. "Let me assure you, your discretion is not in doubt. You are not the one being investigated here."

"Then who is?" She paused. "No, surely not Margaret? That's ridiculous. Anyway, she doesn't work here, so how could she possibly know anything?"

His eyes narrowed. "That's true. But she has been asking a few rather leading questions from certain people lately. Enough, I'm afraid, to raise a few doubts over her intentions. What we now have to do is discover whether they were simply innocent enquiries, or if she has indeed become a genuine security risk."

A disbelieving laugh slipped from Betty's mouth. "The daughter of an earl a security risk? You can't be serious. She's an aristocrat. She's from one of this country's most trusted families."

"So is Diana Mitford, who happens to be the daughter of a baron," he pointed out. "And right now, she is locked up in Holloway Prison because of all her pro-Nazi activities."

"Margaret is nothing like her," Betty insisted. "She's kind, and ever so generous. I know she can afford to be, but not all rich people are like that."

He raised an eyebrow. "Rich? Is that what she told you?"

"No, not exactly. But she pays me very well for the piano lessons. And her father owns that big house as well. Margaret showed me around it the other day. She's already making plans to have it restored once the war is over, and that would surely cost an absolute fortune."

Her final remark drew a look of surprise. He chewed on his bottom lip for a long moment before finally speaking.

"I think perhaps there are a few details about Lady Margaret and her father that you should be made aware of," he began.

ONE HALF OF SIMON HATED spelling out the truth of Margaret's situation. If she wanted to put up a pretence of still being wealthy to her new friend, that was her private affair. Doing so could easily be nothing more than a simple matter of pride. But there was a troubling aspect to this revelation as well. One that was setting his mind off along a path that, although distasteful to consider, was starting to appear disturbingly possible.

Margaret's deep love for Hadley House had always been obvious to everyone who knew her. Given that she could never inherit the place, the fact that she retained such a passionate attachment had always been slightly troubling to her closest friends. Himself included. Even before the earl's financial misfortunes had struck, she still would have had to face leaving the house eventually. A few of their group had even privately speculated over how the emotional impact of this might affect her mind when the time to depart eventually arrived.

And yet now, here she was openly talking about restoring her former home after the war as if it was still their own property. Why would she torture herself by doing this? Unless ....

Unless her mind had already been seriously affected? And if that were true, could she really have reached a stage where she might be prepared to pass secrets over to the Nazis? Like it or not, the possibility of this was suddenly starting to go beyond the point of mere speculation. The loss of the estate and the subsequent collapse of her father's health, not to mention the extensive damage to her beloved Hadley Hall, might easily have been enough to turn Margaret's ire against the government into something far more extreme. Especially if someone working against Britain were to offer her restoration of the family estate in return for a few pieces of vital information about the Park.

But this posed another question. What with all their problems in Russia and the Americans joining the war, Germany was definitely on the back foot these days. Even if they did try to tempt her with the one thing that she wanted more than anything else in the world, why would Margaret risk backing a losing side?

Simon's mind was now racing. The ground beneath Hitler's feet may be looking a little shaky at present, but it hadn't always been that way. During the months after Dunkirk, a Nazi invasion had been a real possibility. Even back in the 1930s, Germany had already begun to look like an invincible force on the rise.

The 1930s! With a rush, Simon recalled how Margaret had accompanied the British eventing team to the Berlin Olympics. Could she possibly have been recruited by the Nazis that far back?

It was certainly a time in her life when anger over the treatment of her father would still have been at its most raw. With hindsight, it was obvious that Germany had been preparing for a full-scale war even then. In those days, from their position of imposing strength, any offer they might have made concerning the return of Hadley House and the estate would have felt like a very tempting proposition indeed to an embittered Margaret.

If all this was true - and at present it was still only conjecture - that opened up another highly disturbing question. Was the earl involved in this as well? In many ways, he had even more cause than Margaret to feel disaffection over the way things had been done.

Most of these thoughts he would keep to himself for now, Simon decided, even though he was asking an awful lot of Betty. But there were some facts that she most certainly needed to know of before progressing any further.

He began to speak.

THE REVELATION THAT Hadley House and its estate had not belonged to the earl for close to ten years stunned Betty. Although thinking back, she could not recall him ever making a single remark to suggest that it did.

But Margaret certainly had. She'd frequently spoken in a way that implied ownership. And this was not restricted to just the mansion. When out riding together over the estate, her brief exchanges with the farmers they came across suggested that all of them still held her in the kind of high regard normally reserved for landowners. Vegetables, fruit, and even a few choice cuts of meat had all been offered up and gracefully accepted.

To discover that Margaret was living in the cottage and using the stables only by courtesy of a temporary arrangement with the government covering the earl's lifetime was astonishing. Even the old groom called Tom she had been introduced to and who had apparently been there for over forty years still continued to address Margaret as 'My Lady'. All in all, Betty felt sure that no one could laugh at her for assuming ownership the way she had.

However, what was far more astounding than any of this, initially to the point of being almost unbelievable, was the news that the woman she was already coming to regard as a close friend might in fact be a Nazi spy. But why were they telling her about their suspicions? Was it simply to order her to end the friendship and keep well away from the woman in future?

She put this final thought into words.

He smiled at her before replying. He was doing rather a lot of that, she felt. Not that it was unpleasant. If he was an intelligence officer, it was probably all part of his technique to relax people when interviewing them.

"Actually," he said, "staying away from Lady Margaret is the complete opposite of what I would ask of you."

Betty frowned, though she did not miss the significance of the word 'ask'. He wanted her to do something, but it was going to be a request, not an order. Strange indeed.

"I'm sorry, I'm not quite sure I understand," she replied. "Are you saying that you want me to spend even *more* time in her company?"

"If possible. But only in a manner that appears to be perfectly natural. She mustn't suspect that it's contrived. Not in the slightest."

The penny dropped with a resounding clatter. Betty was incredulous. "You are asking me to spy on her? Is that correct?"

"In a way... yes."

"What other way is there to describe it?"

He smiled yet again, although this time she felt it was more to ease his own awkwardness than anything else. Somehow, this gave her confidence.

"None really," he admitted.

He pressed on, just as she was about to respond. "I realise that you are totally untrained for this kind of stuff. And that it's a thoroughly rotten thing to ask of you." He gave an almost apologetic laugh. "I mean, no one likes a sneak, do they? Unfortunately, during wars like this, being sneaky is sometimes the only way we have of dealing with certain situations. This is one of those times, and you are the only person we know of who is ideally placed to be that sneak."

In spite of everything, Betty could not help but grin at his analogy. "Is that the best way you have of convincing me to do what you want?"

He grinned back at her. "Sadly, I think it probably is."

She had never met a male officer from any of the services like him before: certainly not one as high up as he was. Normally, senior ranks were unbearably stuffy. Yet here she was – a mere Aircraftwoman - talking to him as though they were military equals.

"Let me understand this fully," she said. "I do have a choice in this matter. I can either volunteer, or I can walk away without a black mark against my name. Is that right?"

He nodded, but all trace of his grin had now disappeared. "That about sums it up. But two things you should bear in mind. Firstly, I cannot stress how important this investigation is to national security. The Prime Minister himself has instructed for it to take place and is being kept fully informed."

His eyes locked onto hers. "Secondly, if you do choose to walk away, no one...not a living soul...must ever hear a word of what we have discussed in this room. I'm well aware that you have been fully vetted and have signed the Official Secrets Act. Regardless of that, I would be failing in my duty if I were to not once again remind you of the need for total confidentiality."

The sudden change in his tone was alarming. For a second or two, Betty felt slighted. One minute he had been sounding almost like a pal, the next he was being unbendingly stern. Of course she was aware of her responsibilities. Hadn't she been reminded of them often enough?

The fact that Winston Churchill himself had played a direct hand in this then fully sunk in. If that was the case, it really must be every bit as important as he'd said.

"If I do volunteer, what exactly will it involve?" she asked.

"At first, nothing much more than cultivating the friendship while keeping your eyes and ears open for anything suspicious." He drew a breath. "I'll be frank with you, Betty. I think it's quite possible that Lady Margaret has deliberately arranged these piano lessons as a way of getting close to you and winning your confidence. Do all you can to make her believe that she has succeeded. Let's see if she is drawn into asking you anything about your work or what you might have seen here inside the Park."

"And if she does. What then?"

"Maybe then we'll test her a bit further by passing on a few choice pieces of false information. See where that leads us to. Our listening stations are confident that there have been no suspicious radio broadcasts originating from anywhere within this area for some considerable time, so the only other way she would have of relaying her messages would be through some sort of personal contact."

Betty frowned. *Passing on false information.* All of a sudden, her role in this was starting to sound very spy-like indeed. How deep might it go? If Margaret really was working for the Nazis, where might her personal contact be? Somewhere close by? And what if she got found out and was suddenly confronted by a great big German agent? One with a gun?

A nervous shiver ran through her. Or was it more than that? Fear possibly?

A memory of the day when she had broken the news to her parents about joining the WAAFs came rushing back. Her father had made a jocular remark about the Germans not having a chance now. She'd told him that she wasn't going to be a hero, just a teleprinter operator.

Her mother had agreed. *'We don't want her to be winning any medals, Dan. We just want her to be safe,'* she'd said.

Betty still did not want to be a hero. But nor did she want to be a coward. From the way she could see it, there was very little wriggle room. It was either all in, or all out.

"Sorry, Mum," she whispered almost silently.

Only then did she realise that, for the last half-minute, she had been lost in her thoughts. She refocused her attention on the Lieutenant-Commander. He was gazing at her, his expression suggesting he could well understand all the possibilities that were passing through her mind.

"It looks like you've got a volunteer," she told him.

His smile returned. "Thank you, Betty," he said. "I had a strong feeling all along that you would not refuse to help us out. Even so, it's still a relief to hear it confirmed. As you must have realised, there is absolutely no one else as ideally qualified as yourself for this particular job. The simple truth is, you'd be almost impossible to replace."

In spite of her still rising apprehension, for some unfathomable reason Betty wanted to make a light-hearted comment in response. Wasn't that what characters in books and films often did before embarking on a risky adventure? Although well aware that this was real life, in a weird kind of way she felt as if she were about to start acting out a role in a story as well.

"I hadn't realised that piano tutors were in such short supply," she remarked.

He laughed, but there was also a flash of admiration in his eyes. "We must get started at once," he said. "When is the next time you've arranged to meet up with Lady Margaret?"

"Not for a week or so. I've got some leave coming up, so I was planning to go home and visit my parents. I haven't seen them for ages."

He frowned and shook his head. "I'm sorry, but you'll have to postpone that for a little while longer. We can't afford even a slight delay on this job. If she *is* passing on information, it's vital that we discover what it consists of as soon as possible, and who it's going to."

His words, although provoking a surge of disappointment in Betty, were hardly unexpected. The war wasn't going to stop just so that she could have her little family reunion.

Another thought then kicked in. Had she gone home, both of her parents would have quickly sensed that there was something weighing heavily on her mind. Solely out of concern, they would have kept niggling away endlessly to discover what it was troubling her.

"I understand," she told him. "It's probably for the best, anyway."

FOURTEEN

For Margaret, the news that Betty wasn't going to be away for a week as first thought had two fortunate aspects.

Her father made no secret over his delight that he would not now be missing out on any of his regular recitals and discussions. Of late, he was claiming more and more of Betty's time during her visits, going so far as to dig out the sheet music for many of his favourite compositions for her to play. Margaret's own piano lessons had become nothing more than a minor sideshow. Not that she minded; it continued to warm her heart just to see him taking such an active interest. He was like a new man, in the last few days even returning once again with renewed vigour to his long-abandoned mobility exercises.

The other fortunate aspect came about when Betty mentioned the reason for the postponement of her visit home. For a few moments she appeared to be almost on the point of tears over missing out on her trip.

"I haven't got a clue why, but all leave in our section of work has been cancelled for a time," she revealed. "Mum and Dad will be so disappointed I'm not coming. We haven't seen each other since just after the Blitz."

Almost at once, she frowned. "Maybe I shouldn't have mentioned that bit about the leave being cancelled. I don't want you to think I'm a blabbermouth or anything. I'm not...honestly."

"Of course I don't think that," Margaret assured her. "Anyway, it's not as if you've told me something that's terribly secretive. And we are good friends, aren't we?"

On hearing this, Betty perked up. "Yes, good friends," she agreed. "And if I can't be at home, then being here with you and the earl is certainly the next best thing."

After she had left the cottage, Margaret further considered what she had learned.

Why had all leave in Betty's section been cancelled? The military did not normally do that without a strong reason, so was there a crisis of some sort going on? It wasn't possible to know for certain unless Betty let something further slip. But even this was useful information that should be added to her latest report. On the spur of the moment, she decided to exaggerate what she had discovered. It would add some much-needed urgency to matters.

She was getting more than a little tired of waiting for Goering to act on her information.

SIMON GLANCED AT HIS watch and then lit a cigarette. With Betty due at his office any minute to make her latest report, he was praying that she would have at least one new insight to pass on. By now, even though the evidence was still mostly speculative, he had already as good as convinced himself that Margaret was definitely guilty of something. The main question was, how damaging that something might turn out to be.

After recalling her visit to Berlin for the Olympics, Simon had immediately arranged for MI5 to have a discreet word with a Colonel Timothy Albriton, the man responsible for arranging the trip and someone who had been in her company for much of the time while they were over there. What the colonel had told them was revealing.

A man of singular memory, he recalled a conversation with Margaret during the pre-Olympic training period at Hadley House in which she stated that some of her friends in London considered Hitler to be: *'Just a strong leader who has performed wonders for the German economy'*. She'd also described him as: *'The very best means available of preventing the spread of communism in Europe'*. At the time, Albriton had put this down to nothing more than youthful naivety. Several of the titled young set had carried similar views back then.

When pressed on Margaret's activities outside of the games, he had been far less precise. No, he stated, he had personally never witnessed her in the wrong sort of company, or indeed doing anything untoward. On the other hand, whilst staying in a reasonably close-knit group during the competition itself, neither he nor anyone else attached to the eventing team had seen anything much of her during their last couple of days in Berlin. They all presumed that she had gone on some last-minute sightseeing and preferred to do this alone. But the plain truth was, she could have been up to almost anything during that time.

The colonel's reference to communism registered quite sharply with Simon. He recalled the earl's well documented anti-Soviet views. Once again he was forced to consider whether Margaret's father might be implicated alongside her.

Acutely aware of the potential seriousness of the situation – not to mention Winston Churchill's renowned impatience - his concern over the lack of progress was growing. More than a week had passed, and despite Betty's calculated mention of her leave being cancelled, Margaret had made no further reference to this. Not even a nibble of curiosity.

Betty came into his office just as he was stubbing his cigarette out, and the wrinkling of her nose when catching a whiff of the fumes was hard to miss. It was a little unusual to see such a reaction. Almost everybody seemed to smoke these days. He then remembered that Margaret had also often found it hard to conceal a similar distaste for the habit.

The relationship between himself and Betty had gradually become even less formal than during their first meeting. Simon had encouraged this; he had asked her to do a tricky job and wanted her to be aware of how much he appreciated her cooperation. He had even told her to address him by his first name if she wanted to when there was no one else about. Not that she had yet chosen to do so.

As she pulled up a chair and sat down, Simon heaved an inward sigh. He could already tell from her expression that she had little of consequence to report.

After hearing this confirmed, he rapped a hand on the top of his desk in frustration. "When are you meeting up with her next?" he asked.

"I tried to arrange a riding lesson for this Saturday," Betty told him. "But it's a no-go, I'm afraid." For a moment she looked genuinely disappointed. "I'm becoming rather fond of this horse-riding lark, and that's the first time she's not gone along with one of my suggestions."

Simon was instantly alert. "You don't think she suspects something?"

"No, nothing like that, I'm sure of it. It's just that she'd already made plans to go to Newmarket on Saturday. Apparently that's the day they're running some quite important race called the Two Thousand Guineas. She said that she really doesn't want to miss it."

He jerked sharply forward. "That's what she said. I mean *exactly* what she said. That she *really* doesn't want to miss it?"

"Yes, that's what she told me." Betty frowned. "What's the matter? Is it important?"

"I certainly think so. You see, I know for a fact that Margaret absolutely hates professional horse racing. She has done so for many years."

A look of confusion came over Betty. "That doesn't make sense. She loves horses, anybody can see that much. Anyway, how do you know what she likes and doesn't like?"

Simon placed a hand on his forehead and remained silent for a few seconds. He badly wanted another cigarette, but did not wish to make the air any more unpleasant for her.

"I think it's only fair that I make a few things clear to you, Betty," he eventually said.

He spent the next few minutes explaining about his past relationship with Margaret, though taking care to speak of her as just one of a sizeable group of friends and leaving out all mention of whatever romantic ambitions he might have had in her direction.

He then came on to why she loathed professional horse racing so much.

"About a dozen of us all went to a meeting at Brighton back in the early thirties," he began. "It was a total disaster. Right from the very beginning Margaret was horrified by what she described as *'the violent and excessive use of the whip'*. I certainly agree there was far more of it than usual that day; you could actually see several of the mounts bleeding from their hind quarters. Then, in one of the races, a horse stumbled over and had to be destroyed. It wasn't so much this as the jockey's attitude to the killing that really enraged her. He simply shrugged and was heard saying something about it only being a bloody horse, and that there were plenty more rides to be had."

"I think I would have felt exactly the same way as Margaret," Betty said in a much quieter yet firm voice. "I hate any kind of cruelty to animals."

Simon nodded approvingly. "Anyway, after that she became totally convinced that horse racing was not a sport at all but a particularly nasty business that was all about the money and betting, with little or no thought given to the horses' welfare. To her mind, this was conclusively proven by what happened just before the last race of the day."

He paused for a few seconds while recalling the sheer violence that had taken place.

"Go on," Betty told him. "What did happen?"

"An enormous fight broke out between two gangs. It was pretty horrific stuff, with hammers, iron bars and razors all being used."

Betty's eyes widened. "What were they fighting about?"

"That's the thing. Just like Margaret said, it was all about the money and betting. They were damn near killing each other just to establish which gang controlled the bookies at the course. The worst part was, several entirely innocent people got rather badly hurt as well before the police moved in."

He sighed. "It was a day I'll certainly never forget. But for Margaret, it went way deeper. She swore that she would never go anywhere near a race meeting again. And yet now you are telling me that—"

"I haven't made a mistake," Betty cut in. "I know what she said."

For a moment he could see indignation in her eyes. He made a calming gesture. "I don't doubt you, I promise. But you can see why this might be so important. If she really is going there, then it's quite possibly for a reason other than the racing."

"Maybe I should ask if I can go along with her?" Betty suggested. "Her reaction to that might tell us something."

Simon shook his head. "No, I've got a better idea. Why don't you offer to play for her father while she is at Newmarket? I'm sure they would both like that very much, and it would also give you a chance to talk to the earl alone for a change. That might help to clear up the question of whether he is involved as well. See if you can get him chatting about the war effort or something."

"Very well, I'll try."

Simon noted the slight lack of enthusiasm in Betty's voice. He had previously told her all about the earl's anti-communist beliefs, and spelled out the reasons why he might possibly detest the government sufficiently to seek revenge. Especially if the return of Hadley House was in the offing.

To his surprise, she'd as good as rejected the possibility out of hand. He suspected that somewhere along the line a genuine fondness had developed between the pair. Another greatly unexpected turn of events given the earl's antisocial disposition ever since his stroke.

"If I do that, what about Margaret going to Newmarket?" Betty asked. "Will someone else be keeping an eye on her while she's there?"

Simon gave her a reassuring smile. "Oh yes. You can be sure of that."

FIFTEEN

A s always, regardless of which race meeting she was at, Margaret did not intend to linger any longer than necessary at Newmarket's July Course. Even before completing her business with Joe, she took little interest in what was happening on the track. She would never forget what she had witnessed on that horrible day at Brighton and had no wish to risk repeating the experience.

Be that as it may, she could not fail to be aware of the huge sense of expectation amongst the near capacity crowd. Big Game, a powerful colt owned by the king and unbeaten in six previous outings, was a red-hot favourite for the Two Thousand Guineas. There had not been a royal owned winner of the season's opening classic for well over thirty years, and sentiment combined with form meant that a large majority of those present had a stake in Big Game's anticipated victory. It would be a very bad day for the bookies if the colt did succeed in pulling off a seventh win in a row.

Margaret spotted Joe strolling around a section of the course close to the paddock enclosure, the leather satchel he used to carry both his tip envelopes and the day's takings slung casually over his shoulder. As usual, a bunch of young children were following in his wake, all of them fascinated by his colourful costume and cheerful banter. Every now and then he would stop to hand out a small packet of boiled sweets for his little band of followers to share out amongst themselves, adding even further to his popularity with children and adults alike.

Sweets distributed, he then set off again, the sound of his rhyming catchphrase carrying clearly over all the other competing sounds.

"I'm the bloke who tells it straight. Come and say hello.

There ain't no better tipster. So give it a go with Joe."

Today, more than ever, he was doing a roaring trade, making everyone laugh while handing out his customary sealed tips, words of wisdom, and even an occasional autograph to the enthusiastic crowd. Margaret found herself wondering wryly if he would dare to tip any other horse but Big Game for the day's main race.

She fingered the envelope tucked securely into the side pocket of her lightweight jacket. The message she had for Goering was longer than usual and had taken quite some time to encode. In it, she claimed to now have the absolute proof he was demanding. She had established beyond any doubt from an inside informer that Bletchley Park was a major codebreaking centre and a very real danger to Germany. He must order its bombing as soon as possible. To further enhance the urgency of the matter, she went on to add that, such was the importance of the place, Winston Churchill himself had made a point of visiting there twice during the past year.

She had no idea if there was even a scrap of truth in this final claim, but it might prove to be the final push that Goering needed to act on her information. Once the full importance of Bletchley Park's wartime role was eventually revealed he would be sure to honour all of his promises regarding Hadley House. Nothing...nothing at all...was more important than that.

Even with the hubbub of a thousand different distracting noises around her, the mere prospect of the estate's permanent return created a flood of happy memories recalling when she and her parents had been one of the most respected families for many miles around. For a tantalising moment, she even had a vision of eventually being able to pass Hadley House on to her own children. She wasn't too old for childbirth yet. There was still time.

The dream quickly evaporated. Before any of this could come about, the war had to end and the right side had to win. She must carry on doing all she could to ensure that outcome.

Joe was wearing a red cravat, which meant he had no message to pass on. Not that she was expecting one. In his last communication, Goering had stated very clearly that he wanted solid proof of Bletchley Park's importance, and that no bombing raid would take place without such evidence. His tone of voice also strongly implied that he had just about lost patience with her continued failure to supply any meaningful intelligence.

You fool, Goering, she found herself thinking. Nothing could be more important than what I've already been trying to tell you. But you'll see soon enough. All you have to do is send your bombers. Then you'll realise how much you owe to me.

Joe was now so busy that he had come to a complete standstill. There wasn't exactly an orderly queue lining up for his services, rather more a cluster of potential customers several people deep, with those at the front waving a hand to be summoned next. As was the accepted custom whenever it became as busy as this, everyone stayed back a regulation six feet from where Joe was standing until being beckoned forward. This allowed each new client at least the suggestion of a brief private audience with the man who many now regarded as a cult figure and an essential part of the English racing scene. Margaret joined at the rear of those waiting.

"Who's next to give it a go with Joe?" he called out as another of his followers moved away to one side clutching their envelope.

"Ow abawt me, Joe?" a rather posh looking man in his early twenties shouted out in an excruciatingly bad fake cockney accent. Pushing his way imperiously past several others in front, he stepped right inside the sacrosanct zone. "'Fink you can show me a 'fing or two."

Giggling loudly, the equally posh looking young lady clinging onto his arm seemed to find her boyfriend's intervention highly amusing.

Margaret had seen it all before. There was nearly always one privately educated idiot who thought it the height of satire to mimic Joe and try to belittle him. She knew he had various ways of dealing with such people.

Joe smiled broadly at the newcomer for a moment before bowing theatrically. "Hey, look over here, everybody," he called out at the top of his voice. "Would you Adam and Eve it? We've got a gen..yoo..ine, twenty-four carat celebrity amongst us."

A brief hiatus followed as people tried unsuccessfully to identify the queue jumper. Several perplexed glances were exchanged.

Joe then shrugged. "Nah, to tell you the truth, I don't know who the 'eck he is either. But he's gotta be someone worth makin' a big song and dance over or else he wouldn't think he's got the right to come bargin' his way past all you others the way he has."

He switched his gaze directly back onto the young man. "I got it! You're someone off the wireless, ain't ya. That's why no one here recognises you. But don't be shy. Tell us all who you are and put us out of our misery. Do you read the news or summit?"

By now, Joe's target had turned bright red with embarrassment. Equally humiliatingly, his girlfriend had released her grip and was inching slowly backwards as if to disassociate herself from him.

"Is this how you treat all of your customers," the young man blustered, his accent now most definitely from the privileged upper classes. "If you must know, I was only having a joke. I didn't want one of your rotten tips anyway. I wouldn't pay even a penny for one."

Joe waved his remarks aside. "That don't matter, my son. I'll give you one for free. It's Joe's tip of the day, and it's especially for you." His voice lowered a couple of notches in volume, even taking on a slightly avuncular tone. "Learn yourself some manners, young 'un. Manners is what separates a proper gent from them who's only pretending to be one."

"Too right, Joe," a man's voice called out. "You tell him, mate."

Several others joined in to express similar sentiments.

Realising that this was a battle he was never going to win, after shooting Joe a baleful look, the young man began to skulk away. His equally embarrassed looking girlfriend tried to renew her hold on his arm, but had it shaken irritably away. Their departure was accompanied by a loud chorus of laughter.

"So, back to business," Joe announced. "Who's next to give it a go with Joe?" He cast his eye about and then pointed straight at Margaret. "Ow about you, young lady?"

Her selection took Margaret totally by surprise. With Joe's audience shifting around to get a better view of the departing couple and call mockingly after them, almost without noticing it, she had somehow drifted close to the front.

A flutter of nerves struck her as she reached to her jacket pocket. At this stage she would normally have had the envelope folded small and in her hand ready to pass discreetly over. But with everybody's eyes already on her, to produce it now was certain to risk attracting unwanted curiosity. She was meant to be simply collecting an envelope, not handing one over.

"What's the matter?" Joe enquired. "Feelin' shy, are we? Come on, I promise I won't bite."

Shut up, you stupid man, she wanted to shout at him. Can't you see I've got a problem? And why the hell did it have to happen for the very first time today of all days? This message was by far the most important one she had ever sent. It had to be delivered quickly. It must be. But people were already staring at her, and the competing urge to simply hurry away was rapidly gaining strength.

At last Joe seemed to realise that something was wrong. Margaret gave a small sigh of relief as the showman in him quickly took over.

"I've got an idea," he told everyone. "Instead of me handin' this lovely lady one of my tips, why don't I get *her* to tell *me* what she fancies for the big race? That'd be a change, eh!"

His suggestion was instantly met with great amusement. Regular racegoers were well used to Joe coming up with an unexpected twist on the usual routine. This unpredictability was a big part of his appeal.

He held out an inviting hand to Margaret. "Come on, love. Step up here and tell old Joe what you think he needs to know. I can keep a secret, honest I can." Raising the other hand up to his ear, he added with an elaborate wink to the audience: "You can whisper it in me shell-like so none of these others can hear."

Tense as she was, Margaret still could not help but feel a flash of admiration for the way he had so smartly adapted to an awkward situation. Stepping forward, she moved in close to speak softly in his ear.

"The message is still inside my jacket," she told him, twisting her body sideways so that the relevant pocket was temporarily obscured from the onlookers by his large leather satchel. "Can you take it out without anyone noticing or should I come back later?"

Joe nodded slowly several times, as if deliberating on the shrewdness of her words.

"Gotcha!" he then announced loudly. "Between you and me, love, I think we're onto a winner. We've got this one in the bag."

Dipping into the satchel, he pulled out a half crown piece. To Margaret's astonishment, he plonked the coin in her hand and closed her fingers over it.

"Don't let anyone say that Joe don't pay for good information," he announced with a grin.

His audience loved it. As she stepped back amongst them, Joe gave a loud chuckle that seemed to hang in the air for an unnaturally long time. "I 'ope she don't ever want to take up this tippin' lark as a professional. She'd put me outa business good and proper."

It was with mixed emotions that Margaret moved away from the scene. Her jacket pocket was now empty, so the vital message was safely on its journey. That was good. On the other hand, she was far from comfortable over the way the handover had been done this time. Yes, she should have been better prepared, but surely Joe could have completed matters without attracting quite so much attention directly at her. Normally their exchanges were done quickly, and she was just one of many who were receiving a tip from him. After today, people were liable to remember her far more clearly. And that was definitely *not* good.

"Why hello, Margaret. How lovely to see you."

Engrossed in her reflections, for an instant the unexpected greeting shook her. She glanced up and saw that the voice belonged to Sir Hubert Harding, an old acquaintance of her father's.

"Hello, Sir Hubert," she responded, trying hard not to let her discomposure show.

He ran his eyes over her. "You're looking well, my girl. But how about your father? I haven't seen anything of him for years, not even at the club. He used to love it in there, you know."

"He doesn't venture out very much these days," she told him. "As for the club, that's probably the last place he would wish to go now. Even after so long, I'm sure that the memory of what happened to him there is still very raw indeed."

He nodded. "That's true. To be honest, the bounder caught me out for a tidy sum as well, although it was nothing like the loss that Henry suffered. The fact is, quite a few members had their fingers burned. The stink it raised caused no end of problems for those of us on the committee. Especially me."

Memories of what Richard had told her in the Tiergarten about the fraudster came flooding back. "It's a pity the committee did not see fit to continue with a 'No Jewish' policy in the same way that many of the other leading clubs do," she pointed out dryly.

"What!" Sir Hubert looked utterly astonished that she should even suggest such a thing. "Of course we bally well do. No Jew has ever been accepted as a member of our club. Not even as a temporary one. As a long-time member of the committee, I can absolutely assure you of that." He snorted indignantly. "The very idea of it is preposterous."

"But I was told that the fraudster was Jewish. So were two leading members who chose to invest with him."

His indignation subsiding, Sir Hubert allowed himself a merry chortle. "Oh, my dear Margaret. Someone has indeed been filling your pretty little head with a lot of nonsense."

Just as he finished speaking, an announcement was made over the public address system, prompting Sir Hubert to pluck a gold watch from his waistcoat. "My word, is it that time already? I must dash. Important matters to attend to and all that. But please do pass on my best wishes to Henry."

Still chuckling to himself, he hurried away.

Margaret watched him go with lips firmly set. Pretty little head, indeed. How dare he suggest that, just because she was a woman, she was automatically more gullible than him. The real proof of gullibility lay in rushing blindly into buying shares in a mine that didn't exist. Which meant there must be quite a large number of fools residing in that precious club of his. She felt she could quite fairly exempt her father from this classification. He had made his investment out of love and a desperate need to provide for her future once he was gone. But as for all those others, greed had almost certainly been their prime motivation.

Pushing these irate thoughts aside, her mind turned to Richard. He had clearly lied to her about the fraudster being Jewish, and his willingness to make use of her father's misfortunes in order to deceive her left Margaret shocked to the core. How could he have been so cynically cruel? This was a man who she'd once considered to be her most trusted friend and confidant within their social circle. Casual boyfriends had come and gone, but the platonic relationship with Richard had outlasted them all. She had genuinely felt a hole in her life after he suddenly disappeared from the scene.

Yet clearly none of this meant a thing to him. It was all so clear now and confirmed what she had suspected all along. That their 'chance encounter' had been nothing of the sort.. His callous deception, and the time he had spent so charmingly showing her around selected parts of Berlin, had obviously been nothing more than a ruse to make her more sympathetic to Nazi doctrine. To make her that much more susceptible to Goering's proposition when it subsequently came. And like a gullible fool, she had fallen for it.

Acceptance of his duplicity gave rise to a host of other considerations, all of which seemed to come rushing into her head at the same time. It was far too much to think about at present. For good or bad, her message had been delivered and was on its way. She could hardly go back to Joe and ask him to return it.

Eager to be gone, she set off across the wide field; it was a good two-mile walk to the railway station. Behind her, a loud roar from the crowd signified that another race had just begun.

FROM THE ELEVATED POSITION of her father's private box and with a powerful pair of binoculars at her disposal, Cynthia Bagsure had an excellent overview of the July Course. After taking a small sip of champagne, she leaned back in her armchair to think for a few moments.

When Simon had summoned her to a small office inside the Park mansion and spoken of his suspicions regarding Margaret, she'd at first been genuinely astonished. Even more so when he went on to tell her how he was now making use of Betty. In spite of the discussion they'd had about Margaret while sitting beside the lake a few weeks earlier, it had never occurred to her that he might actually suspect her sister's old friend of being a spy. After all, this *was* Margaret. And whether or not Simon cared to admit it, everyone knew how deeply he'd felt about her back in the old days.

Gradually though, her astonishment had faded as Simon started going into the details of all the damning little things he'd discovered. Individually, they perhaps did not mean very much. But when put together, at the very least they were certainly substantial enough to cast a huge shadow of doubt over Margaret's recent activities. They were also sufficient to gain Cynthia's cooperation in fulfilling a watching brief today. She did not tell Simon this, but she was a huge racing fan herself and was planning to meet her father at Newmarket for the big race anyway.

From her vantage point she'd had little trouble in spotting Margaret, even amongst all the many others milling about. Not only was she wearing the same rather distinctive tan coloured jacket that she'd worn to the show at Bletchley Road school hall, she also had on what looked like the same blouse and skirt combination as well. Cynthia could not help but briefly wonder how diminished Margaret's wardrobe must currently be when compared with the good old days before misfortune had overtaken her father.

For a short time, Margaret had wandered about the concourse as if keeping an eye open for someone. The tipster everyone knew as Joe Bull then appeared, and almost immediately she began moving over in his direction. This brought a frown to Cynthia's face. Simon had assured her that Margaret would never place a bet on a horse as a matter of principal, so what was the attraction for her with Joe?

Before long, a sizeable crowd had gathered around the tipster, with Margaret remaining amongst them. Through the powerful binoculars, Cynthia was able to see there was much laughter going on. Then, adding even further to her curiosity, she saw Margaret suddenly step forward and lean in close to whisper something into Joe's ear. He responded by apparently cracking another joke and pressing what was possibly a coin from his satchel into her hand. Whatever the joke was, while it appeared to go down well with his audience, Margaret did not look to be very amused at all. In fact, only moments after this she was moving away from the scene with a firmly set jaw.

Then she was approached by Sir Hubert Harding.

For a second, Cynthia felt almost sorry for Margaret. Spending any amount of time with that pompous old fool was not something she would wish on anyone. However, their conversation did not last for long before he scuttled away. Cynthia noted that there had been no physical contact between the pair, excluding the possibility of anything but words being exchanged.

Once free of Sir Hubert, Margaret set off in full stride across a field leading away from the course. She clearly had no further interest in the day's events. Whatever she had come for, it was now done.

Having considered all of this, Cynthia rose from her chair. "I'll only be gone for a few minutes," she told her father before heading off toward the nearest public phone.

With the next race about to get underway and his attention fixed firmly on the track, he barely heard her.

"THANK YOU, CYNTHIA. Well done! Please give my regards to Viscount Holding."

After replacing the receiver, Simon leaned back in his office chair.

One half of him could barely contain his excitement. Put together with everything else that he knew about Margaret, this latest news seemed to pretty much confirm matters. Under normal circumstances, Joe Bull was exactly the type of racecourse character that she would go out of her way to avoid. Margaret's encounter with him could only have been for reasons that had nothing at all to do with tips or gambling. The possibility that he was the personal contact she was using to pass on her messages was now looking to be extremely likely, especially with all of that close contact involved.

He briefly recalled the prime minister's reasons for placing him in charge of this investigation: that he would be ideally placed to quickly spot any little abnormalities in Margaret's behaviour that a stranger might easily miss. Yet again, Winnie's judgement had proved to be spot on.

Simon lit a cigarette. Despite the exhilaration of making such a significant step forward, another side of him could not help but feel a certain sadness. Someone who he had once been especially fond of - he still would not admit to any stronger feelings than that, no matter what Cynthia and her sister might imagine - was now almost certainly confirmed as being a traitor. That was a very hard thing to accept.

But accept it, he must. He stubbed out the less than half smoked cigarette in the already overflowing ashtray. There was only one thing he could do now.

Picking up the telephone once again, he dialled the number that he knew would bring all kinds of extra forces into play.

And once they were involved, the game was liable to get very much tougher indeed.

SIXTEEN

J oe eased his motorcycle away from the road junction. Only another couple of blocks to go and he would be back home.

It had been a highly profitable day at the Newmarket meeting, even though his stream of customers had dried up considerably after the day's big race. By then, most punters were far too busy celebrating their winning bets on the king's horse to bother with him. Their cheers as Big Game romped home by four lengths was possibly the loudest reception he had ever heard given to a winner. With a certain amount of inside knowledge to back up more than mere sentiment, he had even put the hefty sum of fifty pounds on Big Game himself. Despite it being an odds-on favourite, that had still given him a healthy profit of over thirty-five pounds. Shortly afterwards, highly satisfied with the day's takings, just for a change he'd decided to leave a meeting before the final few races.

It was still early evening and broad daylight when he swung the Royal Enfield into the driveway of his lodging house. After pulling the machine up onto its centre stand, he used a padlock and chain from the left-hand pannier box to secure it in place. From the other pannier, he removed his bulging leather satchel.

"Why don't you let me take that bag for you, Joe?" a voice suggested.

He suddenly became aware of two burly men standing uncomfortably close to him, one on either side. He flinched. Where in God's name had they sprung up from? Before he could even begin to think of an answer to this, one of them had his left arm in a half-nelson that, although not quite fierce enough to be painful, was only just short of the mark.

"What the 'ell's goin' on?" Joe demanded. "Get your 'ands off me."

He received no reply other than a brief increase in the pressure on his arm that did actually produce a short stab of pain. Taking the hint, he could only watch in silence as the other man inspected the inside of both panniers.

"Nothing else in here apart from these," he announced, holding up Joe's union jack tailcoat and Tudor rose cap.

The man beside Joe nodded and then released his grip. He leaned in closer, at the same time brushing the sleeve of Joe's leather riding jacket almost as if apologising for the rough treatment.

"Now don't make a fuss, old chap," he said. "You know it won't get you anywhere."

He paused for this message to sink in before continuing. "First of all, I want you to hand that satchel you are still holding so protectively over to my colleague. After that, I'd be most frightfully grateful if you'd just come along with me and get into that car parked on the other side of the road."

The fact that his words were spoken in a quiet and perfectly polite tone somehow made them even more chilling than if they'd been snarled.

Joe could feel his heart suddenly banging hard against his ribs. Plain clothes coppers didn't talk like this. These were almost certainly MI5 agents: more than anyone the very people he had long been fearing a visit from. He'd always known that if British military intelligence got even a sniff of his real identity and IRA activities back in Ireland, let alone all of this secretive message passing he'd been pressured into doing with the posh sounding woman, they would hang him without a second thought. That was the grim possibility he had been forced to live with for close on twenty years.

And now that possibility seemed to be turning into reality.

The quiet residential street was currently empty of any passers-by. Whether anyone was watching from a nearby window, Joe couldn't say. Not that there would be any point in shouting out for help. Not with these blokes on his case. They could do whatever they damn well liked.

After handing over the satchel, he allowed himself to be firmly guided across the road and into the back of the waiting black saloon. There really wasn't much else he could do. Even if he hadn't been handicapped by the slight limp that these days was little more than a minor irritation, this pair were far too strong and capable for him to overcome. With a third man already behind the wheel, the car set off the moment they were all inside.

The vehicle had barely travelled a hundred yards when a black hood was suddenly thrust over Joe's head. However much he had been rattled before, this was now far worse. The feeling of vulnerability that the sudden darkness produced seemed to make everything a thousand times more threatening. It was almost as if they were dragging him to the scaffold already.

Trapped between the pair in the back, his mind was working furiously in an attempt to create a story that might provide some sort of defence for himself. But without knowing why he had been picked up and what they had on him, this was an almost impossible task. There was only one thing he knew for certain; MI5 did not get involved with small time stuff.

He was in a whole world of trouble.

STILL DEEPLY TROUBLED following her brief conversation with Sir Hubert Harding, Margaret arrived back at the cottage to find her father sat in his usual armchair. But instead of gazing out of the window, he was reading a copy of the Daily Telegraph. He placed this down on his lap as she entered the room.

After exchanging a few words with her, he pointed to an article in the centre of the newspaper's front page. "I see that the king has awarded a George Cross to the island of Malta."

Margaret nodded. "Yes, I heard about that on the news yesterday."

She paused, unsure whether to say anything further. This was the very first mention he had made regarding any aspect of the war for as long as she could recall, and at any other time she would have been eager to continue their conversation, But right at this moment she had so much else to think about. Her head was in such a muddle. She needed a spell of peace and quiet to try and make some sense of it all.

"Thoroughly well-deserved too," the earl continued. "Brave people the Maltese. They showed those Nazi swine a thing or two about protecting your home. Just like we will if Hitler ever fancies his chances of having another go at our island. He'll never rule us."

His words slammed into Margaret's already overloaded brain, leaving her stunned. Together with the sudden steely look in his eyes, in just a few short sentences he had told her quite voluntarily what she had been trying so hard to prise out of him ever since her return from Berlin. Now, at long last, she knew the full truth of it. It finally confirmed what she had long come to suspect.

Her father would never accept life under the Nazis, no matter how great the inducements offered to him.

THE CAR PULLED UP AND there was the creaking of a handbrake being applied. To Joe, it sounded disturbingly quiet outside. Had they now arrived at their destination? What felt like no more than half an hour had passed, so they must still be somewhere in London, he reasoned. Other than that, he had no clue as to where they might be.

A hand touched him on the shoulder. "Time to get out," he was told.

Still blindfolded, Joe was guided from the car. A brief walk in the open air was followed by the sound of a heavy door opening. A moment later they were inside.

"Stairs coming up now, so watch your step," his escort informed him.

They climbed two flights then headed along what he imagined to be a corridor. After a few seconds of this he was ushered through another door and pushed down onto a hard, upright chair.

Now they'll take this bloody hood off, he told himself.

But they didn't. Instead, to his horror, his wrists were handcuffed behind his back.

A powerful urge suddenly gripped Joe. "Please, I need the toilet," he told his captors. "You can't leave me like this."

"Sorry, old boy," came the reply. "You'll just have to use a little bit of willpower for now. Someone will be along for a chat with you when they are good and ready."

His escorts' footsteps receded. "Hold on a minute," he pleaded. "At least tell me what ..."

The double clicks of a door closing and then a lock being turned told Joe very plainly that he was wasting his breath.

AT LAST THE PHONE ON Simon's desk rang. While picking up the receiver he offered a quick prayer that this would be the call he'd been waiting for. He should have heard something long ago.

"Stephens here," the voice told him. "We've got your man all safely tucked up with us now. Sorry it took so long, but he'd left the racetrack by the time we got there. We finally picked him up outside his house."

Simon gave a small sigh of relief. "Did he have anything of interest on him?"

"Not found anything yet. But if he is hiding something, we'll find it."

"What are you doing with him at present?"

"Just letting the chap stew for a short while. If someone is guilty, there's nothing like a spot of thinking time to concentrate the mind."

"I've got a car on standby, so I can leave straight away," Simon told him. "I should be there in well under two hours."

ONE HOUR AND FORTY minutes later, Simon's car drew up outside Latchmere House. Or to give it its official name, Camp 020.

A large Victorian mansion set on the edge of Ham Common in south-west London, Latchmere House had been the main MI5 interrogation centre for interned fascists and captured German spies ever since the beginning of the war. Its commandant, the fearsome Lieutenant Colonel Robin 'Tin Eye' Stephens, was reputed to have never once failed to break a prisoner. What made this record even more remarkable was the fact that Stephens was adamantly opposed to using any form of physical violence. Instead, he relied purely on a wide range of psychological pressures: a method that so far had unfailingly extracted every last scrap of useful information from all those who passed through his hands.

It was the colonel himself who greeted Simon at the front door. Although Stephens had no detailed knowledge of Bletchley Park's purpose, he would be fully aware that it was a place of enormous importance. Simon's authority direct from the prime minister to ask for whatever assistance he required in the course of his investigation would have only emphasised this point.

His eyes ran quickly over the colonel. A powerfully built, stern featured man dressed in the uniform of the famously fierce 2nd Gurkha Rifles Regiment in which he had previously served, Stephens presented a formidable sight. This impression was further enhanced by the tin framed, glinting monocle covering his right eye that had earned him his curious nickname. Simon knew that this device was not worn for theatrical purposes, but was the result of exposure to mustard gas whilst serving as a volunteer with the British Red Cross in Abyssinia during the mid-1930s.

"All your man's belongings have been checked and he's just completed a thorough strip search," Stephens told him as they climbed the stairs. "There's no trace of him carrying anything untoward. But of course, he could have easily dropped something off before arriving home."

Simon frowned. "That's my main concern now."

"And that's why I'm going to work on him right away. If he has already made another contact, I'll find out quickly enough."

"How can you be so sure about that?" Simon asked.

Stephens gave him a thin smile. "I've already given him the once over and I know the type. It's plain as can be that he's guilty of something. But whatever it is, it's also obvious that his heart is not really in it. Press the right buttons and he'll talk from now until doomsday."

Given the man's record, Simon was certainly not going to question his confidence. All the same, with nothing incriminating found on Joe Bull, he could not help but worry over the possibility that a message from Margaret might have already found its way into other hands.

WEARING NOTHING BUT his underpants, Joe waited forlornly in the bleak interview room that he had been transferred into several minutes ago. Plain brown linoleum covered the floor, and with the solitary window completely blacked out, the only lighting came from a single low-wattage bulb.

At least that bloody hood was now gone, he consoled himself. But so too were his shoes and the rest of his clothes following a humiliating strip search. Whilst sat on a rickety wooden chair in this new setting under the eye of an expressionless guard standing by the door, he nervously contemplated his short-term future.

There was one saving grace to all of this. Despite their intensive searching, if it was that posh woman's message they were after, they were never going to find it anywhere amongst his things. But so far he'd been told nothing. Not given any clue as to why he had been so roughly grabbed off the street. If only he knew the reason for that, maybe then he could start working on a story to defend himself with. As it was, he'd been kept totally in the dark. In fact, quite literally so until the hood had been removed.

Weirdly, for an instant he found his weak attempt at humour raising a smile. At least his brain wasn't completely frozen yet.

At that moment, the door opened and two men in uniform entered. One was from the army and carrying a briefcase. The other was from the navy.

"On your feet!" the guard barked.

Sharply aware that to ignore this instruction would only make matters worse for himself, Joe did as he was told.

The two officers sat down behind a bare wooden trestle table, on which both placed a notebook and pencil. As they silently ran their eyes over him, Joe did the same in return. He did not know enough about the navy to establish the rank of the man on the left, but could easily tell from the crown and pip worn by his companion that he was a lieutenant colonel. A double row of medal ribbons above his left breast pocket immediately told of his substantial active service experience. Not that this was anything like the most striking aspect about the officer.

Joe recognised a Gurkha uniform when he saw one. Almost every man in the trenches of the Great War had heard stories at some time or another about the men from Nepal's suicidal courage and insane ferocity in battle. Their exploits at the Battle of Loos alone, when a vastly outnumbered battalion of them fought literally to the last man, had given them something close to legendary status. With a regimental motto of *'Better to die than live a coward'*, any British officer serving with such men would need to be among the very toughest, bravest, and best.

Now Joe was being confronted by one of these very officers. Already he could feel himself wilting under the steely gaze of the man's left eye. The right one, also staring at him but through a monocle, was in a way even more unsettling. The small glass disc somehow created a crazy impression that it gave the wearer an ability to see right inside his mind.

Their examination over, the two men each lit a cigarette, with the colonel first of all fixing his into an elegant holder. Leaning back in his chair, he drew in the smoke.

After a few seconds of continued silence, from this apparently relaxed position, he suddenly shot forward to slap a hand hard down onto the tabletop. His voice barked out.

"Stand to attention, man. You look like a bag of shit."

Although Joe had been half-anticipating something like this, he was still unable to prevent himself from automatically reacting to the command. Memories of his service days – a host of places and people he thought were long erased – all came back with a violent rush.

"Name, rank and number," the colonel demanded.

It was on the tip of Joe's tongue to actually start responding. An army number was something that no man who had served a tour of duty was ever liable to forget. The digits were driven hard into your brain, and not being able to recall them instantly when ordered to virtually guaranteed being put on a charge. He stopped himself just in time.

Hoping that his initial reaction had not given the game away, he decided to act out the part of an outraged citizen who'd been wrongly arrested for something he had no knowledge of.

"I ain't never been in the army, nor any other service 'cos of my gammy leg," he claimed. "I just want to know why I've been dragged in here? I ain't done nothing wrong."

His question was ignored. "Name and date of birth then?"

"Joe Mason."

"What about your date of birth? Come on, man. Surely you don't have to think about a simple thing like that."

Under pressure from the colonel's severe gaze, for a few seconds Joe struggled to remember the date listed on his false birth certificate. It came back to him with a rush. "Twenty-ninth of July, eighteen-ninety-five."

"Where were you born?"

"Whitechapel."

"Where in Whitechapel? Are either of your parents still alive? What were their names?"

Joe put a hand to his forehead. The questions were coming too thick and fast. He needed time to think. He had no ready answers.

"Put your hand down and get back to attention," the colonel snapped.

"I never knew me parents," Joe told him. "My mother dumped me in a church straight after I was born."

"Which church?"

This caused another problem. He could hardly name the church in Dublin that he was actually abandoned in.

"How the hell do you expect me to remember that?" he blustered.

The eye behind the monocle seemed to be boring deep inside his head, searching for the truth. "So who brought you up then? I take it you *can* remember that much."

The man's sarcasm bit deep. The sharply creative brain that had been earning Joe his living over the years was now barely functioning at all. "It was...it was...no one you'd know of."

"Why not? If they adopted you, it must be on public record somewhere."

"It weren't like that. They took me in unofficial-like out of kindness."

"Even so, you'd still remember their names. And the address where they lived. How long did you stay there?"

"I dunno. I was still a kid when I left." A stream of air shot from Joe's mouth as his frustration boiled over. "Christ almighty, it was a long bloody time ago. Over thirty bleedin' years!"

"How about your school? Can you remember that?"

"I never went to school very much."

"Really! So where did you learn to read and write so well?"

"What makes you think I can?"

With a mocking laugh, the colonel reached into the briefcase that he'd placed on the floor beside his chair. From this, he produced a copy of the Sporting Life newspaper, which he now spread out on the table. Scribbled in pencil all over the racing pages were Joe's in-depth comments on the strengths and weaknesses of the various runners.

"Quite impressively written for a man who never went to school very much," the colonel remarked. His voice then abruptly hardened. "Don't waste my time by lying any longer. Start telling me the truth or it will go very badly indeed for you."

So they had turned his lodgings over already, Joe realised. With a feeling of despair, he wondered what else they might have found. What else might be inside that briefcase just waiting to pop out and surprise him?

The answer arrived swiftly. Out came his fake birth certificate.

Unlike the more detailed documents currently issued that stated the parents' names and address, this Registry of Birth Certificate dating back to the previous century merely recorded the name of the newborn, the date, and the entry number in the appropriate register book. It was signed by the Registrar of Births and Deaths for the district of Whitechapel.

Except, as Joe knew full well, it hadn't been.

The colonel was clearly thinking the same thing. "If this doesn't check out properly, that will probably be enough on its own to hang you," he said with a grim little smile.

All Joe's worst nightmares were now coming horribly true. "You can't do that," he gasped. "Not just because of a bloody birth certificate."

"So you admit that it's a fake?"

Joe did not have any idea how to answer. The truth could easily be discovered. To lie any further would at best only slightly delay the inevitable.

"We are at war," the colonel continued. "If a man needs to have false identity papers it can mean only one thing. He is an enemy spy. And it is my job to ensure that all spies hang."

"I'm not a bloody spy," Joe protested. "Not like..."

His voice tapered off.

"Not like what exactly?

"Not like one of them bloody Nazis who want to see us invaded."

"Then how would you describe yourself?"

"I don't know. I'm just an ordinary bloke who—"

"An ordinary bloke who just happens to be betraying his country," the colonel cut in sharply.

Yet another denial rose up in Joe's mouth, but this time he choked it back. The cold gaze of the eye behind the monocle was daring him to lie again. It was having an almost hypnotic effect on him. Unable to think of anything to say that might help his cause, he remained silent.

His interrogator stroked his chin. "Of course, there is an alternative. Maybe you are a German? One planted here many years ago as a sleeper spy when the Nazis were first rising to power. That would explain the rather botched-up birth certificate. Abwehr have never been very good at that sort of thing." He gave a hollow laugh. "Some of the documents and cover stories they supplied to their agents were almost laughably bad. That's why we were able to pick them all up so easily at the beginning of the war."

The man's eyes narrowed. "But perhaps you are one that slipped through the net?"

At last Joe found his voice again. His denial shot out at full volume. "No! I ain't no bloody German. I swear to gawd I ain't."

"Then who are you? And don't give me any more of that Joe Mason bullshit. I know a liar when I see one, and I've broken hundreds of them. Some of the best in the business. You, you're a damn amateur who I can break …"

Picking up the pencil in front of him, the colonel broke it in half with only the pressure of his thumb. "Just like that," he completed. "And just like the hangman can snap your neck."

To Joe's surprise, after a moment of unbearably tense silence, the naval officer then spoke for the very first time. In marked contrast, his tone was far less hostile. Almost to the point of being friendly.

"If you are not a German, old chap, then there may be a tiny ray of hope that you can avoid such a fate. But only if you are completely honest with us. Do you understand that?"

Fearing this may be a trick, Joe restricted himself to a nod.

"We'll put aside the matter of your identity for the moment. I know for a fact that you've been passing on messages for the Germans, so I'm now going to ask you about the one that was given to you at Newmarket racetrack this afternoon. I warn you, do not try to prevaricate any longer. I want truthful and accurate answers, and I want them straight away. Your life will depend on the information you give us."

Any tiny amount of resistance that Joe might still have had immediately crumbled. One of their people must have been at the racetrack watching him, he realised. He was done for. His only hope was to spill everything he knew and pray to God that this might be enough to save himself from the noose. In a way, it would almost be a relief to own up. He'd only been doing all this crazy spy stuff under threat anyway. He had no desire to help the bloody Nazis win the war. In a way, he was as British as anyone else these days.

He began talking.

A FEELING OF GRIM SATISFACTION came over Simon. Stephens had been spot-on in his assessment. Whatever their prisoner's reasons for becoming involved, he was clearly no fascist or admirer of Hitler.

Just a few minutes of the colonel's stern interrogation followed by him stepping in to offer the man a glimmer of hope had been more than enough to get him talking. Simon suspected that he'd been somehow pressured into becoming involved, hence his eagerness to now talk in an effort to save himself. Even fringe members of Mosley's BUF party usually put up a little more resistance than this chap before spilling what they knew.

Joe Mason - or whatever his real name may be – was still in full flow. "I ain't never read any of the messages she gave me. Honest I never. All I ever did was—"

Simon cut him off. "Forget all that for now. Just tell me what you've done with today's message. It's not been found on you, and your motorbike has been searched. So where is it?"

"I dropped it off in the usual place on me way home. That old brick khazi on Denmark Hill, right near the edge of Ruskin Park."

"A public toilet?"

"Yeah, that's right. It's got three cubicles, and we leave stuff for each other in the one on the left." He paused to draw a breath. "There's this short length of old pipe coming up out the floor, but it ain't used for anything these days 'cos it's been plugged off at the end. All you need do is unscrew the plug and shove the rolled-up message inside. Fits in a treat."

"And how do you signal to each other that a drop's been made?"

"There's a small fanlight window. It's pretty high up and you need to stand on the pan to reach it properly. It's usually kept shut, but we open it when something's been left. Whoever's collecting then shuts it again after they've made the pick-up."

Simon now had the most pressing piece of information he needed. "Can you get someone straight over to see if today's message is still there?" he asked Stephens.

"They'll need a one-inch spanner or a pair of pliers to shift the plug," Joe chipped in. "We always do it up pretty tight, just to be on the safe side."

With the guard by the door dispatched to arrange things, Simon turned his attention back to Joe. "Now we've got that underway, let's get back to who you really are. Your name and where you are from please?"

There was only a brief hesitation before the reply came. "Joseph Flynn. I'm from Dublin."

In a flash, it all started to make sense to Simon. A sideways glance showed that his fellow interrogator was thinking along exactly the same lines. It was well-known that the IRA regarded Britain's enemies as their friends and were doing all they could to provide a safe refuge for Nazi agents within the Republic. That written messages from Margaret were finding their way across the Irish Sea and from there being radioed on to Germany was an entirely plausible scenario.

After jotting something down with the broken top half of his pencil, Stephens took over with the questions once again. "How long have you been with the IRA?" he demanded.

Joe reacted quickly. "I ain't never been with them. Well...not in the way you mean. I've never planted no bombs over here or nothing like that. Bloody hell, I volunteered to join up with you lot in the last war. Served with the Royal Dublin Fusiliers for three years I did, and went over the top three times. That's how I ended up with this gammy leg. I was at the Somme, and Passchendaele."

Stephen's austere expression did not change. "Very well, I'll ask you again. What was your service number?"

This time the answer came back without delay. It was duly added to the colonel's notes. "I knew it," he murmured while writing. "I can always tell when a man has served."

His eyes then returned to Joe. "Now, Mister Flynn, you are going to tell me everything about yourself. Your full life history. I warn you, leave out nothing, especially the bad bits. You will be talking quite literally to save your life."

SEVENTEEN

Once Joe began, it seemed to get progressively easier. In a ridiculous kind of way, he felt as if he was in a confessional booth purging his sins. Not for his tiny part in the fight for a free Ireland; even now he could not condemn himself for that. No. The burden of guilt came from the almost certain knowledge that he had been helping to pass possibly critical information to the Nazis. Information that may well be endangering the lives of men on the front line in North Africa and elsewhere. His own memories of war's horrors, and of the comradeship between those at the sharp end of things, would never fade away.

After relating his early years and subsequent time in the trenches, he went on to tell them about discovering his previously unknown talent for mimicry whilst recuperating amongst men from all over Britain in the Labour Corps. He even smiled for a moment when speaking about this period. Bitterness and disgust that he was unable to conceal then quickly took over as he recalled the still vivid memory of being told by a British officer from the Travelling Pensions Board - a fat pig of a man who had obviously never seen a single shot fired in action - that he was a coward and would not qualify for any kind of payment or pension.

"I was never a coward," he protested loudly. "I done everything I was ordered to, and falling into that hole was a sheer bloody accident 'cos of the mud. Three years of service on the front line and all that pain I went through, just to have that jumped-up arsehole tell me I wasn't worth a few lousy quid in pension money and should have been shot. No bleedin' wonder I wanted to get back at you Brits by doin' a bit of eavesdropping."

Did he detect just the tiniest nod of understanding from the naval officer after saying that? Although he seemed to be playing a junior role in the questioning, Joe strongly suspected that this was the man he most needed to win over.

For an instant, it then occurred to him that he had used the phrase 'you Brits' just like an Irishman would, but was sounding as London born and bred as the Pearly King of Whitechapel himself. How much of his true heritage was still left in him?

His story moved on to the death of Michael Collins and how, sickened by the continuing violence, he'd been left with only one choice when wanting out. His showmanship on English racecourses had made him a fairly well-known personality following his arrival, so there was little to add about his personal life other than the devastation he'd felt when finding himself being forced back into service after so long.

"I'm just a nobody in all this," he concluded. "All I do is collect and pass on messages. I don't know who the posh sounding woman is, and I ain't never been stupid enough to try and find out who's collecting the stuff I drop off. I've only got one good leg as it is, and I ain't planning to get that smashed up as well."

Stephen's studied him for several seconds before speaking. "Haven't you ever wondered why they picked on you for this job?"

"It was 'cos of the Joe Bull thing. They said it was a good cover for our meeting up."

His suggestion was met with a dismissive wave of the hand. "Perhaps a little bit. But much more important is the fact that you're expendable. Ever since telling them that you wanted out, you've been on their list of disposables."

A surge of indignation rose in Joe. He could see the game that was being played straight away. He wouldn't fall for it. He might be willing to do a lot of things to save his neck, but he'd never become an informer.

"That's a load of old pony," he shot back. "They done me a favour by letting me come over here and start again."

Stephens gave a slow shake of the head. "You said it yourself, Joe. You're a nobody. Look at it their way. If you do happen to get caught collecting messages, what does it matter? You can't identify anyone else involved. As for the bigger picture, you've been out of the game for so long, you don't know anything useful any longer."

"If I don't know anything useful, then what do you want from me?"

"Nothing, Joe. Not a damn thing. If I had my way, you'd already be sitting in a condemned cell. As it is, whether or not you actually will have that fate to look forward to depends on my colleague here."

So it was just as Joe had suspected. His eyes shot over to the naval officer.

The man leaned back in his seat. "Let me think about it for a while," he said to Stephens. "Meanwhile, why don't we send him back to his cell and let him get dressed again?"

After responding with a brisk nod, the colonel stood up and approached Joe. "Let's move it," he snapped.

SIMON HAD ALREADY DECIDED some time ago what path he would take. Naturally, everything that Joe had said would be thoroughly checked out, but there was no doubt in his mind that the man had spoken the truth and told them all that he was capable of.

There were two main reasons why he'd chosen to delay matters. First of all, he wanted to know if Joe's latest message had been recovered before speaking to him any further. Secondly, it wouldn't hurt to let their prisoner dwell on the prospect of the hangman for just a little while longer. There was also the fact that, by being the one to allow Joe his clothes back and speaking to him alone this time, a certain empathy might develop between them. Stephens had set up the fear factor. It was now his turn to see how much this could be capitalised on.

The news was not long in coming back from Ruskin Park. Everything at the small brick building was exactly as Joe had described. The bad news was that the envelope he'd deposited there only a few hours earlier had already been collected and the fanlight window closed up again. Margaret's message, whatever intelligence it contained, was on its way. Worse still, given the Irishman's complete lack of knowledge about how the ongoing system worked, any hope of preventing it from reaching its destination seemed to have gone too.

AFTER JUST AN HOUR alone with Joe in his cell, Simon had gathered as much information as he could have hoped for. Most disconcerting of all was to learn that, over a period of nearly three years, Margaret had sent more than half a dozen previous messages through the same network. He could only pray that none of these had been seriously damaging to Bletchley's security, or indeed, to any aspect of the war effort.

As for Joe himself, as expected, it had taken little further persuasion for him to be talked into acting as a double agent: a decision that Simon suspected had not been driven entirely by a sense of self-preservation. Joe, he felt, was genuinely anti-Nazi and eager to help in possibly undoing any harm he may have caused. In fact, after taking into consideration all aspects of the man's life – especially the raw deal handed out to him following his service on the Western Front – Simon could almost understand why he had initially been driven into the arms of the IRA. With his own quite privileged upbringing within a loving family, it was virtually impossible to imagine starting life as a foundling in a public institution that was probably little or no better than an old-fashioned workhouse.

Not that he allowed any hint of these feelings to show. It was spelled out in clear terms to Joe that he was expected to carry on as normal, and what the penalty would be if he strayed even a touch away from these instructions.

"See this through to the end and you'll be well looked after," Simon told him before leaving.

He responded with a hollow laugh. "What happens if the Germans win the war instead?"

"Then God help us all, Joe. You included."

AFTER LEAVING LATCHMERE House, Simon headed north to a small village in the county of Hertfordshire, eventually pulling up outside a Victorian building bearing the name of Arkley View. It was far better known to him as the primary data collection centre for the country's extensive network of direction-finding and listening stations.

He was now acting on calculated guesswork. If he was right in presuming that Margaret's latest message would soon be transmitted by radio from somewhere in Ireland, his one remaining hope of discovering its contents rested with Britain's army of on-air listeners.

Instructions were issued. Until further notice, all unidentified broadcasts from within Ireland were to be marked for his immediate attention when being forwarded to Bletchley Park.

By the time he arrived back at the mansion it was well into the small hours. It had been a long and exhausting day. Progress was being made, but right now he badly needed some sleep.

ONCE AGAIN MARGARET turned over in her bed. More than twelve hours had elapsed since passing her latest message to Joe Bull, and it was now weighing heavier than ever on her mind.

The twin discoveries of how cruelly Richard had deceived her and then the shattering revelation of her father's true feelings regarding the Nazis left no more room for doubt. It took only a few discreet words with him a little later on that evening to confirm what Sir Hubert Harding had stated. No Jew had ever been permitted to be a member of his former club.

She had been wrong in every single way: both in actions, and in motivation. It was suddenly all so clear. What on earth had possessed her to believe that a man as proud and patriotic as her father would ever accept any kind of gift from a foreign power hostile to Britain? She had allowed herself to be blinded to the obvious truth by an overwhelming desire to somehow make things right for him.

How could the pain of witnessing his downfall have affected her judgement so badly?

"Not that I've ever had anything against the Jews myself," the earl had told her. "It's only a handful of bigoted fools on the committee who have kept that ban in place. Maybe I should have spoken up a bit more about it. As far as I'm concerned, a chap's worth should always be measured in his character, not his heritage. I've always brought you up to believe that as well, haven't I, Margaret?"

This was true, and his words struck deep. Given the Nazi's newly established anti-Semitic laws prior to the Olympics, she had been naïve in the extreme to have so easily swallowed Richard's lie. And as everyone knew, one lie so very often led to another. And then another. This called into question not just everything that he had told her, but quite possibly Goering as well. Even the Reichsmarschall's pledge regarding Hadley Hall and its estate could now be seen as nothing more than an empty promise designed to ensure her cooperation.

Yet even this did not matter any longer. In recent months, horrific tales of torture and mass murder by elements of the German forces had become ever more frequent, and dismissing them all as mere government propaganda was now proving almost impossible to do. If these tales really were true, huge numbers of innocent civilians in occupied countries, especially Jews, were being brutalised in this way. Instead of the economic revival that she had so foolishly envisaged, would similar reprisals be the fate awaiting Britain's population as well?

The bed creaked as Margaret rolled over yet again. How she bitterly regretted sending that last message. But what could she do about it? To confess her activities was not an option. Now fully aware of her father's views on the war, all of her worst fears had been confirmed. The shame of her exposure was certain to be catastrophic for him, quite possibly sufficient to induce a second, this time fatal stroke. As for herself, at best it would condemn her to spending the rest of her life in prison. At the worst, it would mean a date with the hangman.

Everything depended on how Goering reacted. Any answer from him would probably be ready for collection on Derby Day, June the thirteenth. Like nearly all of the classic races this year, this was also to be run at Newmarket rather than its usual venue.

The Reichsmarschall's last message showed quite plainly how little value he had placed on the intelligence she'd so far provided. That was good. If he responded in the same way this time, that would be the end of matters. Despite her still deep-rooted resentment against those in Westminster, and the heartbreak of finally admitting that Hadley House and the estate were lost forever, her conscience was demanding that she should wash her hands of the whole affair.

After having stressed so strongly the importance of Bletchley Park and the need to bomb it, could she dare to hope for Goering's continued indifference?

She would give almost anything to know how he intended to react.

EIGHTEEN

A heavy sigh slipped from Reichsmarschall Hermann Goering's mouth while lowering himself into a comfortable armchair. Ever self-conscious about his personal appearance, he was forced to admit that he was starting to put on far too much weight.

Not that his physical condition was uppermost on his mind as he sat brooding in his apartment at the Reich Air Ministry headquarters. Far from it. That morning's meeting with General Karl-Heinrich Bodenschatz had brought disturbing news. His old friend and former adjutant - still at present acting as the liaison officer between himself and the Fuhrer - had warned him that he was rapidly sinking in the Leader's estimation. Already long blamed for the Luftwaffe's failure to overcome the RAF in the Battle of Britain, he had more recently suffered similar harsh criticism for not eliminating the Soviet Air Force. Now, it appeared, the Fuhrer was also holding him personally responsible for the increasing air raids on German cities.

But there was more. Just before their meeting concluded, Bodenschatz had revealed a real sting in the tail. Goering was well aware that he had enemies in high places, amongst them Chief of the Party Chancellery Martin Bormann and Gestapo head Heinrich Himmler. But it was that poisonous rat Joseph Goebbels, the Minister of Propaganda, that he detested and feared most of all. Apparently, Goebbels was currently creating whispers that the Reichsmarschall might be secretly hoarding a considerable amount of *degenerate* art.

"I don't know if there is any truth in this rumour," Bodenschatz had told him. "As for myself, I don't care. But if there is anything to it, please be warned. The Fuhrer will be most displeased."

Goering was horrified. Whether or not Goebbels had any evidence for his claim was largely irrelevant. It was dangerously accurate. And given his current low standing with the Leader, Hitler being *'most displeased'* could mean anything from public humiliation to a death sentence.

He desperately needed to find a way of regaining favour and killing off these damaging rumours.

Casting his mind back to an earlier part of his meeting with Bodenschatz, he recalled mention of Hitler's concern over the security of their communications. Apparently, Admiral Doenitz had been receiving reports from a number of his U-Boat commanders concerned that their messages were being decoded by the enemy. They felt there could be no other explanation for the number of Atlantic convoys that had lately been able to evade their wolf packs. Though dismissing the idea of their codes being broken as impossible, Doenitz could not deny the existence of these reports when questioned directly about them by the Fuhrer. According to Bodenschatz, Hitler did not fully share the admiral's confidence and had been obsessing about the ability of Allied codebreakers for several days.

Goering agreed with Doenitz about the security of their communications. Enigma encoding was impossible to break, especially with the latest modifications made. So let the British waste their time and resources pursuing the unachievable. More fools them for trying.

Despite this conviction, he knew that it would do much to restore his and the Luftwaffe's standing with the Fuhrer if he were to destroy this alleged top-secret code breaking centre that Lady Margaret kept telling him about. Her latest message had reached him just two days ago. He still doubted very much that the place was as important as she claimed, but her continued insistence suggested that it might after all have some strategic value as a target: both for the war effort, and for him personally. Whatever its real worth, should he be able to oversee its destruction, he would most certainly portray the house as having been one of the main centres for the Allied cryptological work.

Precision bombing on such a small target would be a major challenge though. And given the current strength of the RAF's fighter defences, to mount such a mission during daylight hours with a force of slow-moving conventional bombers would almost certainly end in disaster. No. Only a night-time raid by a small number of his special fighter-bombers had all the requirements of speed, surprise, and low-level capability to stand any real chance of success. Even then, with a blackout in force all over Britain, there would still be the enormous problem of target identification to overcome.

But he was getting ahead of himself. He first needed to check on the doubts he felt over Lady Margaret. Before all this talk of a top-secret code breaking centre, the intelligence he'd received from her had been low grade to the point of being virtually useless. He had to be certain that she had not been exposed as a spy and was now feeding him false information.

The solution came to him quickly. There was a way he might be able to check on this, and at the same time provide a means of making Bletchley Park more easily identifiable for his bombers if it became necessary.

Pushing himself up out of the chair, he reached for the telephone.

YET AGAIN BETTY WAS in Simon's small office at the manor house. Even within the strict confines of Bletchley Park, he had considered it best for them not to be seen regularly talking together outside of this very private room.

Unlike their last meeting when Simon had understandably been frustrated at failing to prevent Margaret's latest message from reaching its destination, this time he appeared a touch more upbeat. After a short chat about how she was progressing, he handed over a sheet of paper.

Betty ran her eyes over the typewritten page. It was covered in sequence after sequence of three number blocks, each of them prefixed by either the letter A or B.

"I take it this is some kind of code," she said.

He nodded, then went on to tell her about a visit he had made to the listening station and data collection centre at Arkley View.

While he spoke, Betty was reminded that she was now amongst the very few people who had any clear idea of what was really happening at Bletchley Park, and of how critical this was to Britain's survival. That she should be entrusted with such a vitally important secret was in a way quite humbling. But as Simon had said only a few minutes ago, at this very moment her role as the pretend friend to Margaret was equally critical. She had to understand the huge importance of what she was continuing to do. And the possible danger that she might find herself in as a result.

His talk of danger had surprised her. Never at any time had she felt even slightly threatened when with Margaret or the earl. Why would she? Apart from keeping her eyes and ears open and reporting back to Simon, there was nothing she had been asked to do that was liable to place her at risk. So why had he mentioned such a thing at this stage? She made a mental note to ask about this before their meeting was over.

"What you are looking at now is what I strongly suspect to be Margaret's latest message," he told her. "As you rightly say, it is in code. And that is where the problem lies."

Betty frowned. "But surely there are people here who can solve it easily enough. That's what they do, isn't it?"

"Yes, and I've already had them take a good look at it." He sighed. "Unfortunately, this is a book code. Or in this case, a two-book code, which makes it doubly difficult. Without knowing what books have been used as the key, it could take a devil of a time to unscramble. Time that maybe we don't have to spare."

"So how does this book code work?" Betty asked, placing the sheet down in front of her.

Simon came from behind his desk to stand beside her chair. Leaning over, he rested his finger next to the first line of type. "The letter A or B before each sequence denotes which book has been used. This one here is for book A. The first figure along from that tells you the page number you need to turn to; the one next to it shows the number of lines down on that page to move; and the third one takes you along that line to the word you are looking for. So the word we want here is from book A on page twenty-two, fourteen lines down, and three words along." He gave a hollow laugh. "It couldn't be simpler. If you know what books to look in, of course."

"Are there no clues to help work that out?"

"Only one so far." His finger moved further down the page. "Take a look at this sequence here for Book B. It begins with page seven hundred and fifty-seven. That makes it a pretty large book: way bigger than anything showing for Book A. It could be a dictionary. Apparently, they are often used for this sort of thing. Which kind of makes sense."

A sudden thought occurred to Betty. "Is there a special reason for you telling me all this?"

Simon hesitated briefly. "Yes, there is actually."

He moved back to his side of the desk and sat down again before continuing. "As I said just now, time could be vital on this. If the chaps here had some of Margaret's previous messages that they could use to create possible matches it would have helped a great deal. But we don't, of course. That being the case, it would speed things up no end if ..."

"If I could find out what books she is using," Betty completed for him.

He nodded. "That's about the size of it. Look, I know this is going rather beyond what was originally put to you. And I wouldn't be asking you to do it if there was any other way. But we can't just charge in and arrest her. At least, not yet. Not until we know what information that last message of hers contained. Whatever harm she might have already done, we need to get the full picture first. There may be others involved who we know nothing about. Her father even?"

"No, I'm positive the earl isn't any part of this," Betty insisted. "I'd stake my life on that."

Even as she spoke this final phrase, it struck a chord with her. "Was this what you meant earlier when you mentioned about me being in possible danger? Do you really believe that Margaret might harm me if she discovered what I was doing?"

He shifted uncomfortably in his seat. "We both know that being caught as a spy in wartime carries a death sentence. So who can tell how she might react if she felt threatened with exposure? I'm not saying categorically that she would become violent. She probably wouldn't. All the same, it's only fair that you fully understand what you might be letting yourself in for, Betty."

The expression on his face told her how much he hated asking her to put herself at risk, however small that risk might be. There was also a look in his eyes that suggested something deeper. A genuine affection that went well beyond what might be expected. Had it ever been there before? If so, she hadn't noticed it.

Whatever the case, she was in far too deep to back out now. She dragged up a smile. "In for a penny, in for a pound, I suppose," she told him. "What exactly do you need from me."

Now she could see something else on his face. Admiration. A second later it was gone and he was down to business.

"They're running the Derby at Newmarket this Saturday, and from what we know, Margaret will almost certainly be going there to check with her contact. Have you arranged to play for the earl on that day?"

"Yes. We always try to do Saturdays whenever possible now. He says it's his favourite day of the week for our get-togethers."

"Then that might be your best opportunity."

She gave him an enquiring look, but said nothing.

"The books Margaret is using will most likely be kept separate from any others in the cottage. Probably somewhere private like her bedroom. If you could grab a quick look inside there, maybe they will be fairly easy to spot."

His suggestion drew a frown. "How will I do that without attracting attention?"

Simon opened a drawer and very deliberately placed a tiny pill bottle on the desk. "With a bit of help from these two little chaps. Just pop them into the earl's cup of tea. He'll drop off to sleep for around twenty minutes quite soon afterwards."

She stared at the bottle in astonished silence. Suddenly, her part in things was taking on a whole new dimension of seriousness. This really was just like in spy stories. There was also an immediate reaction against drugging an old man who she had become very fond of.

Simon's voice broke up these thoughts. "They won't harm him, I promise. I know you're not happy about this, Betty, but it seems to be the only way. Believe me, I wouldn't use them at all if the situation weren't so *damned urgent.*"

The heavy emphasis he placed on the final two words struck home. Betty silently chastised herself for being a bit of a milksop. What should she have expected? This was wartime, and she was in the forces serving her country.

"Just as long as you are certain they won't harm him," she said.

"You have my solemn word on that."

After a second or two, her lack of a reply was taken as an unspoken acceptance of her new role. He continued. "If you do succeed in finding what appears to be the right books, one thing is very important, Betty. You must make a careful note of which editions they are. Earlier or later printings

200

of the same titles might well have a different page layout or sequence. Obviously, these would not work in the same way I showed you."

Her silence continued for a moment longer. "If I do succeed in finding the right books, what then?" she finally asked.

Simon chewed on his bottom lip. "That depends entirely on what we manage to decode. Right now, we've no real idea of how damaging the information that Margaret has passed on to the enemy actually is. Or how they may be planning to make use of it."

He gave a thin smile. "I'd give a fortune to be a fly on the wall listening to whoever those messages are eventually ending up with."

RICHARD FORST'S SURPRISE at receiving a quite friendly worded summons to the Reichsmarschall's private suite at the Air Ministry was considerable.

He was well aware that his network of local informants had produced little of value for some time. Worse still, Goering had come to regard his prized recruitment of Margaret as being a complete waste of time. Even Richard himself was forced to admit that most of the intelligence she'd provided had been a disappointment. That said, he felt quite strongly that her latest couple of messages concerning Bletchley Park should be taken seriously. She knew the area around there better than almost anyone, and would be keenly aware of any unusual happenings taking place. If she really was right about the house being an important code breaking centre, its destruction would be a massive blow to the enemy.

Goering greeted him affably. After they were both seated, his adjutant Teske quickly departed to leave them alone.

"I want to talk to you about Lady Margaret," Goering began.

Richard brightened. Could his boss be thinking along the same lines as himself? Maybe Margaret would prove to be a triumph for him after all.

"Her latest report has caught my interest," the Reichsmarschall continued. "But I still need to be fully convinced as to its value. To mount the kind of bombing raid she has suggested would be a considerable risk. You can see that, can't you?"

Richard nodded, but remained silent. What was this leading to?

"I also need convincing that she has not been caught and turned into a double agent."

That Goering was even thinking along such lines horrified Richard. If that were proven to be true, no matter how unreasonable it was, he would be the one to carry the blame.

"No! I'm sure that she is still fully committed to us," he protested.

The smile Goering gave him lacked any trace of warmth. "I'm glad you have so much confidence in the lady. That being the case, you won't mind personally checking it out for me."

"But how am I to do that?"

"By going to England and speaking with her, of course."

A wave of astonishment swept over Richard. For a short time he thought he must have misheard. "Going to England?" he repeated.

"Certainly. What more accurate way is there to ascertain the situation?"

Richard's scrambled mind was still trying to come to terms with this development. "Are you sure I am the best person for the job?" he asked.

As soon as he finished speaking, he realised what a damn stupid question that was. Goering's response merely confirmed this.

"Who could be better? You know both Lady Margaret and the country well. Intimately, in fact. Also, you speak the language fluently with no hint of an accent, so you can pass yourself off as an Englishman without the slightest trouble. And it's not as if anyone other than Lady Margaret is aware of your allegiance to us. Your face is hardly liable to be featuring large on any wanted posters, Richard. With new identity papers, as long as you don't do anything stupid, you should be able to come and go with reasonable ease."

He could not argue with any of these points, so remained silent and allowed Goering to continue.

"You have had an easy war so far here in Berlin, especially compared with those men serving on the eastern front. Now it is time for you to make yourself useful to me in another way. The Fuhrer himself has taken a strong personal interest in your mission and has ordered that you should be provided with the maximum assistance available. If you are successful, I can promise that you will be very well rewarded."

The Fuhrer himself had taken a strong personal interest.

Any lingering shock that Richard felt was now swept away. The mention of a substantial reward was intriguing too. If he could pull this off to the Leader's satisfaction it would do a lot more than just repair his status with the Reichsmarschall. This was the kind of work that could make him a hero of the Reich. For a brief moment he pictured himself receiving a high-ranking medal and personal congratulations from the Fuhrer. Suddenly, he was fired with enthusiasm. Not that he had any real choice in the matter. To refuse would be embracing disaster.

"I will be honoured to play my part," he said. "How will I communicate? Through the established channel?"

Goering shook his head. "No, we will need something far more immediate than that. You will be provided with a suitable radio."

On the surface, this should present no difficulty to Richard. Over the last eight years of establishing networks he had become familiar with CW communications and could work competently at twenty words a minute on the Morse key. There was a problem though: the not inconsiderable one of concealment. The usual radio-in-a-suitcase type of issue issued to spies was becoming far too well known. The Gestapo had successfully identified several Allied agents in France recently just for being in possession of a suspicious looking suitcase. It could be a real giveaway.

In spite of this concern, he said nothing of it for now. He would wait and see what he was going to be given before raising the issue.

"While I would like to see this mission successfully completed as quickly as possible, do not risk transmitting until you are certain of Lady Margaret's information," Goering continued. "Once you are fully convinced of her continuing loyalty and that an air raid is justified, a single codeword can convey this. Given where and when the lady's recruitment took place, I think Olympus would be appropriate. Just remember, the British have listening stations everywhere and are quite excellent at direction finding. Transmissions must be kept to just a few seconds to avoid being located."

"And after this is done?" Richard asked. He had a feeling there was more to come.

"Yes, there is one final task after that I will require from you, Richard."

He paused before going on to explain why any attack had to be done at night. On hearing this, Richard could already make a good guess at what was coming next. He guessed correctly.

"One or both of you will need to illuminate the target for my bombers," Goering told him. "How you achieve this is your choice, but as a suggestion. you might like to consider starting a marker fire as close as possible to the house the moment you hear our planes approaching. In addition to this, as a back-up, you will also be supplied with three of the very latest Luftwaffe issue twin-barrelled flare pistols to use as you see fit."

Richard frowned. "Timing is obviously critical here. How will I know when the planes are due to arrive?"

"There will be six Messerschmitt 109 fighter bombers on standby at Saint-Omer airfield near Calais. Once I have received your codeword, I will arrange for the raid to be timed for one o'clock that same night. Listen to your radio for confirmation of this two hours beforehand at exactly eleven o'clock. After that, both I and my pilots will be depending on you. This is highly dangerous work I know, but the mission cannot hope to succeed without your help."

Dangerous work? To Richard's ears, it was now sounding rather more like a suicide mission. And there was one aspect that Goering had not yet made any mention of.

"How will I enter England?" he asked, silently praying that he would not be expected to parachute in. His fear of heights was considerable. "From what I hear, their coastal defences these days are strong. Sneaking in undetected might prove to be difficult."

"Not at all. We have established a point on the south Wales coast where you should be perfectly safe to land. Admiral Doenitz has even been heard boasting that some of his U-boats actually send men ashore at this spot occasionally to obtain fresh supplies of drinking water."

Goering allowed himself a small chuckle at the cheek of this scenario before continuing. "As you might guess, this is also a popular spot with our friends in the IRA. You will be met on arrival by two of their men and driven to the town of Swansea. From there you will be able to catch a train for your onward journey."

"And once my mission is completed, how will I return home?"

The Reichsmarschall's good humour continued. "A successful outcome will most certainly ensure you a safe and speedy return, Richard." He paused before adding: "Do you happen to know anything of the Westland Lysander aircraft?"

Although wondering why he had been asked this, Richard was keen to impress. "Yes, I have heard stories of it. It's a two-seater plane that the British use to drop off and pick up their spies in France. Much like our own Fiesler Storch, it has exceptionally short landing and take-off capabilities. It is also reasonably fast."

Conscious that he was addressing the commander-in-chief of the Luftwaffe, he did not further elaborate by adding that the Lysander was considered by some to be almost twice as fast as the Storch.

Goering merely nodded. "You might be interested to know that we captured a Lysander just over a week ago. Despite the pilot's best efforts to destroy his aircraft, he failed. It is now fully serviceable and has been transferred to northern France awaiting ...."

He gained direct eye contact with Richard and gave a small nod.

"You would use it to bring me back to France?"

"Certainly. In fact, the Fuhrer has demanded it. As I said before, he has taken a great personal interest in your mission. I gather you know of a suitable place in the Bletchley area where the plane could land?"

Richard nodded eagerly. Ideas were already taking shape in his mind. "Yes. I can show you exactly where on a map."

"Good. The Lysander will arrive thirty minutes after the target is hit. I would advise you to put aside one of your flare guns to guide its landing."

The whole idea was making perfect sense to Richard. No one would fire on a Lysander. At least, not until being absolutely certain that it was in enemy hands. The Messerschmitts would be attracting most of the defending night fighters' attention anyway. There would also be utter chaos around the Bletchley Park area once the bombs had been dropped. With the Lysander's top speed of around two hundred miles an hour, he could be safely back across the Channel in no time at all.

"When do you want me to leave?" he asked.

"Today."

Richard blinked. "Today? What about—?"

"Colonel Teske has already arranged for you to be provided with all the papers and equipment you will need. You can report to him immediately to finalise arrangements."

A flick of the Reichsmarschall's hand indicated that their meeting was now over.

Still trying to fully grasp the enormity of what he was about to undertake, and even more so of the potential rewards should he be successful, Richard rose to his feet. It was time for formality.

His arm thrust out in a stiff Nazi salute. "I won't let the Fuhrer down," he promised. "Nor you, Reichsmarschall."

With his elbows still resting on the edge of his chair, Goering merely raised a palm in acknowledgement. "I know you won't, Richard."

ONLY AFTER THE DOOR to the room had closed did Goering allow himself a satisfied smile. For someone who had proved himself to be quite skilled at deceiving others, Richard Forst could be surprisingly gullible himself.

It was true what he'd said about the captured Lysander, but did Richard really believe that such a valuable asset would be placed at significant risk just to extract him from England? As for his belief that the Fuhrer was taking a personal interest in his mission, that was simply laughable. Hitler knew nothing of it. Nor would he ever do so unless this supposedly top-secret Bletchley Park was destroyed. Only then could Goering reveal the intelligence his agents had provided regarding the code breaking efforts taking place there, and tell of how his very own Luftwaffe had completely eliminated this threat in order to ease the Leader's latest concerns.

Richard had no training or experience in espionage work and would almost certainly be captured or killed. Quite probably, Lady Margaret as well. None of that mattered; they would have both served their purpose. As for her believing that a simple letter of intent from him would restore Hadley House to her ownership once the war was won, that was in some ways even more ridiculous than Richard's naivety. This was war, and a promise made to secure what you wanted during such times was the most expendable currency of all.

It wasn't his fault if people nearly always believed what their hearts wanted them to.

NINETEEN

Margaret drew a deep breath. She did not particularly like being in dense crowds, and at this moment the crush of people milling around the paddock area of Newmarket's July course was the worst she'd known since her association with Joe Bull had begun. Finding him was proving to be rather more difficult than usual.

Naturally, it was always going to be packed on Derby Day. This year though, the enormous expectation surrounding Big Game seemed to have attracted even more punters than usual. After the colt's massively popular Two Thousand Guineas victory a few weeks previously, there was only one question now on virtually everyone's lips. Could the king's horse make it eight wins in a row and win the Derby as well? The fearful bookies had made it a heavy odds-on favourite to do so.

At last Margaret caught sight of Joe. As usual, he was surrounded by people eager to be entertained by his cheerful banter. It was, she supposed, all part of the traditional race day experience for them: one that most were quite willing to part with a few shillings to enjoy.

Butterflies danced around inside her stomach as she threaded her way closer. Since realising Richard's deception, the feelings of guilt over the path she'd chosen had become ever more disturbing. How she longed for a chance to take back that last message. But that wasn't going to happen. It was done, and now all she could do was try to live with the consequences. It wouldn't be easy. In recent days, the damning word 'traitor' had started to figure with uncomfortable regularity in her thoughts.

Moving closer still, her eyes searched to see which colour cravat Joe was wearing. Fully expecting it to be green to signify that he had something for her, it came with a jolt of surprise to see a red *'no message'* silk scarf around his neck. Only a black cravat warning her to stay well away from him could have made more of an impact.

A jumble of possibilities began racing through her head. Had a reply merely been delayed for some reason? Maybe Goering was still considering what action to take? Or perhaps he had simply been too busy to respond yet? Either way, it did not suggest any great urgency on his part to follow her advice.

From this, a flicker of hope rose. Was it possible that the fool had now completely lost faith in her intelligence and discarded her without even a curt message to say so? Despite the strength of her last message, might Bletchley Park still be safe from attack? If so, that would be a massive weight off her mind. Please let it be so. She'd then be free to continue with her life and do her best to pretend that none of her treacherous actions had ever taken place.

Although she was still at the rear of Joe's audience, his eyes seemed to instantly pick her out. For a split second she thought she saw something odd in his expression, almost as if he was afraid of her. But that was ridiculous. Why would he be? Given her current unsettled state of mind, it was far more likely that she was imagining things.

As if deliberately designed to take her mind off this, a completely separate thought then dropped into her head.

The horses!

She had grown so used to relying on Tom to provide them with their two daily feeds, she needed to remind herself that he had gone away for a few days that very morning. An older brother of his in Liverpool was seriously ill and was not expected to last for very much longer. Although they had never been particularly fond of each other, with no other close family to speak of, Tom felt it his duty to be there with him.

Margaret chastised herself. How could the welfare of her horses have slipped her mind, even for a minute? She must get home immediately. Without so much as another glance at Joe Bull, she hurried away.

DESPITE SIMON'S ASSURANCES, Betty had still felt quite powerful reservations over using the two pills he'd provided her with to coax the earl into sleep. In the end she settled for stirring just one of these into his tea, and even that compromise produced several pangs of guilt. He was, after all, a quite elderly man who had suffered a serious stroke in the past.

As it turned out, one little tablet and fifteen minutes of her playing Beethoven's beautifully soporific Moonlight Sonata proved quite sufficient to have him snoring gently in his armchair. Moving close, she spoke to him twice. There was no response. Now was her chance. Treading as lightly as possible, she hurried upstairs.

There were only three doors leading off the landing: two bedrooms and a bathroom. Margaret's room turned out to be the last door along.

Aware that her heart was beating much faster than usual, Betty made straight for the wardrobe. If the books were anywhere in here, reason told her that this was the most likely place. On the surface they would appear to be perfectly innocent items, so Margaret was unlikely to go to the trouble of hiding them away.

In spite of this logic, it was still with a sense of near disbelief that Betty saw exactly what she was looking for straight away. Sitting there in full view on the top shelf were two books kept completely separate from everything else. And just as Simon had suggested, one was quite slim and the other bulky enough to contain possibly a thousand pages. What's more...yes, it was a dictionary.

Could it really turn out to be this easy?

Lifting both books down, she saw that the smaller one was a copy of Black Beauty. This was a quite famous novel, although not one that she had ever got around to reading herself. Mindful of Simon's instructions, she made a careful note of the publishing details of each work before placing them back exactly as she'd found them.

Having got what she needed, common sense told her to get straight back downstairs. But a desire to make the most of this opportunity was also strong. What else might she find that may be of help to Simon? For no obvious reason, she felt a powerful need to prove her worth to him.

After checking the rest of the wardrobe and finding nothing of interest, her attention switched to the dressing table. Was there time for a quick look through the drawers in that as well? Yes, she decided. A glance at her watch showed she had only been up here for a little over five minutes.

While moving across the room, a floorboard suddenly creaked beneath her foot. To Betty's ears it sounded frighteningly loud. Sharply aware that the bedroom was directly above the living room where the earl was sleeping, she froze, listening hard for any sound of a reaction.

She remained locked into position for a full minute. Only then, after hearing no sound coming from below, did she feel confident enough to move once again. But her attention was no longer on the dressing table. Aside from the creaking, Betty had also felt a small but definite movement of the floorboard when making contact. It probably meant nothing. All the same, her curiosity was aroused.

Sliding aside the thin mat covering the area, she looked closely. The offending board – just a short section about eighteen inches long - wasn't just loose, it was completely unnailed. A tentative prod with her finger showed that it could easily be lifted up and removed completely.

The perfect hiding place for something? Or maybe just a board that no one had bothered to fix properly? There was only one way to find out.

Once again Betty became aware of her rapid heartbeat while looking down into the newly exposed space. Sitting there neatly between two joists was a square-shaped tin box that the lid informed her had once been packed full of shortbread biscuits. Not that it was full of anything very much now. In fact, it felt completely empty as she lifted it up and placed it on the bed.

She sat down beside her new find. Despite its lightness, there must surely be something inside, she reasoned. Why would anyone take the trouble to hide an empty tin? Drawing a deep breath, she removed the lid.

Just a rolled-up document secured with a rubber band lay inside. Betty's eyes narrowed while unrolling it. Whatever this was, the high-quality feel of the parchment certainly gave it an air of considerable importance.

No sooner had she flattened the document out than her eye was captured by a heavily embossed black logo at the top of the page featuring what looked to be an eagle with widespread wings. Directly below this, almost as if clutched in the giant bird's talons, was the unmistakable symbol of a swastika. Dated August 1936, the letter was designated as being from Hermann Goering, Commander-in-Chief of the Luftwaffe and addressed to Lady Margaret Pugh of Hadley Hall, Bletchley, England. A shiver ran through Betty.

Despite its German origin, the entire letter was hand-written in English. Betty could barely believe what she was reading: incredible promises from Goering that, in return for Margaret's *esteemed assistance in securing victory for German forces in any future war against Britain',* Hadley Hall and all of its estates would be fully restored to the earl, and thereafter to Margaret herself.

For a short time, Betty felt in a complete daze. To think that Margaret had been working for the Nazis even before the war began. For the last six years, in fact. How much damage might she have done in all that time? It was impossible to guess. There was also that reference to the earl in the letter. Was he, in spite of everything Betty believed, involved in this treachery as much as his daughter?

She read the letter again, slowly this time so as not to miss any clue that might point to the truth of the matter. There was none that she could see. Nevertheless, she still wanted to believe in the old man. She had developed a fondness for him that ....

"Betty! What on earth are you doing in here?"

The sudden sound of the earl's voice shattered her thoughts. She glanced up to see him standing in the open doorway, the look on his face suggesting a mixture of puzzlement and annoyance rather than outright anger. How could she have not heard him coming up the stairs? Had she really been so preoccupied with her discovery?

"I'm sorry," she began, desperately trying to think of what else to add.

It didn't matter. The earl's gaze had already shifted to the gaping hole in the floor and then back to the document. "And what is that you are holding?" he demanded. "I think you have some explaining to do, young lady."

This time his tone was far more accusing, cutting deep into Betty. "I wasn't trying to steal anything," she assured him.

"Then I'll ask you again. What is that document you are holding so protectively?"

Stepping fully inside the room, he moved up close and held out his hand. His voice, though now softer, was heavily tinged with disappointment. "I've always trusted you, Betty. In fact, I thought we had become rather good friends. But if you don't feel you can allow me to—"

213

"I'm trying to protect you," she jumped in.

"Protect me? From what?"

All her confidence in the old man came rushing back. Whatever Margaret had done, the earl was innocent of any involvement. Betty had never been more certain of anything. The thought that he might now be regarding her as a petty thief was tearing at her heart. She offered no resistance when he gently removed the document from her grasp with his good left hand.

Too late did the possible repercussions strike her.

The earl could not fail to spot the Nazi emblem so clearly embossed at the head of the page. "What the devil?" he began, but then fell silent as his eyes moved down the page.

Betty watched his face closely for the inevitable reaction. He began shaking his head, as if in denial of what his eyes were seeing.

He gazed at her in astonishment. "But this has been written by...by Goering of all people. He's Hitler's number two, for God's sake. How could he and Margaret possibly have had anything to do with each other?"

Betty frowned. "I don't know. Has she ever been to Germany? Before the war, I mean."

There was a long moment of silence.

"Berlin in thirty-six," the earl then murmured, as much to himself as anything else. "She went there for the Olympics."

He tossed the document onto the bed and his voice rose. "No! I refuse to believe it. This must be some kind of forgery, although why anyone would wish to create such a vile thing is beyond my understanding."

"It was hidden under the floorboards," Betty pointed out. "Margaret is the only one who could have put it there."

He once again began shaking his head in denial. "You...you're supposed to be her friend. We both trusted you and welcomed you into our home. Yet you repay us by sneaking around and accusing Margaret of being a spy. A traitor! How do I know that you weren't trying to plant that letter there yourself? That you have some twisted plan in mind to incriminate her."

Betty felt herself wilting under his gaze. All the same, she could not prevent herself from blurting out: "I'm so sorry, My Lord, but we have lots of other proof apart from this letter. We know for certain that Margaret has been passing messages to the enemy."

The earl blinked in astonishment. "We? Who the hell is *we*?"

He sat down heavily on the edge of the bed. "Are you telling me that Margaret is being officially investigated? And that you are a part of this investigation?"

The cat was now well and truly out of the bag. There was no possibility of evading the truth. "In a way...yes...I suppose I am," Betty admitted.

He snorted, as if to ridicule such a preposterous idea. Nonetheless, during the lull that followed, she could see that this did not really reflect his true feelings. Faced with such a damning document, he was at least being forced to consider the possibility of his daughter's involvement with the enemy.

"And if that is to be believed, have I been under suspicion as well?" he asked after a few seconds. With a look of disgust on his face, the old man nodded toward the letter, still where he had dropped it. "After all, according to that thing, I stand to gain every bit as much as my daughter should the war go against us."

Betty could not bring herself to lie to him. "Your involvement has been suggested, My Lord. But I've never doubted you. Not really. And your reaction to all this proves that I was right."

"But Margaret is as good as convicted? Is that what you are telling me? That it's just a matter of time before she is arrested?"

"Possibly. It's not for me to say."

The earl's eyes strayed once more to the letter. After drawing in a deep breath, he picked it up again, this time examining it closely through reading glasses produced from his top pocket for nearly a minute.

"Very well, I accept that this document has the appearance of being genuine," he eventually conceded. "However, what I do still doubt very much is the value of the promises made in it, even if the Nazis were to triumph. Which of course, they never will. Churchill and the Americans will see them off eventually, especially now that fool Hitler has got himself bogged down in Russia."

As he removed the glasses, Betty saw a tear running down his cheek.

The earl angrily brushed the drop away. "Yes I hate the bloody communists. I've never made any secret of that. But that doesn't mean I want the Nazis to take over our country. Not at any price. How could Margaret think for one second that I would ever accept any favours from such swine? What would drive her to such madness? If she is as guilty as you say, she has ruined both the family name, and her own life. All for the sake of a worthless—"

This was as far as he got. A few mumbling sounds followed, but nothing even vaguely coherent. He then began to sway from side to side so badly that he looked to be in imminent danger of tumbling to the floor.

Betty rushed over to first of all steady him, then to lay him out properly on the bed. Given his medical history, she was certain that he was suffering another stroke. There was no time to lose. With the nearest phone box she knew of nearly two miles away, she breathed a quick prayer of thanks for the fact that there was a telephone in the cottage.

Racing downstairs, she grabbed up the receiver and began dialling 999.

THE TRAIN CARRYING Richard from Swansea to Oxford pulled into the station only three minutes past its scheduled arrival time. After donning his cap, he stepped onto the platform looking every inch the English army officer.

He could not fault any of the equipment he'd been supplied with. The uniform of a major in the Royal Signals was a perfect fit, and the officer-issue canvas kitbag he carried had been stencilled with the same name, rank and service number that each of his identity documents bore. Only if someone were to dig beneath all the personal effects inside would they discover a remarkably compact SE 98/3 radio, three double-barrel flare guns, and a Luger pistol.

The kitbag was a far more convincing cover for such incriminating items than the notoriously suspect 'radio in a suitcase' he had initially been fearful of. Better still, this concealment would only be needed for as long as it took to reach Bletchley. Once there, he now knew exactly where he intended to base himself until the job was completed.

His U-boat rendezvous at a deserted inlet quite close to the small Welsh city of St David's had gone smoothly enough, even though the two IRA men he'd met up with had viewed the uniform with a large degree of suspicion and animosity. In fact, throughout the two-and-a-half-hour drive to Swansea in the early hours of the morning, neither one spoke barely a word to him. Not that this was of any great concern. They delivered him safely to Swansea railway station, and that was all that mattered.

From there onwards his assumed identity worked perfectly, and buying a ticket had presented no problem. As he'd been assured by Teske during his briefing, an officer in uniform travelling about the country was far less likely to attract attention than a civilian of conscription age would. He'd even affected a slight limp to suggest that he was still 'doing his bit', even though he could probably have been excused military service if he'd sought to. Several friendly smiles from older citizens suggested that this message had indeed been taken on board.

Once in Bletchley, having served its purpose, the uniform could then be dispensed with. But before any of that, there were two more things he needed to equip himself with. And with a bit of luck, he knew exactly where to get hold of them both.

WHENEVER TRAVELLING anywhere by train, Margaret regularly rode the five or so miles to Bletchley station on a bicycle that she had owned ever since she was sixteen years old. Here, it would be left under the watchful eye of the ever-helpful stationmaster until her return.

Today, concerned that her horses' afternoon feed would be late, the ride home was done at a rather more rapid pace than normal. As she began down the long, straight approach to Hadley Hall she found herself breathing heavily. Then she saw the ambulance parked directly outside their cottage. With jolting abruptness, her heart went from beating rapidly to feeling as if it had stopped altogether.

Father!

Somehow finding the energy to pedal even faster, she was less than fifty yards away from the cottage when the front door opened and two medics carrying a stretcher emerged. Betty followed closely behind.

Allowing the bicycle to simply fall to the ground, Margaret dashed over to intercept them. Once close, she could see no flicker of comprehension on her father's face. His pallor was deathly pale. A flashback to that awful time of nine years ago returned with startling clarity. Even though one of the medics was talking to her, she did not need any telling that he had suffered a second stroke.

She felt a hand on her arm. "We can't waste any time," Betty told her. "They need to get him to hospital as quickly as possible."

The urgently spoken words cut straight through the rising panic in Margaret. She stepped back so that the stretcher could be placed into the back of the vehicle. Suddenly, she was in full control of herself. "Yes, and I will go with him in the ambulance," she informed the medics.

"Of course, My Lady," one of them responded.

Even now, in the face of this dire emergency, other matters were not forgotten. "Tom is away for a few days and I fully expect to be staying at the hospital overnight," she said to Betty. "Will you please see to it that the horses are watered and fed before leaving here this afternoon? It's quite simple, and I know you've watched me do it a couple of times before."

"Of course I will," Betty assured her.

"Tell me quickly before we go. Do you have any idea what might have brought on father's stroke? Was he upset about something perhaps?"

Betty shook her head. "No, not that I know of. One minute we were just talking, and the next ..." She spread her hands. "I called an ambulance immediately. Thank goodness for your telephone."

"And thank goodness you were here to use it," Margaret added.

She felt an irony attached to these words. She cared a lot about Betty - she really did - and could not have been more grateful to her for what she'd achieved. Lately however, despite knowing that it was wrong, she'd been unable to prevent a slight but persistent feeling of jealousy over the amount of time Betty and her father were spending together. They had obviously created quite a bond. Almost certainly to the point where he now held a considerable affection for the girl.

When was the last time her father had been so relaxed and talkative in *her* company?

"We're ready to go now, My Lady," the medic stood by the ambulance rear doors told her. The other one was already in the driving seat.

There was no time to gather a few things. Margaret hurried into the back of the vehicle and sat down on a stool beside her father's stretcher. As the door closed, she just had time to raise a hand in Betty's direction.

"Thank you so much," she called out.

BETTY WATCHED THE AMBULANCE drive away with a sense of both sadness and guilt. Sadness, because a fine old gentleman who she had become extremely fond of was now critically ill. Guilt, because it was her actions that had undoubtedly provoked the earl's condition.

A disturbing question was also forming. Suppose the earl did recover, even just enough to speak with some small sense of coherence. What would his reaction to Margaret be now that he knew of her arrangement with Goering? Judging from his response to the letter, it was unlikely to be a particularly understanding or forgiving one. Especially after accusing her of ruining the family name.

Even though her feelings of guilt persisted, Betty refused to shirk away from what she knew must be done next. Returning inside the cottage, she dialled the special telephone number that Simon had given to her. He replied after only two rings.

As concisely as possible, she related everything that had happened and asked for further instructions.

"Stay right where you are," he told her. "I'll be there as quickly as possible."

SIMON ARRIVED TWENTY minutes later, just as Betty had finished attending to the last of the three horses. He was driving one of the military staff cars that she had often seen coming and going at the Park.

They headed straight into the cottage living room and sat down at the dining table. Betty had already placed Goering's letter down on this, together with the two books she suspected of being the key to Margaret's code. From a small briefcase, Simon added to these items the same sheet of paper he had used when explaining to her how the code worked.

As Betty expected, his attention went first to the damning letter.

Once he had finished reading he gave a soft whistle, at the same time shaking his head. "I can certainly see how this might have caused the old chap to have another stroke. If he really is as innocent as you insist, it must have been a terrible shock to his system."

Betty did not respond. She had no wish to be further reminded of her part in the earl's collapse. Instead, she slid the two books closer. "I hope these are the right ones. I didn't find any others that seemed to fit the bill."

All trace of Simon's reflective moment disappeared. Digging into his briefcase again, he produced a notepad and pen. "Yes, let's get on with it and discover the worst."

After only ten minutes of working together on the code, two things became apparent. Yes, these were the right books. And yes again, the worst possible scenario had indeed developed.

"What do we do now?" Betty asked once the message had been fully decoded.

He sighed. "For your side of things, I want you to put these books and this letter back exactly where you found them. Do your best to make it look as if no one has been in that bedroom."

"And for your side?"

He gave another sigh, this one much deeper than the first. "Once back in the office, I need to call some very important people. And believe me, that's something I'm not looking forward to in the slightest."

IT NEEDED TO BE DARK before collecting what he needed, so Richard had several hours to kill. A couple of these were spent checking that the place he had in mind was still there and serving the same function. To his relief, it was. Three more hours were then passed in a city centre cinema where he mostly dozed through an entirely forgettable black and white comedy film and several newsreels informing the gullible British public of how well the war was going.

Hunger then took him to a nearby pub where the dubious sounding rabbit stew was the main dish on the menu. To his surprise, it actually tasted quite good, encouraging him to mop up every last drop with a bread roll. While eating, much of the conversation going on around him centred on the shock defeat of the red-hot favourite, Big Game, in that afternoon's wartime Derby run at Newmarket. According to one disgruntled punter who had actually been at the course, such was the disbelief amongst the crowd at seeing the king's previously unbeaten horse finish in a distant sixth place, the result was met in almost complete silence.

With his meal finished and the daylight fading, it was time to make a move. He headed toward the west of the city, keeping going for the best part of three miles. By now, the kit bag was starting to feel particularly heavy. Richard was thoroughly sick of lugging the damn thing around, but he would never risk parting with it. Not even for a second. Without the radio, he would have no hope at all of achieving his mission. Nor of returning home to Berlin. To be stuck in England, praying for the invasion to come quickly, was his very worst nightmare. Much better to think of the positive things. Yes. The prospect of a personal audience with a grateful Fuhrer and the rewards that he would likely bestow were more than enough motivation for him to see this thing through to a successful conclusion.

By now he was in a mostly rural area, with only isolated houses scattered about. Moving away from the road and down a dirt track, he headed closer to the dwelling that was his target. A combination of blackout restrictions and sparse moonlight meant that he had to pick his way carefully. But yes, he had the right place.

As a young man in the days when he was motorbike crazy, Richard had often made the journey here. The owner of the secluded house and ramshackle barn nearby was Hughie Carter, a temperamental character who'd lived in this same spot on his own for more years than most people could recall.

Although never a man to back away from a shady deal, there was one quite legal skill that Hughie was the absolute master of. There was not a thing in the world that he did not know about motorcycles. The trouble was, he had some weird kind of inner selection process for those he deigned to help. Far more customers were turned away than were ever accepted. Nobody understood what criteria the grumpy old sod used, but if you did not fit them, the only spanner Hughie was liable to pick up on your behalf was one thrown across the workshop to help you on your way off his premises.

Fortunately, without knowing how, Richard had passed the test that allowed him to become one of the chosen few. As a result he'd learned much, and the successive bikes he owned were never in anything less than peak condition. In fact, three of them were rebuilds bought direct from Hughie himself. Now, more than a decade after that last sale, he wanted another. The only difference this time was that he did not intend paying for it.

He'd viewed Hughie from a distance when checking the place out earlier that day. The man had to be at least in his mid-seventies by now, and did not appear to be moving with anything like the same fluency as before. With luck, his hearing would have deteriorated as well. Knowing that Hughie was a habitually early sleeper and riser, Richard sat on an old tree stump and watched the house, waiting for the dim flicker of light creeping from behind a ground floor blind to go out.

He did not have to wait for long. The man often used to remark in his own cantankerous way that: *"Ten o'clock's my bedtime, and I don't work late for anyone."*. It seemed that little had changed.

Just to be on the safe side, Richard waited for another thirty minutes before approaching the old barn that served as Hughie's workshop. The flimsy Yale lock on the double doors was easily slipped open, allowing him to step inside. Only after closing the doors behind him did he switch on the lights. With no window in the premises, little trace of these shining would be visible from the outside.

Apart from the variety of motorcycles that were currently for sale, nothing much else had changed. One machine immediately caught Richard's eye - a Vincent Rapide combination. The low slung, single-seater sports sidecar would be a godsend. He'd been hoping to find a bike with decent sized panniers to carry his stuff, but this would serve the purpose much better. It would also allow him to take a more plentiful supply of what he'd be needing to ensure the success of his mission: petrol for a fire to mark out Bletchley Park for the incoming bombers.

His eyes moved around the workshop until spotting a dozen, one-gallon cans in the far corner. A quick inspection confirmed their contents. He smiled. Without special coupons or some kind of official authority, Richard knew that petrol was almost impossible to get hold of in England. The same was true in Germany. Yet, as anticipated, Hughie's dubious connections had allowed him to remain well stocked with the stuff.

After locating the correct ignition key from amongst several others hanging on a board and checking that the Vincent had enough fuel in its tank, Richard loaded six cans of petrol deep into the leg space of the sidecar. From a nearby shelf he then took down two boxes of coarse grade steel wool and added these. Finally, his kitbag served to wedge everything securely into place. Satisfied that he now had all he needed, he switched off the workshop light and opened the doors.

It was time to go.

Unless Hughie was a very heavy sleeper, starting the engine so close to the house was sure to wake him. That left only one option. He would have to push the bike at least a hundred yards down the lane first. The old bastard would be furious on finding it gone, but given his many shady deals, it was most unlikely that he would be reporting its theft to the police.

Returning to the Vincent, Richard grabbed hold of the handlebars and drew a deep breath. At least the lane ran slightly downhill going away from the house. That was something to be grateful for. Perhaps it wouldn't take too much of an effort after all. Once he got the thing outside and moving, he might even be able to freewheel for most of the way. That would ....

"What the bloody hell are you doing in here," a voice growled.

Richard's heart gave an almighty jolt. Even though there was little light to see by, Hughie's voice was unmistakable. So too for that matter was the silhouette of his figure that had suddenly appeared in the open doorway. He was holding what looked terrifyingly like a shotgun.

Before Richard could even begin to answer, Hughie reached across to flick on the light. It took only a second or two for recognition to dawn.

"I remember you," the old man stated. "Richard...Richard Forest. And look at you all dressed up like an officer." His tone hardened. "You were one of them I took a liking to and helped out. Is this how you repay me? You come sneakin' back here looking to rob."

Richard could already feel sweat forming on his brow. The shotgun was pointing directly at his chest, and Hughie's double-handed grip on the weapon was rock steady.

He said the first thing that came into his head that might sound even vaguely plausible. "It's not like that, Hughie. I've got a car now, and I ran out of petrol a couple of miles up the road. I know you always keep a few cans here, so I came to see if you'd sell me a couple."

"And when you thought I'd gone to bed, you decided to just help yourself."

"No! I didn't want to wake you up, that's all. I was going to leave you a note and some money. I give you my word on that."

"Like an officer and a gentleman, you mean?"

"Yes. If you like. Come on, Hughie. You know I wouldn't lie to you."

With the shock of discovery now subsiding, Richard's mind was starting to work more clearly. Hughie might have that gun, but he was unlikely to use it unless seriously threatened. Hell, the thing might not even be loaded. He had an enormous advantage of strength and agility over the old man. All he needed to do was keep him calm; an opportunity to grab the weapon would come along soon enough.

Hughie spat on the floor. "I always sleep with one ear open. Can hear a pin drop anywhere on this property whatever the time of night." His gaze shifted briefly over to the far corner. "There's nothing wrong with my eyes either, and I can see there's a damn sight more than two of my cans gone missing."

He gave a sharp flick of the shotgun. "Move away from that bike. Let's see what you've been doing there."

Richard backed away a couple of paces from the Vincent.

"Further. Up next to that bench."

The workbench indicated was at least fifteen feet away. Much too far to safely make a rush for the old man, even if his attention were to be momentarily diverted. Richard's eyes scanned around for a weapon of some kind. There was only one thing he could see that was near enough. Lying on the bench, just out of reach, was a wooden handled mallet with a solid rubber head. It was a hefty item, weighing probably close to two pounds. Hughie had often referred to it as his 'persuader'.

Now standing next to the sidecar, the old man stooped to inspect what had been put inside. At the same time, Richard inched slightly closer to the mallet. He then watched as his kitbag was yanked out and barely glanced at before being dropped onto the floor. He found himself praying that the radio had not been damaged.

With the petrol revealed, Hughie fixed him with an unforgiving glare. "So much for wanting only two cans, eh. Not to mention taking off with the most valuable bike in here right now." He nodded downwards. "Maybe you've got something else of mine in this here kitbag as well."

Keeping his eyes flicking rapidly between Richard and the bag, he began to unfasten the top buckles with just one hand. Although this was making the task awkward, he obviously had no intention of putting the gun down to make it any easier for himself. Not even for a moment. Richard silently cursed. That's what he'd been hoping for. But then a break came in another way. As Hughie's gaze shifted back to the bag for the umpteenth time, he suddenly spotted the name stencilled across the end.

A frown formed while shifting slightly to get a better look. "Who the hell is Major Roberts?" he began. "Have you been—"

That was as far as he got. Fully aware this might be the only chance he'd get, Richard had already snatched up the mallet and hurled it at Hughie. For a despairing instant he thought his throw was too high. But then, initially aware only of a flurry of movement and not the onrushing missile itself, the old man instinctively began rising from his crouch. By the time he might have realised his mistake, it was too late. Two pounds of brutally hard rubber smashed into the side of his head. With barely a sound he crumpled to the floor, the shotgun slipping from his grasp.

Richard closed in at full speed. Not that his haste was necessary. An ugly mark on the side of Hughie's head showed that the missile had struck him directly on the temple in an apparently fatal blow. After only a few seconds, there appeared to be no sign of him breathing. Nor could Richard find any trace of a pulse.

He stepped back, struggling for a short time against waves of nausea. Although probably responsible for a considerable number of deaths through the network of spies and informants he'd set up for Goering, he had never actually killed anyone with his own hands before. Yet what had he expected? He was here in England as an enemy agent to perform a task that would result in the deaths of many. This wasn't some damn game. He needed to toughen up fast.

Gradually, he pulled himself together. Although unexpected, he could now view what had just happened as being a good thing. Having killed once, he should be able to do so again without hesitation if the mission demanded it. In fact, the more he thought about this, the possibility that he might be forced to kill several more times yet before heading back to France was starting to look very real indeed. He'd already selected a perfect place for his pick-up plane to land. Only if conditions there had changed quite dramatically would an alternative spot need to be sought.

Calm now, he regarded Hughie's body once again. There was no harm in leaving it exactly where it was. He would be well away from here by the time the old man was discovered. As a further precaution, he picked up an oily rag from the floor and wiped the mallet handle clean of any fingerprints. Not that the police had his prints on file anyway, but it made him feel better. Now there was nothing to connect him to the crime.

After placing his kitbag back in the sidecar and wheeling the Vincent outside, Richard switched off the workshop light. He closed the doors so that the Yale catch engaged enough to superficially lock the place up. Given Hughie's legendary temper, few people would dare to push on them hard enough to force their way in without good reason.

The bike started on the second kick. With two-thirds of its headlight taped over to comply with blackout restrictions, Richard was well aware he needed to ride cautiously. Not that this was a concern. It was only forty or so miles to Bletchley, and he had all night to get there.

TWENTY

S imon leaned back in his office chair, yet again wondering if there was something more he could be doing to aid the situation.

The Prime Minister's reaction to his decoding of Margaret's message had been swift. Expert opinion deemed that a daylight raid was highly improbable, and that any night attack on Bletchley Park was almost certain to come in the form of a conventional force carpet bombing the entire area. To clinically pick out such a small target in the dark without ground assistance would be virtually impossible, even for a group of small fighter-bombers in a low-level attack.

Based on this reasoning, an entire squadron of the very latest Mosquito night fighters at nearby Cambridge was being held on standby for the sole purpose of intercepting any bomber stream heading in the direction of Bletchley. Large numbers of Hurricanes had also been issued with similar instructions, and even though a daytime assault was considered improbable, several Spitfire squadrons were alerted just in case of the unexpected.

As for measures on the ground, three Royal Artillery regiments creating a total of seventy-two anti-aircraft guns were in the process of being transported to strategic locations in order to form a circle completely around Bletchley Park. This twenty-mile-wide defensive ring would be able to intercept any bombers that managed to evade the night fighters, no matter which direction they approached from.

Yet even with all this deployment, Simon remained troubled. The experts might think that a low-level night attack was out of the question. Even he couldn't see how such a strike might be made successful unless there were others working with Margaret, and there'd been absolutely nothing to suggest that this was so. Nevertheless, the possibility continued to play on his mind. As did the fact that Goering had still not responded to her latest message. After being presented with such vital intelligence, why the continuing silence? Did the Luftwaffe chief doubt its truth? Or was this simply a lull before the storm?

The fact that Bromley Home Guard night patrols around the Park's outer perimeter were to be replaced by a company of experienced regular soldiers until further notice did little to ease his concern. For the sake of local gossip, word had been put about that this was merely a training exercise.

He glanced at his watch; it was nearly 1.00am. Perhaps he should try to get some sleep? The camp bed in the corner of the office suddenly looked very tempting. Betty was back at her digs and no doubt already catching up on some well-earned rest. As for Margaret, she was still at Northampton hospital. He would be informed the moment she left there, and of any change in her father's comatose condition. The old chap must not be allowed to speak with her and reveal what he'd discovered. If that happened, she would need to be arrested immediately. All good sense said that this should be done regardless, but Simon could not shake off the disturbing suspicion that there was something critical yet to discover, and only by allowing Margaret to remain at large for a time longer might this be revealed.

She was a resolute woman who would not be easily shaken. However, if he could do something to seriously unnerve her, maybe that would push her into making a rash mistake?

After a few minutes of pondering on this, he reached for the telephone.

FEW WORDS WERE EXCHANGED between Margaret and Doctor Grant during the drive from Northampton Hospital back to Hadley Hall. While the doctor's black Austin Seven chugged steadily along, Margaret stared silently out of the window contemplating her father's plight. Right at this moment, nothing else was of any importance.

At the hospital that morning, the hard facts had been presented as gently as possible. The chances of him ever regaining consciousness were exceedingly slim. Even if he did somehow manage to come out of it, extensive brain damage would leave him with little ability to function for himself. Although they were doing everything they could for the earl, she should prepare herself for the worst. Meanwhile, it was pointless for her to remain at the hospital. Any change in his condition, however slight, would be reported to her immediately.

After being at his side in the ambulance and detecting barely a flicker of life throughout the forty-minute journey, Margaret had been half-expecting this prognosis. Now that it was confirmed, her emotions were surprisingly well under control. In fact, she soon found herself accepting that it would be far kinder if her father were indeed to slip away now rather than wake up and remain lingering on in a vegetative state unable to perform even the simplest task. He would despise that, even if he was unaware of it.

Of course, his death would mean losing all rights to remaining at the cottage. Yet this was far from uppermost in her mind. Her first thoughts were for her horses. What would become of them, especially Soldier, if she no longer had the stables?

She was still dwelling on this when the car arrived at Hadley Hall.

"Are you sure you will be all right on your own," Doctor Grant asked.

His question snatched her back into the present. "Yes, I'm fine, thank you," she assured him.

"Well, if there is anything you need, you only have to ...."

She held up a hand to stop him. "Thank you for the lift, doctor. However, all I want at the moment is a bath and some sleep." She stepped out of the car, closing the door firmly.

He took the hint, and with a final sympathetic smile, drove off down the long driveway.

Margaret headed straight for the stable block. Yes, she did want a bath and some rest, but not before attending to the horses. It was ten o'clock, and well past time for their morning feed. They would all need exercising as well, but she was way too tired for that. It would have to wait until after she'd caught up on a few hours of sleep.

She had completed the feeds and was filling the last of the water buckets when a brief noise that seemed to be coming from Tom's small apartment directly overhead caught her ears. No, she decided, he could not have returned already. Anyway, even if he had, he would have come down to inform her of this. Almost certainly the noise was nothing more than some of the old timbers shifting slightly.

But then came another noise, and this time there was no mistake. It was footsteps. She hurried over to the bottom of the stairs to call up. "Tom. Is that you?"

There was no reply.

She called out again, this time much louder. Still there was no response. A deep frown formed. He must have heard, and Tom would never deliberately ignore her. Unless ....

Unless it wasn't Tom up there.

Suddenly aware that her breathing had quickened, Margaret's eyes swept around for something to serve as a weapon. They settled on a shovel used for mucking out the stalls. If this was some low-life sneak thief up there, she was damned if she would run off and make it easy for them to get away.

With her makeshift weapon grasped in both hands she tip-toed up the stairs, although having already announced her presence, treading softly now felt somehow pointless. She paused at the top. The door leading into the apartment was ajar. She drew a deep breath. Would it be better to rush straight in and hope to gain an element of surprise, or should she ease the door more fully open first to see who she was dealing with? She was still debating on this when a man's voice called out to her.

"Come in, Margaret. It's been a long time, and I've missed your company."

Although she recognised the voice almost at once, for several seconds she thought she must be hallucinating. Richard couldn't be here. Not in England. It wasn't possible.

And yet there he was. A simple push on the door confirmed it. He was lounging on Tom's little two-seater settee. What's more, he was dressed in the uniform of a British Army major. The shovel slipped from her grasp.

"Come in," he repeated. "We've got a lot to talk about."

ONLY AFTER SEVERAL late-night telephone calls and pressure from the very top in Whitehall had the senior staff at Northampton Hospital eventually agreed to go along with Simon's deception. In truth, the earl's condition was nowhere near as bad as the consultant had gravely informed

Margaret. Quite astonishingly, he was now conscious and showing no evidence of any further brain damage. After explaining this to Betty, Simon could see a wave of relief wash over her.

"Thank God," she breathed. "But why make Margaret believe differently? I know she's a traitor and all that. Even so, surely that's just being cruel."

"Possibly," he agreed. "But an air raid may be coming at any time, so all tactics are permissible. If she's emotionally stressed then she might just let something slip when you next talk to her. I've a suggestion on that front that I'll tell you about later."

"Can't you tell me now?"

"There's something else I want you to do first."

He leaned forward. "I need you to go to Northampton Hospital and speak with the earl. It's important that we keep him and Margaret well away from each other until we know how he's coping with the situation, and you're the only person he might be prepared to open up to."

Betty nodded. "That makes sense. When do you want me to set off?"

"Straight away. I've already arranged for a car to take you there. It should be waiting directly outside. It's still quite early, so with a bit of luck you'll be back here by mid-afternoon."

She rose from her chair. "I'll let you have a full report as soon as I return."

"Yes. And then I can brief you about that other stuff."

What a change in her, Simon reflected after she had left the office. Gone was the apprehensive recruit unsure of what she was becoming involved with. In spite of her youth and inexperience, Betty was now absolutely indispensable to Bletchley's security. He wondered if she was aware of exactly how much he was depending on her. Most likely she did. The fact that she had recently been taken off all other duties and was at present answerable only to him must have provided quite a strong clue.

That the fate of Britain's most vital war asset could well rest on the inexperienced shoulders of just one young WAAF was a truly daunting thought. Nonetheless, it was a fact. With Margaret as yet oblivious to the true nature of their friendship, her undoubted affection for Betty was the one thing that might yet be exploited to save the situation.

MARGARET STEPPED INTO the room, her mind still struggling to come to terms with Richard's sudden appearance. Why had he risked everything by coming here? And where on earth had that British officer's uniform come from?

Her thoughts quickly switched to the glib lies he'd told her and how much she despised him. To Richard, and to Goering, she had been nothing but a useful fool. A damned fool whose faint hopes that she would never hear from them again had now suddenly been crushed. For a moment, utter despair gripped her.

He rose to his feet and moved closer. "You don't look all that happy to see me, Margaret. Is something wrong?"

Sharply aware that she must not give him any reason to doubt her ongoing commitment, she forced a smile. "No, nothing is wrong. But I'm finding it incredibly hard to believe that you have risked coming to England. You can't blame me for being surprised. How on earth did you get into the country?"

He smiled in return. "That's not important. What matters is what we are going to do together now that I am here." He waved a hand toward the settee. "Come and sit down with me. There is much we need to discuss."

Margaret allowed herself to be ushered onto the seat.

Once settled beside her, he asked: "Where is Tom? Did he die?"

"No, but his brother in Liverpool is seriously ill. He went there yesterday morning and I'm not expecting him back for several days."

"Ah. I wondered why the apartment was unoccupied. The cottage also when I first arrived."

She lowered her head. "Father had another stroke yesterday. He's not expected to survive this time. I've been at the hospital all night."

"I see. That explains everything."

A cold fury raced through Margaret. Was that it? Not even a brief expression of sympathy. My God, how he had changed. He was literally unrecognisable from the Richard she'd known in the old days. Or at least, the Richard she had thought she'd known. There was even a look on his face that suggested he found this development convenient. Which of course, it probably was if he intended to remain here for any length of time. Her father would certainly have had a lot of awkward questions for him.

A short silence followed. Richard then said: "However, I bring you good news. Reichsmarschall Goering is most impressed with the intelligence you have provided concerning Bletchley Park. So much so that, subject to my confirmation, he has agreed to follow your recommendation that it be bombed."

Margaret was aghast. But if she had only taken time to think about it, that could be the only logical reason for Richard being here now.

"Subject to your confirmation?" she said, striving to conceal all trace of her alarm.

"A small reconnoitre of my own that I will do later today. Just to check the lie of the land."

Margaret's initial reaction was to blurt out that she had made a mistake and since discovered that the place was far less important than she'd first imagined. But he was unlikely to believe her. Not after the emphatic tone of her last message. Also, a last-minute change of story was sure to arouse his suspicions. More than anything, she now wanted to stop what she had set in motion. But how? Exposing Richard would only serve to reveal her own treachery.

Much as it disgusted her, she had little choice but to play along with him. At least for a while until she knew more. Most importantly, she needed to discover exactly when the bombers were coming. Maybe then she could make an anonymous warning to someone. It was all a bit vague at present, but the best her exhausted mind could come up with until she'd had some sleep.

"And after you have made your check, what then?" she asked.

"If all is satisfactory, I will summon the bombers. That's when I'll be needing your help."

"Help to do what?"

"To illuminate the target, of course. Even a Luftwaffe pilot would be unable to locate a single house in the blackout. I'll explain about that later."

"And when will the bombers actually come?"

Margaret held her breath. Could she really get an answer to this key question so easily?

He regarded her sharply. "Why are you so keen to know that?"

"I'm not keen," she told him. "I'm concerned...concerned for your safety." She shifted just a little bit closer on the settee. "How are you going to get away once the bombs start to fall? Remember, if you are caught, that could lead back to me. There are a lot of people who'll remember how much we used to hang around together before the war."

He appeared to accept this explanation. His frown disappeared. "Don't worry, that's all been arranged. Another plane will follow shortly after the bombers to take me back to France."

Margaret was astonished. "Really! Where will this plane land? There is no suitable field for miles around. All the flat ones have been ploughed up and are growing crops to meet government quotas."

He smiled. "There is a place not far away. In fact, if your father is going to die soon then you might want to think about coming with me. You'll have nowhere to live once he's gone. At least, not until Britain surrenders and you get Hadley Hall back once again."

A fresh surge of hatred for him seized her. That he could so casually dismiss the death of her father was sickening. Nazism had turned Richard into a loathsome monster. It was almost impossible to keep her revulsion from showing.

Somehow though, she *had* to keep it hidden. She touched his arm. "Let me think about that. Right now, I just need to sleep. I didn't get a wink all night at the hospital."

He nodded. "Yes, go to bed. I'll come over later and we can talk some more then."

She had just reached the door when he spoke again. "I trust you completely, Margaret. Believe me, I do. However, the Reichsmarschall prefers to leave nothing to chance. He is committing some of his most valuable aircraft and pilots to this mission, so it is vital to him that it succeeds. He instructed me to inform you that ...."

He paused, prompting Margaret to look at his sharply. "Inform me of what?"

His expression was deadpan. "That should the bombers fail to destroy Bletchley Park, a radio transmission 'accidentally' naming you as an accomplice to the raid will be broadcast. One that is certain to be picked up and decoded by the listening stations here."

For a second or two, Margaret was speechless. For what felt like the thousandth time she asked herself how on earth could she have been so damned stupid as to fall for their sweet talk and empty promises in Berlin? Only an all-consuming desire to find a way of gaining revenge prevented her from exploding in a flash of temper.

Drawing on resources buried deep inside, she forced an air of nonchalance and even the hint of a smile. "Forgive my initial look of surprise, Richard. I believed I had already done more than sufficient to earn Herr Goering's confidence. But don't worry, I understand that this is not of your doing. I'll assist you in whatever way I can to ensure a successful outcome. Who can tell? Maybe circumstances will dictate that I must join you on that plane?"

Her smile was returned. "Indeed. Who can tell?" He made a shooing motion with both hands. "Now go...go, catch up on your sleep. Don't worry about the horses. I'll see to their afternoon feed. I need you to be fully rested for what lies ahead."

Margaret made her way over to the cottage. Unwilling now to wait for the water to heat up, all thoughts of a bath were postponed. Instead, she settled for a quick wash at the sink before crawling wearily into bed. Get a few hours rest, she told herself. Then maybe I'll be able to start working on a way out of this terrible mess.

But what if there wasn't one? Richard's last-minute revelation meant that he held all the aces.

What if she was forced to see this thing through? How many people might die if Bletchley Park were to be destroyed?

Could she really live with that?

RICHARD PEERED OUT of the apartment window to confirm that Margaret had entered the cottage. Not that he seriously considered her resolve to be weakening. Yes, she had shown alarm for a few seconds on first seeing him, but that was to be expected. She had also quite rightly pointed out that if he were to be captured, that would put her at risk as well. Once over the initial shock, he thought she had sounded as determined as ever. And even if she wasn't, Goering's threats would be more than enough to ensure her full cooperation.

Of course, he had no real intention of taking her back with him on the Lysander, whatever her decision on that. The plane was only designed to carry one passenger, and to squeeze in another would be sure to slow it down at a time when as much speed as possible was needed to get safely back across the Channel. Nevertheless, if she believed there was an escape route available, that should increase her willingness to play a full part. With her father on the point of death, what did she have to lose? Richard was surprised that the old man had lasted out as long as he had since his first stroke.

He returned to the settee. Yes, he had changed a lot since those days when he and his parents used to be guests at Hadley Hall. He'd had to. Only by being ruthless and dedicated to the Nazi philosophy was the world ever going to be made fit for decent Aryan people. Scruples were for the weak. Although he might once have been a little fond of Margaret, he strongly suspected that there would be no happy ending for her when this war was finally over.

He'd arrived at Hadley Hall not sure what to expect. The stable block apartment was the perfect place to base himself, so he'd been quite prepared to dispose of old Tom if he was still around. Or anyone else there who might present a problem. As it was, a fortunate set of circumstances had made this unnecessary. He'd be long gone before the old groom returned. With the earl conveniently out of the way as well, it was a sure sign that the gods of fortune were all working hard in his favour. He could not – *he would not* – fail.

Everything was now ready. His radio was already set up in the adjoining bedroom, its internal batteries capable of providing infinitely more user time than he was ever going to need. As long as his reconnoitre of the target this afternoon did not throw up any unexpected problems, he could transmit the codeword straight away.

By tomorrow morning, Bletchley Park would be nothing but rubble.

TWENTY-ONE

U ncertain of how he may greet her, it was with a rising sense of trepidation that Betty entered the earl's private hospital room. He was lying motionless in his bed with eyes closed. Only a shallow rising and falling of his chest indicated that he was still actually alive.

"Are you awake, My Lord?" she asked in a voice that was somewhere between a whisper and her normal volume.

"Yes, Betty, I hear you," he responded after a moment of silence.

His eyes opened. "That MI5 chap hanging around outside brought me a message from young Simon Straw of all people to say you were coming. I've been trying to gather my thoughts ever since. Such as they are, that is. It's damnably difficult to make sense of anything at present."

His speech, although slightly more impaired than before, was still comprehensible. Equally encouraging, his tone didn't sound especially hostile either.

"That's only to be expected, My Lord," she said. "I know how hard this must be for you." She sat in a chair alongside his bed. "Do you mind if I ask how much you remember?"

His eyes misted over. "Enough to know that I have almost certainly lost my daughter. I take it there is a lot more evidence against her aside from that foul letter. That the proof is incontrovertible."

"Yes, My Lord. I'm afraid that it is."

"Has she...has she been arrested?"

"Not yet. But very soon, I think. At the moment she is unaware that we know of her spying."

With his head still resting on the stack of pillows, he gave the slightest of nods. "I should have seen it. All those damn fool questions she kept asking about Hitler and the Nazis. She was never the same after going to Berlin in

237

thirty-six. Someone over there must have filled her head with all kinds of nonsense." A deep sigh slipped out. "I suppose there is one consolation. I doubt she was ever able to give the buggers anything useful. Not that this is any kind of excuse."

Betty made no reply.

"Anyway, if she hasn't been arrested yet, where is she? Why hasn't she come to see me?"

"Lieutenant-Commander Straw thought it better to keep you two apart for the time being. You know, until things are more settled."

He gave another slight nod. "That's probably for the best. Margaret might be my daughter, but right now I don't think I could bear to look at her."

A short yet difficult silence developed.

Out of the blue, he then asked: "Tell me, were you ever really her friend? Or were your visits to the cottage always just a contrived arrangement to catch her out?"

Although the question took Betty by surprise, there was no hesitation in her reply.

"Absolutely not! I knew nothing about Margaret's spying at the beginning. The piano lessons started out as more of a business arrangement than anything else. But we did become proper friends rather quickly, especially after I started playing regularly for you. We even went riding together several times. She was so happy to see you finding some pleasure in life once again. It was only after Lieutenant-Commander Straw asked me to assist him that it became …."

She paused to wave a hand, searching for the right phrase. "Well, I suppose you can guess how it was. But you must know one thing. I became genuinely fond of you…I still am. No matter what else was going on, I always looked forward to playing for you, and to our discussions afterwards."

"So did I, Betty. You can't possibly know how much. You have an amazing talent for someone so young. That Steinway and you were made for each other."

Several seconds passed before the earl spoke again. This time it was in a reflective tone. "I met young Simon several times back when he was just starting out in the navy. Smart chap, as I remember. I always knew he would do well for himself. To tell you the truth, I think he used to have quite a soft spot for Margaret. Not that they ever actually got together as far as I know. A shame really. I think they would have probably fitted together rather well."

Only then did the bitter irony of the situation suddenly seem to strike him. "And look where they both are now. Him about to have her arrested, and she to be tried as a traitor to the country."

At this point, everything suddenly became too much. A loud sob escaped, and the tears that he had been so grimly holding back came flooding out. It broke Betty's heart to see him in such despair. Instinctively, she took hold of his hand resting on top of the bed covers. There was nothing useful she could say at this point, so she waited for him to compose himself once again. He was a man of powerful will. She knew that, no matter how fierce the pain, his pride would not allow any public display of anguish to linger for an instant longer than he could help.

And so it was. He was soon trying, without much success, to brush away the tears with his one good arm. Betty produced a clean handkerchief from her pocket to help him.

"Thank you, my dear," he told her. "And now, if you don't mind, I'd rather like to be on my own for a while."

"Yes, of course," she responded, rising to her feet.

She paused by the door to glance back. "If there is anything else that..." she began, then stopped herself. The earl's eyes were already closed again, and this time he gave no indication of having heard a word.

She closed the door gently behind her.

SIMON GAVE A NOD OF approval as Betty finished making her report. There had been a moment of slight embarrassment when she spoke of the earl's remarks concerning himself, especially the mention of his 'soft spot' for Margaret. But that aside, everything was as he hoped for. The old boy was obviously not going to cause them any difficulties. At least, not in the short term.

That side of matters concluded, he told Betty of all the extra security measures now in place to protect the Park. Although he had no binding obligation to do so, he felt a compulsion to tell her anyway. She was his right arm in all of this, and he wanted her to feel as safe as possible.

She grinned. "It sounds as if even a gnat couldn't slip through."

"Absolutely," he agreed, "But it would help even more if we knew exactly when an attack is due. Or even if one is coming at all. There's still been no reply to Margaret's last message, so perhaps Goering isn't convinced by what she's told him. Our air defences are strong, and he'd be well aware of the risks. It could cost him and the Luftwaffe dearly to act on what he must surely see as no more than one person's unsubstantiated information."

"So it's possible that even Margaret herself doesn't know what's on the agenda," Betty said.

"That's right. Even so, I can't shake off this feeling that she's still got an important part to play, and that arresting her now will do more harm than good. It could be a massive risk I'm taking. Winnie will have my head on the block in an instant if it goes wrong. All the same ...."

He lapsed into a brief silence.

"You said earlier that you want me to talk to her again," Betty prompted.

Simon nodded. "Go to see her this evening at around eight o'clock on the pretence that you want to know about the earl's condition. But before you leave, make a point of dropping it into the conversation that you've now been put back on night duty for the foreseeable future. Watch her closely when you tell her that."

"And am I? Back on night duty I mean."

"No, of course not. But from everything you've told me, Margaret seems to have developed quite an affection for you. Would you agree?"

"I think so. Especially after the business with her father."

"So if she does happen to know that a raid is due at the same time that you'll be on duty, it's likely to spark a reaction. At least a fleeting one."

Betty nodded. "Yes. That's possible."

"Then it will be up to you to spot it. If there is any sort of response, let me know straight away. We can take that as a pretty definite sign that something is coming very soon."

"And if there isn't?"

"In that case, go back to your lodgings and get some sleep. We'll talk again in the morning."

"And what about Margaret?"

He sighed. "Maybe it will be time to bring her in. I'll have to sleep on it."

IT WAS LATE AFTERNOON when Richard, now dressed in the drab clothing of a farm labourer, began a circuit of Bletchley Park's perimeter astride the Vincent combination. What he witnessed appeared to substantiate everything that Margaret had told him.

It all looked a lot different to how he remembered the place. For a start, the amount of activity going on around the main entrance was astonishing. Half a dozen buses had pulled up, and together with the scores of disembarking passengers, they were pretty much blocking the entire road. He was forced to pull up for a time, allowing him to take in the scene more fully without appearing to be deliberately loitering.

Virtually all of the bus passengers were Wrens. Richard looked at his watch; it was approaching four o'clock. Could this be the changing of a shift? The timing suggested that it may well be. Also arriving were several groups of WAAFs, together with clusters of both men and women in civilian clothing. Unlike the Wrens, all of these were making their way to the gate either on foot or by bicycle. However, one thing was absolutely consistent. No one was being permitted entry without first having their security pass checked.

After a minute or so, a suitable gap in the road appeared, prompting Richard to move on. One of the soldiers at the gate had already eyed him a couple of times. Given that he'd been pretty much forced to stop anyway, it was probably nothing. All the same, he was relieved to be away from the man's gaze.

Further along it was much quieter, with just a perimeter fence of closely spaced iron railings topped with barbed wire on one side of the road, and open farm fields on the other. He'd had no idea the place was so large, or that so many people were working there. He'd imagined that everything would be centred on a few dozen highly skilled codebreaking experts working within the mansion itself. That was the impression Margaret's messages had suggested. But this was clearly a far more widespread concern incorporating all manner of ....

Of what exactly? Even at a leisurely pace it was hard to see anything much on the other side of the fence because of all the trees and dense vegetation. Only occasionally was he able to catch a glimpse of a drab looking hut or brick outbuilding, but their purpose was unclear.

After completing his circuit of the grounds, the bike's mileometer showed that he had covered very nearly two miles. For some strange reason, he found himself making a mental comparison. Whatever top secret intelligence work was going on behind all the security at Bletchley Park, it was requiring an area that was comparable to the vast Olympic stadium back in Berlin. So much for preconceived ideas.

By now, the coaches had departed from the main entrance, meaning that there was no reason for him to stop this time around. All the same, there was a significant number of people leaving the place. This was taken in at a quick glance and only served to confirm in his mind that a change of shift had indeed just occurred. Coupled with the obviously tight security, Richard was now as certain as he could be that Bletchley Park was every bit as important as Margaret had claimed. And even if it wasn't, the bombing could go ahead anyway. After having taken so many personal risks, he had no intention of missing out on the Fuhrer's gratitude.

He rode on until arriving at a spot that he'd made a note of during his first time around. Here, a five-bar gate led into a deeply ploughed field full of a potato crop that was only a few weeks away from harvesting. On the far side of this field ran a narrow lane that he'd established earlier would take him back onto the main road leading away from the town of Bletchley. As an escape route, he could not have expected to find anything much better.

Even so, time would be tight. He'd have just thirty minutes after the bombers arrived to be in position ready to guide the Lysander in. He wasn't fool enough to think the plane would risk waiting very long for him in such dangerous skies, so there could be no delay in getting to the rendezvous point. He would need to be on his way there the moment the first bomb fell.

Richard cast an eye carefully about. Aside from two figures so far away that they were little more than specks, there was no one else in the surrounding fields. He rode the motorcycle through the gate, taking care to close it behind him, then removed the six cans of petrol from the sidecar. These were slid down into a drainage ditch next to the hedgerow and covered as best he could with a mixture of earth and bits of shrubbery. They would be there for only a few hours, so it was highly unlikely anyone was going to come across them before he returned.

Satisfied, he eased the Vincent back onto the road, taking care to check that the gate was securely fastened. One left hanging open was just the kind of thing that might attract unwanted attention to the spot.

While heading back to Hadley Hall, he resolved to wake Margaret immediately. There was a lot for them to discuss.

MARGARET WAS ALREADY awake. Barely had she opened her eyes when all the harsh realities of the situation returned to assail her.

Her first thoughts were of her father. Despite what the surgeon at the hospital had told her about his condition, she longed to see him. Even though he was in a coma and wouldn't know she was at his bedside, there were still things she felt she must say to him before he died. But Richard's sudden arrival had put a stop to that. The bombers would be coming very soon, possibly even tonight, and he was sure to demand that she stay close at hand.

She was still dwelling on this when she heard the sound of a motorcycle approaching. On looking out of the bedroom window, it was with only a small sense of surprise that she saw it was Richard astride the machine. She continued watching as he parked the bike inside one of the old Nissen huts and then approached the cottage. He walked straight in through the front door. His voice carried easily up the stairs.

"Margaret. Are you awake?"

"Wait in the living room. I'll be down in a minute," she called back.

She drew a deep breath in an effort to compose herself. He must not suspect her change of heart. Yet even if she did succeed in retaining his trust, that would be only one small step. In spite of a quite lengthy sleep, the far greater challenge of how on earth she might be able to prevent the air raid without incriminating herself still seemed to be insurmountable. An awful truth was starting to dawn.

Maybe incriminating herself *was* the only way to stop things?

If the doctors were right about her father, it was unlikely that he would ever get to know of her shame anyway. As for her own fate, with so much now lost to her, did she really care all that much any longer? Wouldn't it be better to try and make amends for her foolishness? It was either that, or she would have to do whatever Richard required of her and somehow live with the consequences.

On entering the lounge, she found him stretched out in her father's armchair by the window. Even this simple act felt somehow disrespectful, driving her loathing of him to an even greater pitch. It became physically painful to produce a friendly smile.

"Have you been for your inspection?" she asked.

He nodded. "And now I have an important question for you. What do you know of the night-time security there? I assume you have checked on all of that."

She wanted to tell him that it was heavily patrolled by professional soldiers, but he would only have to return there after dark to easily expose that as a lie. Maybe this was even his way of testing her truthfulness and commitment?

She sat down on one of the upright chairs at the table before replying. "I have no knowledge of what measures there are inside the grounds, but as far as the outside perimeter is concerned, the only patrols I know of are those done by the Bletchley Town Home Guard."

He laughed. "The Home Guard...really? We have heard all about them in Berlin. A bunch of old men, the infirm, and conscientious objectors with no stomach for a fight. We should have no problem in dealing with them."

"But inside the grounds might be very different," Margaret pointed out in an attempt to deter him, if only for a little while longer. "It's quite possible that there are highly trained troops on patrol there. It's impossible to see in the blackout."

Her remarks drew a careless flick of the hand. "Whoever is on the far side of the fence will present little problem. We will be gone well before they are fully aware of what is happening."

This was the second time that he had used the word 'we' in the conversation. "So what is it you are expecting from me?" Margaret asked.

"I told you before. To help me illuminate the target for the bombers."

"Yes, I know. But how will we do that?"

"I have petrol, and I have flare guns. These will serve our purpose admirably. You need only concern yourself with the flare gun that I will supply you with."

Rising from the armchair, he produced a small notebook and pencil from his pocket and then joined her at the table. Margaret watched as he began to draw a rough outline of Bletchley Park and the surrounding roads.

Once finished, his finger indicated an area directly behind where the mansion was situated. "This is where I would like you to take up position. The trees in this spot are quite dense and will provide you with more than sufficient cover in the blackout."

Margaret nodded, but remained silent. He was absolutely correct, so there seemed little point in debating the matter.

"I already have petrol in place and intend to start a large blaze on the perimeter right here," he continued, now indicating a point further to the north. "But wait until you see my flare go up. It should last for nearly a minute. When it seems to be fading, fire your two flares and then leave immediately on your bicycle. As long as you follow my instructions there will not be any danger. I will meet you at the road junction here. What with all the confusion once the bombs start to fall, no one will be concerned about two people on a motorcycle."

"And what then? Where will we go?"

He smiled. "That will be up to you, Margaret. I can either drop you off at home, or, if you wish, you can return to Berlin with me and enjoy a good life until such time as the war is won. The Fuhrer himself has promised to reward us well for our work here tonight, and Hadley Hall will still be waiting for you at the end of it all."

He paused to touch her lightly on the arm. "On the other hand, I know how you must feel about your father. So if you prefer to stay here and try to carry on as normal, that's understandable. No one is ever going to suspect such a well-regarded member of the aristocracy of having had any involvement with the bombing."

Margaret looked into Richard's eyes and knew at once that he was lying. It was all way too glib. He had no intention of taking her back to Germany with him. Not that she had any desire to return there anyway. After having done what he wanted, she would be abandoned to flee the scene as best she could. And even if she did manage to make it safely home, he would be long gone by then.

Yet in spite of all this treachery, and her longing to stop what she had set in motion, what else could she do? There was no possible way that she could prevent Goering from issuing that damning radio message. At least by pretending to go along with things she stood a chance of evading the hangman. Much as she fought to dismiss it, the prospect of a sudden drop into oblivion through a scaffold trapdoor had never before figured quite so prominently. Or seemed so horribly real. She touched at her neck for a moment, sure she could feel coarse rope hairs rubbing against the skin there.

A second consideration also arose. What if the doctors were wrong and her father did recover sufficient awareness to become aware of her crimes? How terrible would that be for him? There was no possible way she could prevent Goering from making good his threat of the radio broadcast.

Richard was looking closely at her, no doubt taking her short silence as evidence that she was actually considering the two escape options he'd presented.

Somehow forcing a hint of enthusiasm into her voice, she said: "That sounds like a very good plan, Richard. You have obviously thought of everything. And maybe we *can* leave together. When will the bombers be coming?"

"I see no reason to delay. It will be tonight at precisely one o'clock."

"So soon?" Margaret struggled to keep the alarm from her voice.

"Yes, why not? You said yourself it is a good plan. Besides, the longer I am here, the greater the risk of detection."

It was impossible to argue against either of these points. A feeling of inevitability swept over Margaret. If she was doomed to go through with this terrible thing, perhaps it might indeed be better to get it over and done with quickly? Thinking for too long about the many deaths her actions were liable to cause would surely drive her mad.

"Tonight it is then," she agreed.

TWENTY-TWO

The loud knock on the cottage door startled Margaret out of her almost trance-like state.

Despite struggling not to, she realised that for the last half an hour she had been totally lost in fearful thoughts of what might develop during the coming night. The arguments for and against her participation had raged incessantly inside her head, leaving her feeling mentally battered. Now she wondered who could possibly be knocking. It wouldn't be Richard, even though he had left her more than an hour ago and disappeared into the stable block apartment. No, he would have simply walked straight in as if he owned the place.

Opening the door, she found that it was Betty standing there. Surprisingly, she was in her WAAF uniform. Margaret had not seen her friend wearing this for quite some time. Her still muddled mind tried to recall the reason for this. It didn't come.

Betty gave a hesitant smile. "I'm so sorry I haven't had a chance to catch up with you before. How is the earl now? Please tell me he's recovering."

The girl's concerned look reignited the heartache that Margaret had been trying so hard to suppress. At least until Richard was gone. "I'm afraid not," she said in a low voice.

Betty's hand flew to her mouth. "My God! He hasn't ...."

"No, not yet. But it will only be a matter of time according to the specialist. He's unlikely to come out of the coma he's in."

Her friend reached out in a comforting gesture, but Margaret drew back. Richard might appear at any moment. She had to get rid of the girl as quickly as possible.

"If you don't mind, Betty, I'd rather be on my own right now. Perhaps you can come back again in a day or two?"

She nodded gravely. "Yes, of course. If that's what you want. Although I'm not sure how much spare time I'm going to have for a while. I've just been dumped back on night duty. You know, the dreaded midnight to eight o'clock shift. That doesn't leave very much time for anything other than working and sleeping."

Her words crashed into Margaret's already overloaded brain. She blinked. "You can't be. I thought you told me you'd been reassigned to regular day shifts. Just Monday to Friday. That's what you said."

Yes, she realised with a rush. That was why she had not seen her friend in uniform very much recently.

"I thought so too," Betty replied, pulling a disappointed face. "But then my old department head asked to have me back."

All kinds of horrible thoughts were now whirling around in Margaret's head. "When do you start your first shift?" The question came out as an automatic response. She already knew the answer. The renewed sight of the uniform told its own story.

"Tonight," the girl confirmed.

For several seconds Margaret found herself completely unable to speak. Betty was looking at her closely. "Are you alright?" she asked. "You've gone rather pale."

At last Margaret found her voice. "Don't pay any attention to me. I get these silly turns sometimes, but they're nothing to worry about. I'll be right as rain in a tick."

"I should go then," Betty stated. "You've already told me you'd rather be alone for now, and I can understand that. Your father is such a dear man. It must be so hard for you."

"No, I've changed my mind," Margaret responded quickly. "I *would* like you to stay for a little longer. In fact, there is something very important I need to show you."

There was no mistaking the spark of curiosity that appeared in Betty's eyes. Not that Margaret had any idea of how she was going to follow this up. All she knew for certain was that she could never allow her dear friend to be placed in such terrible danger. It was traumatic enough having to contemplate the possible deaths of so many people that she didn't even know. But for Betty, the girl to whom she owed so much, to be amongst those casualties really would be more than she could ever live with. No matter what the risk to herself, she had to do something to prevent this.

But what?

"It's over in the mansion," she continued, a vague plan forming.

"I'm not sure." Betty glanced at her watch. "Maybe it's best if I get going. Besides, I thought you'd already shown me everything there is to see over there."

"Not this. It's been stored away in the cellar for a long time now. It's a special secret that only father and I know about."

After her brief hesitation, the curiosity was back in Betty's eyes. "You certainly make it sound intriguing," she said.

Margaret cast an anxious eye in the direction of the stable block; there was no sign yet of Richard emerging. Even so, they must get over to the mansion as quickly as possible. Stepping out from the cottage door, she took Betty by the arm.

"Come on. You won't be disappointed, I promise. And it will only take a few minutes."

Walking as briskly as possible without giving cause for alarm, she guided Betty toward the big house. Once inside and out of sight from the stable block, she paused to look the girl directly in the eye. "You do know how much our friendship means to me, don't you, Betty?"

She appeared a little puzzled by the question, but answered quickly enough. "Yes, of course I do. I feel exactly the same way. Surely you must know that by now."

The reply removed any trace of lingering doubt in Margaret's mind. She gave a fond smile. "Come on then. It's this way."

They moved on toward the rear of the house, eventually stopping at a solid oak door secured with sturdy bolts at the top, middle and bottom. After sliding back all three of these, Margaret reached into a cupboard fixed to the wall nearby. Inside were half a dozen switches, each one designated to a separate part of the house by a tie-on label. She pulled down on the switch indicated as being for the cellar. Light immediately showed through the partly open door.

"Be careful of the steps," she warned, leading the way down a wooden staircase.

The huge cellar was packed with old furniture, crates, and general household equipment. Gazing down at all of this, Betty hesitated on the top step.

"What are you waiting for?" Margaret asked her.

"I'm just wondering what you could possibly want to show me."

"Well, if you don't come down, you'll never find out."

With her friend clearly unsure of things, Margaret produced what she hoped was a reassuring smile. "But here is a clue. If I said the name Beethoven and then added the word autograph, what would you think?"

There was an unmistakable note of anticipation in Betty's response. "You mean a letter written by him? Or even a signed manuscript?"

Margaret's smile persisted. "Why don't you come and see for yourself?" She pointed toward a mahogany roll top bureau nearby.

With knowledge from several remarks Betty had made in the past, she knew that Beethoven was one of the girl's most admired composers. Quite possibly her most favourite of all. The lure of seeing something hand-written by the great man would surely prove to be irresistible.

But it did not work out that way. To Margaret's astonishment, Betty abruptly stiffened. "No, that can't be right," she said. "A document like that would be worth a fortune. If you really owned one, there would never have been any need for this house and the estate to be sold."

For several seconds, Margaret was too stunned to respond. Before she could, Betty added: "I'm sorry. I've heard people in the town talking about how the government and tax people took everything away from your father. It was such an awful thing to happen. I can understand why you don't ever want to talk about it."

The sharp riposte came without thought. "Can you? Can you really? What they did to him was unforgivable. After all the time you've spent together, you must know for yourself what an honourable man he is. Yet now he is lying in a hospital bed with little hope of survival and I don't know what to do for the best. How can I ever make things ....?"

Margaret's voice faded away and her fists clenched tightly as all the pent-up emotions seized her. For a long moment there was absolute silence. Betty then advanced slowly down the steps and held out a hand.

"There is something very bad troubling you, Margaret. I can see that. Why don't we go back to the cottage and talk things over? You never know, maybe I can help."

"Help me?" Margaret wanted to laugh out loud. "I was the one trying to help you. I was trying to save your life."

Betty's hand dropped, a look of disbelief forming. "Save my life? How?"

"Yes, why don't you tell her, Margaret?" said a voice coming from the doorway at the top.

Her eyes darted upwards and a small gasp slipped out. Standing there was Richard.

The pistol in his right hand was pointing directly at the pair of them.

AFTER LIGHTING ANOTHER cigarette, Simon's thoughts yet again turned to Betty.

She had not reported back to him, and it was now just after nine o'clock. It seemed as if the news about her change of shifts had not drawn any significant reaction from Margaret. Together with the lack of further messages from Goering, this helped to reinforce the idea that the Reichsmarschall was not prepared to sanction such a risky bombing raid on Margaret's word alone.

All this should have been a big relief. Yet it wasn't. The feeling there were developments taking place that he knew nothing of persisted to trouble Simon. Then, half an hour later, the telephone rang.

A voice from Arkley View data collection centre informed him that an unidentified radio transmission of just one word – Olympus - had been picked up a short time ago. The transmission had been too brief for accurate direction finding, but it definitely originated from a point somewhere within twenty miles of Bletchley Park.

Simon found his hand shaking as he replaced the receiver. Olympus had to be a codeword for something. And given that the message was from an unidentified source, the potential risk it presented could not be ignored.

What if there was an attack coming tonight after all? One that Margaret had no knowledge of. It suddenly appeared horribly possible. In spite of all the defensive measures in place, he couldn't help but wonder if there was more that could be done. *Should* be done. Only one person could decide that.

He reached for the telephone again, this time dialling a special number he had been given for direct communication with the Prime Minister. His final thought before a voice answered was one of enormous relief that Betty should be back at her lodgings by now.

If an air raid really was coming, then at least she would be a darn sight safer on the far side of town than bang in the middle of the target area.

RICHARD LOOKED DOWN at the two women, the Luger in his hand not wavering. "So, Margaret. Do you want to explain to me what is going on? Who is this, and what is she doing here?"

"Her name is Betty. She is a friend of mine. That's all."

"And the uniform?"

"She's a WAAF. She works at Bletchley Park."

"Ah, I see. One of your impeccable sources of information, no doubt."

Betty glared up at him. "I never talk about my work. Never!"

He glanced at her for only a moment before returning his attention to Margaret. "In that case, if she has been of no help to you, why would you wish to save her life?"

Margaret shifted uncomfortably. "She's been a most marvellous friend to both me and father. That's why she came to the cottage: to ask me about his condition. Then she said that her shifts had been changed and that she was going to be on duty tonight. I had to do something."

"So you thought you could lock her safely away in the cellar here until the bombing is all over. Is that it?"

His words slammed into Betty. "Bombing! What bombing?" She rounded on Margaret. "Is he saying that Bletchley Park is in for an air raid tonight?"

Despite all the terrible damage that she knew the bombs might do to the war effort, the first thought that leapt into her head was for Simon. Would all the defensive measures in place be enough? The mansion would likely be a prime target, and his office was right there on the top floor. If any of the German planes did succeed in getting through?

She forced this awful prospect from her head.

Margaret could not meet her gaze. "I just wanted to protect you," she mumbled. "I thought that if—"

"You thought too much," Richard cut in. "It would have been better if you had just let your friend leave and carry on as normal. That way she might have stood a slight chance of surviving the raid. As it is, I am now forced to kill her." He made a small flicking motion of the hand. "Stand aside please."

To Betty's astonishment, Margaret did the exact opposite, stepping quickly across to place herself directly in the firing line between them. "No! You mustn't harm her," she told Richard.

He frowned in bemusement. "You would protect this girl with your own life? Your friend is a risk, and this mission is vital. It *must* not fail. I will simply shoot you both if necessary."

"Maybe. But if you kill me, who will help you to illuminate the target?"

His frown grew deeper. Encouraged, Margaret pressed on.

"You need me, Richard. You need me to be sure that the bombers can identify the manor house clearly. That's why you want me to be stationed so close by. It is by far the most vulnerable position to be in, any fool can see that. I accept the risk anyway. But I'll tell you this: I swear on my family name that I won't lift a finger to help you if you harm Betty."

"So you do not care about being exposed as a spy yourself?" Although he huffed a laugh, there was an uncertain edge attached to it.

"Of course I care. And I still want to help you make this mission a success. It's just that I have to live with my conscience afterwards."

Realising that her life was hanging on the result of this conversation, Betty remained absolutely still and silent. Even so, her mind was racing. So much so that fear for herself had not yet had a chance to fully take a grip. All she could think of at the moment was the confirmation from Margaret's own lips that the manor house was destined to take the main force of the attack. There had to be a way she could do something to stop this.

"In times of war, a conscience is for fools, Margaret," Richard remarked. "Many people die. That is the natural way of things."

Her tone was resolute. "Maybe so, but that is my final word on the matter. It's your choice how you wish to continue."

"You are making things very hard for yourself...and for me," he said after a few seconds.

She responded quickly. "I don't see how. Just think about it for a minute. If we leave Betty locked in here, how can she possibly interfere with anything? And as soon as the raid has taken place, you have another plane coming to pick you up. We can be safely on our way back to Germany long before anyone is able to stop us."

He raised an eyebrow. "You said *we*'. Does that mean you've definitely decided to come back with me?"

"I haven't really got any choice now that Betty knows about our plans. She might be a good friend, but she would never be able to stay silent over this. In any case, as you pointed out yourself, Richard, once father is gone I'll have nothing here. No family and no home. Not a damn thing apart from a possible date with the hangman. On the other hand, life in Germany until the war is over might be quite good. You've already said that Herr Hitler himself will be only too happy to look after us both well enough if tonight goes as planned."

He nodded. "That's true. But what about your friend? It might be many days before anyone finds her. I can't believe that you'll just leave her here to die of thirst. Not after everything else you've just said."

"No, of course I wouldn't let that happen. I've already thought about it. I'll write a note to my solicitor telling him where she is and pop it in the post box at the crossroads just a mile away. There will be a collection there first thing in the morning, and because the letter is local it will be delivered the same day on the second post."

She swung around to face Betty. "You'll be uncomfortable for a while, but Mister Bridle is sure to see my note by lunchtime tomorrow. Someone will come soon after that to free you."

While speaking with her back briefly to Richard, she gave a rapid wink. There was no clue as to what this was meant to convey. All the same, Betty felt a flicker of hope.

After turning once again, Margaret looked directly up at Richard. "So, are we agreed? Betty stays here, and we leave together on the plane. It's either that, or you'll have to kill us both and hope you can manage things all on your own."

For what seemed like an eternity to Betty, Richard stood there expressionless while considering matters. The hint of a smile then formed.

"You know what, Margaret?" he began. "I really should have taught you how to play poker. You would have been an absolute natural."

THE CELLAR DOOR SHUT with an ominous thud. This was followed by the rattle of the three bolts being pushed securely home. A moment later the lights went out, plunging Betty into darkness.

She had noted the stoutness of the door when entering; it looked to be at least four inches thick and would be impossible to break through without some kind of heavy cutting implement. There was the darkness to contend with as well. Even if there was to be a highly convenient axe or something like that amongst all the other stuff here, she would never be able to find it.

Yet again, her fears for Simon returned. The thought of him dying was unbearable. If only she had reported back immediately after seeing Margaret's quite obvious reaction to news of her night duty. But she had lingered, thinking perhaps Margaret might be about to reveal some other vitally important detail that he should know about. By the time this proved to be a false hope, it was too late.

If only...if only.

She had never doubted Margaret's genuine affection for her. Her friend's attempt to lock her up safely out of the way of the bombing had simply confirmed that. Yet in spite of this, the fact that Margaret had apparently been willing to go way further – as far as to risk her own life in order to protect her – that was truly staggering.

Based on this revelation, there was now just one thing to help keep her spirits up. That secretive wink. What exactly it was meant to convey could only be guessed at. Could it be a sign that Margaret had some hidden agenda that her accomplice knew nothing about?

Right now, this seemed to be just about Betty's only hope.

TWENTY-THREE

Richard switched off the radio. Confirmation had been received in the form of a second codeword: Marathon. The bombers would be arriving in exactly two hours. If all went well, he'd soon be returning to Berlin acclaimed as a hero of the Reich.

Much as he longed to be such a hero, Richard had little appetite for becoming a dead one. He'd selected a position for himself on Bletchley Park's perimeter that was relatively safe, and provided the means for a rapid getaway. Margaret was the one left with the vitally important and dangerous role of illuminating the mansion house. Though the camp was far more widespread than anticipated, he was still convinced that this was where the most important work was being done. In any case, a large country house was specifically what the Luftwaffe pilots had been ordered to look out for and concentrate their bombs on.

That Margaret had realised so easily that hers was by far the most dangerous role had been a touch disconcerting at first. However, she'd accepted this and was still prepared to play her part. Not that she had very much choice in the matter, especially since this friend called Betty had become aware of her activities. He was still incredulous that Margaret should even want the girl to remain alive, let alone that she'd been prepared to risk her own life in order to save her. In his eyes, this once again proved how emotionally unstable women could be when firm decisions were required. And it would cost her dearly. He was now more certain than ever that leaving her behind to face the consequences was the right thing to do.

By the time her flares went up, he would already be back across the field to where his motorcycle waited. With any luck he might just have time to see the first bomb fall before heading off to meet the Lysander. As for Margaret, even if she wasn't killed by the blast of a near missing strike, she would be most unlikely to escape the area undetected with only a bicycle to rely on. Especially if she was fool enough to wait around for any length of time in the expectation that he would be picking her up as promised. For a supposedly well-educated and intelligent woman, she had always been a little bit too trusting for her own good. He'd known as soon as he'd seen her in Berlin that she was the perfect subject for recruiting.

And now that intuition was about to pay off in the most rewarding way imaginable.

EVEN THOUGH AT JUST twenty-three years old he was already a hardened veteran of air combat, it was with a greater sense of excitement than usual that Oberfeldwebel Erich Kimmel eased himself into the cockpit of his Messerschmitt 109F-4. With routine thoroughness, he ran through his pre-flight checks.

For several days he and five other specially chosen pilots from his staffel had been on standby for a mysterious mission that was said to have the close attention of Reichsmarschall Goering himself. Now the details had been disclosed, although why a manor house in the middle of the English countryside was so important remained a mystery to him. A direct hit, or probably even a near miss, from just one of their 250-kilogram bombs should be more than enough to completely obliterate such a small building. To send six planes made it a very important mission indeed.

Night raids often presented a number of problems in identifying the right target. But not in this case, apparently. They had been promised that assistance on the ground would make certain the correct house was clearly illuminated for them. How this was to be achieved had not been stated. Kimmel suspected that no one at the briefing actually knew for certain.

He was to be the last to take off from Saint-Omer and would be at the rear of a loose line astern formation as they flew up the North Sea at an altitude of just fifty metres. Only when north of Felixstowe would they turn west and head inland toward the target, still maintaining low-level flight so as to avoid radar detection. With luck they would catch the British night fighters unprepared, especially the formidable new twin-engine Mosquitoes.

As the moment for take-off arrived, Kimmel wondered if his position in line might be symbolic of his entire Luftwaffe career. Here he was playing catch-up yet again. Despite all his experience during the Battle of Britain and on the Eastern Front, he was still an NCO with apparently no hope of ever receiving a commission.

But then again, given his less than wholehearted enthusiasm for much of what had been done in the name of National Socialism, it wasn't really surprising. Even though he took care not to openly voice criticism, he suspected that sufficient doubts had been placed against his name to hold him back. There was also the matter of his quite modest family background; his father was a tailor and his mother a librarian. Perhaps he should have been born a count or baron?

These thoughts were rapidly pushed aside as he became airborne. There was a job to be done, and despite any feelings of resentment, he would be doing it to the very best of his ability.

IT WAS 11.29PM WHEN Simon received a second call from Arkley View. Another single word transmission had been intercepted, this time originating from somewhere in northern France. The codeword used on this occasion had been Marathon.

The connection between Marathon and Olympus was obvious. However, it was the alternative connection that suddenly dawned a second or two later that really shook Simon.

Margaret's trip to the Berlin Olympics. The time when she had almost certainly first been recruited by Goering.

This could not be a coincidence, he decided. Despite not having heard back from Betty, it looked as if Margaret must be fully in the picture about the timing of the raid after all. It was hard to believe that she was prepared to let her young friend die without revealing a flicker of emotion, but there was no other conclusion he was able to draw.

Now the seed was sown, Simon could not prevent other desperate thoughts from developing. He'd assumed that Betty was safely back at her lodging house. But what if she wasn't? What if Margaret had seen through the subterfuge and done something awful to the girl in order to cover her tracks. The mere thought of any harm coming to Betty was almost too painful for him to bear. He had to know that she was safe.

There was no telephone at her lodgings. Only a personal visit to the house would be sufficient to calm his mind.

"IT'S TIME TO GO," RICHARD told her. "We need to be in position early."

Margaret, dressed in black riding trousers and a dark jumper as instructed, did her best to look eager. "Yes, let's get it done."

They had been sitting in Tom's apartment for the last half an hour. Richard's tension was clear. He had repeated yet again in detail what he was expecting her to do, then lapsed into a long silence. She felt she could make a darn good guess at what was going through his mind, and none of it boded well for her.

There was just a slender crescent moon outside, making it impossible to see clearly for any great distance. The motorcycle, with her bicycle already loaded into the sidecar, was parked just by the entrance. Margaret climbed onto the pillion seat behind Richard, much like she used to do back in those carefree days of just a decade or so ago. It was a bitterly ironic moment. So much had changed since then, it felt more like fifty years had elapsed.

Richard set off at a cautious pace, partly because of the severely restricted headlight, and partly because of the steel wool she had seen him push into the exhaust to reduce the sound of the bike's approach.

Margaret could not even begin to count the number of times she had either ridden or walked along these lanes and fields; every small feature of the area was indelibly etched into her brain. When they eventually pulled up on a fairly narrow lane rarely used by anyone other than local farmers in their tractors, in spite of the darkness and featureless landscape of potato fields, she knew exactly where they were. He had picked his spot well. Absolutely no one was liable to be coming along here at this late hour.

After they'd dismounted, Richard pulled her bicycle from the sidecar. He then pointed to the far side of the field next to them. "Over there is where I'll be starting the fire," he told her. "I already have plenty of petrol in place, so that will not be a problem."

Margaret could easily picture his plan. He would soak all around the hedgerow and as far as he could through Bletchley Park's railings directly opposite with petrol, then retreat a safe distance before firing a flare into the centre of this. He could probably do it even from as far back as where they were standing right now. After then firing a second flare into the sky for her benefit, he could be away on the motorbike literally within seconds of the blaze igniting. For a moment she wondered where his rendezvous with the rescue plane would be. She still couldn't think of any field nearby that would be suitable for one to land.

His voice interrupted her thoughts. "I know it's only the Home Guard, but keep well away from where you know they patrol. Even so, it shouldn't take you more than fifteen minutes from here to get into a good position. Then it will be just be a matter of waiting for my signal."

He paused to touch her encouragingly on the arm. "This mission is vital and must not fail, Margaret. I know we've discussed your task many times already, but do you have any last-minute questions?"

She shook her head. "None at all. I know exactly what I must do."

IT WAS WITH NO TRACE of a welcoming smile that Betty's landlady, bleary-eyed from sleep, opened the front door of her house in response to Simon's loud and repeated knocking.

"What the heck is going on?" she demanded. "It's darn near midnight."

As calmly as he was able to, Simon enquired whether Betty was at home.

"Not as far as I know," the woman responded. "But you people at the Park come and go at all kinds of funny hours. Hang on there while I go and check her room."

She returned a couple of minutes later with a shake of the head. "No sign of her, I'm afraid. She's definitely not here."

Something that felt very much like a hard punch to the chest struck Simon. He raced back to the staff car parked by the gate.

"Where to now, Sir?" asked the driver, a tough looking RAF corporal. "Back to the Park?"

Simon fingered the Webley .38 service revolver he had so hurriedly shoved into his pocket before leaving the office. "No," he said. "Hadley Hall. And make it as quick as you can."

RICHARD WAS REACHING inside the sidecar for the flare guns when Margaret seized her opportunity. She had already taken note of what looked like a broken fence post lying on the ground just a couple of yards away. The moment he turned his back on her she quickly grabbed this up and swung it with all her might.

Some sixth sense must have warned Richard of the danger, but he had only half swung around by the time the post crashed down onto the top of his head. Fragments of wood flew in all direction, suggesting that the post was at least partly rotten. For a horrible moment Margaret thought he was going to simply shrug off the blow and rear up at her. His chin then sagged to his chest. Encouraged, she swung again. This time it was more than enough. Richard slumped forward, settling in a heap near to her feet.

The first thought that flew into her head was to wonder whether or not she had killed him. An instant later she realised that she didn't really care if she had. If that was the only way to prevent a mass slaughter at Bletchley Park, then so be it. What happened to herself wasn't important any longer. Her life was ruined anyway.

After rolling his body over, she leaned closer and pressed a finger to his neck. It was almost with a sense of disappointment that she felt a pulse. For a second or two she was actually tempted to strike him again to finish him off. Then something of the old Margaret returned and she knew that she couldn't do it. Not while he was already unconscious and no threat to her. In any case, for all she knew, he might already be dying. It was well known that head injuries often had delayed fatal consequences.

She quickly found the Luger, which she hurled away as far as possible into the hedgerow. The two flare guns then followed the same path.

Her only thought now was to get back to Hadley Hall as quickly as possible. She looked at the Vincent, then remembered what Richard had told her years ago about how much more difficult it was to steer a combination than it was a solo motorcycle. This was certainly not the time to be risking an accident. Besides, in the current darkness, she was sure she could get back home more quickly on her bicycle. Especially as she knew a couple of shortcuts through fields that she could push the bike across. Even if well ridden, the combination would find it impossible to follow the same path.

After a final check to ensure that Richard was still unconscious, she swung into the saddle and began peddling.

THE CAR WAS STILL COMING to a halt when Simon leapt out from the rear and raced up to the cottage to give three resounding thuds on the front door. He waited for only a few impatient seconds. With no sound coming from inside and finding the door locked, he ran around to the back. The door here was also secured, but gave way surprisingly easily under a bit of firm pressure. Pausing only to pull the Webley from his pocket, he stepped inside.

Passing through the small kitchen, he flicked on the light in the living room. An open notebook on the dining table immediately caught his eye. On the exposed page was a crudely drawn map that, on closer inspection, was clearly meant to be of Bletchley Park and the surrounding roads. Two crosses had been marked on this: one in the area of trees directly behind the mansion, the other further north where there were open fields beyond the perimeter fence.

Two crosses?

The niggling possibility that Margaret might have an accomplice somewhere in the background suddenly felt like a very real prospect. Maybe it was even a second person who had drawn this rough map? It certainly did not look as if it had come from her usually neat and quite fussy hand.

The voice of his driver sounded from behind just as he was shoving the notebook into his pocket. "Is everything all right, Sir? Do you need a hand with anything?"

Simon turned to face the man. "Thank you, corporal. I'm going to check if anyone is upstairs. Perhaps you would like to wait in the hallway just in case I need you."

After all the noise he had already made, there seemed little need for stealth. In any case, the urgency to reassure himself that Betty was not in any kind of danger would not allow him to hesitate for a moment longer than necessary. He mounted the stairs in a few rapid strides.

With just two bedrooms plus a bathroom and toilet to check, the search was completed in only a couple of minutes. Finding no trace of anyone or anything that might offer a clue, Simon rapidly considered where to go next. To thoroughly search the big house would take an enormous amount of time. Time that he might not have if a raid was imminent. On the other hand, he recalled Betty telling him that the groom Tom was away for a few days. His living quarters was clearly the next place to look.

While the corporal set about searching the stables, Simon dashed up to the apartment.

The discovery of a uniform and identity papers for a major in the Royal Signals, together with what he recognised to be an Abwehr issue radio in the bedroom, confirmed all too clearly that the intercepted codewords reported by Arkley View had been sent and received on this set.

With the compact radio weighing less than ten pounds, Simon was easily able to pick it up before heading back down to the stables. At least there would be no more messages coming from this damn set, he told himself. But this was little consolation. The sense of impending disaster was now overwhelming, and his concern for Betty had risen to an even greater pitch.

He *had* to find her.

"All clear down here, Sir," the corporal called out while approaching. The sudden boom of his voice drew a few nervous whinnies from the stalls, but they quickly settled down again.

"Put this in the car," Simon told him, handing over the radio as they stepped outside. "Then come over to the mansion. We need to search that as well."

"Blimey, Sir, that's going to take just the two of us a fair bit of time," the man said, eyeing the vast shadowy shape in the gloom ahead. "Do you think maybe I should go off and see if I can rustle up a bit of help?"

An uncharacteristic surge of irritation ran through Simon. "We don't need any delays. Save me your suggestions and let's just get on with it, eh corporal."

He regretted the sharp words at once. The man was only trying to be helpful. He knew nothing of his concern for Betty, or of the rapidly approaching threat to Bletchley Park.

At that moment, his eye was caught by a small movement further down the lengthy driveway. In the near darkness, it at first appeared as no more than a tiny speck of light. Then, on drawing closer, he could see that it was the shielded headlamp of an approaching bicycle.

It was Margaret, and she was peddling furiously in their direction.

WELL AWARE OF ROUGHS Tower, a spotting station and anti-aircraft gun platform situated seven miles off the Suffolk coast, Oberfeldwebel Kimmel and the five other Messerschmitt pilots were aiming to fly well to the east of this defensive fort before turning west and heading inland to their target. What they were not quite so informed about was of a second sea fort six miles south of Roughs that had been grounded and made operational only two weeks previously. Sunk Head Tower was also a few miles further out to sea. Far enough out for the passing of the low flying attackers to be duly noted and reported by telephone to the mainland.

There were already Mosquitoes circling at 30,000 feet ready to swoop should a conventional bomber stream be detected. Now the Hurricanes were scrambled.

SO INTENT WAS MARGARET on getting back to Hadley Hall in order to release Betty, she did not spot the two figures and black military staff car looming up in the darkness until less than thirty yards away. Even then she did not recognise the taller of the two figures until almost right on top of him. Not that it would have made any difference if she had. Self-preservation was the last thing on her mind right now.

"Simon," she gasped, struggling for a moment to catch her breath. The bicycle's worn brake pads squeaked loudly as she pulled up. "What...what are you doing here? I thought you were down in London."

Her question was brushed aside. "Just tell me where Betty is," he demanded. "What have you done with her?"

If she had been surprised by his appearance, she was now truly astonished. "You know Betty? How?"

"Never mind all that. Just tell me where she is."

"She's in the cellar." Margaret jabbed a hand toward the gloomy outline of the big house. "I thought that was the safest place for her."

"So she's not been harmed?"

"Of course not. I wanted to protect her."

For a moment she thought she spotted a look of comprehension on Simon's face. As if something important had been explained. But it was quickly gone.

"Take me to her...now!" he instructed. "Corporal, you wait for us here."

"But you need to know about—" Margaret began.

"Now!" he repeated.

He was clearly in no mood to listen to anything else until assured of Betty's safety. Forcing aside the mystery of why he was here and how the pair of them obviously knew each other quite well, Margaret shoved her bicycle inside the stable door and set off toward the big house, rapidly assessing the situation as she went.

There was no denying the force of the two blows she'd struck Richard with. As long as he remained unconscious, there was little immediate danger. With no one to illuminate Bletchley Park, the Luftwaffe pilots would never be able to identify their target. As for Simon, it would take only a few minutes for them to release Betty. Once that was done, then she would be able to warn him about Richard and the bombers. He would know exactly what to do.

The interior of the house was in such deep gloom that it was difficult to see anything very much. Nonetheless, Margaret led the way confidently forward until reaching the cellar entrance. After sliding back the bolts, she eased the door open just a few inches.

"Betty," she called. "I'm back. I'm going to turn the light on now."

266

There was no reply. Margaret began to call again when Simon moved her briskly aside.

"Betty. It's Simon. You're safe now."

Just as he finished speaking, Margaret flicked down the light switch.

Only now did Betty respond. "Is that really you?" She sounded very close.

As Simon pulled the door fully open, it was revealed exactly how close. She was standing on the small platform at the top of the steps with an old cricket bat grasped in both hands. Margaret recognised it as the one her father had owned way back in the days when she was a little girl and he had turned out regularly for a local village team. Given his present condition, the memory of him as a fit young man produced a sharp stab of ironic pain.

Simon held out a hand to Betty. "Are you hurt?"

The bat, which had been raised as if ready to strike, fell to one side. Still squinting against the sudden light, she spoke quickly. "Don't worry, I'm fine. But the air raid is coming tonight. And the mansion is the main target."

"That's what I've been trying to tell you," Margaret added. "You also need to know that Richard Forest is a Nazi spy. He's here to light up Bletchley Park for the bombers."

"Richard Forest? You mean that chap you used to go around with who liked motorbikes?"

Her words began tumbling out at a frantic pace. "That's right. I knocked him out and left him beside a field opposite the Park. But he might wake up at any moment. I'm not sure. I threw away his flare guns and pistol, but he's still got petrol to start a fire with. He has a motorbike as well, and there's a plane coming to take him back to France. I don't know exactly where it's going to land, but—"

Simon gripped her hard by the shoulders to stem the flow, then dug into his pocket. A familiar looking notebook was thrust in front of her eyes. "This field where you left Forest. Is that it? The one marked with a cross?"

"Yes, that's it."

"And there is no one else working with him?"

"He's on his own. You have my word on that."

She took a quick look at her watch. "But you must hurry. The bombers are due to arrive at one o'clock. That's less than twenty minutes away."

Seeing him hesitate, she added: "You don't need to worry about me. I'm not going to run off anywhere. I've got nothing left now and nowhere to hide. I'll still be here to face the music when you come back."

"I'll stay with her," Betty volunteered. "It's the least I can do after what she did for me."

Simon frowned. "What she did? You mean locking you down there?"

"No. More than that. Much more. Forest was going to shoot me, and it was only Margaret who stopped him by saying he'd have to kill her as well. I'll explain about it later on, but she really did save my life."

There was obviously little time for Simon to consider the situation. After only a second of thought, he gave a nod. "Very well. The pair of you remain here until you hear from me."

The two women met eyes. "We have lots to talk about, don't we?" Betty suggested.

Something very close to relief washed over Margaret. There was so much she needed to get off her chest. There was also a lot to discover. As much as she had been keeping secrets from her friend, it was now clear that Betty had been doing exactly the same to her.

A wan smile formed. "Yes. We've a great deal to talk about," she agreed.

THE FIRST OF THE HURRICANES zoomed in from behind just as Kimmel's line was preparing the turn inland. Caught by surprise and outnumbered, he watched in horror as two of his comrade's 109s were sent plunging into the inky depths of the North Sea.

As the vulnerable man at the rear, Kimmel could hardly believe he had survived this initial assault. Not that there was time to dwell on his good fortune. The Hurricanes had peeled away and were no doubt already turning for a second attack. There would be more of them arriving very soon too. Now that their line had been spotted, flying low was no longer a necessity. With a superior climb rate to the Hurricane, and at least fifty kilometres an hour speed advantage in straight and level flight, there was only one logical tactic.

The order came over the radio from his Staffelkapitan, Hauptmann Rudolf Wrick, even before this thought had fully formed. "Climb to five thousand metres."

Kimmel responded immediately.

Less than five minutes later he was at the required altitude, but in the darkness could not see any of his comrades. On the good side of things, there was no sign of any Hurricanes either.

Their instructions at the briefing had been clear. The mission must come first at all times. No unnecessary dogfights, and if their line were to become separated, it was every pilot's responsibility to continue on to the target area alone. Turning back was not an option.

After a final check of the surrounding sky that continued to show no sign of either friend or foe, Kimmel headed west toward the English coast.

EVEN AFTER REGAINING consciousness, for a moment or two Richard had no idea where he was or what had happened to him. Then the pounding in his head served as a painful reminder.

With a loud groan, he struggled to his feet and squinted at the luminous dial of his wristwatch. It was fifteen minutes before one o'clock. He still had time...just.

The flare guns were gone, as was his Luger. That bitch Margaret must have done something with them. The only relief was on seeing that the Vincent hadn't been touched. Without that, he wouldn't have had a hope of meeting with the Lysander on time. The petrol would also still be where he had left it. A fire on its own this far away from the mansion wasn't a perfect marker, but it was the best he could give them under the circumstances.

It took precious time to cross the field in the dark. Twice he stumbled over particularly deep furrows, and more minutes were lost trying to locate the hidden cans once he got there. After splashing the contents of the first can through the railings of Bletchley Park's perimeter, another glance at his watch warned him that he had virtually no more time to spare. As if to confirm this, he caught his first faint sound of rapidly approaching aircraft.

With their distinctive, high-pitched whine, even from a distance he could tell that they were Messerschmitts.

His elation was short-lived. Sounds that were far less welcome suddenly reached him, and these were a whole lot closer. First there was the rhythmic stomping of many boots moving along the road in his direction at a pace that was far too rapid to be the old men of the Home Guard. Then came a series of sharply barked orders that were both concise and explicit. The type of efficient commands used by highly trained professional soldiers. Margaret must have known about these troops and had them alerted. He could not believe that she had so easily fooled him. Given the chance, he would surely make her pay for her treachery.

There was no time to use any of the other cans. But the ground was dry. With luck, the petrol he had already put down would be sufficient for the fire to spread naturally once it got a grip.

His original plan had been to ignite the entire area from a distance using one of his flares. Now, the only way remaining was to do it up close. He briefly gave thanks for the whim that had made him buy a box of Swan Vestas matches while at the pub in Oxford. Just in case of complications, he'd thought. Well things were now a damn sight more complicated than he could ever have imagined. Aside from the troops rapidly closing in, if he didn't move fast, he might even find himself caught up in the bombing. That would be truly bloody ironic!

Standing several feet back, he flared up half a dozen matches at once and tossed them through the railings. A whoosh of flames instantly flared up, causing him to hastily jump back even further. He smiled. The Luftwaffe pilots were the finest in the world. This would surely be sufficient to mark their target for them.

With escape now the only thought on his mind, he set off as rapidly as possible back across the dark field to the waiting motorcycle.

TWENTY-FOUR

After making a rapid phone call from the cottage, Simon was driven off in his waiting car, leaving Betty and Margaret alone in the big house to talk. They sat down together on two wooden office chairs just inside the foyer. It was Margaret who spoke first.

"How do you know Simon so well?" she asked. "Have you been working with him?"

There was now no point in telling her anything but the truth, Betty decided. As succinctly as possible she revealed all that had taken place, from Simon's initial recruitment of her, right through to how she had searched Margaret's bedroom and the decoding of her final message to Goering. The only things she omitted to mention were the earl's discovery of his daughter's activities – and therefore the catalyst for his second stroke – plus the truth about his current condition. Simon might well wish for this to remain a secret for a little longer yet.

She had been half-expecting an embittered reaction: possibly even a brief display of temper. But once she had finished, Margaret simply let out a self-deprecating laugh. "And to think I was the one who started out by using you to gain information. There's certainly a lot of truth in that old saying about reaping what you sow."

A brief, introspective silence ensued. Betty then suggested that they might be more comfortable if they went over to the cottage, but Margaret shook her head.

She now appeared utterly resigned to her fate. "I'd rather not," she said. "Hadley Hall has always been so dear to me, and this is probably the last chance I'll ever have to spend any time here. Even the foul damage done by those builders can't destroy the memories. This is still the home I was born and raised in. My family have lived here for over three hundred years."

There was a hint of tears in her eyes as she added: "I'm sure you can understand how I feel."

"Of course I can," Betty responded. A thought quickly formed. "Look, why don't we go up to the ballroom? At least that part of the house escaped the builders and is still as it used to be."

The suggestion drew a hint of a smile. "Yes, I think that would be a wonderful idea."

With just a few dim candle-like wall lights showing the way, they climbed the mighty oak staircase together to the third floor. Betty well remembered her sense of awe when first setting eyes on the ballroom. This time after stepping through its doors the sensation was equally captivating, albeit in a much different way.

Her first visit had been made in bright daylight, with the sun lending a dazzling brilliance to the vast overhead dome. Now it was the faint rays of the crescent moon bringing a gentle glow into the room. The thin shafts of light were seemingly enhanced by the curvature of the glass, causing them to shimmer with a life of their own as they weaved their way down through the countless individual lights of the chandelier. Whereas before there had been brightness that roused mental images of vibrant music and gay dancing couples, an aura of peace and calm now existed. To Betty's mind, there was an almost holy serenity about the room.

And then came the distant sound of approaching war planes.

Both of them rushed to opposite windows, each searching for a sight of the aircraft. From a brief state of make-believe tranquillity, Betty was thrown violently back into a world of harsh reality. Her heart began racing as she thought of Simon. He must be back at Bletchley Park by now. He might be in terrible danger, especially if this Richard Forest had not yet been caught. What if he had recovered consciousness and had been able to start his marker fire?

A gasp from Margaret had Betty spinning around and rushing across to join her. Through the open window she was pointing into the distance, her face contorted with anguish.

A flickering red glow on the near horizon confirmed Betty's worst possible fears.

"That's where I left him," Margaret moaned. "That's Bletchley Park." She thumped the windowsill with her clenched fist. "Why didn't I finish him off when I had the chance?"

For several moments Betty could only stare, frozen by dread and a feeling of total helplessness. Then, from out of nowhere, a wild thought formed. Maybe there was something she could do, after all?

Grabbing hold of Margaret's arm, she squeezed hard to get her full attention. "The mansion at Bletchley is the bombers' main target. That's right, isn't it?"

"Yes, that's what Richard told me."

"And how far away from there is his fire?"

A puzzled frown appeared on Margaret's face. "Nearly half a mile I would say. But there are six planes coming. If they can't see the mansion clearly, they'll just bomb all around the area of the marker. One of them is bound to hit it."

"Not if we give them a better target to go for."

"A better target? What on earth are you ...?"

Realisation came with an almighty rush to Margaret. "Hadley Hall? You want them to bomb Hadley Hall instead?" Her voice rose to a shout that echoed all around the vast room. "No! Never. I won't allow it."

Undeterred, Betty continued. "If we were to switch on that chandelier, the roof will light up like a huge beacon. We're only five miles away from the Park. The bombers will never know the difference, especially on such a gloomy night."

"Didn't you hear me? I said no."

"So you're quite happy to allow Lord knows how many people to die because of what you've done. That's almost certain to include Simon, remember. Unlike a lot of others, he remained a good friend to you even after your father had his estate so cruelly taken away."

Seeing the anguish of indecision on Margaret's face, Betty strived to press home her advantage.

"You said to Richard when we were in the cellar that you had to live with your conscience. Well I don't see how you can. Not if you're prepared to sacrifice Bletchley Park and all the people working there tonight just for the sake of a ruined old house that you don't even own any longer. Nor will you ever do so again. I thought you'd accepted that, Margaret."

Much as Betty's words continued to make an impact, they were still not enough to stir Margaret into action. She shook her head several times before turning away and gazing out of the window once again. It was clear that she was in tormented denial. Much as she wanted to save Bletchley Park, over three hundred years of Pugh family history was still clinging to her heart. Hadley Hall was demanding that she did not sacrifice it.

Time was running out. There was only one card left to play. Betty's eyes raced around the room. Where were the damn light switches?

Her gaze settled on a small wall cupboard a few feet to the right of the ballroom entrance. It was similar in appearance to the one she had seen by the cellar door. That had to be the place. Dashing over, she yanked the door open and a gasp of relief shot out. Inside were three switches, with the middle one significantly larger than the other two. Each of these was set in the 'up' position. Using both hands for speed, she pushed all of them down.

For a couple of seconds nothing happened. Then the wall lights, probably fifty or more of them in total, flickered into life. A moment later, as if having waited for its minions to suitably prepare the way for its grand entrance, the mighty chandelier burst into incandescent brilliance.

The sudden brightness snapped Margaret out of her trance-like state. She rushed over toward Betty, her hands waving in a desperate criss-crossing motion. "No! Switch them off. You must switch them off."

Betty's fear was mounting. The bombers were sounding much closer now. Every instinct she possessed urged her to get out of the house and run for her life. But if she did that, she knew Margaret would only switch the lights off again.

She raised a hand that felt far from steady to the advancing woman. "I'm staying here until you agree to come with me. I'll fight you if necessary, Margaret, but these lights have to remain on."

"Are you mad? The bombers will be here any minute."

"We can leave together right now if you want to."

"Just turn them off. Then we can talk about it."

Betty shook her head. "There's no time left for that."

Her voice softened. "I know you are a good person, Margaret. You were prepared to die in order to save me when we were down in the cellar. Now my life is in your hands again. We can both stay here and almost certainly get blown to hell, or we can run for it. It's your choice."

Even as she spoke the words, Betty wondered if she could actually stick to them. Only a mental image of Simon had kept her resolve firm for this long. Now, with the bombers virtually on top of them, even this crutch was failing her. Thoughts of her parents raced through her mind. They would be shouting at her to run. What was it her mother had said that time?

"We don't want her winning any medals, Dan. We just want her to be safe."

Margaret's voice broke the tense silence that, although it felt agonisingly long, had probably lasted for no more than a few heartbeats. "To be honest, Betty, I don't care if I do get blown to hell. I've nothing left to live for anyway, so it's probably as good a way as any to go."

A loud growl of frustration then slipped out. "On the other hand, I can't let you throw your life away, you stupid bloody girl. Certainly not because of a situation that I created. And you are right. Hadley Hall will never be mine, so why should anyone else ever get to have it?"

Moving toward the open doorway, she held out a hand. "I suggest that we run as fast as we can."

Betty needed no second invitation. With hands clasped firmly together and Margaret leading the way, they raced down the stairs. But had they left it too late? Just as they reached the entrance, a low flying fighter plane, the swastika on its tail clearly visible in the light thrown out from the blazing skylight, zoomed over the house at little more than rooftop level. Both of them froze, waiting for the inevitable bomb. Yet none came.

"He'll be back. You can be sure of that," Betty yelled, tugging at Margaret's hand. In spite of the danger, there was a fierce elation inside. Her plan seemed to be working. At least they had drawn the bombers' attention.

Margaret resisted her pull, tugging hard in a different direction. "We can't leave the horses," she shouted. "We must get them out of the stables."

Betty wanted to tell her there was no time, but she knew she would be wasting her breath. So fierce was Margaret's pull and so determined her expression, nothing in this world was going to change her mind. The choice was clear. Run the other way and leave Margaret to it, or ....

Or what?

Glancing up, she saw the plane that had passed overhead was at present circling and obviously preparing for a second approach. And now it wasn't alone. Other aircraft could be heard in the near distance, some with the same high-pitched tone of the attacking German, others with a deeper, throatier roar. Adding to the cacophony of noise, every few seconds there was also the staccato rattle of machine guns.

The chances of Margaret clearing all three horses away from the stables on her own before the threat returned was virtually zero. Betty could hear the startled animals already snorting and squealing in agitation. Would they simply bolt when the doors were opened? Perhaps even trample all over them in their frantic desire to escape the commotion?

She yielded to Margaret's tugging. What else could she really do? The woman had already saved her life, and was now making what for her must be the most heart-breaking sacrifice imaginable of her ancestral home.

As they raced toward the stables, Margaret began shouting instructions.

DESPITE ORDERS TO KEEP radio broadcasts between themselves to an absolute minimum until actually attacking, Kimmel had somehow managed to link up with the remaining members of his staffel shortly after crossing the Suffolk coast. Even so, how he had made it unscathed all the way through to the target area was almost beyond his understanding.

Although it was only a country house they were attacking, it must surely be of the most vital importance given the abnormally large amount of aircraft that were being thrown into defending it. There had been anti-aircraft guns and searchlights as well as they drew close. Only by using every bit of their flying skills had he and two of his comrades managed to survive this far. A third casualty in their long-since broken line formation had gone down in flames under a barrage of fire from a trio of Hurricanes just five minutes ago.

Without knowing exactly what kind of signal or illumination they were looking for, there had been a moment of confusion. First of all a small fire had been spotted. But the glare from this did not reveal any sign of a mansion house, just some trees and a few hut-like buildings. With only three bombs remaining between them, Staffelkapitan Wrick had initially been reluctant to use any of these until being certain this was the right place. Kimmel could understand why. He too suspected that the fire might be a decoy designed to draw them away from the real target.

But the pressure of constantly having to take evasive action and fight off the defenders was relentless. Then, just as they were about to bomb on the fire anyway, a far brighter light suddenly appeared just a short distance away. Wrick immediately veered toward this.

With Kimmel and the other remaining Messerschmitt doing whatever they could to draw fire away from their leader, Wrick made a low pass over this new light. His radio broadcast quickly followed.

"This is your target. Ignore all other lights. I will go first...bomb here."

Following up as third in line, Kimmel just had time to see the outline of a magnificent country house before Wrick's bomb fell. The staffelkapitan had been so right to be cautious, he acknowledged. Given the intense fire they were under, it had taken great courage not to bomb blindly on the first light they had seen. For a moment Kimmel forgot his customary resentment of officers who he felt had gained their status aided by a fortuitous accident of birth. Wrick fully deserved his commission, and the Knight's Cross that he wore so proudly.

The leader's bomb was a direct hit. One second the mansion house stood tall and proud in the brilliant glow of its spectacular roof dome; an instant later the light was snuffed out. With a mighty boom, the entire edifice was reduced to an ugly heap of stonework, timber, and glass. Kimmel, highly skilled in air-to-air combat but slightly less comfortable with his role as a bomber, could almost feel a certain sadness at the destruction of such a fine historic building.

Not that there was time to dwell on this. A fresh wave of Hurricanes swept into the attack, this time focusing their guns on the 109 in front of him that was now lining up for its bombing run. This was Oberleutnant Stoller's plane, number three in their original formation. Kimmel managed to pick off one of the Hurricanes, but not before the RAF pilot had put a three second burst from his 20mm cannons into Stoller's cockpit. It was inconceivable to Kimmel that anyone could have survived such a devastating volley.

Forced to break away and take evasive action, his next view of Stoller's plane was as it closed in on the devastated mansion, all the time rapidly losing height. In what was obviously the final action of a dying man, the oberleutnant released his bomb. It was to little effect, landing well short of its target and disturbing nothing more important than what was most likely a field of crops. The 109 then continued on in a straight line for a short distance further before ploughing into the ground. The Messerschmitt instantly erupted into a ball of flames.

Barely had this happened when Wrick's voice came over the radio. He was now circling an erratic but calculated path over the target to direct operations. "Make your run now, Kimmel. I'll cover you as best I can."

Taking virtually the same flight path as Stoller, Kimmel began his attack. Some military style huts caught his eye at the last second. Yes, he decided. They might also be of significant importance. Instead of aiming his bomb at the already ruined house, he directed it at these.

Even though he was already halfway to the point where Stoller's plane had crashed when the bomb detonated, a brief series of shock waves from its blast still travelled far enough to rock his aircraft. For an instant, he struggled to steady the 109. Then, just as he had succeeded in this, from the light of his comrade's brightly burning aircraft he caught a glimpse of movement on the ground nearby. A closer inspection showed that it was two people attempting to scramble onto the back of a horse. Women by the look of it. One of them was wearing a uniform.

The orders to all of the pilots at the briefing had been explicit. Any sign of life on the ground once the bombs had gone should be strafed with their machine guns to ensure maximum damage. No exceptions. It was an order that did not sit well with Kimmel. Air battle was honourable. Bombing, though distasteful, was often essential. But shooting defenceless women who were clearly fleeing for their lives?

On the other hand, if Wrick was still watching from above, he would most likely report him should he fail to follow orders.

He had just a split second to make his decision.

TO BETTY, HOW THEY had got the horses away from the stables before the first bomb fell was a miracle in itself. Margaret was now the one entirely in charge. As expected, two of the horses bolted off into the distance the moment they were free enough to do so. Soldier, however, though alarmed, clearly had no intention of abandoning Margaret.

"There's no time to saddle him," she had shouted over the screaming of the aircraft, jumping astride the stallion and then pulling Betty up behind her. "Hold onto me tightly."

Betty did not need any second telling. She clung on to Margaret for all she was worth. Never before during their rides together had her mount been allowed to go at anything like a full gallop. Nor had she ever sat on one without the aid of a saddle and reins. Just staying on the back of Soldier as he pounded along the driveway was taking almost every bit of her strength.

They were close to three hundred yards away from the house when the first bomb fell. In the momentary lull before it exploded, the weirdest of feelings seized Betty. It was as if all the air had been sucked out of the atmosphere and the entire world was holding its breath.

The colossal roar of noise that followed was both deafening and terrifying. Dirt and dust together with small pieces of stonework carried on waves of concussive energy enveloped them as they galloped on. Some of these flying fragments dug spitefully into her back. Her instinctive reaction was to cup both hands over her ears to protect them from the continuing blast of noise. Only at the very last instant did she manage to stop herself from actually doing so. To release her hold on Margaret, even for a moment, would be certain to send her crashing to the ground.

The rattle of machine guns was followed by the boom of a second bomb detonating, although this time the explosion sounded further away and there were no shock waves. Not that this offered any respite. Instead of veering away like the first bomber, this one continued straight on, as if intent on pursuing them all the way down the long driveway. Ever lower it came, passing over their heads so closely that Betty felt she could almost reach up and touch it.

Only at the very last second did she realise that the plane was about to crash. All at once, Margaret was calling out to Soldier and straining every muscle to pull him to a halt.

The aircraft hit the ground no more than a hundred yards in front of them. With a great whooshing roar, a barrier of flames spanning almost the entire width of the driveway erupted. Although now virtually at a standstill, Soldier reared sharply as the blast of heat rushed back at them. Even Margaret was caught unawares, and once she started to slide backwards, there was nothing else Betty could do but release her hold and twist sideways in order to break her own fall as much as possible. Both of them landed heavily on the tightly packed gravel.

The stallion hovered over them, almost as if apologising for having reacted the way it did.

"Are you all right?" Margaret asked as Betty scrambled to her feet.

She nodded. "Just a bit winded and bruised, that's all."

Margaret gave Soldier a rub on the neck. "Best get back on board as fast as possible then. We'll head for that small lodge up where the gates are. We should be safe inside there until—"

She was cut off by the sound of a third bomb exploding. Now far enough along the half mile driveway not to be seriously affected by the blast, it was still daunting to see the enemy plane heading at low level straight toward them. Betty had heard several frightening stories about people – even innocent civilians - being gunned down in the wake of a raid by some of these small fighter-bombers. Exposed in the open as they were, they stood little hope of survival if that was this pilot's intention.

As if in silent agreement, they automatically joined hands and simply stood there beside the now equally calm stallion to await whatever fate had in store.

It may not have been at the last instant when the plane veered to one side and climbed rapidly away. But if it wasn't, it certainly felt like it. Their gasps of relief burst forth simultaneously.

"Do you think he was going to?" Margaret asked in a hushed voice.

"I suppose we'll never know," Betty replied.

There seemed little more to add. In silence, they remounted Soldier and headed for the lodge.

JUST AS RICHARD HAD been counting on, the guards' concern over the sudden blaze took priority. Even so, several speculative shots were fired in his direction before getting fully across the field. Had the handful of pursuing soldiers caught a better sight of him, it might have been a different story. As it was, thanks to the gloom of the night and the reliable Vincent starting with the very first kick, he was soon well clear of the area.

Now for his rendezvous with the Lysander. He prayed it would arrive on time. He had done all that he could under the circumstances, and the bombers were almost here. As long as they did their job well, he would soon be bathing in the glory of the Fuhrer's personal congratulations. The thought of this was sufficient to raise a grim smile of satisfaction.

The smile was still lingering when the sound of the first bomb exploding reached him. Though it was close, he couldn't be quite sure where it was coming from. What he did know, beyond any doubt, was that it wasn't coming from Bletchley Park.

Muttered curses slipped out. What the hell were the fools doing? Hadn't they seen the marker fire he had set for them? The fire that he had risked his life to start.

It wasn't long before a second explosion came, and this time he was alert to its direction. In a flash, everything became devastatingly clear. They were bombing Hadley Hall instead of the mansion at Bletchley. How could they possibly have made such a mistake?

Unless...unless Margaret had done something to divert them?

Surely she wouldn't though. That house was her passion – her life. The very reason why she had become a spy for him in the first place.

His mind then switched to that other young girl. Betty! He almost spat out her name. She had no such sentimental attachment to Hadley Hall and might well have found a way to divert the bombers there in an attempt to save those she worked with.

But there was a new fear now eating away at Richard. What neither of those women could have known was that the driveway at Hadley Hall was the arranged place for his Lysander to touch down. He could only pray that the Luftwaffe pilots had been accurate with their bombs and not caused too much damage to his intended runway. Taking Goering's advice, he had already put aside his one remaining flare gun to guide thc plane in. It was waiting for him inside the small lodge near to the end of the drive.

That was where he must get to as quickly as possible.

TWENTY-FIVE

S imon paused for a moment to wipe his sweat-soaked brow, at the same time offering a quick prayer of thanks that he'd been able to raise the alarm in time. Thanks to a combination of rapid measures by the Park's internal firefighting team and then a liberal coating of a special foam by the Bletchley Town Fire Brigade, the blaze was now as good as extinguished.

Far less satisfying was the fact that Richard Forest had somehow managed to slip away. Margaret had said that there was a plane coming to pick the man up, but so far no one had been able to suggest any suitable field nearby where a small aircraft might be able to land. Motorised patrols were now scouring the area for any sign of the fugitive or his motorcycle.

There had been one tense moment when, with the flames still burning, a lone Messerschmitt passed directly overhead. Thankfully, for some reason known only to himself, the pilot decided not to drop his bomb on the marker. Just seconds later he came under heavy fire from a small group of Hurricanes and veered away to the east. Two more enemy planes followed him.

Not that the attackers had withdrawn very far. Gunfire suggested that quite a battle was taking place a few miles away. Bombs could soon be heard exploding. Simon frowned. The Luftwaffe pilots, realising their task was a hopeless one, must have decided to ditch their loads in order to make good their escape. With their much-lightened aircraft and superior air speed to Hurricanes, they stood a good chance of doing so as well. The new Mosquitoes, which were more than a match for anything in the sky, were currently being held at thirty thousand feet just in case this attack turned out to be a decoy for a force of heavy bombers following later.

After a time, an almost unnatural silence settled over the area. With the danger seemingly having passed, at least for the moment, Simon's thoughts immediately turned to Betty. She would be safe, thank God. As for Margaret, he did not know how to feel.

Over the years, his emotions concerning the woman had swung from a deep affection - he still could not bring himself to admit anything more than that - to utter contempt for the way she had betrayed her country in the pursuit of personal gain. Infuriatingly, she had even sought to use him as a source of information. And yet now, just when she was in a position to strike a crippling blow at the very heart of the Allied war effort, there had been a last-minute change of heart. Thanks to her, what would have been an unimaginable disaster had been avoided. On top of that, she had apparently placed her own life at great risk with Forest in order to save Betty.

How could he hate her after she had done all that?

The two women had said that they had a great deal to talk about, and this was obviously true. Perhaps he should give them just a bit more time to resolve things before returning?

He fully believed Margaret's promise that she wasn't going to run off anywhere; to do so now would be futile. Besides, capturing Richard Forest must be his current priority, and only by keeping himself contactable here would he know as quickly as possible of any success on that front.

Yes, he decided. Delaying his return to Hadley Hall for a little longer would be the best thing for everyone.

THE LODGE WAS NOTHING more than a one-room wooden shack that in past years had served as a conveniently located second office for the estate manager, who in the latter days had pretty much been Margaret herself. The only furniture was a desk, two upright chairs, and a filing cabinet long since emptied of any documents relevant to the estate. Rarely used outside of daylight hours and with no mains electricity connected, a broken old oil lamp in the corner had once been the only means of artificial lighting. However, a decent sized window at the front was allowing most of the sparse moonlight to trickle inside. For now, that was sufficient.

With the sounds of aircraft now gone, Soldier wandered off into the night. "He won't go far away," Margaret told Betty. "He's probably gone to look for the two mares."

They each flopped down onto a chair, silently reflecting on the catastrophic events. Although the drama and danger had felt virtually endless, in truth barely fifteen minutes had actually passed since the first bomb had fallen.

It was Margaret who spoke first. "I've a confession to make," she began.

Betty could hardly hold back an ironic laugh. "Only one?"

"No. It's nothing to do with what you're thinking. This is about us. Or to be more accurate, us and father."

"I don't understand."

"It all seems so petty now, but do you know there were times when I was jealous of you. I mean *really* jealous, yet at the same time pathetically grateful. How can that even make sense?"

Betty frowned. "Are you talking about my playing for him?"

"In a way. But there's far more to it than that. After his first stroke, I spent years trying everything I knew to bring him out of his depression without so much as a glimmer of success. Most of the time he would barely speak to me at all. Then you came along, and just by being blessed with an abundance of the musical talent that I so obviously lack, in little more than one hour you had gained his rapt attention."

Betty made to say something, but Margaret pressed on. Even in the dim light it was possible to see the determination on her face. This was something she had long been keeping suppressed. Now the floodgates had opened, nothing was going to stop her completing what she had to say.

"It didn't bother me at first. I was just so enormously grateful. I would have felt the same toward almost anyone who had given father back a purpose in life. Slowly though, as you began spending more time together and became increasingly close, things started to feel different. He used to speak so fondly of you, I couldn't help but wonder sometimes if you were the daughter he really wanted. That I had turned out to be nothing but a disappointment to him."

This time Betty was determined to break in. "That's not true. You mustn't think that way. Yes, we did spend a fair bit of time together in the cottage when you weren't there, but I'll tell you this. Whenever he spoke about you, there was always the deepest love in his eyes. Never did he consider you a disappointment. Not in any way at all."

Margaret sighed. "Maybe you are right. Anyway, what I really wanted to do was apologise to you for allowing my jealousy to get the better of me. You didn't deserve that."

A second, far deeper sigh slipped out. "As for father, it's too late for me to tell him how I feel. Thank God he isn't aware of what I've been doing. If he could see me now, then I really would be a disappointment to him. I think death is going to be the kindest thing for both of us."

These final words struck Betty like a spear to the heart. Although she could understand Simon's reason for doing it, she had never been comfortable with allowing Margaret to believe that the earl was still comatose and close to death. Every instinct was crying out to tell her the truth. What possible harm could it do now? She would most likely be facing execution very soon anyway, and who could say if she'd even be allowed to see her father again?

A warning thought then flashed. Margaret currently seemed to be accepting of her fate. But if she became aware that the earl was conscious and lucid, it was impossible to tell how she might react. She had already expressed her vast relief that he wasn't aware of her treachery. To suddenly discover that he did actually know all about it might well change everything.

The muffled sound of a motorcycle approaching snatched away any necessity for a response from her. Alarm instantly appeared on Margaret's face. Without a word, the pair of them rushed over to the window.

"He's come back here," Margaret gasped. "Why would he do that?"

Keeping low so that only the top half of their heads were above the glass, they watched as Richard dismounted and then stared down the devastated driveway. After a few seconds of this he released a stream of curses, even shaking his fist at something invisible in the sky.

The penny finally dropped for Margaret. "The driveway!" she whispered. "That's where his rescue plane was going to land. Why didn't I think of that before?"

It did not need Betty to point out that no plane of any description would be able to use the drive in its present condition.

"Do you think he's coming in here?" she asked.

"He may do. Take a look around and see if you can find anything we can use as a weapon. I'll keep watching and warn you if he comes any closer. At least he hasn't got his gun now."

"It's a pity you didn't think to keep it for yourself instead of chucking it away," Betty remarked. "It would have come in very useful right now."

"Oh, you're wrong. I did think of keeping it." Margaret gave an ironic little huff. "About one second after I'd thrown it somewhere it would be impossible to find in the dark."

In spite of the tension, Betty chuckled softly. She regretted her brief admonishment and was glad Margaret had not taken it to heart. "We could always break the legs off one of these chairs and hit him with those as he comes in the door," she suggested.

"That's not a bad idea. No...wait. He's getting back onto his bike."

A short pause followed while Margaret continued watching. "He's heading down the drive toward where the house was," she then said. "Why would he go back there?"

"Never mind about that," Betty told her. "Look what I've just found in the filing cabinet."

THE RIDE BACK TO HADLEY Hall had taken Richard a lot longer than planned. After barely a mile along his intended route, it suddenly became clear that there was already a whole fleet of vehicles out scouring the countryside for him. It was an unbelievably rapid reaction, forcing him into making several frustrating and time-consuming detours before finally managing to slip through the net.

There was just one consolation as he drew near. Margaret was almost certain to have spoken about his rendezvous with a pick-up plane, so Hadley Hall was probably the last place anyone would be thinking of looking for him. She'd wrongly assumed he had found a quiet field somewhere in the area that would serve as a landing site, and he'd encouraged her to continue with that belief. With luck, the search patrols would be putting most of their efforts into locating the imaginary field. At least long enough for him to get away.

That was, always assuming his makeshift runway had not been put out of action.

Ever since hearing the bombs, this had been his one great fear. And as he turned onto the driveway, it was instantly confirmed. The still burning plane and the widespread lumps of smouldering debris scattered by the crash – it was impossible to tell if the wrecked aircraft was German or British – said without a shadow of doubt that nothing could ever land here. He was over fifteen minutes late for their rendezvous anyway. For all he knew, the pilot had already arrived, realised at once that a pick-up was impossible, and departed again. He sure as hell wasn't going to hang around for long with so much RAF activity in the area.

All of Richard's frustration exploded in a torrent of obscenities aimed at the Luftwaffe pilots for their incompetence in ignoring what had been a clear marker for them. To think he had always rated them as being the finest in the world.

Quickly, he realised that he was wasting valuable time. His first instinct was to flee the area immediately. Then he checked himself. The search for him was bound to intensify very quickly. Even now it might be impossible to break clear, especially in his current identity.

But what if he were to revert to being Major Roberts of the Royal Signals? That might at least give him a chance. The uniform and ID papers, not to mention a good supply of British money, were all still in the stable block apartment. So too was the radio. It was vital he contact Berlin to let Goering know that his planes had bombed the wrong house.

Their mistake wasn't his fault. He'd done everything asked of him, and established that Bletchley Park was probably even more vital to the British war effort than Margaret's messages had stated. Goering would surely understand all of this and arrange for an alternative way to get him back home. He would just have to keep his head down for a time. Maybe he would be supplied with an IRA contact to help with that?

Like the cottage, the stable apartment was close to two hundred metres away from the mansion. Only three bombs had fallen, so it was perfectly possible it might have survived.

Hoping desperately that he was right, Richard climbed back onto the Vincent. While skirting around the burning aircraft, he noticed a swastika on a section of the tail that had become separated. So it was a Luftwaffe plane, he thought bitterly. Serve the damn fool right.

It was with similar feelings that he regarded the massive pile of rubble that had once been the mansion. One or both of the women had been responsible for this disastrous outcome. How he would like to believe that they were now buried somewhere beneath all that remained of Margaret's precious house. It would be a fitting reward for their interference.

He almost sobbed with relief on finding the stable block still standing. There was much scarring on the outside, mainly from being struck by small chunks of flying masonry from the devastated mansion; all of the windows had been blown out as well. But none of that was important. It still looked structurally secure. The only odd thing was the lack of horses and the wide-open doors to their stalls. Not that the locks on these were very substantial. He could only imagine that, in their panic when the bombs started to fall, the horses had kicked their way free and bolted. Yes, that made perfect sense now he thought about it.

On entering the apartment, the first thing he noticed was the kit bag and officer's uniform on the settee where he had left it. Now feeling a lot more confident, he rapidly stripped off and changed into this before stepping through to the bedroom.

The realisation that the radio was gone literally stopped him in his tracks. He squeezed his eyes tightly closed for a moment, hoping ridiculously that when he opened them again the set would magically be restored. It wasn't, of course. Only the wire aerial dangling forlornly from the ceiling served as a taunting reminder that it had ever been there at all.

What on earth had reduced him to such stupidity?

The answer came back almost at once. It was desperation.

Yes, he *was* getting desperate now. Without a means of contacting anyone, how the hell was he ever going to get out of England? Once again, thoughts of the IRA surfaced. But he had no names...no addresses...no telephone numbers to contact. Just a story about some stupid made-up character called Joe Bull who appeared at most of the big race meetings.

When would the next meeting take place? He had no idea, but it shouldn't be too difficult to find out.

Still dwelling on his predicament, he picked up the kit bag and returned to the Vincent outside. One thing was obvious; he couldn't stay around here for much longer. Sooner rather than later the emergency services would become aware of what had happened to Hadley Hall and be arriving to check out the scene.

Hiding in plain sight would be his best option. He doubted that those searching for him would have the faintest idea that he might have assumed the identity of a British officer. Should he be forced to stop at a checkpoint, all of his papers were in order. It would just need a bit of good German pluck to bluff his way through.

Heading back to Oxford felt like a good plan; the rail links there would give him several choices. Continuing all the way back to Wales might even be an option. If he could find a way of getting across the water to Ireland, most of his problems would likely be solved.

The Vincent though, was a sure giveaway. It was damn near out of petrol anyhow, so it was time to dump the thing. He recalled seeing Margaret's bicycle lying on the ground just by the stable door. A quick inspection showed that, although covered in dust and bits of glass from the shattered window nearby, it was still in good working order.

This then, would have to be his transport for a time. He had the ID papers and banknotes in his tunic pocket: they were the important things. The cumbersome kitbag would have to go. Not that he could simply leave it behind. Not with the name and number of the identity he would be assuming stamped all over it. Rapidly, he gathered up several handfuls of hay and stuffed these inside the bag. Another of his Swan Vestas matches did the rest.

Only when fully satisfied that the bag was burning properly did he mount the bicycle and set off back down the driveway, all the time weaving carefully around the lumps of masonry strewn along the way. He was approaching the still smouldering Messerschmitt when the unexpected happened.

With a clearly audible whoosh, a flare shot up from the far end of the driveway into the night sky, its brilliant white light creating a glow that could be seen for miles around. A renewed stream of curses flew from Richard's mouth. Nothing was more certain to bring the search parties rushing over in this direction.

It must have come from the gun he'd left in the lodge. He also knew that it was one of those bloody women who had fired it. They were behind all of his troubles. Yet again, thoughts of violent revenge rose up. If only he'd shot them both when he had the opportunity to do so.

With a huge effort, he eased his temper. Concentrating on survival was the important thing. Nothing else mattered. He increased his speed until practically level with the lodge. As expected, there was no sign of the women. Having made their signal, they would be hiding somewhere well out of the way until help arrived. Hugely tempting as it was to spend a few minutes seeking them out, he put it from his mind. He had to keep going. Once free of the mansion grounds, there were any number of lanes and tracks he knew of that could be used to evade the patrols.

He was almost there – had just thirty yards to go - when the unexpected happened for a second time. Two figures rushed out from the bushes on his left to place themselves directly in his path. The one nearest was Margaret. She was pointing the flare gun straight at his chest.

"Get off the bike," she told him. "You're not going anywhere."

UNABLE TO FULLY CONVINCE himself that the danger was now over for the night, Simon continued to prowl about Bletchley Park grounds while waiting for any further news in the search for Richard Forest. He eventually sat down for a while on one of the benches beside the lake. It was, he recalled, the same one that he and Cynthia Bagsure had sat on when the first real seeds of doubt had been sown about Margaret. So much had happened since then, both in what he had learned about her, and in many ways, what he had discovered about himself.

It was hard to believe how fond he had become of Betty. Ever since his youthful infatuation with Margaret had foundered in the face of numerous competitors, his confidence in affairs of the heart had gradually deteriorated to such an extent that he ceased to view women in that way very much at all. He'd remained on friendly terms with most of those who came within his social circle, but that was always the extent of things. His career had taken over virtually every other aspect of his life.

And then, purely in the line of his work and national security, Betty had entered his world and won him over completely with ....

With what? That was the ridiculous thing. He had no clue how to define the reason for the way he felt. She was honest, smart, dependable and pretty, but so were countless other girls. Apparently, she was also an exceptionally talented musician, though he had yet to hear her play for himself.

Not that there could ever be anything between them. According to her file she was just twenty-one years old, making the age gap eleven years. That in itself should be a warning. Also, she had never given even the slightest hint that the attraction might be mutual. No, he had to put such thoughts out of his head. Once this current situation with Margaret was finally resolved, he would be returning to the Admiralty and Betty to wherever her WAAF duties took her. And that would be the end of that.

He gazed up at the sky for a minute, as though bleakly seeking some kind of divine confirmation that this was how things were destined to finish.

The flare that suddenly shot up instantly banished any melancholy thoughts. Jumping to his feet, he shifted to one side in order to get a better look at the direction from which it had been launched. Almost at once he realised that it had to be somewhere close to Hadley Hall.

Had the flare been fired by Richard Forest? Given that the man was hoping to rendezvous with a plane to extract him, it appeared highly likely. But Hadley Hall?

Simon clapped both hands hard to his head as the blindingly obvious answer came to him. Everyone was assuming that a quiet field somewhere would be the natural pick-up location; that was what Margaret had stated, and the way such things were nearly always done by the SOE. But the driveway at Hadley Hall would be absolutely perfect for the job.

And that was where Betty and Margaret were.

With heart racing, he ran over to the transport section. The garage was deserted. Where the hell was a vehicle when you needed one the most? He knew the answer. They were all out assisting in the search for Richard bloody Forest.

There was only one other hope. Swinging toward the left-hand side of the mansion, he headed as fast as he could for the despatch riders' entrance. He spotted just one motorcycle parked in the narrow lane there. Without pausing to think, he jumped astride the machine and swung the kick-start. The engine fired at the second attempt.

The guard at the gate was already moving across to block his path as he approached, but a brief inspection of the special pass bearing the prime minister's official stamp and signature that Simon carried with him at all times was sufficient. Such passes gave the bearer almost limitless authority. The iron railing gate was opened without further question.

Praying that he would not be too late and heedless of the poor visibility, Simon twisted the throttle fully open.

DESPITE MANAGING TO keep both her voice and hands relatively steady while pointing the flare gun, all kinds of uncertainties were eating away at Margaret. At first it seemed like a simple enough plan that she and Betty had agreed on. They would fire one of the flares to summon help as quickly as possible, then save the second one to prevent Richard from leaving if he attempted to come back this way.

But now that moment had come, things did not feel anything like so straightforward.

How would she react if Richard refused to do as she said? Much as she hated him, could she really fire a mass of blazing magnesium into another human being? And even if he did force her to do so, could she rely on the gun to work as it should? She had received hardly any instruction in its use.

"I've set your gun to fire both barrels at once," he'd told her just before they'd set off for Bletchley Park earlier. *"There's no point in complicating matters, so all you need remember is to pull both triggers all the way back. It's that simple."*

Working on that principle, she had used just one of the two triggers to fire the first flare from this other gun. That had gone without a problem, she reminded herself. So why was she worrying unnecessarily? If the situation did become desperate, all she had to do was make sure the second trigger also went fully back.

Richard dismounted from the bicycle as ordered, allowing it to fall to the ground. Even in the dim light, the hatred and frustration on his face was clear to see.

"Do you really think you are going to keep me here?" he snarled. "Do you even properly understand how that gun works?"

Margaret's uncertainty returned tenfold. How had he managed to do it? Just by looking at her, he had tapped into her greatest uncertainty. Had she really made it so obvious? Or was he simply making a blind guess?

Betty moved alongside Margaret, raising the broken chair leg she was clutching. "You won't get past both of us. Not before the troops arrive."

"And they will be here any minute now," Margaret added.

As if to confirm this, the sound of an approaching vehicle reached them. Richard began to inch forward.

"Don't come any closer," she snapped, holding the gun with arms fully extended.

He was no more than six feet away when he stopped, raising both hands up to shoulder level in a gesture of submission. "All right, Margaret," he said in a surprisingly quiet voice. "You win."

And then he rushed straight at her.

For an instant Margaret's mind froze. This was the very thing she had been dreading. Instinct then kicked in. She pulled hard on both triggers, forcing them all the way back.

Nothing happened.

A heartbeat later he was upon her. The gun was wrenched from her grasp and a solid punch to the stomach drove her down onto her knees. Gasping for air, she looked up to see Betty swing her makeshift club at Richard's head, but he shifted slightly to one side and the blow slid harmlessly off the edge of his shoulder. A violent shove then sent her friend staggering several yards back before crashing down onto the hard gravel of the driveway.

In one quick movement, Richard flicked a small lever at the back end of the gun over to the left. He gave a mocking laugh.

"You stupid bitch, Margaret. I knew you wouldn't think to change the selector. But it's done now, and this one cartridge will be more than enough to burn you all the way to hell."

She could see in his eyes an almost insane lust for revenge. He was going to kill her. There was not a trace of doubt about that. She wasn't afraid of dying. In fact, like her father, she would be better off dead now anyway. But for it to be at Richard's hands and to see him revelling in the moment...that was just too much to bear. She closed her eyes, waiting for the inevitable.

A loud screeching of tyres jerked them open again. A Jeep carrying four soldiers swung off the road and onto the driveway. At the astonishing sight of a British officer standing over two women lying on the ground, the corporal driving slammed on the brakes immediately. All four men jumped out of the vehicle.

"What's going on, Sir?" the corporal called over.

A growl of frustration came from Richard. For an instant Margaret thought he was going to fire the flare anyway, but then he checked himself.

A prod from his boot had her scrambling to her feet. He made a flicking movement with his free hand toward the lodge, which was only a few yards away. "Inside," he ordered.

He glanced at Betty, who by now was almost back on her feet. "Get over there and tell those soldiers that if they try to come in after us, I'll kill her without a second thought. Is that clear?"

"If you do, you'll never get away," she told him.

He made a small spitting motion. "I just wish I had a spare cartridge for you as well."

Margaret started to say something to her friend, but a firm shove in the direction of the lodge cut her off before she'd hardly begun.

Just seconds later they were both inside and the door had slammed shut.

TWENTY-SIX

O nly a few minutes had passed since entering the lodge, but already Richard could see from the window that there were now three Jeeps and a dozen soldiers gathered at the end of the driveway. More were almost certainly on the way.

As anticipated, none of the soldiers had yet tried to force their way inside. For now, they seemed content to keep him bottled up where he was until someone of senior rank arrived to take charge. Even then, an attempt at negotiation was sure to be their first move. Until that option had failed, a direct assault was most unlikely.

Even so, they would not hold off indefinitely. The situation was bad: maybe impossible to escape from. But one thing was certain. Margaret was going to pay dearly for all her interference. Had it not been for her, he would already be on his way back home to a hero's welcome from the Fuhrer. Margaret would remain alive only as long as she was useful, and fully deserved what would undoubtedly be a most excruciating death.

She was sitting on the floor with her back against the far wall as instructed. He regarded her spitefully. There was still one more way in which he could increase her torment before things came to an end. He was going to extract enormous pleasure in this final twisting of the knife.

He moved closer and sat down on the one undamaged chair. "I've got something to tell you," he began. "Something about your father that you really need to know."

He could see that she wanted to ignore him. Or more likely, tell him to go to hell. But she was unable to do either. Her curiosity demanded that she hear him out, just as he knew it would. Despite her silence and hostile expression, she was listening closely.

Richard allowed a smile to form. This was his moment.

"It was me," he told her. "I was the one who came up with the idea of the fake gold mine that ruined the earl."

This time Margaret was not capable of holding her tongue. "You're lying," she retorted. "Your own father lost money in that as well. Not even you would have—"

"My father was a fool," he cut in. "I tried to convince him when Hitler first began rising to power that here was the man to restore Germany's fortunes, and that we should return there permanently to support him in this venture. Father refused, so I cared little for him after that."

"No, that's not right. I remember how devastated you were when your parents were killed in that car crash."

He shrugged. "For my mother perhaps. She could see the virtue in National Socialism. But as for my father," he huffed a short laugh, "he was pathetically weak."

The look of devastation on Margaret's face as she was forced to accept that he was probably telling the truth brought a rush of enormous satisfaction. He was so glad now that he hadn't killed her earlier. Dying with this knowledge would make her death infinitely more painful.

He continued, determined to plunge the knife ever deeper. "There was one useful purpose my father served, however. Thanks to his loose talk, I got to know the inner workings of his club quite intimately. Most of the members there were actively looking for ways to recoup their losses after the stock market crash, and none more so than the earl. He really was the perfect, ready-made victim."

Margaret shook her head. "No! No! Don't you dare mock him. Whatever he did, he did it with the best of intentions."

"And with the worst kind of judgement, wouldn't you agree?"

She made no response, though the effort it was taking to contain her fury was plain to see.

Richard pressed on. "I had a friend I met at university who came from the gold producing region of South Africa. We came up with the idea together of how easy it might be to sell shares in a fake mine to the greedy. At first it was just a bit of a joke: no more than idle speculation. But then he introduced me to his uncle, a man who was able to get his hands on all the right kind of paperwork to convince investors that everything was authentic. The chap was a real smooth talker as well. After that, it was just a case of me putting him in touch with a couple of club members who'd be prepared to nominate him for a temporary membership. That old fool Sir Hubert Harding was most helpful with that."

He paused. As it turned out, he'd been a fool too. Not that he had any intention of revealing how his partners in crime had subsequently disappeared, taking all of the proceeds with them. Just for an instant, the memory of this caused anger to flare.

It faded just as quickly on spotting Margaret's reaction to the mention of Harding's name. That was good. The more anguish he could inflict on her the better.

"He was the one who told me that the club had never allowed any Jewish members," she said after a short silence. "That's when I first realised what a lying swine you are."

He laughed. "I did rather enjoy our day out in Berlin. You were so pathetically eager to believe everything I said. To tell the truth, I'm not sure who is the most gullible, you or your father. I suppose it must be something in the Pugh family genes."

Her look of rage was especially gratifying. With teeth bared and fists clenched, had it not been for the flare gun in his hand, he was sure that she would have launched herself at him.

The sound of a new arrival outside destroyed the moment, dragging Richard out of his triumphant little world and back into the harsh aspects of the real one.

Leaving Margaret to her misery, he moved across to peer from the side of the window. A motorbike had pulled up. Although the rider was wearing civilian clothes, the soldiers' reaction to him suggested that he carried a lot of authority. The girl Betty rushed straight over to the newcomer and they became locked in conversation. Richard had a feeling he had seen the man before, but in the difficult light and from a distance of nearly forty yards, he could not make out his features clearly enough to be certain.

After a quick glance behind to check that Margaret had not moved, his attention then shifted to the man's motorcycle. It was a BSA 500cc by the look of it, with a top speed of around sixty miles an hour. Which was probably five miles an hour faster than those Jeeps. Not that speed was everything for the plan that was now starting to form. Manoeuvrability was equally important.

If he could only get hold of that bike, he'd make a run for it back down the driveway toward Hadley Hall. In his hands, the BSA could weave easily around all the obstacles along the way. But the Jeeps would be slowed right down. Better still, as they got nearer to the ruined house, it would be impossible for them to continue at all. If he made it that far without incident, he could be sure of a fairly big head start.

Despite having visited the mansion a number of times, Richard had only a vague idea of what lay in the grounds to the rear. Maybe beyond that massive pile of rubble there was still a way through to one of the roads beyond. Of course, it was just as possible that there wasn't. It was a gamble. But anything was better than being trapped inside this damn lodge. If he stayed here, he'd be captured or killed for sure eventually.

, Instinct suddenly made him turn around. Margaret had crept to within three feet of him, the chair she was holding raised high to strike.

With only an instant to save himself, he lunged forward to grab hold of her leading arm before she could muster any downward force, twisting it savagely. She gave a cry of pain as the chair clattered to the floor. Enraged, he delivered three violent slaps across the face before dragging her back to her original position against the far wall.

The temptation to kill the bitch immediately was enormous and took several seconds to smother. He needed her alive to bargain for that motorcycle. But once that was achieved, any thoughts he might have had of sparing her in order to facilitate his escape were banished.

Whatever the risk to himself, she was definitely going to burn.

A SURGE OF RELIEF RACED through Betty on seeing Simon arrive. As soon as he had identified himself to the only officer present - a lieutenant - she rushed over to tell him of everything that had happened.

His look of horror as she began relating all that she and Margaret had faced, not to mention his overwhelming sense of relief on finding her safe, told her far more clearly than any words of the enormous affection he felt for her. Surprise and delight rose up. Not that there was any time to dwell on this revelation. Not with Margaret in such terrible danger.

"What are you going to do?" she asked.

"Naturally, I'll try my best to settle this peacefully," Simon assured her. "With Forest's link to Goering, he could be a mine of information. MI5 are desperate to question him, and there's a chap I know of who is certain to extract every last scrap of whatever he knows."

He drew a breath. "All the same, if Forest decides to dig his heels in, we can't wait forever. We'll have no choice but to go in there and drag him out."

Betty gasped. "But what about Margaret? You know he's threatened to use his flare gun on her if anyone tries that. He means it as well. I know he does."

He sighed. "Look, I know that you two still have some sort of friendship going on. That's hardly surprising after what you've told me. But Margaret has brought all this on herself. She's a traitor. You mustn't forget that."

"No! Not any more she isn't. If it wasn't for her, the Park would be in ruins by now."

"Maybe that's true. But that still doesn't cancel out all the other things she's done. And remember, even if she does survive this, she's most likely going to hang quite soon anyway."

"But there will be a trial first. There must be. I'll testify in her defence. I'll tell them how she stopped the bombs falling on Bletchley Park, and how she risked her own life to save me from being shot. That's got to count for something."

He looked directly into her eyes. "You really do care for her an awful lot, don't you?"

"Yes, I do. Almost as much as I care for you, you stubborn bloody man."

The frustrated words came out with a rush. Betty immediately felt her cheeks burning. "In a different kind of way, naturally," she hastily added, as much to cover her own embarrassment as to clarify matters.

His look of astonishment quickly turned to a smile. "Really?"

There was no going back now. "Yes! Really."

His smile widened. "Then I think we have a lot to talk about, don't you?"

Before she could respond, he touched her on the arm. "But that must keep for later. For now, I promise I'll do all I can to get Margaret out of there alive. At the same time, you must understand that I can't guarantee anything. Most of this is in Forest's hands."

Betty nodded. It was true. She was placing him in an impossible situation.

She watched as he issued some instructions to the lieutenant, then advanced alone toward the lodge at a pace slow enough to indicate that this was not an attempt to rush inside. He stopped ten yards short of the entrance.

"Richard Forest. Can you hear me?"

Betty realised that she was holding her breath.

AT FIRST THERE WAS no reply. Simon was on the point of calling again when a voice responded.

"Well, if it isn't Simon Straw, the chap who used to moon after Margaret back in the days when she and I ran around together. How fitting it should be you who's come riding up like a gallant knight to her rescue."

The mocking words bounced off Simon with little effect. His mind was totally focused on ending the situation as painlessly as possible. He'd given his word to Betty that he would do his best to achieve this, and allowing Forest's taunts to antagonise him would only make matters a thousand times more difficult.

"There's no chance of you escaping, Richard," he said, even though it sickened him to be using the man's first name as if they were friends. "There are a dozen rifles waiting to fire the moment you step outside. But if you give up now, no one will shoot. I guarantee your safety."

A chuckle sounded. "Ever the optimist, eh Simon? You really believe I'm going to walk out of here and give myself up just because you've asked me to. I'm not a fool. I know you'll do everything you can to keep me alive for questioning, so you're not going to shoot anyway. Not unless you have absolutely no other choice."

"So what do you want? Or are you just going to stay in there until we have to force our way in. Because that's what will happen. And it will be sooner rather than later."

"No. I've got a much better idea. I want your motorbike. That BSA you arrived on."

Although the demand at first caught Simon by surprise, he quickly acknowledged that there was no reason why it should have done. In many ways it was damned obvious. Forest's obsession with motorcycles, not to mention his undoubted vanity over his riding skills, had often been remarked on within the old social group.

Before he could come up with a suitable response, the voice continued. "I want you to park the bike directly outside the front here, up on its stand and with the engine left running. Margaret won't come to any harm if you do exactly as I say. You have my word on that."

After a few seconds of consideration, Simon gave a nod. "Very well. If that's the only way there is to save her, I'll give you what you want. I mean, it's not like you're going to get very far anyway, Richard. You must know that there are patrols everywhere. Not even you are a good enough rider to evade them all."

Casually dismissing Forest's ability to make good his escape was a deliberate ploy. Not only might it provoke him into an act of recklessness, it also lent plausibility to Simon's own apparent climbdown: that the decision to hand over the machine was made solely in an attempt to save Margaret. In truth, the beginning of an alternative plan was already starting to form.

Under no circumstances must Forest be allowed to escape. But if the motorcycle could be used to entice him out of the lodge, that would create many new possibilities. It might also prove to be the saving of Margaret, although there was no guarantee of that. All Simon could do was fulfil his promise to Betty by trying to give her as good a chance as possible. In the end though, circumstances would dictate how she emerged from all of this.

For an instant, he wondered what decisions he would be making had Forest chosen to take Betty hostage instead. If it were her life at stake, would he still be quite so immovable in his determination that the man must be captured whatever the cost?

This awful possibility was rapidly forced from his mind as Forest spoke again. "Just bring the bike over here like I said. I'll worry about the rest."

There was little else for them to discuss at this stage. After returning to where the BSA was standing, Simon gathered everyone around him. Keeping his voice down so that there was no possibility of it carrying any distance, he explained what he wanted one of the soldiers to do.

RICHARD WASN'T SURE whether or not to feel elated over the way things had developed. Had getting what he wanted been just a little too easy? Under different circumstances he might have felt a lot more suspicious, but with Simon Straw it was hard to tell. He'd always considered the man to be a sentimental fool. It was quite possible that, even after all these years, he was still nurturing a secret love for Margaret and would be prepared to make almost any concession in the hope of saving her.

A glance in Margaret's direction showed her to be still slumped on the floor. He sneered. She didn't look so bloody attractive and self-assured now. In fact, she appeared to have given up completely ever since her failed attack on him. Either that, or maybe she was clinging desperately to the final hope that hero Simon would come to her rescue?

Not a chance, you bitch.

His gaze shifted back to the discussion taking place outside. He'd made his demand clear enough; what the devil was there to talk about? Then, just as he was beginning to worry that maybe things were not going to be so easy after all, the group dispersed and Straw started the bike up. Less than a minute later it had been left outside the lodge exactly as instructed and Straw had withdrawn back with the others.

He dragged Margaret to her feet. By now she was literally shaking with terror, as if knowing full well that he never intended keeping the promise he'd made to her precious Simon. She was right to think that way. The moment he was astride the BSA and ready to go, he would then give her the most painful death imaginable.

Even after that, he still doubted that anyone would fire on him. At least, not initially. With his high connections in Berlin, the need to take him alive for questioning was always going to be their top priority. Straw's failure to contradict him on that point just a few minutes ago as good as confirmed it. And once he'd got moving on the bike, he'd show the bastard how good a rider he was.

He grinned while regarding Margaret's wretched features. "I really thought you had more courage than that, My Lady," he mocked, the flare gun held threateningly at the ready.

With a yard between them, they stepped out of the lodge door and over toward the waiting motorcycle. They were nearly halfway there when the still violently shaking Margaret abruptly dropped to her knees, her wild scream of despair cutting through the still night air like a thousand tiny shards of flying glass. So shrill and desperate did the pitch of this ever-rising cry become, at its zenith it seemed to achieve an almost whistle-like quality. Then, as if this wasn't sufficient to complete her humiliation, she quickly followed up with a series of loud sobbing pleas apparently directed toward the heavens.

"God can't help you now," Richard sneered.

Heedless of his taunt, she gave two final pleas at the top of her voice. "Save me," she begged.

Nobody responded, and Richard noted that not a single rifle was raised. Everything was going to plan, and seeing Margaret reduced to this snivelling state really was the icing on the cake. It was going to make killing her an even greater pleasure than ever.

WHEN SIMON GATHERED the others around him for their apparent discussion, the true reason had been to temporarily obscure the BSA from Forest's sight. As instructed, one of the soldiers who had earlier scooped up a large handful of dirt from the side of the driveway, was then able to drop this unobserved into the machine's petrol tank. If Simon's calculations were correct, it would take somewhere between three and five minutes of fairly gentle running before the gravity fed fuel supply filter became totally blocked. At a higher speed, Forest would not get any distance at all before the bike came to a possibly quite abrupt standstill.

Its engine had already been running for nearly two minutes when the pair emerged from the lodge. He was appalled by the sight of Margaret. She had always been such a strong and proud woman; to see her in such a pathetic state was barely believable. Her desperate cries for help merely compounded Simon's sense of shock.

The importance of capturing Forest alive had been powerfully stressed, and everyone was under strict orders not to take any action unless directly ordered to. This was especially true over the firing of shots, even if Forest did resort to using his final flare on Lady Margaret. Left without a weapon and on a motorcycle going nowhere, it would be a simple task to subsequently capture him. Perhaps quite badly bruised, but still in a perfectly fit state for interrogation.

He waited to see what Forest was going to do next.

CONTRARY TO APPEARANCES, Margaret was in perfect control of herself while pleading to the heavens. It sickened her beyond belief to feign terror and listen to Richard's taunts without reacting. But pretended fear was the only way she could disguise what she was really up to.

There was not a shadow of doubt that he intended to kill her before attempting to escape. And she was equally determined to kill him should an opportunity arise. Even more so after hearing his foul boasts about being the one to have caused her father's ruin. Never before had she experienced anything like the virulent hatred that was now raging inside.

Richard made no attempt to pull her to her feet. With the gently running motorcycle just a few paces further on, the look of contempt on his face while circling around her very nearly drove Margaret into leaping up and attacking him with her bare hands. But he was keeping a cautious distance between them, and the flare gun in his left hand was still pointing directly at her. She could only wait.

Wait and hope.

She watched him climb onto the saddle. After quickly checking how much fuel there was in the tank, he gave a sharp twist of the throttle. The engine roared in response. Satisfied, Richard placed both feet on the ground and leaned forward to ease the bike off the stand. But then the engine spluttered. He gave another twist to the throttle, and this time after giving a loud cough, it cut out completely.

Swearing loudly, he jumped down twice on the kick-start to no avail. More curses flew from his mouth. Then, as if realising his efforts were futile, the swearing abruptly stopped. Very deliberately he passed the flare gun over to his right hand, his eyes glaring venomously at Margaret. She knew at once that the moment had come.

But she now faced him defiantly, with chin raised and no trace of fear or intimidation. His expression of unbridled hatred gave way to a blink of surprise. He had clearly been expecting her to beg and cower – that was what he wanted to see - and confusion as to why she wasn't doing so had caused a momentary hesitation. It was a hesitation that, from the corner of her eye, Margaret suddenly knew would cost him dear.

Her prayers had been answered. Although she had chosen to disguise it as a wild scream of terror, she knew that her whistle-like cry would be recognised for what it really was by the one it was intended for. It was a summoning call to the one true friend who would never let her down in her time of need...Soldier.

The stallion's huge shadow emerged from the darkness at the end of the lodge like an avenging giant. Snorting with rage and with hooves kicking up large divots from the earth, its hindquarters thudded into the side of a visibly astonished Richard long before he had time to react, sending both him and the motorcycle toppling heavily to the ground. The flare gun flew from his hand. Stunned by the impact, he lay there with one leg trapped beneath the fallen machine.

In a flash, Margaret jumped forward to snatch up the grounded weapon, immediately checking the selector at the back. This time there would be no mistake.

"No, Margaret! Don't kill him."

The desperate cry came from Simon. She glanced over her shoulder to see both him and Betty running toward her. The soldiers were following close behind.

She gave no indication of having heard his plea. Facing Richard once again, she looked him directly in the eye. "This is for father," she shouted, carefully aiming the gun with both hands. "Because of you he is dying. I want you to burn in hell for what you did to him."

This time it was Betty's voice that interrupted her. She was standing alongside Simon only a short distance away. "No, you are wrong, Margaret. The earl isn't dying. He's awake and recovering well. It's true, I swear it is."

Margaret shook her head. "It can't be. The doctor said he would never recover. Why would he tell me such a terrible lie?"

Betty offered no immediate response. Despite this, and against all common sense, Margaret still found herself for a few seconds clinging to the faint hope that there might be a small amount of truth in what she had just been told. The moment quickly passed. Even if there was hope, it still did not change the fact that Richard had been the cause of all her father's misfortunes, both medical, and financial.

"He still deserves to die," she insisted, her grip on the flare gun tightening.

"And he will do," Simon assured her. "He will hang for what he has done. There is no doubt about that. But first of all we need to question him and find out everything he knows. What he will be able to tell us about someone as important as Goering will be invaluable."

Richard shifted slightly under the weight of the motorcycle. "I won't tell you a damn thing," he growled. "Why should I if you're going to hang me anyway?"

"You know, I'm actually rather pleased you feel that way," Simon responded. A tight little smile formed. "I'm sure Colonel Stephens will be as well. There is nothing he enjoys more than a challenge to his interrogation skills. He has never yet failed to break a man, and you certainly won't be the first. That much, I can guarantee."

He switched his attention back to Margaret. "He'll suffer far more...and for much longer...if you let me take care of things. Isn't that what you want for him? The most painful and humiliating departure possible? Hand that flare gun over to me and that's what he'll get."

It was everything she could wish on Richard. Nonetheless, she shook her head. The need to be the one to mete out justice to him was still burning strongly inside.

Fear was now rapidly overcoming Richard's brief show of defiance. "You can't do that," he told Simon. "Physical torture is against the Geneva Convention."

The protest merely drew a shrug. "But you are not a combatant, Richard. You are a spy, so you are not protected by such rules."

Simon paused briefly for this to fully sink in before continuing. "Besides, who said anything about physical torture? No. Thumb screws and electric shocks are not the way the colonel does things. What he most definitely will do, is break your mind. No matter how much you resist, he'll break it bit by bit until he's extracted every last bit of information out of you. Only after that will the hangman be allowed to break your neck as well to finish the job. But by this point, you'll probably have little recollection of who or what you are anyway. Death will probably feel like a wonderful release."

Margaret watched Richard's face closely as the full horror of what his slightly longer-term future might consist of struck home. She delighted in his anguish.

He glared back at her. "Go on then," he suddenly urged. "Pull the damn trigger and finish me off. That's what you want to do, isn't it?"

Yes, the temptation was still powerful. In fact, had he not urged her to do so, she almost certainly would have gone through with it. As it was, the sudden realisation that perhaps Richard genuinely would prefer to die here and now rather than face whatever degradation and agonies awaited him under interrogation was enough to stop her.

Why the hell should she do anything he wanted?

Let the bastard suffer for as long as possible.

He could see that her resolution was fading. His voice rose to a desperate shout. "Kill me, you bitch. Don't you want your revenge? I'm the one who ruined your father."

"Yes, and I'm the one who ruined you," she replied coldly before lowering the gun.

TWENTY-SEVEN

U nable to sleep, Erich Kimmel settled into a small folding chair on the grass outside his quarters to reflect on the night's events. After lighting a cigarette, a glance at his watch told him that it was just after 5.30am.

The fact that he and Hauptmann Wrick were the only survivors of the raid was a sobering thought. There had been times during the flight back to Saint-Omer when he felt sure that neither of them would make it either, especially after being ambushed by a large group of Hurricanes shortly after passing the Thames estuary. One of these fighters had got onto Wrick's tail and looked certain to bring him down. Only a desperate burst from Kimmel with the last few rounds of his ammunition had saved his Staffelkapitan. Thankfully, after that, the 109's superior air speed had proved sufficient to see them both safely home.

During their debriefing, they were each able to report that the target had been completely destroyed. Wrick had even taken several photographs to confirm this. In spite of the heavy losses, the general feeling seemed to be that it was a job extremely well done.

Kimmel was just about to light a second smoke when he spotted Wrick approaching. Returning the cigarette to its packet, he stood up and came to attention as the man drew close.

The Hauptmann made a brisk movement with his hand. "No need for such formalities at present, Oberfeldwebel. I just want to have a private talk with you."

Although Kimmel relaxed his stance slightly, inside he was still tense. So far, nothing had been said regarding his failure to follow standard orders. He had hoped it might have escaped Wrick's notice. Now though, he sensed that it had not.

The Hauptmann's next words confirmed this. "Tell me, Kimmel, would you like to explain why you did not strafe those two people on the ground at Bletchley Park when you so clearly had the opportunity to do so."

Kimmel had been pondering on what he might say if asked this question. He now responded with the only plausible explanation he could think of.

"I fully intended to, as was my duty," he began. "However, on realising how low I was on ammunition, I reassessed the situation. As the only survivor of the raid apart from yourself, I felt it was my far greater duty to protect the rear of my Staffelkapitan during what was certain to be a difficult flight home. It was a decision that, especially with the benefit of hindsight, I was most glad to have made. The lives of those two women would have been small compensation indeed if I'd not had ammunition still available to deal with the situation that arose on our return past the Thames Estuary."

Wrick remained silent for an uncomfortably long moment. He then gave a sharp nod. "Yes, on reflection I think I can understand your reasoning, Kimmel. Even in the face of standing orders, sometimes a man does have to exercise a little personal judgement. Flexibility in small doses can occasionally be a good thing."

Kimmel knew that this was the nearest he would ever get to an outright expression of gratitude for having saved the man's life. It didn't matter in the slightest. He was simply relieved not to be facing a formal charge of dereliction of duty.

"I'm happy that the Hauptmann agrees with me," he said.

"Oh, and there is one other thing you should know, Kimmel. Reichsmarschall Goering has been in touch during this last hour. He is said to be thrilled with the success of our mission. So much so that we have both been invited to Berlin to receive his personal thanks. It is hinted that we may even be honoured with an audience in front of the Fuhrer himself."

"Truly a great honour," Kimmel responded almost automatically.

"There is also a strong possibility of a promotion for us both. Perhaps you may finally be elevated to officer status? I will certainly make a recommendation to that effect if given the opportunity."

"The Hauptmann is most generous."

He watched Wrick walk away into the slowly breaking daylight before resuming his seat.

Yet again he wondered why Reichsmarschall Goering had been so very interested in this particular mission. And why he was so greatly thrilled at its success, despite the loss of four fine and highly experienced pilots. What was it about a single house in the English countryside that was so vitally important? Perhaps the trip to Berlin might provide a few answers.

For some strange reason, the prospect of this trip - even the possibility of his much longed for commission - was not filling Kimmel with the amount of excitement that it should do. Maybe he was just tired?

Or was he just sick of fighting for something he did not truly believe in?

He once again removed a cigarette from the packet. After he had smoked this, he would then make another attempt to grab a few hours of sleep.

For now, he was just grateful to still be alive.

IT WAS A LITTLE AFTER mid-day when Betty finally woke up. For a moment she wondered where she was, then she remembered collapsing exhausted onto the earl's bed. Margaret had gone to her own room next door. From the sound of things downstairs, she had already risen.

The cottage had suffered a fair amount of scarring to the exterior, but as in the case of the stable block, it was far enough away from where Hadley Hall had once stood to save it from any serious structural damage.

It must have been close to five o'clock when the pair of them had eventually put their heads down. With Richard ready to be transported down to an ominous sounding place in London called Latchmere House, Simon had agreed that they could stay together at the cottage until his return. That though, was the limit of what he could allow. He made it perfectly clear that, once back in Bletchley, he would have no choice but to place Margaret under arrest. Whatever else the two of them had left to discuss, it would be best to have it completed before then.

Predictably, Margaret's first thoughts after Simon's departure were for her two missing horses. She even managed to recruit a jeep and several of the soldiers, none of whom knew anything of her activities or impending arrest, to assist in her search for them. Only when both of these animals, together with Soldier, were safely back in their rather battered stalls was she prepared to rest herself.

Betty rose from the bed. After splashing some water over her face and running fingers through her tousled hair in a vain attempt to tidy it up, she went downstairs to find Margaret in the living room. Betty took a seat beside her at the dining table.

Not at any time during the aftermath of Richard's arrest had Margaret spoken a word about her father. Betty speculated that she'd been deliberately avoiding any mention of him to spare herself the pain. In the daylight however, all that appeared to have changed.

"You can tell me everything now," she said bluntly. "Does father know the full enormity of my crimes?"

At this stage, there seemed little point in withholding any of the truth. Filling in the gaps she had omitted the last time, Betty revealed how the earl had caught her reading Goering's letter, and how he had reacted on discovering the extent of his daughter's treachery. The sudden knowledge that it was her own actions that had induced his second stroke brought Margaret to near total despair. For more than ten minutes she did nothing but heap curses upon herself for her stupidity, refusing point blank to listen to anything further that Betty tried to say.

Then, for no apparent reason, she suddenly became coherent once more. "Tell me, is it really true what you said about him being awake and recovering?" she demanded.

"I wouldn't have lied to you about that," Betty assured her. "I spoke to him myself only yesterday morning."

"And he hates me for what I've done, doesn't he?"

"No, not hate. Never that. Saddened...disappointed...angry. All of those things and lots more besides. But never hate. You are still his daughter, Margaret. Perhaps after a time he might ..."

A hollow laugh slipped out. "That's the one thing I don't have though. Time. I can't imagine that they'll keep the hangman waiting very long for my company."

"I'll do whatever I can to help you at your trial," Betty promised. "I'll tell them about all the good things you've done. How you saved my life. And how Bletchley Park would never have survived if you hadn't stopped Richard when you did."

She sighed. "Stop fooling yourself, Betty. In our hearts, we both know that nothing is going to save me. And even if they were to grant permission for me to see father before they do the dirty deed, I couldn't possibly face him. The shame would be too much for both of us to bear." She gave a sad shake of the head. "No, it would be far better if we never see each other again."

"Are you really sure you mean that?" Betty asked.

"Absolutely! I don't wish to discuss it any further."

Unsure what to say next, Betty remained silent.

A full minute elapsed before Margaret spoke again. "But there is one last thing I want to do before I have to leave here. I wonder, would you be prepared to have a word with Simon on my behalf? I can see how close you two have become, so he may be willing to listen."

"Of course. What is it you want me to ask him?"

Margaret began to explain.

IT WAS WITH MIXED EMOTIONS that Simon left his car at the end of the driveway and began the lengthy walk down to Margaret's cottage. It was true that a disaster of unimaginable proportions had been averted. What's more, thanks to Betty's bravery and resourcefulness, the Luftwaffe had almost certainly been fooled into thinking they had destroyed the correct target. A couple of messages that were sure to be intercepted and decoded by German listening stations referring to the loss of 'a major asset' would help to confirm this belief. Goering would be delighted.

The damnable thing was, none of this could have happened without Margaret. And yet now he had to arrest her for a crime that carried an almost certain death sentence. Yes, he detested her for her treachery. But at the same time, much as he fought against it, he was equally unable to force the Margaret he had once cared for completely out of his mind. It was tragic that the earl's misfortunes had damaged her so badly.

On nearing the cottage, he saw Betty emerge from the front door and head toward him. Even though her uniform was in a terrible state and her hair looked as if it had not seen a comb for several days, his instinctive thought was that she had never looked more attractive.

Throughout the drive back up from London he'd been thinking about that brief awkward moment when they had declared feelings for each other. Could it really be true that Betty felt the same way as he did? Circumstances at the time had made it impossible to establish anything for certain, but once he'd got this depressing business with Margaret over and done with, then they would be able to get together for a proper talk.

She stopped just a few feet in front of him, a welcoming smile on her face. He longed to reach out and give her a hug, but there were still matters of propriety to observe. Apart from anything else, he was a mid-ranking officer and she an aircraftwoman WAAF. He had to be certain that he wasn't reading too much into the situation.

She spoke first. "I need to ask you something before we go inside. It's about Margaret."

The mention of her name brought him sharply back to the reason for his being here. "What about her? I thought I had made it clear, Betty. I really can't delay her arrest for any longer."

"Not even for one more hour?"

"One hour? What can she possibly hope to achieve in that short time?"

"She's asked to go for one final ride around the estate on Soldier. You must know how much she loves that horse. Surely you can't deny her the chance to say goodbye to him properly."

"She could have done that earlier today. Why wait until now?"

"Because she wants us both to go out with her. Apparently, there's something she needs the two of us to see." Betty touched him lightly on the arm. "All the horses are back now, and Margaret says you ride very well. I've had enough lessons with her to pass muster as well, so there shouldn't be a problem."

He sighed. "I'm not sure. There's been enough delay already."

"You used to be in love with Margaret once, didn't you?"

The question came out of the blue. He felt the colour rushing to his cheeks. "Who told you that? Was it her?"

Betty shook her head. "That wasn't necessary. I've seen it in your eyes several times when you've spoken about her." She smiled. "Even a working-class girl from south London learns to read the signs, you know."

For several seconds Simon did not have a clue what to say. Should he deny it? After all, he'd denied it to himself enough times. Then he remembered how easily Cynthia Bagsure had spotted the same thing in him, and she had been little more than a child at the time.

"Even if that was true," he finally said, "those feelings left me a long time ago. All trace of them. I was a lot younger then and—"

"About the same age as I am now, I would imagine," she pointed out.

The reminder of their age difference shook him. Betty, however, merely laughed. "Don't worry, it's the nineteen-forties now and there's a war on. Women these days mature a whole lot faster. We've had to."

Her laughter faded and a serious expression formed. "I know my own mind, Simon. I was deadly serious when I said how much I care about you."

"I meant every word of it as well," he quickly responded.

A sudden awareness then dropped into his head. "That's the very first time you've called me by my first name. Do you realise that?"

"Of course I do." Her smile returned. "And now that I've started, I'm not planning to stop any time soon. At least when we are together in private."

His own smile was now matching hers. "I'm glad to hear it. Can I give you a hug now?"

She spread her arms wide in silent answer to his question.

It felt so good to be holding her close. How long had he been subconsciously dreaming of this moment? Only with the greatest of willpower did he finally force himself to release her. There was still a job to be done.

Sensing his intentions, Betty took him by the hand. "Please give Margaret this one last thing. You know as well as I do that she isn't going to run away. If she'd been planning that, she would have done it long ago while you were down in London."

Simon could not argue with this. He was also well aware of Margaret's close bond with Soldier. That had been displayed in the most dramatic way possible only hours earlier.

"Very well," he agreed. "But just one hour. No longer than that."

MARGARET THANKED THEM both profusely for allowing her what she termed as: 'My final request'. In the stables, the three horses were quickly saddled.

Once clear of the wrecked driveway, the three of them set off at no more than a gentle trot. At frequent intervals Margaret leaned forward to whisper words of love and encouragement into Soldier's ear. Each time she did, the big stallion nodded its head as if in acknowledgement.

Although almost every field on the estate was by now ploughed and growing crops for the war effort, there was one field in particular that Margaret was deliberately heading for. It took them fifteen minutes to reach it. At last they were able to turn off the lane and pass through the gate.

What made this field different from all of the others was a fairly wide path of firm ground at its far boundary. Had it not been for the path's relatively short length and the towering obstacle that stood at its end, it might have even been a suitable landing strip for Richard's rescue plane. Not that this was of any concern to Margaret now. The obstacle itself, however, was of paramount importance.

Stanley's Folly.

It wasn't just the generations of her own family that held tradition dear in their hearts. So too, in their own way, did all those families who had been long-standing tenants and employees of the Pugh family. Virtually all of them looked back fondly on the days before the government had assumed ownership and saw Stanley's Folly as being an essential part of local history. Margaret's request to keep it trimmed to its original dimensions had always been honoured. As had a firm grass approach of fifty yards long on either side of the tall hedge.

So far, not even the frequently visiting government inspectors had raised an objection to this. Margaret often wondered if their tiny concession was due to pangs of guilt in Westminster over the way her father had been so cruelly treated by their political predecessors. Or maybe they would, after all, soon be demanding that the carefully preserved approaches be cultivated as well. All in order to grow just a few hundred more potatoes.

It made no difference. Today, the conditions were perfect.

And that was all that mattered.

"WHAT THE DEVIL IS SHE trying to do?"

Simon's astonished voice sounded loud as Margaret suddenly steered Soldier away from the field's edge and onto the firm level ground of the pathway. From here, she immediately urged her mount into a gallop directly toward the towering hedge.

"Surely she can't be hoping to ..." he continued.

His words faded away as he and Betty watched the stallion launch itself upwards. Even though she had been told in advance all about the Folly's history and made aware of Margaret's burning desire for one final chance to claim the cup, Betty still found herself holding her breath. She sensed that Simon was doing exactly the same thing.

Higher and higher Soldier rose, climbing to what seemed to be an impossible height for such a large and heavy beast. And then, in the blink of an eye, he was sailing clear of the top with several inches to spare.

"Yes!"

Even as Margaret's cry of triumph was echoing out, just before she disappeared from view on the far side of the hedge, she appeared to stand up in the stirrups, and, to Betty's horrified eyes, deliberately throw herself head first out of the saddle. Only seconds later, a distraught whinnying that sounded eerily like a human crying shattered the silence of the countryside. These sounds of anguish continued as Betty and Simon headed as quickly as they could for a gap to ride through further down the field.

Once on the other side they could see Margaret lying motionless on the ground. Her beloved horse was standing immediately alongside the body, gently nudging her face with its nose in a vain attempt to stir her. As they drew nearer and dismounted, Soldier turned his head toward them. Betty was sure she could see an unmistakable plea for help in the stallion's eyes.

But there was nothing they could do. Margaret's head was twisted sideways at a grotesque angle, telling them both beyond any doubt that her neck was broken.

"She did that on purpose, I'm sure of it," Betty whispered in a deeply shocked voice.

"I agree," Simon told her.

After a moment of silence, he drew a deep breath. "But I don't think that is what the world needs to know."

THE OBITUARY IN THE Times newspaper carried the bare facts, stating that Lady Margaret Pugh, the only child of Henry Pugh, the twelfth Earl of Dewksbury, had suffered a fatal accident while out riding on their former estate. Details of the funeral arrangements followed.

It was the Bletchley Gazette that painted a more fulsome picture. Lady Margaret, it told its readers, was a much-loved personality who'd been a patron of many charities within the area. Her death at the tragically young age of thirty-two was a deep shock to all who'd known her.

The feature went on to describe the well-known local legend of Stanley's Folly, and of how Lady Margaret on Soldier had become the first of the Pugh family in 150 years to clear the fearsome obstacle. As the rules required, her accomplishment had been certified by two independent witnesses, so entitling her to the trophy put up by her great-great-grandfather. This, it had been jointly decided by her father and the family solicitor charged with the trophy's safekeeping, would be placed in her casket and buried along with her in the family plot.

In a footnote, it was mentioned that the gallant mount Soldier, along with Lady Margaret's two other horses, had all been found an excellent new home together in the Buckinghamshire countryside by a Colonel Timothy Albriton. The colonel, who had worked closely with Lady Margaret during the British eventing team's preparations for the 1936 Olympics, said he remembered with gratitude all the assistance she had freely provided him with at the time. This small favour was the least he could do in return to honour the memory of a fine lady.

AT THE EARL'S REQUEST, the funeral was delayed for a few days so that he was able to attend. It had been feared that the twin blows of losing his daughter and the destruction of his former ancestral home might provoke a third, and this time fatal stroke. As it transpired, on the surface at least, he received the news with astonishing calm. Betty suspected it was almost as if, after learning of Margaret's agreement with Goering, there was little else that could genuinely shock him. Although still confined to a wheelchair for the immediate future, when he arrived at the small church it was with his head held proudly high. No one, not even Betty when she greeted him, could tell what was going through his mind.

With a short time yet before the service was due to begin, she and Simon wandered over to a quiet corner of the churchyard. Both of them had chosen to wear civilian clothes for the occasion, she in a suitably dark dress and matching jacket, he in a smart black suit. They stopped beneath the shade of a large oak tree.

Betty glanced briefly across at the large gathering of local people who had come to pay their respects. "I know that what Margaret did was unforgivable," she began, "but I still think she went a long way toward redeeming herself at the end. After she died, I couldn't see any point in dragging it all up and making it public. I'm so glad those people over there will never know the truth about her. Thank you for that."

He gave a rueful smile. "To be honest, I had nothing to do with it. I'm not *that* powerful, you know. Nowhere near."

"But I thought you said that the world didn't need to know about what really happened."

He touched her on the arm. "That was only concerning the manner of her death. No one needed to know that she deliberately set out to kill herself rather than face her father and the shame she'd bring to the family name. Having said that, I do rather feel that the old boy has his suspicions. Not that he'll ever breathe a word to anyone about them."

This was the first time Betty had spoken to Simon about what was an obvious cover-up. She waited, knowing he would soon enlarge on matters.

"Apart from us two and Cynthia, less than half a dozen people know the full extent of Margaret's deeds," he began. "The brutal truth is, she did us an enormous favour by taking the alternative way out. Had she lived and been put on trial, even one held in–camera, the complications would have been enormous. You know as well as anyone how desperately important it is to keep the Park's activities under wraps. How can you accuse someone of plotting against a place that officially doesn't even exist?"

Betty nodded. "So it was someone at the top who hushed it all up?"

"At the very top. Winnie demanded it. And there's another thing. Apart from the obvious aspects, there is also the matter of public morale to be considered. We've already had two Mitford girls and that Mosley chap stirring things up. If yet another member of the aristocracy was seen to have been cosying up to the Nazis, it could do incalculable harm to the mood. The very last thing this country needs right now is more class divisions forming. Not when we all desperately need to be pulling together."

There was a short reflective silence. Betty then asked: "Do you really think we will win this war? I mean, honestly."

"Absolutely," he told her, his voice now much lighter in tone. "As long as we've got people like you on our side, the Germans haven't got a chance."

She grinned. "It's funny, my dad said something daft like that on the day I joined up."

"Well, he sounds like a very smart man to me."

He hesitated, then added: "Look, you're overdue some leave anyway. Why don't we pop down to see your folks at the weekend? What do you think?"

It suddenly occurred to Betty that she had not visited home even once since being posted to Bletchley. With a rush of emotion, she realised how very much she was missing her parents.

"I think that's a splendid idea. Especially now you've decided to give up smoking; mum and dad hate the smell of it even more than I do. But before you say hello to them ..."

She glanced over once again at the gathered mourners, who by now were starting to trickle into the church. "Perhaps we should first say our goodbyes to someone else."

His expression gave just a hint of the conflicting emotions that Betty knew must be passing through his mind.

"Yes, let's do that," he agreed.

PART FOUR

Reflections

TWENTY-EIGHT

From the outside, it was just another of the many four-bedroom houses found in the leafier suburbs of north London.

The ding-dong of the front doorbell sounded just as the clock in the living room began striking three o'clock. Betty smiled while making her way along the hallway. Her visitor was certainly punctual.

Her smile widened on opening the door. "Cynthia Bagsure. How lovely to see you again."

"It's jolly lovely to see you as well," she responded.

They walked together through to the living room. Tea and biscuits had already been placed on the table.

"I'm so glad that you've agreed to let me come here and tell you all about my little proposal," Cynthia began after the tea was poured. "You do know what I'm doing these days, don't you?"

Even though they had not seen each other for a long time, Betty felt quite amused at the absurdity of the question. "I could hardly *not* know," she pointed out. "Not with that show of yours being on the television twice every week. Over the last few years you seem to have interviewed just about everyone there is to know about in the arts and entertainment world."

"Everyone except you, Betty."

"And now you want to?"

"Yes, why not!"

"I'm more inclined to ask why."

Cynthia smiled. "That's easy. You haven't done an interview in more than fifteen years, and yet people still talk about you. One minute you were the toast of the classical music world: its brand-new shining star bursting onto the scene from relative obscurity and winning all kinds of highly prestigious competitions. Then, just when your fame and reputation was at its brightest, you simply stopped performing altogether. Not even a farewell concert to explain why."

She paused before adding: "Would you like to tell me what happened?"

Betty thought for a long moment. Living in relative obscurity during an important period of her life had been the right thing to do. If it had been anyone else but Cynthia asking the questions, she might still have been tempted to keep it that way. On the other hand, the longing to play in public once again was undeniably growing stronger.

She began slowly. "At the start, my retirement was only ever intended to be temporary so that Simon and I could have at least one child before it was too late. I'd already passed my thirtieth birthday by that time, and then there's that age gap between us as well. It rather felt like being a case of now or never. In the event, a year later I had twin boys, Stanley and Arthur."

Cynthia nodded. "Yes, I remember hearing about them being born. That makes them fourteen now, I take it?"

"That's right, and growing up fast. They both want to join the navy like their father."

After taking a sip from her cup, Cynthia probed a little deeper. "You said temporary. So I imagine once the birth and all that stuff was over, you originally intended to return to concerts? Why didn't you?"

"The truth of the matter was, I just couldn't bear to be away from the boys for any length of time. If I'd gone back to the tours and all that travelling I would have hardly ever seen them grow up. Simon was quite prepared to leave the navy and be there for them as a full-time parent, but they needed both of us."

"So in your eyes, the music had to go. I can understand that easily enough."

Cynthia waited for a moment before asking: "Are you considering a return to performing now that the boys are well on the way to growing up? Is that why you agreed to our chat?"

Betty nodded. "I've been considering it for a few weeks. That's why your call was so timely. It won't be like before though. There'll be no more long tours and months on end away from home. But an occasional performance might be nice. That is, if people still want to come and hear me play."

"You bet they will."

All of Cynthia's natural exuberance came rising to the fore as she continued. "We could make the interview all about your comeback. For the sake of younger viewers who won't remember, we can pick up your story at the end of the war. Tell them how, after leaving the WAAFs and getting engaged, you went off to New York for two years to continue your musical education. With Simon getting promoted to Commander and shortly afterwards being handed a post as an Assistant Naval Attaché in Washington DC, even then it seemed as if fate had decided that the pair of you shouldn't be kept too far apart."

She gave an elaborate wink. "Or was it Mister Churchill showing his gratitude for services rendered? Best not touch on any of that, eh."

"Most definitely not," Betty agreed.

"Never mind. The news of your comeback will be a plenty big enough story on its own."

"Nothing is decided for certain yet," Betty warned her. "I'll have to talk to Simon and the boys about it first." She grinned. "That is, if I can get them to stop going on about this football world cup thing that's taking place at the moment. All three of them seem convinced that nineteen sixty-six is going to be the year when England finally win it."

"How is Simon?" Cynthia asked. "It's been absolutely ages since we last saw each other."

"He retired from the navy a long time ago, still as a commander. Once the boys came along, he had no further desire to commit himself to it as a long-term career. They're all out together somewhere right now. I think he's teaching them how to play golf." A fond expression formed. "They couldn't ask for a better father."

"I was rather hoping to catch him," Cynthia admitted. Her voice dropped a touch. "There are a couple of things I thought he might be able to tell me concerning all that terrible business at the Park." She rolled her eyes. "You know me and my insane curiosity."

"Why don't you ask me instead?" Betty suggested. "Simon kept me up to speed about most things I wasn't directly involved with."

"To be honest, it's more a case of what came about afterwards. I take it they did hang that awful Richard Forest. I never heard anything more about him after he was taken away. Even now I can barely believe how he turned against us the way he did. He came to our house several times back in the day, you know. He was always so polite to me."

"Oh yes, he got what he deserved," Betty confirmed, deliberately omitting any mention of Richard's lengthy and decidedly uncomfortable stay at Latchmere House prior to execution. "What else were you curious about?"

"This is really silly, but I can't help wondering whatever happened to that wonderfully quirky character Joe Bull. Do you know who I mean?"

"Oh yes. I never actually saw him myself, although as you might guess, I did hear all about him as things progressed. Quirky he might have been, but he was still working against us."

Cynthia frowned. "Does that mean he got the rope as well?"

"Actually, no. Although he spoke like a true cockney, in reality he was an Irishman. When MI5 discovered that he had such a brilliant talent for copying accents and other people's voices, they thought he was too good to waste. They made use of him right up until the end of the war. Don't ask me how exactly, but I do know that he more than earned his reprieve."

"A reprieve? You know, in a strange kind of way I'm rather pleased about that. I spoke to him several times on the racecourse. He was so funny to chat to, and he was absolutely brilliant with all the children. I wonder where he is now."

"Simon said that after VJ Day they gave him a new identity and shuffled him off to Australia." Betty laughed. "They say the Aussies love a bet, so if he's still alive he's probably wearing a big bush hat with lots of corks dangling from it and handing out horse tips sounding like he was Sydney born and bred."

Cynthia joined in with her laughter. She then turned back to the main reason for her visit. "I've just one question about this possible comeback of yours, Betty. Is your playing still up to scratch? I don't mean to sound insulting, but it's been such a long time. And I do know how much people at the very top level need to practice."

Betty had been wondering if this question might occur. "I'm not quite up to concert standard at the moment," she admitted, "but I do still practice for at least three hours most days."

Rising from her seat, she walked over to the corner of the room and placed an affectionate hand on the top of an upright piano. "This old thing still plays as beautifully as it did the first time I ever sat down in front of it. That was nearly twenty-five years ago in Margaret's cottage."

She noted the look of surprise on Cynthia's face. "Her father left it to me in his will. It was the only possession of value he had left. He was most insistent that it should not pass into anyone else's hands."

"I know that you visited the earl whenever you could before he died," Cynthia remarked. "To tell the truth, I was quite surprised that the government were so generous in providing him with a new home, not to mention all the private care he needed from day to day. He lived on for nearly ten years after that second stroke. It must have cost them a fair bit."

But not as much as if he had chosen to speak openly about what he knew, Betty considered.

It seemed as if Cynthia had read her thoughts, because a moment later she said wistfully: "You know, it's a terrible shame we can't tell people about all the incredible things that happened at the Park, and how they played such a key part in us winning the war. Now that *would* make a sensational programme. Why, they could even make a major film out of it."

"Maybe they will one day," Betty told her. "But I don't think it's going to be for a good number of years yet."

She settled on the piano stool. "Would you like me to play something for you? Just to prove that these ageing fingers of mine can still do it."

Cynthia thought for a moment and then grinned. "Tell you what, how about a quick rendition of Down at the Old Bull and Bush? After all, I was the one who gave you your first big break in show business remember."

"You were indeed," Betty laughed, recalling immediately that this was also the evening when she'd first encountered Margaret. Without that fateful meeting, her life would have certainly taken a vastly different path. The music would always be with her, but there would have been no Simon, nor their two wonderful sons.

Also, given what Margaret had already set in motion, there would quite possibly have been no Bletchley Park for very much longer either.

Raising the Steinway's lid, she added with a fond smile: "Very well, Cynthia. Down at the Old Bull and Bush it shall be."

A FINAL WORD

I'd just like to say a big thank you for reading this novel. I really do hope it provided you with a few hours of enjoyable escapism. If you did find it an entertaining read, would you please consider leaving a review on Amazon, or indeed any other relevant website or blog? Reviews are the lifeblood for all authors, and you will have my sincere thanks if you take the trouble to write a few words on your thoughts about this book.

You may be interested to know that I SPY BLETCHLEY PARK is a companion novel to BURIED PASTS, a similar fictional tribute that I wrote to my Canadian father, a pilot who flew 28 missions with RAF Bomber Command during World War Two.

Here's the blurb.

NOTHING STAYS BURIED FOREVER

EVEN AFTER 18 YEARS, Canadian pilot Mike Stafford still carries an overpowering sense of guilt for the death of his best friend during a huge RAF bombing raid on Berlin in 1944. He eventually returns to England for an inaugural squadron reunion full of apprehension over what the visit may produce.

Berliner Siggi Hoffman, then just twenty years old, also has terrible memories of a personal loss from that same air raid. She too is unable to forget. Nor has she ever yet been able to forgive.

When fate throws these two together in a small north Yorkshire town during the summer of 1962, the past collides devastatingly into the present. And as long buried secrets are finally revealed, so a new enemy closes in.

PUBLISHERS WEEKLY REVIEW: *'This page-turner blends suspense with a cast of characters who genuinely care for each other. It's an engaging and satisfying novel for fans of adventure stories with a heart.'*

THANKS ONCE AGAIN FOR your support. It really does mean a great deal to me.

George Stratford
www.georgestratford.com[1]

---

1.   https://www.georgestratford.com

Printed in Poland
by Amazon Fulfillment
Poland Sp. z o.o., Wrocław
22 October 2021

c3bf3b47-6e1b-45ab-83d8-a708ee66c4eaR02